To YOU, the reader.
Thank you for taking a chance on us.
Thank you for your support.
Thank you for the emails.
Thank you for the reviews.
Thank you for reading and joining us on this road.

* * * *

SEASON TWO

YESTERDAY'S GONE

SEAN DAVID
PLATT WRIGHT

::EPISODE 7::
(FIRST EPISODE OF SEASON TWO)
"SANCTUARY"

CHAPTER 1
MARY OLSON

Billings, Alabama
March 20, 2012
Five months after the events of Oct. 15

Mary woke up sticky. Another dream about Ryan.

Though he was little more than an echo of the past during her waking hours, there wasn't a thing Mary could do to keep him from haunting her sleeping ones. Odd how the past forgot its place in dreams, where old friends, lovers, and ex-husbands held court on equal footing with the present.

A flash of sudden sorrow, then a current of guilt flooded Mary's guts. She turned over, adjusting her eyes to the early morning that spilled through the thin opening in the thick, dark curtains. A shaft of light fell on what she assumed to be Desmond's sleeping form, but when her eyes met his she saw that he was wide awake. Watching her again.

"Morning, sleepyhead," he said.

"What time is it?"

1

Desmond turned and picked up his watch from the nightstand. "Quarter after 6."

"You realize we don't actually have to rise before the roosters anymore, right?"

"Old habits," he said. "Besides, when else can I get a peep show?"

"I can't imagine there's anything interesting about watching a log."

"You have no imagination," he smiled. "Or any idea how dirty I can make mine."

Mary blushed, like she did several times a day beneath the glow of Desmond's compliments, though he didn't usually start so early.

She had no idea what the last five months would have been like without him. Desmond was a godsend – smart and a natural leader — but more than that, he had a way of untangling the knots of their hardships, no matter how thick the gnarls. Without Desmond, they never would have left the Drury alive and never would have found sanctuary in their new Alabama home.

"You're doing it again." Desmond rubbed his hand on the ball of her knee.

"Sorry," she met his eyes, "I was just thinking about the last few months."

Mary was getting lost in thought a lot more often lately. Too often. She'd been known to go deep, and had her whole life. It's what made her a good, if not great, artist. She had a way of pulling whimsy from nowhere, then displaying it in a way no one had ever seen before. But that took time and space. And now, with all the time and space in the world, it seemed as if Mary's mind was always being pulled off to plunge deeper into her thoughts - deep enough to drown the outside world. Desmond said she could stare into the nothing for hours if he let her. If Mary didn't trust him as much as she did, she'd swear he was lying. It never felt like more than a few minutes. She would simply start thinking about something trivial, until her mind started chasing memories down the rabbit hole, taking her in different directions each time: worrying about Paola, conflicting thoughts about Desmond, odd ideas about Luca and Will and everyone they'd met in Alabama. These thoughts had less shape and left her far from understanding, especially the thoughts about Will.

John was there sometimes, too. Like a shadow.

"What about the last three months?" Desmond kept rubbing Mary's knee, his fingers drifting higher.

"Everything," she said, "and all at once. But most of all I guess I'm wondering if it's really over. Is this it? Is this our life now? Is this what it's going to be like forever?"

"Maybe," Desmond smiled. "But it's not so bad, right? I'll never have to go to another boring cocktail party. You'll never have to worry about shipping in time for the holiday rush. And it looks like the universe finally took care of Facebook once and for all."

Desmond's hand had crawled all the way up Mary's inner thigh, his fingers grazing the edge of her gummy middle. Desmond smiled again, this time more like a wolf.

"Jesus," Mary said. "You're like a teenager. Wasn't last night enough?"

"You have something better to do?" He rolled on top of her. Her knees lifted in the air as she pulled her legs back toward the bed.

"Never," she said.

His teeth touched the edge of her ear. Mary moaned slightly, then whispered, "You don't need to warm me up, Tiger. Just go."

"When I'm ready," he said playfully, rock-hard but taking his time. "Good things come to those who ... "

A gunshot finished his sentence, followed seconds later by the ringing of the alarm bell on top of the grain silo where one of the men was on watch.

Desmond rolled off of Mary and onto the floor. She bolted from bed, threw on a sweater and sweats, then grabbed the pistol from the nightstand. Desmond threw on his pants, grabbed the rifle in the corner of the bedroom, bolted into the hallway, down the stairs, into the living room, and to the oversized window overlooking the front yard of their four acres of farmland.

Mary ran to Paola and Luca's room, two doors down, and threw open the door. Both children were wiping sleep from their terrified eyes. "Stay in here! Remember the plan." Mary shouted a few decibels shy of a scream, meeting her daughter's eyes. "And lock the door."

Luca leaped from the top bunk, then went to the door. "Thanks, Mary," he said, closing the door and turning the latch. Though he looked like a young teen, he was still a child who needed to be locked away.

Mary ran downstairs where Scott and Desmond were staring out the window, a few feet from Linc, all three with rifles ready. She saw the long-limbed black monsters outside, the things that had nearly killed them back at the hotel, and that stalked her dreams nightly.

"Bleakers!" Scott said, his mid-adolescent voice a crack of excitement.

"Who's on watch?"

"Will," Desmond said. "He's on the silo."

"How many are there?"

"I see four, just inside the gate," Desmond said. "What about you, Linc?"

"Your four, then one in front of the barn," Linc said, peering down the scope of his rifle, which he aimed out the open window.

A gunshot, from Will, thundered outside, immediately followed by a second and third.

"One by the barn is down," Linc said, "Will needs backup. Let's get out there now."

Desmond was first out the door; Linc just a step behind that. Scott tried to follow, but Linc held up a palm, "You sit this one out, kid."

"Come on," Scott pleaded, looking at Mary, who shrugged, deferring the call to Linc. If she had it her way, Scott would be up in the room with the other kids. But that was the mother hen in her, something that she was trying not to push on Scott, who was striving to be seen as a man in the group.

"I said no," Linc's deep voice and former linebacker's body was intimidating, even if everyone knew he was a bigger teddy bear than Mary. "I can't be keepin' an eye on you right now. Maybe next time."

Scott's eyes narrowed behind his thick glasses and under his straw-colored bangs. He opened his mouth to protest, but Linc wasn't waiting for an answer. And now was obviously a bad time to make a stand. Scott swallowed and held his rifle in the air. "OK, I'll hang here, make sure the kids stay safe."

Linc nodded, slapped Scott on the shoulder, then he and Mary joined Desmond racing towards the gate, 50 or so yards from the house and 200 from the silo at the other end. Two of the dark monsters had broken off from the pack and were circling the silo, screeching and clicking at Will, safely out of range, unless one of the creatures started climbing the ladder, which no one had seen them manage to do. Yet.

The pair of bleakers by the gate turned their oversized, black eyes toward Desmond, Linc, and Mary, who took steady aim and opened fire, emptying their guns on their way to the barn where they could shoot from more safely. Like the bleakers they'd seen in small clusters over the last couple of weeks, these were faster and able to take more bullets than the ones they'd grown used to. Their mouths, holes with rows of jagged teeth, were wide open, wailing an unholy clicking shriek that drilled into Mary's brain like the sound of a baby screaming for its mother.

"Shit!" Linc screamed at a bleaker that had taken a bullet straight to the face but still kept walking, without half its head; a horrifying first. Linc threw down his rifle and reached into the holster at his belt and grabbed the Glock. He squeezed off three shots until the fucker fell to the ground, twitching and clicking.

"Inside, now!" Linc ushered Desmond and Mary inside the barn, pulling a second pistol from the other holster and firing at the three new bleakers that had appeared from nowhere. Linc, an ace shot, managed to hit the first two in the forehead, then slipped inside the barn and locked the door behind him, but not before he saw something that widened his eyes and sucked the life from his face.

He stood at the door, frozen, staring at nothing.

"What is it?" Desmond asked.

Linc shook his head, not looking at them.

"I don't even know where to start, man. I wanna say there are dozens, but that's just to make us all warm and fuzzy. Truth is, looks like those giant-faced fuckers are oozing out of the forest right now. Definitely the biggest swarm we've seen so far. Maybe a hundred of 'em."

Mary looked out the small barn window toward the house, then over at Will - a speck on top of the silo - but said nothing. Everyone knew the only thing guarding the house and the children inside it was an old man standing on top of a silo 600 or so feet away, and Scott, who was little more than a child himself. Stating the obvious wouldn't help a thing. Besides, even if she opened her mouth, Mary was half certain all she'd manage was a whimper.

Six shots popped through the air in neat succession, exactly two seconds apart. Will pulling the trigger from atop the silo and hitting his targets, by the sound of it. The final shot finished with a thud as a bleaker's body banged against the side of the barn.

Mary found her voice. "We have to get back to the house," she said. "They're dead if we don't."

As if to prove her right, another shot rang loud; closer, from inside the house. Mary looked back out the window. A bleaker was pushing its way in through the front door of the house; another four were thrashing wildly a few feet behind.

"Desmond!" Mary threw him a sharp look, but he raised his arms in the air, helpless. They were reloaded, but the barn was surrounded. And with only the one small window facing the silo, they had no idea how bad it was behind them. Judging by the visible clusters storming the gate, and the speed with which the bleakers were moving, opening the barn door would be almost certain suicide.

"Let's give it a second, so we can get our bearings." Desmond's voice was cool, but his hand was shaking as he cocked the gun.

"We don't have a second, Dez!" Mary shrieked, "THEY ARE IN THE HOUSE!"

Thunder battered the barn from all sides as dozens of bleakers banged against the outside walls. Another round of shots rattled the air and hammered their nerves, while also sending them a sliver of hope as more bleakers fell.

"It's now or never," Desmond said, looking at Linc. "You ready?"

Linc nodded, though he looked like he was holding his shit together with floss.

Desmond opened the door firing, kicked the closest bleaker to the ground, aimed his gun at the creature's mouth and pulled the trigger, coating the dirt in a putrid brew of chunky black.

Two bleakers rushed Linc, knocking him to the ground as his shots misfired into the air. Mary stepped toward the fallen trio and popped both of the bleakers in the back of their heads. Linc looked up, and despite all the chaos, managed a grin.

Desmond was too busy emptying his Glock into the approaching swarm to notice anything but the roar of Will's rifle from the top of the silo, and another half dozen perfectly punctuated shots. Will was keeping them alive. But he only had so many bullets. And in the moments between reloads, they were on their own. As Mary, Desmond, and Linc pressed their way into the front yard, they got their first real glance at just how many they were dealing with. A hundred was a conservative guess. It was as if someone sent out a beacon calling every creature within miles to home in on the farm. There was no way Mary could see them getting out of this alive.

The creatures were still pouring in from the woods on either side of the farm.

When will it stop?!

They were going to die today.

She looked over to Linc and Desmond in desperate search of some sign of hope in their eyes. All hope was gone.

Another gunshot from the house pulled Mary's attention back to the children. She had to get in there. Now!

She raced straight at - and around - a bleaker, racing to the house. She raised her pistol and fired at two of the creatures blocking her path to the house. They fell, but her clip was empty. She stared at the porch where the bleakers were trying to get in the front door, which was somehow blocked, but for how long she had no idea. Nor did she know if any had already breached the door before it became blocked, as she couldn't see Scott or hear anything in the house.

Suddenly, shots screamed out from behind, and the two bleakers in front of her fell to the ground, heads splattered.

She spun around as a midnight-blue SUV charged the gate, tearing through a huddle of bleakers, sending three to the dirt before the truck screeched to a halt, stopping with a squish as it landed on top of a bleaker's head, popping it like a grape.

Two armed strangers — decked out in black outfits that looked like SWAT gear — leaped from the truck and opened fire on the bleakers. The driver stayed inside, threw the car in gear, then raced toward the thickest part of the swarm, mowing bleakers a handful at a time, covering the windshield and sides of the otherwise spotless SUV with gooey slop.

Linc fell into formation with the two soldiers, both clearly trained, picking off bleakers shot by shot.

Desmond raced to Mary, handed her a clip for her pistol, and they ran to the porch where three bleakers were trying to open the front door, which had been blocked by a fallen light fixture. All the bleakers had to do was kick the obstacle aside. But they kept opening the door over and over, expecting the same movement to yield a different result. Mary was glad to see the bleakers' brains were still moving slow, even if their legs had learned to go faster. Desmond and Mary opened fire from behind and painted the porch in black.

"You've got this," Desmond said. "I'll cover the outside, make sure nothing else gets in. You get to Scott and the kids, okay? Scream if you need me."

Mary nodded, then stepped inside the house, gun raised, looking first toward the living room on the right, then toward the kitchen on her left. Two pairs of bleakers; four total. The first two were rifling through the kitchen; one was pulling out a butcher knife, looking at it with its head turned like a dog trying to figure out Algebra, while the two in the living room were roaming in circles, seemingly lost.

Relieved by their lack of attention, Mary flew up the stairs, hoping none had thought to hit the second floor. Her hopes were dashed when she saw the trail of blood on the wooden floor leading to the end of the hall where Scott lay in front of Paola's door, trying to fight off two bleakers with his bolt action rifle. His shirt was bloody, and he looked minutes from bleeding out.

"Paola?!" Mary screamed, "Are you okay?!"

"MOM!" Paola's panicked voice yelled from the other side of the door.

Scott looked up to Mary, eyes glazed. "I'm so sorry, Mary," he sobbed when he saw her.

Mary said nothing, just opened fire on the pair of bleakers at the bedroom door, then shifted her aim to the third bleaker, which managed to take the rest of her bullets without having the decency to drop.

FUCK!

"Stay inside!" she yelled again, then ran to the end of the hallway, swinging her arm in a wide arc and lodging the butt of her gun into the surprisingly soft back of the bleaker's skull.

The bleaker turned to Mary, its mouth agape, with its jagged rows of malformed teeth. She took another wide swing, making matching entry and exit wounds on each of the bleaker's cheeks, chunks of wet, black flesh and teeth hitting the wall and floor. What was left of the monster's mouth collapsed on itself as it rattled a wretched sound of surprised anger, stumbled, then fell to the floor, thrashing.

Scott slid the rifle along the floor to Mary. She picked it up and swung down, taking out the rest of the creature's skull until it stopped moving.

"Where are the bullets?" she asked, sure that she'd drawn the attention of the four bleakers downstairs and would need to be armed.

Scott pointed to his duffel bag at the end of the hall – the same bag they'd found him with two months ago when they first saw him, dehydrated on the side of the road in lower Tennessee. It was a kid's bag, black, with white lettering that read *BOMB TECHNICIAN: If you see me running, you'd better start running, too!*

Mary stepped past him, feeling a bit shitty not to bend down to check his wound but also recognizing that she needed to prepare for the other monsters or none of them would get out of the house alive. She reached into the bag, retrieved the box of bullets as sounds of the bleakers stumbling up the stairs caused her hands to shake. She slipped the first bullet into the magazine, then the second. A bleaker was at the top of the stairs, clicking and shrieking, mouth open wide.

She slid the third bullet into the magazine, then tried to squeeze the fourth, but it was a tight fit. She struggled, hands shaking, fingers betraying her, pressing hard to get the bullet into the chamber as the creature moved closer. She wished like hell that the boy didn't have a bolt action. But that's what she had. Four bullets. Four bleakers.

Fuck!

The fourth bullet slid into place, and she clicked the magazine into the gun's stock, glanced up to see the bleaker barreling towards her, slid the bolt back and forth loading the chamber, then raised the rifle as the bleaker was nearly on top of her. The shot ripped through the bleaker's chest and launched it back into a second bleaker that had come into the hallway.

"Desmond," she screamed, "I need you up here NOW!"

No reply. She fired a second shot, taking out the second bleaker's face.

Outside was a thunderstorm of chaos. It sounded like more bleakers, more engines, more gunfire, more shouting.

More of everything.

Mary managed to squeeze off two more shots, bringing down the third bleaker, before the final one — that she knew of, anyway — got through and was on her. The monster clawed at her arm, tearing the fabric of her sweater, but narrowly missed her flesh as she squeezed out of the way. Her rifle fell, just out of reach, as the creature stood to its full length and glared down at her with its alien eyes. Its mouth opened wide, and it leaned over, shrieking so loud that she had to cover her ears or risk her eardrums being burst.

The bedroom door behind the bleaker swung open, and Luca ran into the hallway, screaming.

"NO!" He charged toward the bleaker, punching the back of its body. Luca looked to be 14, rather than the eight years his lifetime provided. And though 14 was bigger than 8, it wasn't big enough to stand against the 6-foot-5 or so bleaker that turned around and swatted an angry black fist at the boy, sending him sprawling back along the bloody hardwood floor. The bleaker turned back to Mary, who watched as Paola slipped into the hall and put her arms under Scott's armpits and dragged him into their room. Scott's eyes were closed, and Mary feared the worst.

Once she had Scott inside, Paola cried out, "Luca, come back!"

Mary screamed. "Do what she says, Luca! Now!"

The bleaker turned its attention back toward Luca. The boy got up, sliding in Scott's blood, then scrambled into the bedroom, buying Mary a half minute to grab her rifle from the floor. Luca slammed the door shut a nanosecond before the bleaker slammed the weight of its body against the door, clicking and shrieking. The door burst in, and the creature lunged towards the opening.

One bullet.

Mary aimed and pulled the trigger but missed.

She cried out as the creature stepped into the room with the children. With her child.

"No!" she screamed, jumping up.

Just then Desmond appeared with two of the black-outfitted men, all armed.

The three men raised their weapons in unison, took careful aim, then fired into the room. The creature fell to the floor with a thud as Mary screamed out, "Paola!"

Mary stood up and ran into the room as Paola ran into her arms and buried her head in her mother's chest, sobbing. Luca wrapped his arms around Desmond's waist. "Sorry I couldn't help," he said.

"You don't need to be sorry for a thing," Desmond said, then put his hand on the back of Luca's head.

"What happened?" Mary asked Desmond.

He shook his head. "You don't even want to see what's outside. If these men hadn't shown up when they had, we'd all be dead."

"Who are they?"

"Don't know yet, but there are a lot of them. Six cars and more than a dozen men, at least. And it looks like another car was coming when we came inside."

"I think Scott might be dead," Mary said, trying not to cry as she gestured to the boy lying on the floor. She knelt next to him, feeling for a pulse and shook her head. Blood soaked the floor beneath him. Even if they managed to start his heart, there was no way to replace the lost blood.

The sound of several sets of heavy footsteps echoed into the living room, then fell quiet. Seconds later, footsteps creaked up the stairs. Two tall men stepped into the hallway and in front of Paola's room. The taller of the two — a near giant with a broad face and crooked nose — studied the room, then nodded his head. He approached one of the two men with Desmond — a tiny soldier with a thick Brillo of chestnut hair — and said, "Looks like we lost Rutu and Sal."

The soldier shook his head. "They'll be missed," he said.

Desmond looked down to Scott. "We're down one, too."

Without a word, Luca knelt by Scott.

Mary started towards Luca, but Desmond squeezed her hand, pulling her back.

"Let him try," he said.

Luca sat down on the floor, legs crossed, and closed his eyes, going to a place in his head no one understood.

The hallway settled into a lingering silence, most of them likely believing that they were witnessing one child mourning another.

Desmond waved a hand to the new people to indicate that everything was fine. The morning light poured through the window as if Luca were drawing it in and turning up its volume until it obscured him, and Scott, in its brightness. The air crackled with electricity, making the slightest of hums. This was the second time Mary had seen Luca work his magic, yet it seemed no less amazing than when he'd saved her daughter.

When he finally stood, Luca was a full foot closer to the ceiling.

Luca's hair, cut by Mary just three days before, fell in wild tufts to the base of his neck. A thin line of stubble lined his upper lip and the base of his chin. His baggy pajamas were now long shorts, straining their seams. No one could say when his shirt had fallen to the floor, but Luca was bare-chested. Strong, tight muscles replaced the soft flesh of moments ago. Luca faced the onlookers, embarrassed, then walked slowly to Desmond, slipping his arm awkwardly around his waist.

Scott stood, still bloody, but only on the outside. "Wow," was all he managed to say.

The front door slammed downstairs, sending a roll of thunder through the awkward silence. There was no pause, just a single set of footsteps from the front door to the stairs, ending with a face in the hallway that made Desmond and Mary gasp in unison.

"Hello," John said, "It's been much, much too long."

* * * *

CHAPTER 2
BRENT FOSTER

Manhattan
March 20

Manhattan was surreal from the interior of a chopper.

All the intricate plumbing systems man had set into place to keep the island dry had surrendered within days. With nobody left to keep nature at bay, much of the city looked as if it were a Venetian waterway. Except Venice had boats. Manhattan was riddled with floating bodies and the rotting remains of humans and animals. The only living things were the aliens, which was the unofficial label that Black Island Research Facility had given the creatures.

Some of the carnage came from whatever happened on Oct. 15; some of it was from the nuclear fallout that happened after the nuclear power plant meltdowns that began shortly after Brent arrived at Black Island. The fallout and acid rain had subsided considerably, but there were pockets of the world that would be uninhabitable for centuries due to radiation leaks, which poisoned land and water for miles.

They hadn't found a single soul for months, yet the Black Island Guard continued to send teams into the city once a week in hopes of finding survivors, a hope that dulled by the day.

The strange fog that had hovered above the city for several weeks after The Incident had cleared, but the city still seemed off, as if something had permanently shifted the New York Brent once knew into an alien landscape he could barely fathom. It would be easy to blame it on the city being underwater, submerged up to the second floors of most of the downtown buildings, but that wasn't it and Brent knew it. There was something else he couldn't put his finger on. Something else crawling beneath the city's landscape, like spiders under a rock, which made it far more sinister.

"You regret coming?" Michael asked from the seat across from Brent. Michael was one of the first Guardsmen to befriend Brent when he first arrived at the island. Michael was in his mid-40s, a pudgy police officer from Brooklyn before Oct. 15 and one of the first to get drafted into the Black Island Guard, which now stood 30 strong, including Brent, the latest recruit.

"No, I had to see for myself," Brent said through a lie. He did regret it. Whatever hopes he had that they might find Gina and Ben standing on top of a building, waving for help, were murdered the second he saw the vacuum of life.

No people, and no red on the chopper's infrared screens. At least, nothing human.

This is what was left. *Nothing.*

Brent had become almost numb to this new reality without his family, but it didn't make the realization easier to swallow. It was another nail in two coffins he had tried to bury months earlier.

"I'm sorry, Brent," Michael said. "I know how hard it is."

"It is what it is," Brent said, staring out the window. He caught movement out of the corner of his eyes, a pack of aliens scrambling across the rooftops, fleeing the chopper. They moved fast, leaping with almost graceful execution like a herd of gazelle.

"You hear that the alien they had in Level 7 is dead?" Michael asked.

"No. What happened?"

"Just died. Nobody's sure why. Pembrook said the scientists want two more caught and brought back. They're gonna send a unit out tomorrow. Probably gonna send half the squad to make sure there's not a repeat of last time."

"Last time?"

"Two months ago. We lost four guys on that mission."

"I had a friend, Luis, who took down a pack of them in Times Square all by himself," Brent said with a slight smile. It was the first time he'd spoken of Luis since arriving on the island, but probably the hundredth time he thought of the man who'd saved him more than once, and in more than one way. "He would've been one helluva Guardsman."

"What happened to him?"

"He got bit, and a Guardsmen killed him on sight."

"Shit, I'm sorry."

"Like I said, it is what it is."

**

He was an hour late, and the moon was already peeking over the horizon when Brent arrived at Jane's house for dinner. The house, one of 50 on Black Island (now unofficially called New Eden by some), was where the civilians lived. He, however, stayed inside the underground base — a sprawling bunker and laboratory, most of which extended several levels beneath the sea floor — along with the other Guardsmen, scientists, technicians, and the de facto President, Andre Pembrook.

17

New Eden was, at least as far as Pembroke said, the last place on Earth to have power, water, and enough supplies to last at least a hundred years. Brent wasn't sure what supplied the power. There were solar panels on the homes and atop the research facility's above-ground levels, and rows of them on the east end of the island, but he couldn't imagine that these alone could supply such an immense operation.

"Sorry I'm late," he said, as Jane answered the door in a floral print dress.

"Brent!" Emily cried out, running toward him, pigtails bouncing.

He swept the girl in his arms, pulling her into a hug as she plastered his face with kisses.

"How was your day?" Jane asked, as he made his way to the dining room, the table set and ready for dinner. The house smelled delicious, like lasagna, which sat in a casserole dish on the table. Jane was incredibly resourceful, and it was amazing what she could do with the rations allotted each island home.

"Good. Dinner looks great!" he said, taking a seat at the end of the table across from Jane. Emily, her daughter, sat in a chair between them. Though the house was in great condition, especially compared to the city, it reminded him of a home straight out of his childhood, in its out-of-style furnishings. It was as if all the homes on the island were decorated in the '80s and never upgraded.

"Are you ready to say grace?" Jane asked, and Emily began reciting a prayer.

Brent clasped his hands together and closed his eyes, going through the motions. He might not believe in prayer, but he didn't want to offend his hosts or interfere with how Jane was raising Emily.

"How was your day?" he asked, as Jane scooped pasta onto Emily's plate.

"OK. The kids were good."

Jane, who was a teacher in her former life before she quit two years ago after her heart attack, taught the kids at the island's daycare/school. There were six children on the island other than Emily, and Jane taught and looked after them until everyone else returned from work. Everyone on the island was assigned a job based on their skills. There were cooks, maintenance people, farmers, a medic, a seamstress, mechanics, welders, custodial and laundry workers, an electrician, tech people, and others whose jobs helped keep the island running.

There were also a group of scientists Brent had heard of but never met. They never surfaced from Level 7. Their work, and existence, were shrouded in mystery.

Not everyone was suited for their jobs, but the island was stocked with training materials for nearly everything you needed to know about anything. There was little, if any, need for a journalist in the post-apocalypse, so Brent wound up working with the island's Guardsmen, thanks to Michael, who helped ensure he was up to speed on gun training. Michael was no Luis, and given his laid-back personality, Brent didn't think he'd fired too many rounds in the line of duty, but he was a decent shot in practice.

"We painted pictures," Emily said, with a big smile. "I made something for you. May I get it, Mommy?"

"Yes," Jane said, handing Brent a plate of lasagna. "It's still warm; I got a late start."

Brent scooped a forkful of lasagna into his mouth as Emily ran to her bedroom. "This is delicious," he said.

"Thanks, though I would kill for some fresh mozzarella."

"No, it's perfect as is."

"Here you go!" Emily said, running to the table with a huge smile and a painted picture in her hands.

The painting was of a man and woman on a playground with a little girl in a swing. He recognized the blue swing as the playground on the island they'd gone to every weekend since their arrival. "It's Mommy, me, and you!"

Emily stared at him, eyes glimmering with joy, waiting for his response.

"Thank you," he said. "This is great work. I'm going to hang it in my room." He gave Emily another big hug, and caught Jane giving him a weird look, as if to apologize for Emily's exuberance.

"OK, eat your dinner before it gets cold," Jane said.

"I like it cold," Emily said, smiling.

"Should we get some ice cubes for your lasagna, then?" Brent joked.

"Yeah! That would be yummy."

Brent shook his head, laughing, then took a sip of wine. Despite all that had happened in the world during the last five months, Emily was resilient, often silly, hyper, and at times, pouty like any normal little girl. While Jane put on a good show, he could tell that she was having a tougher time. But she was practical, and appeared upbeat most nights when he came over for dinner.

Brent enjoyed being with them, though at times like this he worried that Emily was looking to him as a father figure. They'd grown close over the past few months, bonded by shared tragedy and the human need for companionship in a world circling hell's drain. But there was no romance between Brent and Jane. They were good friends, with similar interests in books and movies. That was it. But Brent wasn't certain Emily understood the distinction. And he wasn't about to say anything to either the girl or her mother for fear of alienating Jane or crushing Emily. So, he simply enjoyed the relationship for what it was, a quasi-family unit that they'd successfully avoided delving into or discussing in any depth at all.

"What did you do today?" Emily asked from behind a mouthful of lasagna.

"Michael and I flew over the city looking to see if we could find any other people."

"Did you?" Emily asked, half-chewed lasagna rendering her question barely intelligible.

"No," Brent said, "Not this time."

"Do you think your family is still alive?" Emily asked.

Jane's face went red. "Emily Rose!"

"What? I was just asking . . ."

"It's okay," Brent said. "I don't know. I don't think there's anyone else out there, at least not in the city."

Emily's eyes were big and sad. "Are you going to keep looking?"

Jane's face grew redder, but it was too late to say anything, so she said, "I'm sorry, Brent. Let's change the subject, shall we?"

"She's curious," Brent said in the child's defense. "It's okay. I don't think the helicopters are going to go out too many more times. And it's too dangerous to go by myself. From what Michael says, they've pretty much scoured the city and gotten everyone they could."

"I don't want you to go back there," Emily said. "They're probably in heaven, anyway."

"Emily!" Jane said, "I want you to apologize to Mr. Foster right now."

Emily looked at him, confused at what she'd said wrong, doe-eyed and adorable. It was impossible to get mad at a face like that – for him, anyway.

"I'm sorry," the girl said. "I just don't want anything bad to happen to you. I don't want to lose you, too."

Brent leaned over and hugged Emily, his eyes welling up. Jane's eyes were red, too, as she excused herself and went into the kitchen, out of sight.

"It's okay, Emily." Brent said, giving her a kiss on the top of her head. "Wait here, I'm gonna get some more to drink, okay?"

"Okay," she said, pushing the food around on her plate with the fork.

Brent went into the kitchen and found Jane leaning against the fridge with her face in her hands, shuddering. She hadn't noticed Brent in the room yet, and he worried that maybe he should go back into the living room so he wouldn't embarrass her. She obviously wanted privacy. Before he could leave, she turned, looked at him, eyes red, cheeks wet, and blew her nose into a napkin.

"I'm sorry," she said.

The awkwardness of the moment deepened. He had no problems showing affection to Emily, but he and Jane were more like two male friends, avoiding anything close to intimacy. As she stood there, vulnerable and crying, he felt stupid not embracing her. He surrendered to his instinct, walked to Jane, and put both arms around her.

She fell into his chest, crying and sniffing louder. Her warmth and lightly perfumed scent reminded him how long it had been since he'd touched another woman. He thought of Gina and how much he missed her, then found himself inappropriately aroused. A flush of guilt flooded his body.

Jesus, Brent, what the hell?

"Are you okay, Mommy?" Emily asked, standing at the kitchen's entrance.

Jane pulled away, leaned down, then hugged her daughter, "Mommy just got sad. I'll be okay."

Brent stared at his "family" as they held their embrace and felt even more like an outsider.

**

After Emily went to bed, Brent and Jane sat on her couch together watching a DVD of some comedy show neither of them had ever seen, nor remembered being on the air. He had no idea whether the show was funny or not because all he could think about was the fact that Jane was just inches away. He grabbed a few looks at her whenever he could, trying not to be too obvious, something Gina said he was horrible at hiding whenever he'd look at another woman on the streets.

Brent was surprised that he'd not really noticed Jane's beauty before now. He'd recognized that she was pretty, of course, but dismissed it as one might recognize their sister as pretty, yet not be attracted to them. But he hadn't really thought of her sexually until their embrace in the kitchen. He hadn't thought of any woman other than Gina, in fact. But now, he found himself intoxicated by the woman's beauty as if she'd just removed a mask and was revealing her true self for the first time. Jane's father was Irish and mother Japanese, leaving her with beautiful fair skin, long, dark hair, and oversized, but gorgeous brown eyes.

As he was looking at her eyes and trying to figure out if it was merely his imagination that had filled them with flecks of gold, she turned and caught his gaze. He meant to turn away, flushed with embarrassment, but instead leaned over, cupped her face in his hand, and kissed her. Softly at first, then passionately, as she fell back and he, on top of her, hands running down over her breasts, down her sides and back up again, kissing her the entire time.

Neither said a word. She let out a sigh as his mouth found her neck. He licked, sucked, and nibbled as his hands moved down, hiking up her dress, then unbuttoning his pants. He was about to slide her underwear aside when Emily screamed.

Jane bolted upright, eyes wide and darting back and forth, avoiding eye contact with Brent. "She gets real bad dreams sometimes," Jane said, even though Brent knew it, and raced into Emily's bedroom.

Brent buttoned his pants and sat up, uncomfortably, on the couch, wondering what the fuck he was doing.

They're still out there.

He closed his eyes, trying to will the nagging thought into submission.

No, they ARE gone.

Stop it. Just . . . stop.

Jane's voice carried from her daughter's room and cut through the inner battle in Brent's head. "It's okay, baby," she said, "Mommy's here."

Brent stood, went to the doorway, and peeked into Emily's room. A blue nightlight lit just enough of the room for him to see Jane sitting at the edge of Emily's bed, stroking her daughter's hair as the girl lay on her side, facing the wall. Jane looked up at him. Again, he felt like an outsider.

He whispered that he needed to go.

She nodded, then waved awkwardly.

Once outside, Brent locked her door with his copy of her key, then headed toward headquarters, a quarter mile away. He wished he'd thought to bring an electric cart, but then again, Brent didn't want to push his privileges too far as a recent recruit.

The air was crisp, cool, and the wind tinged with salt from the ocean, reminding him of the few times he'd taken his family to the shore. And how much more often he wished he had.

* * * *

CHAPTER 3
CHARLIE WILKENS

Dunn, Georgia
March 20
8:40 p.m.

Three flashes of light were followed by a second set before they went black.

The signal outside the gate was Adam's code to enter, but the vehicle wasn't the truck he and Jeremy had left with. Charlie stood from his chair on the second-floor balcony where he'd been waiting nearly two hours for the guys to return.

"You got eyes on the gate?" Charlie called into the radio to Vic, who was on watch in the cupola. "Can you see inside?"

"Hold on, it's dark, but looks like him."

"Wait here, okay?" Charlie said to Callie, half asleep in a lounge chair beside him, where she'd been staring at the stars and engaging in her usual what-ifs. She sat up in her seat, staring at the front gate.

Charlie grabbed the shotgun, ran inside, down the stairs, and out the front door with Boricio, who was holding his trusty bat, and Vic, with his Colt Python.

"Where's the truck?" Boricio asked.

"I dunno," Charlie said as they drew closer to the car, still a blur in the dark, though they were close enough to see it was some sort of dark sedan. The car's interior was bathed in darkness, causing Charlie to silently curse himself for not thinking to bring a light. He hoped Boricio wouldn't notice his lack of planning. There was no room for errors on Team Boricio, even if they'd been safe for nearly three months since finding the compound. And Charlie already felt like the weakest link, aside from maybe Adam. Vic and Jeremy were constantly teasing him, calling him by girls' names and giving him the same shit that Bob did, though they claimed they were just playing. Charlie thought he'd settled the issue of his supposed weakness with what he did to Bob, but most of them hadn't been there to see that, and only Boricio really knew what happened.

In their eyes, Charlie was the kid, the baby of the group. Never mind that Adam was actually weaker, younger, and more timid than Charlie. Somehow Adam got a pass, for reasons Charlie didn't understand. Perhaps it was because Adam was so nice to everyone, practically fawning over them. Or maybe there was some target painted on Charlie that always made him the butt of the jokes, the one most likely to get bullied. The one who couldn't do anything right. The pussy who always chose the path of least resistance. Whatever the case, he found himself in the familiar position of trying to fly under the radar in a pack of wolves. Trying to avoid scrutiny. Trying not to fuck up.

By the time they reached the gate, they got a clearer look inside the car's cabin. Whoever was inside was slumped over the steering wheel, unmoving.

"Who is it?" Charlie called, shotgun raised.

The shape in the car moved, slowly, and the driver's door opened. The shape stepped out, and into the moonlight.

Adam's face was bloodied, his left eye swollen shut, shirt shredded and covered in blood.

"Jesus!" Vic said, "What happened?"

Adam stumbled forward as Boricio unlocked the gate and pulled it open.

Adam shuffled forward then leaned against the car; his hand slipped on the hood, and he nearly fell to the ground. Charlie rushed to his aid and put an arm around him, helping him stand upright.

"They killed Jeremy and took the truck," Adam said, eyes on the ground.

"Who did this?" Boricio asked, enraged.

Adam's eyes wouldn't leave the ground. Charlie couldn't tell if he was afraid to report the bad news to Boricio, or if he was simply too weak to look up. "It was that crew we ran into on the road last week, the pale guys on the motorcycles."

Boricio stared at Adam, laughed, then glared at Charlie. "I told you we shoulda killed those cum-colored fuckers!"

"They didn't do anything," Charlie said defensively.

"Tell that to the walking roadkill," Boricio said, pointing at Adam.

"I meant they didn't do anything last week. They didn't pose a threat."

"This ain't a fucking Sadie Hawkins dance," Boricio yelled, "and we don't fucking wait for invitations or for motherfuckers to 'pose a threat.' We strike first so we can stay alive."

Charlie shook his head, not wanting to have this argument again.

"Let's get you inside," Vic said, helping Adam towards the house.

"Lock the gate," Boricio barked to Charlie, throwing him the keys, as he followed Adam and Vic inside. Charlie shook his head, then caught a glimpse of Callie standing on the balcony, looking down, concerned. He sighed, then turned back and closed the gate, taking an extra moment to lock it, knowing that once inside, he would get an earful from Boricio.

By the time Charlie made it back inside, Adam was sitting beside two battery-operated lanterns at the kitchen table, shirt off, as Callie cleaned his wounds with a rag and a fresh bowl of water. Adam's face was bruised and his nose bloody, probably broken. Blood seeped from a thin, red line slashed across his chest courtesy of the sharp side of a knife. The wound looked scarier than it was, though, as it didn't seem to run too deep.

Adam cringed as Callie hit a tender spot. "Sorry," she said.

"They got you after you made the pickup, or before?" Boricio asked, pacing back and forth.

"After," Adam said.

"Fuck!" Boricio slammed a fist on the black granite kitchen counter. "So they got the truck *and* the supplies."

"Yes, sir," Adam said.

"OK, Lone Ranger, I want you to start from the beginning and tell me exactly how in the fuck this shit went sideways."

"Well, everything was normal. We hit the store, loaded the truck, and were about halfway back when all of a sudden we heard the motorcycles and saw the lights behind us. At least six of them, all on bikes. They drove in front of us and blocked the road, with guns aimed at us."

"And you didn't just run the fuck through them?" Boricio asked, "Jesus, Mary and Joseph, that's a holy trinity of fucking stupid. Why wouldn't you floor it?"

"I was afraid they'd shoot us if we didn't stop."

"Well fuck a duck, son." Boricio said. "Looks like you just screwed the pooch. What happened next?"

"We got out of the truck and one of the guys, the bald one with the patch, asked us what we had in the truck. I'm pretty sure he knew, though. So I told him 'supplies' and he said they didn't belong to us, that we'd stolen them from the store, and he was gonna take them back and we ought not to get in his way."

"And then?" Boricio asked, full attention on Adam's story while Vic paced in the shadows where the kitchen opened to the dining room.

"Well, Jeremy said 'Hell no', so the guy with the patch shot him right in the head. I wanted to shoot the guy, but there were six of them and I knew I couldn't get them all. He told me to give him my gun."

"And you did?" Boricio's upper lip twitched.

"Yeah," Adam said, eyes on Boricio, like a child afraid he was about to see the slapping side of a belt. "So, the guy took my gun, then hit me in the face with his shotgun. All the other guys started laughing. He asked me for the keys, and I asked him if he was gonna shoot me. He laughed and said if he'd planned to do that, I'd already have maggots making babies in the holes. So, I handed him the keys, and he was all, 'See, I told you I wasn't gonna shoot you' then headed to the back of the truck to see what was inside. The other guys followed, except one, who stood over me. I don't know what took so long, but they seemed to be looking in the back of the truck forever. Then the guy who was watching me went to join them. I got up and ran into the woods, but they came after me, and knocked me down. I thought for sure that was it. The bald guy came over, leaned down, slid the knife across my chest, and said, 'Tell your people that we own Dunn, and we'd better not see them again.' Then they left me there. I walked a half a mile or so, without a gun or anything, praying I wouldn't run into one of them monsters. Then I found a house, went inside, got the keys to a car, then drove back here as fast as I could."

"Thank God you're alive," Callie said, looking up at Charlie, quietly urging him to say something.

"You did a good job," Charlie said, figuring someone should praise him if Boricio wasn't.

Boricio laughed, "If shitting the bed and losing a truck along with one of our men is what constitutes a good job these days, well fuck me in the face and show me where I can sign up for the union." Boricio laughed, then added, "My, my, how far the mighty Team Boricio has fallen."

Charlie looked up. "Do we really want to bag on him while he's down? I'm sure he feels like shit enough already."

Boricio's eyes drilled into Charlie. He seemed like he wanted to say something, but kept his mouth shut in a rare moment of silence.

"So, what are we gonna do?" Vic, the walking steroid case, asked. "We're not gonna take this shit, are we?"

"I dunno," Boricio said. "Let's ask Prince Charles, here. Do we want to make this shit straight, or should we just pack our bags, tuck our dicks in between our legs and cluck the fuck out of Dunn because One-Eyed Willy and his gang of cum-colored fucktards said to get off their turf?"

"There's enough homes and stores for all of us," Callie said, ignoring Boricio's usual ranting. "Why did they rob us? It's not like there's that many people competing for resources, right? They're the only ones we've seen, right?"

"Well, them and The Prophet's compound, but that's about an hour away," Charlie said. "Maybe supplies are drying up around Dunn? Or maybe they're just acting now to get what they can before they do? Maybe they've run into other people left behind?"

"Who gives a dickstick dipped in twat oil WHY they robbed us," Boricio said, swinging his hands theatrically. "It's Top-of-the-Food-Chain time, kids! That means kill or be killed, whether you're human or monster. I know Charlie and Adam here have this cozy notion that people are 'nice' and we ought to be a happy band of Mr. Rogers types, taking off our shoes and wiping survivors' asses if they can't do it themselves. But when the cosmic shit hits the fan, people ain't nothin' but animals – hunter or prey. And in case any of you fuckers were in the bathroom tossing one off during intermission, Boricio is a hunter. The only question is what do you all wanna be?"

"Hunters!" Vic shouted as he came back into the kitchen, fist in the air like he was rooting for his favorite wrestler.

Boricio smiled. "What about the rest of you?"

Charlie and Callie were silent. Adam whispered, "Hunter," avoiding eye contact with anyone.

Boricio looked at Charlie, eyes wide and smile manic. "Well, what say you, Charles in Charge? Hunter or hunted?"

"Hunter, but ... "

"Nope, nope, nope. No buts! Predator or prey. No middle ground, no gray areas, no nothing. Kill or be killed."

"I'm not down with killing people for no reason," Charlie said. "When we passed those bikers on the road, there was no reason to do anything. Not at the time. Yeah, they gave us dirty looks, and there was a tense moment where it looked like they might make a move, but they didn't do anything. They kept on going."

"Yeah, but apparently, they circled back," Boricio said. "Maybe they followed us back here and have been watching us since, waiting with fangs. Fuck, maybe they're in the bushes ready to rattle right now. Maybe *they're* the smart ones here, and Team Boricio is a drooling bunch of dumbasses riding the short bus to the graveyard."

Vic looked like he'd been smacked in the face, then ran upstairs, back to his lookout post.

"Listen, Charlie, I appreciate you've got a nice pink pussy side. But that's the same side that had your stepdaddy beatin' the shit out of you, right? There's no place in this world for nice; not no more. We're an endangered species, and there ain't no place for the weak. If you can't pull the trigger, you're already extinct."

"We all know what I'm capable of," Charlie said, glaring back at Boricio. "Just ask Bob if I can pull the trigger. Oh yeah, you can't. Can you?"

Boricio smiled. "Fair enough, Chucky. Fair enough. But not everyone's gonna give you an excuse like Bobby Big Boy. Sometimes, you're gonna have to find a reason. And most times that reason boils down to whether your hard-on to live is fatter than the next fucker's. So, are you two with me? You hunters? Are you gonna help me hunt these fuckers down, get our truck back, then shove a shit sandwich straight down One-Eyed Willy's throat?"

Charlie swallowed, "Yes."

"Definitely," Callie said. Though she was tough, she wasn't bloodthirsty. But seeing her friend Adam injured sparked her fiercely protective streak. "Let's get these fuckers."

**

Midnight

The house was silent. Callie had retired to the bedroom a half hour earlier. Boricio had been down for an hour or so while Vic was still upstairs in his spot, supposedly wide awake on red alert. Charlie found Adam alone, sitting in an overstuffed recliner in the living room, reading a book by lantern light.

"How's it going?" Charlie asked. "Feeling any better?"

"Yeah," Adam said, "Feeling stupid more than hurt."

"Don't let it get to you. I would've done the same thing," Charlie said, sitting on the couch across from Adam. "No way you could've known they'd kill Jeremy."

"Worst thing is, Jeremy actually told me I ought to run them down."

"No shit?"

"Yeah, but I didn't want to tell Boricio or he'd blame me even more."

"Yeah, he can overreact sometimes," Charlie said with a grin.

Adam laughed, then coughed and winced.

"Jeremy was a good guy," Adam said. "I mean, I know he was kinda an asshole sometimes, and Boricio didn't care for him, but he was always nice to me."

"I hear you," Charlie said, though if he was being honest, he would have said good riddance. Jeremy was nice to Adam because Adam kissed his ass. Otherwise, the guy, a 38-year-old former stockbroker on vacation when shit hit the fan, was a raging douche bag who always had to have his way. The only good thing the guy had ever done, as far as Charlie was concerned, was find the three-story house they called, half-jokingly, their compound.

The home was huge, three stories, 12 bedrooms, five baths, and a separate five-car garage, but it wasn't a true compound like The Prophet's, where they'd been held as prisoners. The home had a wrought iron gate, a well, and a generator that they were able to use when they had fuel. Best of all, the home was located in the middle of nowhere, and they'd avoided detection by man or monster . . . until now, perhaps.

Charlie wondered if Boricio was right. Had the bikers followed them to the compound? Were there enemies hiding in the dark, waiting to strike? Charlie wondered how the hell Boricio could sleep with all the uncertainty in the air. He considered talking to Adam about the matter, figure out whether or not Adam thought anyone had followed him, but the kid was feeling shitty enough without adding the worry of an impending enemy strike to his plate.

"Why don't you get some sleep?" Charlie suggested.

"I've got lookout in a few minutes."

"I got it."

"You sure?" Adam said, "Isn't Callie waiting for you?"

"She's passed out," Charlie said, not bothering to clarify a misconception in the house that he and Callie were an item. Though they'd gotten close, and they slept in the same room, oftentimes in the same bed, Charlie was imprisoned behind the Friend Zone. And to be honest, he didn't care. Having Callie in his life was enough. Or at least that's the lie he kept telling himself. He maintained the lie partly to appear like less of a loser, but also as a way to protect Callie from the others. They hadn't seen another woman in a long time. While Charlie trusted Boricio as much as a guy like Boricio could be trusted, and Adam seemed harmless enough, he didn't trust Jeremy or Vic. Well, Vic, now that Jeremy was gone. None of the others needed to know the details of his relationship with Callie, so let them believe whatever they wanted if it kept them from sniffing around her like dogs in heat.

"You sure?" Adam asked.

"I'm up," Charlie said. "No problem. You catch some Z's and get better. God only knows when Boricio and Vic will want to hunt down the fuckers who did this to you."

* * * *

CHAPTER 4
RYAN OLSON

Brentwood, Missouri
Oct. 14, 2011
6:27 p.m.

Ryan Olson knew shit would splatter fan blades the second he saw Pete's car mulling about the Shop N' Save parking lot.

What the hell is he doing here?

Ryan glanced back at the registers; five lanes open. While the lines were maybe a little longer than they were supposed to be, and two cashiers had called in sick, he didn't need to take a register yet. Plus, Becky and Rosa were due back from break in 10 minutes. So, things *should be* cool, and he could slip outside without it turning into the end of the world. Of course, when it came to the grocery store, the end of the world happened at least twice a shift.

He grabbed the intercom microphone on the wall and called for the head stock boy, Bill, to come to the front end.

Bill appeared a few minutes later, mopping a hand across his sweaty brow. "What's up, Ryan?"

"I'm taking my lunch break now, I need you to watch the front end, okay?"

"Sure," Bill said, eagerly peeling off his blue apron, and tucking his white shirt over his big gut and into his pants. "Who's on break?"

"Becky and Rosa; they should be back soon, then Dex will probably want his break. But if we're in the weeds, he can wait."

"K," Bill said, taking over the captain's spot on the front end, the one that allowed him to see the entire front of the store. Though Bill didn't know it, he would never make management. Despite being a great worker and always on time, he was too sloppy and awkward with people, especially women. He was a 35-year-old who still lived at home with his mother and lacked the skills needed to be much more than a cog in the retail machine. To be management, you had to be great with people. Bill was scared of them. However, his eagerness to rise from the ranks of stock boy, where he'd been for 11 years, meant he would do whatever was asked, eager to prove himself to management, even the assistant manager, Ryan. Which was great when Ryan needed to break for longer than usual.

Ryan clocked out, but instead of heading straight out the front doors, he took the long way. Murphy's Law: When employees saw you were about to go on break, they quickly developed last minute emergencies requiring urgent response.

Ryan, a customer said the strawberries taste off.

Ryan, the bathroom is flooded; we need to call a plumber.

Ryan, my baby's got a sore throat; I need to take off, and no, it doesn't have anything at all to do with that concert I have tickets for.

That was just the employees. Customers were worse. Ryan was amazed that most people managed to get through the day without his help.

Ryan slipped on his black jacket and made his way to the back of the store before sneaking out the front doors. He found that the fewer people who knew he was on his way to lunch, the quieter his break would be. And when it came to dealing with a problem like Pete, the less attention on Ryan, the better. Once he was certain the cashiers and stock boys were otherwise engaged, he made his way out the front doors and scanned the parking lot for Pete.

Pete was sitting in his black sedan about 10 rows back, listening to loud rap music, bouncing his head under a black skull cap and dark shades, looking as suspicious as, and not unlike, a drug dealer in a family park.

Ryan glanced around to make sure nobody was paying attention to him, then approached Pete's car and squatted on his knees beside the driver's side.

"What the fuck are you doing here?" Ryan asked.

"Viktor wants to know your answer."

"I said no, the answer's not changing," Ryan said, through clenched teeth.

"I was really hoping you wouldn't say that," Pete said, taking a deep drag on his joint. "He's not gonna be happy."

"I don't care if he's unhappy. *This* isn't an option. I'll pay him back, but it's gonna take time. Another week, at most. What's seven days to Viktor?"

"I don't get it, man," Pete said, taking his shades off and meeting Ryan's eyes. "The dude is giving you an out. An EASY fucking out. Most people would kill for this, and you're saying no?"

Ryan shook his head, refusing to waver. "I'm not putting innocent people at risk. You tell him I said no. He will HAVE to wait."

Pete shook his head. "Don't be stupid, Ryan. We'll be in and out, nobody gets hurt, nobody knows you were involved. Easy. As. Shit."

Ryan closed his eyes, stared at the pavement, littered with chunks and slivers of broken glass. Pete had a point. The problem of Viktor could turn to vapor if Ryan would just play ball. No more debt. No hovering threat of Viktor's goons. It would all go away. But the risk was too great. He couldn't live with himself if something went wrong. He couldn't look Mary or Paola in the eyes if innocent people were hurt because of him.

"I can't." Ryan said. "Tell him no."

Pete let out a deep sigh. "Shit, dude, you are either the dumbest fucker ever, or the ballsiest. You sure you want me to make this call?"

Ryan nodded yes and watched as Pete dialed Viktor on his burner cell.

"Hey, it's me . . . No, he's saying no deal. He wants another week."

Ryan couldn't hear what was being said on the other end, and Pete's face was blank, save for his usual stoner expression.

Then, something Viktor said dilated Pete's eyes.

He handed Ryan the phone. "He wants to talk to you."

Ryan felt the acid in his chest rise as his pulse quickened. He reached for the phone, then stole another glance around the parking lot to make sure nobody was watching.

"Yes?"

"Am I to understand you're saying no?" Viktor's voice said, smooth and reptilian.

"Yes, sir," Ryan said. "It's too risky. We don't need to do it like this. I just need one more week."

"No, you've had enough time." Viktor said. "It's time to pay. You either pay now, or we'll have to settle. How we settle is up to you, but I'd take the easy way if I was you."

"It won't work," Ryan said. "Someone could get hurt. Someone will find out I was involved. Too much risk. If you can't wait a week, just come and get me. I'm tired of living under the threat that you're gonna send someone after me. You're a businessman; you realize if your guys come after me, you'll never get your money. So why not just wait another week?"

Viktor settled into a quiet that lingered too long; every silent second twisted the anxiety rising in Ryan's gut.

Finally, Viktor spoke. "You're right; if I hurt you, I won't get my money. But I have a feeling that if I send some of my men to Warson Woods, pay a visit to your family, maybe *that* might change your mind?"

Ryan froze, rage threatening to boil over.

"You stay away from my family," he said, doing his best to keep his anger contained.

"Then you pay me tonight. Your choice. Put Pete back on."

Ryan handed the phone to Pete, hand shaking. Pete listened for 10 seconds or so, then said, "OK, boss" and hung up.

"So, what's it gonna be? You in?"

Ryan stared, paralyzed by fear. He knew Viktor was dangerous. Knew he'd gone in too deep with his gambling. Knew that someday his luck might run out, and maybe he'd get a beat-down. But never did he consider that Viktor would go after his family. Hell, he didn't even think Viktor *knew about* Mary or Paola.

This was it.

Ryan was finally out of options.

He'd gone too far this time, and now there was enough shit to make sure the fan stopped spinning forever.

He nodded to Pete, "I'm in."

* * * *

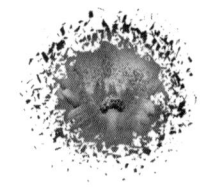

CHAPTER 5
LUCA HARDING

Luca moved his bishop in a diagonal line across the board, removed a black knight from the other side, and settled his bishop in its place. There was silence in his head. The Black Pieces weren't talking. They were probably mad because Luca had just taken the knight.

The Black Pieces were like that sometimes, even when they weren't playing chess with Luca. Sometimes they would start talking from nowhere, capturing his attention and demanding that he keep it. There were four of them, so far as he could tell. They all sounded similar, weird and kind of high-pitched in voice, almost like he imagined elves would sound. They said they didn't have individual names, and instead called themselves Black Pieces because that was how he'd first noticed and thought of them during a game of chess. Luca thought it weird that they didn't have names before now. But that was the least of all the weirdness in his life these days, so he didn't fight the idea.

Most of the time the Black Pieces said the same sorts of things; things he mostly understood, though every once and a while they said something that sent a cold chill through Luca's body.

The Black Pieces came back and told Luca to move one of their pawns two spaces to make room for a rook. Luca moved the pawn, then returned to his thoughts while pondering his own next move.

The Black Pieces were nicer than most of the voices. Always calm and reasonable. And they always answered back. The other voices ignored his responses and questions. They were like TV or the radio since he could only hear the voices, and they only went one way. Luca could sometimes see them, too, but only when he slept.

The Black Pieces were always around. That's why they could play chess together.

Luca moved one of his pawns forward, then waited for the Black Pieces.

Luca caught his reflection in the mirror on the far side of the room, then quickly looked away. He hated his reflection. It was worse than the worst scary movie he ever saw, which was probably this movie called *The Lovely Bones* he saw last summer. Mom said he shouldn't see it, but Dad insisted he was old enough. Mom was right because *The Lovely Bones* had given him nightmares for a month.

Luca hated how old he looked. It was weird. Paola had been looking at him like he was from another planet since they met. Now that he looked like the college kids who hung out at the Town Center in Las Orillas, she probably wouldn't want to be around him at all. Paola laughed at his jokes and seemed to enjoy being around him, but Luca was sure that if the world was filled with more people, she wouldn't care about him at all. They were probably just friends because Paola didn't have a choice.

He caught his reflection again, but this time he held it. Not because he was comfortable ~ the mirror still made him feel yucky ~ but because looking into the mirror gave him a view of a younger but still breathing version of his father, and he suddenly couldn't bear to turn away.

Luca moved for the Black Pieces, still transfixed.

Even if Luca looked just like his father, he had still only been on Earth for eight years. It was making him feel weird; how the thoughts in his head were starting to feel so much older than his eight years. Luca didn't *think* as old as he looked, but he also didn't *think* nearly as young as he was.

Luca took the final black knight and wondered again what Paola really thought of him. He loved playing with her. Mary and Desmond were like his new mom and dad, or at least the closest thing to parents that he had now. So, that meant Paola was like his sister. But he didn't feel about Paola like he did about his sister, Anna. Not at all. Paola gave him a weird feeling, and reminded him of something his dad once said:

Young love softens the mind too much to control the body's tingles.

Luca hadn't really known what it meant; still didn't. But he was somehow sure it had something to do with how he was feeling now, sure it had to do with the weird feeling he never had before tingling in the place he wasn't supposed to talk about.

Luca moved for Black Pieces again, taking his own white knight with the Black Pieces' rook.

He wished Jimmy were still alive. Jimmy probably would have had good advice on the subject. Luca didn't have the courage to discuss his feelings with any of the grown-ups, though he did manage to ask Will if he thought Paola might ever like him as more than a friend. Will said, "Chicken pox and puppy love are both terrible after 20, so you're definitely in the right time frame." Will's answer mostly confused Luca, so he asked Will about the funny feelings he was getting. Will laughed and said, "Girls will melt your brain and make blood run to your lips, cheeks, and everywhere else. You can't and won't ever be able to do anything about it. Might as well stop trying now." That left Luca more confused than ever.

That was a month ago; after they'd found the house and farm but before Will started acting weird. Luca thought Will was weird most times now, even though no one else really seemed to notice. Will hadn't acted weird today, though. Will had been all business. Like the old Will who found him in California and flew him to Missouri.

He'd come up the stairs a step behind John, just after Luca healed Scott. There was no mistaking the looks Will traded with Desmond. Neither knew what to think about John coming back, but one thing was certain – neither liked it. Luca overheard Desmond saying, "This scene seem a bit too well written for you?" Will barely nodded, but his eyes were burning.

Luca moved his rook to the top of the board.

John had been insistent:; They had to leave immediately. They weren't safe. The bleakers who breached the gate were only the beginning, he said. More were coming, too many to count. It was easy to believe. The outside looked like burned food. The black bodies of the dead bleakers were in gross piles everywhere. Bullets usually ripped them to pieces because their bodies were so soft. All their arms and legs and insides on the ground looked like a nightmare exploded.

John told them about a place in Alabama where he had been living for the last few months; a place where they would be welcome and safe, with plenty of food, supplies, and good people – some of whom had come to help them today. They would be well taken care of, he promised.

Luca listened to everything John said, just like everybody else. He couldn't tell what Desmond and Mary were thinking even though he tried to read their faces. Paola didn't like it at all, he was sure of that. This was her new home, and she wouldn't want to leave. It didn't take Luca long to decide he didn't like it at all. Listening to John talk about Alabama only made him suddenly miss Jimmy all over again. And worse, it got him thinking about Dog Vader.

Just like the nightmare piles outside.

Luca's rook disappeared; Black Pieces had infiltrated the back row and put Luca's queen in jeopardy.

Paola told Luca that after John left she heard Will whispering to Desmond and her mom. Will said he'd been dreaming of the place John was talking about; said John showing up was odd, no doubt, but the place John was talking about seemed like the same place they were supposed to go. It'd been the place he'd been thinking about night and day for nearly a month but didn't know how to get to. Luca protected his queen with his remaining knight, then waited for the Black Pieces to tell him their next move.

Paola sounded scared when she told Luca what she overheard. Luca said not to worry, it was a good thing John had come back. They were going to be saved. Paola believed him, even if he didn't even know whether or not he should believe in John himself. John made him think about Dog Vader an awful lot, and several of the voices agreed that John shouldn't be trusted, which was funny since the Black Pieces rarely agreed on anything.

Thinking about Paola made the funny feeling come back. Though, if Luca really thought about it, it had never gone away. Ever since healing Scott, and him getting old fast again just like he had back at the Drury Inn, the feeling had never left. But now it was stronger than ever. It used to feel like part of his body was waking up from sleep. Now it kind of hurt. Luca felt a need to touch himself, which is why he kept his hands at the edges of the chessboard.

Luca thought of Paola, and for the millionth time wondered what she would have thought of him if they met under different circumstances. He imagined her standing a few feet in front of him, so pretty, with her dark hair and big eyes and lips. Her lips were usually ready to smile and loved to tell the jokes that made him laugh. Her lips were also fierce with her mother, but in a way that Luca liked. Paola said the sorts of things that Luca felt, but would have never been able to say to his own mom.

 He hadn't thought much about her body before, but waiting for the Black Pieces to make the next move made Luca imagine the slight curve of her hip. And that made him feel the uncomfortable tingle below his waist again.

He turned his attention to the chessboard - moving for the Black Pieces and then immediately moving for himself, getting his queen to safety again - when there was a slight knock on the door. Mary poked her head inside.

Luca looked up, surprised. "Just checking on you," Mary said behind her smile, laced with its usual little bit of sadness. "Are you coming out? Desmond told everyone you needed a minute, but the natives are getting restless. There's seven cars ready to take us."

Mary glanced at the board and saw both sets of pieces. Luca could feel her eyes on his right hand hovering just above the Black Pieces' queen, ready to make his next move; could feel her trying to ignore it. Luca suddenly realized how pretty Mary was, how much she looked like Paola. He felt the funny feeling again, followed by a wave of guilt.

"The clothes fit okay?" she asked.

"They're a little big," Luca said, "but not too bad." He smiled awkwardly, trying to ignore the funny feeling, waiting for Mary to leave and hoping the Black Pieces wouldn't get impatient and disappear again.

There were plenty of grown-up clothes in the house. Even though Luca had grown several inches, he was much skinnier than everyone else and swam in the grown-up clothes.

"I'm glad," Mary said. "Let's give it another five minutes, okay? We're loading up now. We're in the last car, the burgundy van at the end of the line." Mary smiled once more, then shut the door behind her.

Paola's mom was harder to read than anyone else in Luca's new family. She loved Desmond and had an overwhelming need to look out for everyone else, but the only thing she ever really thought about was protecting Paola. Other stuff mattered, but not as much. It reminded Luca of when he was 5 and the only thing he wanted to watch was *Return of the Jedi*. Other movies were good, too. And he liked them when they were on, but he was always thinking about the Ewoks and Luke's final battle with the Emperor and his dad, Darth Vader.

Luca moved for the Black Pieces, then quickly made his own move to keep the game going so the Black Pieces wouldn't have to wait.

Luca closed his eyes and waited for the Black Pieces, but they seemed to have disappeared. Luca called out in his mind but heard no response.

Luca wasn't sure what to do. If the Black Pieces were done playing, he could go downstairs and get going. Maybe they would finish later. But if the Black Pieces came back and still wanted to play but Luca was gone, they would be mad. And that wouldn't be good.

The Black Pieces were usually nice. Luca had only seen them get mad twice before. The first time was back during February's incident; the one Desmond promised they would never have to talk about. The second was earlier this morning, right before the bleakers came.

When the Black Pieces got mad, they didn't even act like the Black Pieces anymore. They acted like the *Man in the Center* instead.

He couldn't help but notice that he was just a couple moves away from checkmating the Black Pieces. Luca wondered if that was why they had disappeared. The Black Pieces hated to lose.

The Man in the Center had been in Luca's head ever since the Drury. *The Man* wasn't the boss of all the other voices, but he seemed to always be in the middle.

Luca scratched his head. This was always so hard, trying to figure stuff out and have it make sense.

The Man in the Center was like the sun. The sun wasn't the boss of the day, but if it didn't come out, the day didn't exist. The voices liked to tell him stuff, especially about Will, but Luca somehow knew they weren't allowed to say anything without the *Man's* permission.

Except for the Black Pieces. Luca was pretty sure the Black Pieces were allowed to say whatever they wanted.

The voices had told Luca a lot, but they hadn't told him what he should tell the rest of his new family. He didn't want to tell them anything, really. It would only scare them. And everyone was already scared enough. So, he would continue to wait. He could always tell everyone if it looked like they were about to step into any danger. Besides, Will knew everything already.

The Black Pieces returned to the board.

Luca moved the Black Pieces' queen into his white rook's square.

Check.

If Will wanted everyone to know, he would have told them. There was a good reason he hadn't, Luca was sure. Will had to know that Luca knew, too. He would've seen it in the dreams. Hardly a night went by that they didn't share the same dreams.

Luca moved his king a square to the left, then moved the Black Pieces' bishop.

Check.

Unless Paola, or anyone in his new family, was in danger, Luca would stay quiet. After all, Will knew the secret, the same secret the Black Pieces and *The Man* both knew.

The secret they said would change everything.

Luca realized he was trapped. He moved his king one final square to the left, two away from one of the Black Pieces' more aggressive pawns.

Checkmate.

* * * *

CHAPTER 6
BORICIO WOLFE

Dunn, Georgia
March 21
6:29 p.m.

Boricio, Charlie, and Vic roared down the highway in what Charlie had nicknamed "The Boriciomobile" a few minutes after it was first unveiled by Harry, their resident welder back at the compound.

There couldn't have been too many assholes left breathing who could do what Harry could do. When it came to tricking out cars, the fucker made the impossible possible, and did it with a shit-eating grin. He used to have a warehouse-sized garage in Houston, but his last customer picked up their custom Porsche Cayenne — iPad console freshly installed — on Oct. 14. Boricio was happy to make his acquaintance about two months after that. Harry had made it to Alabama with his own pimped-out Land Rover, but Boricio wanted something custom-made and Harry was happy to comply.

Harry got started with a Ford Expedition chassis, then leaned on Boricio's scribbles and profanity-filled instructions, followed by hundreds of hours of welding.

Harry was building the first car they'd need; the one that was safe to travel in as a group. Now that it was finished, the real Boriciomobile was also being finished — built on the body of a beautiful, gloss-black BMW Z8 Boricio had brought back from a luxury dealer in Montgomery. Boricio spent a lot of the seconds when he wasn't lamenting the lack of fresh, pink meat to think up new ways to make the Z8 cooler than anything that little bitch James Bond had ever driven. But until then, he'd stay slap happy with the current model Boriciomobile.

The Boriciomobile was bulletproofed from head to toe and outfitted with side-mounted machine guns on each side. The car only had four homemade missiles in its rear launcher, but that was all they'd been able to make and enough to demolish anything in their way. And like they were playing an old game of Spy Hunter, the Boriciomobile had a built-in oil slick that dropped a thick layer of oil on the road behind the truck, giving any dumb shit dumb enough to follow a detour onto Fuck You Road. The Boriciomobile also had a smoke screen and spiked wheels; the only thing Harry said was a no-go were the caltrops. Boricio insisted Harry figure out a way to make the spiked metal motherfuckers launch from their built-in chamber in the Expedition's side panel, even though Harry didn't have the springs he needed. He worked on it for two weeks straight, but Boricio finally listened to reason once Harry told Boricio that, yeah, he could eventually figure it out, but it would delay him getting started on Boricio's Z8.

Boricio said, "Do the fuckers still drop?"

Harry said, "Yeah. They'll drop. Tear the tires behind you to shit."

"Well then," Boricio winked, slapped Harry on the back, and laughed loudly. "Let's call this project complete, fully gassed, and ready to drive 95 miles an hour to Fuck-All."

They'd been driving all day, searching for the gang of bitches who had robbed Boricio's boys. Boricio wanted revenge, and hell if he wasn't happy to get the fuck out of the compound for a hunt. And a group hunt at that! Boricio hadn't really allowed the rest of the team to see the real him, the one that killed or fucked anything he wanted. The one that would scare the shit out of all of them except maybe Vic. If he ever allowed the fully unfiltered Boricio to be seen, he could have a hard time holding onto them all. And while he had originally intended to fly solo in the post-apocalypse, he was sort of enjoying this new role as leader. Plus, given enough time, they wouldn't think twice about his predilections. Or so he figured.

Tonight would offer him the opportunity to kill with unbridled glee and nobody would think twice. They were there for revenge, after all. And in the guise of revenge, Boricio could do whatever the fuck he wanted short of skull fucking a corpse. *That might draw some odd looks.*

Boricio laughed when they found the truck and motorcycles parked in front of a warehouse, 17 miles east of his compound.

"We're heeeere," he said to the passengers and took out his binoculars and surveyed the area.

Shit.

Boricio handed the binoculars back to Charlie. "We need to go."

"We're not doing anything?" Charlie said.

"What the fuck?" Vic shouted in the back seat.

"Did you see those fuckers out there? Cocky as a bunch of bayou crocodiles, what with four guards standing in front of the warehouse in broad daylight. Must think themselves the Justice League. We could've popped those four fuckers into the ever-after without even getting out of the truck. But we ain't got no idea what's waiting inside. And I'd like to know what the hell four guards are waiting for. Makes me think they know something Boricio don't. If we don't know what's in their playbook, we should probably just piss on the pages. So, let's lay out what we do know: dumb shit fuckers usually don't know how to get four, even when they've got two and two staring them in the titties. If we want them drinking, we've gotta give 'em Cinco de Fucking Mayo in their backyard."

Vic and Charlie nodded. Even if they didn't know exactly what Boricio meant, and they looked like they didn't, they'd been with Boricio long enough to follow his lead. Fuck it. They would figure it out one way or another before shots were fired; that was all that mattered.

Vic was a born hunter. Daddy gave him a .22 for his 10th birthday, and the giant fucker had been shooting into the trees ever since. The dude brought down his first deer before he turned 12; the bullet had struck home right between Bambi's pretty little eyes, he'd said. That made his daddy proud. Unlike the rest of Team Boricio, Vic actually liked his old man, and in a way that made Boricio leave him alone. The other boys would've been heckled to death, talking about how they loved their daddies. But when Boricio had asked Vic if he swallowed his daddy's spunk, or just spit it into a napkin like his baby brother, Vic looked at him with the same brand of boiling rage that washes the face of someone about to put a bitch six feet beneath the daisies.

"How many you think are in there?" Charlie asked.

"You ain't scared, are ya?" Vic asked, laughing. "Shit, Boricio, maybe you shoulda made Charlie stay home instead of Callie."

"I'm not scared," Charlie said. "Just trying to think of the best way to do this."

"Good point, Charlie Brown, which is exactly why we're gonna liven this party up a bit," Boricio said. "And nothing livens a party up like a few dozen uninvited party crashers. And I've got just the plan."

**

An hour later, Boricio and the boys were descending rapidly upon their designated sides of the warehouse, each behind the wheel of his own steel stallion: an old Honda Prelude, a new Honda Pilot, and a shiny, red Dodge Charger Boricio had a hard time not just taking back to the compound.

With all three cars parked, they bolted back to the Boriciomobile, hit the alarms on the key chains, and waited as the sirens wailed.

Two more bikers came outside to investigate the noise. One looked Hispanic and the other even darker. *A half-black?* That surprised Boricio; the group he'd seen on the bikes looked like skinheads who generally didn't take to partnering up with brown people. Boricio looked through the binoculars. "Two shit smears added to party," Boricio said. "Looks like we hit our minimum."

Boricio's minimum, conveyed to Charlie and repeated to Vic, had been: *No less than six dumb fuck bikers before we start shooting, got it?*

"Now?" Vic asked.

Boricio nodded.

Charlie was the first to pull the trigger, though only by a half second. His shot was good, hitting the biker closest to the door directly in the shoulder. He fell back as Charlie's second bullet tore through the guard's skull. Vic nailed three in a row, sending the two soldiers on the roof spiraling over the side before training his sights on the ground, clearing the fourth soldier before sending an unnecessary bullet into the fifth Charlie had already finished.

"Well lookie who's been learning to bull's eye something besides Callie's face," Boricio said, slapping Charlie hard on the back. Charlie grunted and turned to the warehouse.

Boricio had called dibs on "whichever fucker was stupid enough to talk into a walkie-talkie." Vic and Charlie were silent as he took careful aim.

Boricio pulled the trigger, and the walkie-talkie flew to the concrete, followed a second later by its handler. The scream was deafening as the team leader's kneecap shattered, pooling the already bloody parking lot with a new, wider river of blood. Boricio pulled the trigger again, turning the guard's hand into a sloppy slab of meat. Boricio started to laugh. "You see that fucker flapping like his hand was made of fish. That's what happens to stupid fuckers who start shit they don't know how to finish."

Boricio was cut off by the sudden screeching of monsters, clicking in deafening waves surging toward the still-screaming cars and crashing through the center gate of the warehouse, which the dead bikers had left open.

"Ramblers, let's ramble," Boricio said, pointing to the Boriciomobile.

A whole lot of pants must've been meeting a whole lotta shit from behind the warehouse walls, judging by the way the bikers started pouring out the open bay door. And they were armed a lot more elegantly than Boricio expected: Agrams and Bruggers and Hecklers; expensive foreign shit Boricio hadn't expected to see in the sticks.

Boricio gunned the engine and rolled down the ravine, smashing through the chain link fence surrounding the warehouse before plowing into the warehouse door, which crumpled like a beer can beneath a boot.

"Well, how about that!" Boricio screamed. "They sure don't build shit like they used to." Boricio laughed to himself, slapped his knee, then revved the engine in reverse, running down a pair of the monsters, tearing their leather with a sickening THWTHWIIIPSH.

"The fuck you pureed pussy meat waiting for?" Boricio yelled. "Shoot some fuckers!"

Vic and Charlie lowered their windows and fired their guns, barely taking aim. Monsters and soldiers dropped into piles while Boricio continued to laugh, firing the side machine guns until they were empty, then launching a missile into an adjoining garage just because he could. He would've sent the missile sailing straight into the warehouse, but he didn't know if there was a prize inside the box and didn't want to ruin it if there was.

"Stop!" Charlie yelled, pointing out the window to a huddle of three women and several more children hunched low and moving fast behind the smoke to count. They were headed toward the tree line. "There are children out there," he said. "We don't kill kids. We can't kill kids."

"Kids ain't nothing but future adults waiting for pubes. That makes them early bird fucking specials."

Charlie said nothing. Boricio ignored the huddle, parked the truck, and jumped from the cabin of the Boriciomobile. The three of them stood, guns raised, waiting for more men to come pouring out of the warehouse, which was now burning. Dark smoke began to billow out, and Boricio smiled. "That ought to drive the rats out."

A figure appeared in the smoke, then rushed out of it and toward them.

It was an 8-year-old boy, rushing the three of them, waving a Beretta in the air. Boricio, without hesitation, pulled the trigger on his .45 and sent the 8-year-old into a bloody skid along the cement floor. He turned to Charlie.

"See that shit? He was gonna shoot me! There's your fucking kids for ya."

Boricio went back to the car, fished out his megaphone, turned it on and spoke into it.

"Bring me One-Eyed Willy or I'm gonna shoot every one of you fuckers in there. And I ain't gonna save you a trip to the Pearlies just because you ain't voted or you happen to be wearing a pussy in your panties. My bullets will fuck your shit up with equal opportunity, and that's as real as the cousins you think about while fucking your brothers."

Flames licked the warehouse walls, causing many of the monsters to flee the warehouse and run back into the woods.

"You're running shy on time," Boricio said. "There's only one way out that ain't got monsters waiting, and that's the front door. And I'm gonna shoot every last one of you fuckers unless you send One-Eye out. You got to the count of three! One . . . Two . . . "

A bald guy in his late 40s, with an eye patch, came out of the smoke, hesitantly.

"And circle gets the square!" Boricio said, smiling.

One-Eyed Willy stood in front of Boricio, shaking. Boricio kicked his feet from under him, sending the bald man to his knees. Vic and Charlie tied the man's ankles and arms while Boricio sang nursery rhymes, starting with *Itsy Bitsy Spider.*

Boricio threw One-Eyed Willy into the back of the van while flames spread and smoke billowed out of the warehouse.

"Okay, we got what we came for," Boricio said into the megaphone. "Olly-olly oxen free, you can all come out now. If I see any guns, I'm gonna assume you're hostile and will shoot you. So come out, with your hands up, if you want to live."

Men, women, and children poured from the warehouse, hands up.

Boricio, Charlie, and Vic kept their guns aimed and ready.

"Is that everyone?" Boricio asked, speaking through the megaphone at the 25 or so people in front of them.

A chorus of heads nodded yes.

"Good," Boricio said, and turned to Vic and Charlie with a smile.

"Kill the men."

Boricio and Vic opened fire as the women and children screamed, helpless.

A woman scooped up a young girl and headed to the tree line. Vic trained his rifle on them and took aim.

Charlie stepped in front of the rifle, "What the fuck?!"

"Outta my way, boy!" Vic screeched.

Charlie stepped aside. As Vic took aim, Charlie pressed his pistol against Vic's head. "Let them go."

With all the men now dead, Boricio turned his attention to the scene brewing between Charlie and Vic and smiled.

Boy had balls; was just takin' a bit longer for them drop was all.

Vic's eyes were bulging, rage coursing through him as he glared at Charlie. "You best put that fucking gun down."

"Now, now," Boricio said, "Can't Daddy leave you two alone for a second?"

"You said just the men," Charlie said, looking back at the woman and child running into the woods. "He's trying to shoot them."

"Let 'em go, Vic. They won't last five minutes once they run into monsters, anyway."

Vic smiled at that, and Charlie swallowed, putting his gun down.

Vic refused to break Charlie's stare.

"Come on, boys, we've gotta head back home," Boricio said, putting an arm around Charlie's neck and leading him back to the truck. Vic sat in the back with the prisoner and Charlie took the passenger seat up front. As they drove away, Charlie stared into the rearview as fire engulfed the warehouse.

**

Back at the compound, Boricio marched One-Eyed Willy into the kitchen at gunpoint where Adam, Harry, and Callie were sitting at the table, drinking.

Boricio dropped the man down in a chair and then went to the butcher block, retrieved a large knife and slid it across the table to Adam.

"Give him a second smile, right there below his chin."

The bald man's eye widened, and he cried out something incoherent behind the rag stuffed in his mouth and taped over.

Adam's lip quivered, then he shrunk back. "I can't do that, Mr. Boricio," he said.

"Do you think this fucking summer camp, boy? This is Camp Boricio, and fun time is over. You created this problem. You end it. I'm getting a bit goddamned sick and tired of having to be the only one around here with the guts to do what needs to be done."

One-Eyed Willy started to cry.

Adam looked at Callie and Harry who were both staring at the prisoner.

Boricio turned to Charlie who was standing at the entrance of the kitchen.

"Well, if Adam can't do it, maybe you'll pull the tampon out long enough to take care of business."

Vic snorted a laugh. "Yeah, right."

Charlie stomped over, grabbed the knife from Adam, pulled One-Eyed Willy's head back, his eye widening into shock, then slit his throat.

Charlie left his hand under the man's throat as blood pumped out in hot spurts. He glared at Boricio and then at Vic, then shoved the blade deep into the bald man's skull, and stomped out of the room.

* * * *

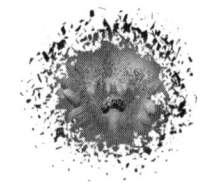

CHAPTER 7
RYAN OLSON

Ryan watched the front end as the post-dinner rush died down and nightfall turned the parking lot black. They'd be storming in any minute now, guns drawn. He might not be able to do anything about it, but he could at least minimize the risk of shit going bad.

He glanced at Clarissa, the youngest of the cashiers. She just turned 16 two weeks ago; she landed the job on her birthday. She was nice, cute, bubbly, and the kind of cashier that made his job easier. She showed up on time and actually did her job, unlike a lot of the high-schoolers who either acted like they were too good to work at the store or had attitude about having to work at all.

He walked up to her register, looked back, and saw she had only one other person in line, a young woman with a small basket of stuff. He clicked off her lane light and said, "Take your 15 minute after our next guest, okay?"

"OK, Mr. Olson," she said, smiling.

Ryan glanced up and down the front end. Three other cashiers on: Gladys, who was as old as the hills and twice as slow; Billy, a 25-year-old drama queen who'd not dream of stopping a robbery; and Ellen, a 28-year-old woman who was just kinda there most days and was far too self-concerned and lazy to get involved in anything that didn't immediately involve her.

That left the stock guys, who he had unloading pallets in the back; produce, who was likely hanging out shooting the shit; the bakery and deli departments, who never left their sections in the back of the store; the pharmacy, which was already closed; and of course, the customer service desk. That was where his real problem could emerge. There were two cashiers on duty, both older women who had been there longer than him. One of them wanted his job so bad he sometimes felt he should check to make sure his lunch wasn't tampered with.

Customer service was trained to hit the silent panic button the minute they sensed anything. After that, they'd be cooperative, but they might also try to trick the robbers. Tell them they didn't have access to the safe when they did, had less money on hand than they did, or anything else that might make the robbers pissy.

Of course, the robbers were the biggest variable in the robbery. Ryan's only instructions were to cooperate and make the entire thing quick, easy, and painless. If someone did something stupid, surprised the robbers, or tried to play hero, then this could all get scary. Ryan didn't know who would be staging the robbery. He figured that it wouldn't be too bad if it were only Pete and one other person. Though he didn't like Pete, he knew Pete wasn't likely to turn a bad situation worse. But if Viktor got some fucking meth heads to pull a robbery, all bets were off.

Ryan glanced back to Clarissa's lane to see that she had allowed a fat family with a cart full of at least $400 worth of stuff to get in line behind her last customer. And, of course, the woman had a purse stuffed with so many coupons they threatened to spill out in a sea of paper when she opened the purse.

What the fuck?

That order would take five minutes, easily, assuming the coupon queen didn't want to sit and argue about half the coupons that would likely be expired or for different items. Coupon people could be nearly religious in their fervor and rage when they felt entitled to something not stated in the coupon.

Ryan hated customers who took advantage of his cashiers. Whether it was the assholes who crowded the *10 items or less* lane with a cart full of shit, or the ones who jumped into a closed lane, the customer knew the cashiers wouldn't give them a problem. That whole "customer is always right thing" gave assholes license to treat cashiers, and the customers behind them, like shit. Finding people who wanted to work for the shit pay the store offered was hard enough. Expecting them to take mounds of abuse from the customers was another hurdle altogether.

Ryan raced over to the lane before the woman took the first item out of her cart, and said, "I'm sorry ma'am, this lane is closed."

"Excuse me; I'm already in this line, and I'm not getting into another. Your cashier should've told me that when I got in line." The woman hoisted a case of soda from her cart and slammed it on the conveyor belt in a silent *fuck you.*

Clarissa glanced at Ryan, eyes wide, not sure what to do.

"Ma'am, there are three other lanes open, and nobody in line on lane four, let me help you ... "

"What's the problem?" the woman's fat husband said, pushing his way toward Ryan. The guy was big, bald, and mean-looking. The two made a lovely couple. Their obese son with an unfortunate haircut and a face smeared with chocolate cookie from the bakery watched with anticipation.

"It's okay, Mr. Olson, I don't mind," Clarissa said as Ryan's eyes locked with beefy baldy.

Ryan sighed, "Okay. Thank you, Clarissa."

"Yes, thank you," the woman said, glaring at Ryan.

Ryan held his tongue. The taste of shit was familiar in this job; no use spitting it out now when he was about to assist a heist. *Just keep things humming along.* Ryan turned, reluctantly, and headed back to the front of the store.

That's when all hell broke loose.

Three men in black ski masks and matching outfits rushed through the front doors, armed with shotguns.

"Everyone on the fucking floor! You, take me to the safe!" one of the men yelled, staring straight at Ryan.

Screams erupted along the front end as customers and cashiers alike stirred, confused, and were slow to fall.

"Now!" one of the men said, firing a shot overhead. The shot punched a hole in the tiles, sending a rain of white dust to the ground. The cashiers and customers hit the ground. Ryan took some pleasure in seeing the annoyed and panicked looks on the couple he'd just argued with. Then he caught Clarissa's face, struggling not to cry, and his stomach turned.

"Come out of there, hands up!" a gunman shouted at the two cashiers at the customer service desk.

The two women came from behind the counter and stepped to where the gunman was pointing, a front-row seat at the head of the express lane. One of the cashiers, Carolyn, caught Ryan's eyes and nodded slightly, as if to indicate she already hit the panic button.

Fuck, not much time now.

"What do you want?" Ryan asked.

"All your fucking money!" the man said, shoving Ryan toward the office, just past the customer service desk. "Tell your people to cooperate, and nobody gets hurt."

"Do whatever they say," Ryan said to his cashiers as one of the gunmen went to the cashiers with a black sack demanding they fill it up. "Remember your training. Your life is more valuable than any dollar amount the store will lose. So, just give them what they ask for."

Well, that sounded stupid.

"Let's go. Hurry!" the gunman yelled at Ryan, leading him through the door to the manager's office.

Once inside the manager's office, the gunman said, "Open the safe."

Ryan realized then that it was Pete behind the mask.

Ryan hoped like hell Pete would keep his mask on, or not say anything stupid, as there was a security camera just above, filming their every move and sound.

"Okay, okay," Ryan said, as he removed the keys from his pocket, inserted it in the safe, then punched the security code into the safe's keypad.

"It's gonna take 90 seconds to open," Ryan warned as red numbers on the digital display began the countdown from 90.

"Fuck, you didn't tell us we'd have to wait!" Pete said.

Ryan's heart nearly stopped dead. He pursed his lips and glared at Pete, hoping what the idiot had said so far wasn't enough to implicate Ryan's part in the robbery whenever the cops reviewed the security footage. Ryan couldn't believe Pete could be so fucking stupid. He had to alert Pete to the camera's presence before the fucker started using names, removed his mask, and invited Ryan to meet for drinks later.

"Don't shoot me," Ryan said, "There are cameras in here, and they'll catch you."

Pete glanced around, then found the camera above them. He looked back at Ryan, eyes narrowed, then said, "Just hurry."

The clock read 20, 19, 18 ...

Ryan's heartbeat raced as he hoped to God that the cops wouldn't arrive before he was able to give the men their money and get them the hell out of the store.

14, 13, 12 ...

The clock is taking forever!

Finally, it hit zero, then read, "SAFE OPEN."

Ryan turned the thick metal handle, pulled the safe open, reached inside, grabbed all three of the deposit bags, then handed them to Pete.

"Anything else?"

"Nothing of value," Ryan said, pointing at the receipts and lotto tickets.

"Thanks," Pete said, turning around and leading the way out of the office.

Just as he stepped through the doorway, gunshots erupted. Two quick ones from a shotgun. Then a third, deafening blast from another gun.

Shit just got bad.

"You stay here," Pete said to Ryan. "We'll call you when needed."

Ryan stayed in the office listening to the volleys of gunfire from the other side of the wall, which were rapid at first but gradually slowed to a few scattered inconsistent sounding pops, then finally to nothing.

Ryan crept from the office and into the chaos of the now mostly empty grocery store. Shelves were overturned, cans rolled along the linoleum, and cereal carpeted the floor, causing Ryan to detour around Aisle 7 so he wouldn't crunch the sugary grains under his feet.

What the hell happened?

Pete and one remaining officer were the only men standing, pistols in one another's faces. Ryan stepped back, trying to make his way to the back of the store so he could escape unseen. As he was backing up, his foot slipped on something and fell backward, right into a display of glass Ragu jars that fell to the ground in a crash.

He looked up as the officer turned, startled by the noise. The punk made the most of the cop's split second distraction, pulling the trigger and splattering the cop's brains out the front of his skull.

The officer fell as Ryan screamed.

Pete said, "Shut the fuck up, Pollyanna, and go make yourself at home in the back of the Lincoln. Otherwise you can join Johnny Law on the floor." He waved the gun in the air. "So, what's it gonna be?"

A siren blared in the distance. Several more immediately echoed. Ryan chewed his lip, then walked the rest of the way down the aisle, over the dead officer, past Pete, then to the front of the store where he saw two of his people on the ground. One was Bill, face down in his own blood. And then he saw her ~ Clarissa, lying on the ground and staring straight up, blood bubbling in her mouth. Her eyes met Ryan's, and she tried to speak.

"Oh my God," he said, kneeling down.

"Come on!" Pete screamed.

"She's still alive!" Ryan said, "I have to help her."

Pete marched over, looked down at the girl, and aimed the gun at her face.

Ryan screamed, and tried to reach out, but was too late. Pete pulled the trigger.

"Come on!" Pete said, grabbing Ryan by the back of the neck, forcing him to the front doors and out into the parking lot.

It was a short drive to Viktor's pad, surprisingly close. Ryan always thought the guy lived further out. They were inside the house for five minutes or so, Pete explaining things to Viktor in a whisper on the other side of the door. Viktor's anger was nearly silent, but fuming and thick in the air, even with an oak door between them.

Another guy, Ryan had once heard Pete call Stink, came out of Viktor's room, walked up to Ryan and slid a needle into his neck before Ryan even noticed what was happening. Ryan felt a few seconds of familiar euphoria, then his eyes rolled to the back of his head, and his face fell flat on the cream-colored shag carpet.

**

Ryan opened his eyes to darkness. He had no idea how long he'd been out, only that his head was pounding and the room was pitch-black. He heard a whistle-like thunder outside, then a deafening crash that shook the walls.

"Anyone here?" Ryan cried, voice hoarse. "Someone wanna tell me what the fuck that was?"

He stood up, groggy, then fell to the ground again.

More darkness.

When he woke again, it was morning.

He made his way to the hallway, down the stairs, and out the unlocked front door. The sky outside was a weird shade of purple, and smoke billowed from three different directions.

What the hell?

He had to get out of there. Now.

Ryan thanked Christ there were keys in the Mercedes. He figured stealing Viktor's car was a one-way ticket to the graveyard, no doubt about it. But then again, Ryan figured that ticket was already punched. Best to get to Mexico, Canada, or anywhere else where they had good, long distance and cheap plastic surgery. First, he'd have to get Mary and Paola to come with him. They were sitting targets as long as Viktor was alive.

He pulled away from Viktor's estate, shuddering at the plumes of smoke and vaguely remembering the sound of explosions in the night.

I'm free now. None of that matters.

Ryan kept driving, and didn't stop for 212 miles. He was well into daylight before his mind surfaced the shocking reality: The roads were void of motion, and vacant cars littered the asphalt.

The world had died; he was alone.

* * * *

CHAPTER 8
DESMOND STRONG

Desmond filled a duffel bag with the things that mattered most, finishing with an 8 gig memory card. While he used to love taking photos, he'd nearly forgotten cameras existed until about six weeks earlier and felt ridiculous for having waited as long as he had. It was still too early to tell if this was the end of forever or the beginning of a global reboot, but either way, if the survivors didn't document it, who would?

Desmond would give anything to have pictures of the first month: their flight from Warson Woods, the wreckage of the storms that looked as if the world had stacked an entire city into a pile, the bodies in the river, and their time at the Drury; the frantic search for John, the horrific, ghostly flight from the inn, and every rancid minute stumbling through the following month until everything finally fell into place in their newfound home.

Pictures were evidence, and evidence was data. Data made decisions easier to make. Data could help you swallow the stuff your instinct begged you not to.

Stuffing the duffels was horrible. Worse this time than the last. Was this how it would be forever? Always running, never stopping, hanging their hats until the horizon lined with the undead . . . or whatever they were?

Desmond shuddered. In five months he'd grown accustomed to much of the new world, but the bleakers still made him feel every bit as sick as they had on first sight. Most of the new world was still a mystery, but the bleakers were a mystery that wanted to kill you while they rotted in front of your face.

What are they?

Are their numbers growing?

Were they once people?

Was it possible for him, and the others, to become bleakers, too?

Desmond couldn't help but feel that if he'd taken pictures back at the Drury he'd have more answers now. And how hard would it have been to find a quality camera in an empty inn? But the truth was, answers weren't why he started taking pictures.

It was Mary.

First, it was just pictures of her and Paola together, then he added pictures of their surroundings, the compound, the surrounding woods. Once he felt his old groove, the groove that had filled his old hard drive with 100 gigs of gorgeous photos, Desmond moved the lens into the bedroom.

At first, Mary was shy. But not for long. The curve of her breasts; the slightly wide hips that made her self-conscious, but made her look like a real woman to Desmond. Her neatly trimmed pubic hair. Desmond found it extra sexy, looking as neat as it did at the end of the world.

Desmond connected with Mary the way he'd always wanted to, but never could, with a woman. The way he imagined it could be. The way he saw his Uncle Jeremy connect with his Aunt Hazel, his mom's sister.

Part of the problem had always been Desmond. He figured if a woman was into him, at least part of it had to be for the money. Most of him knew it was ridiculous – he was reasonably smart, handsome, and funny – but the rest of him couldn't help the uncharacteristic self-doubt.

But at the end of the world, money didn't matter, which meant his guard was dropped where it belonged. His relationship with Mary had been born in an instant, three weeks away from the Drury, smack in the middle of a hard snow without any food and little hope for survival. Their mouths met before either knew what was happening. It was over in minutes, maybe seconds. But it was only the beginning.

When the snow thawed, so had something frozen inside Desmond. Mary, too. It was plain to see. She didn't try to hide it, not even in front of Paola, who clearly didn't care for the coupling.

Paola was nice enough to Desmond; she might have even loved him. But that didn't mean she wanted him with her mom. Not that Desmond blamed her. Her father, Ryan, deserved the loyalty. But he was gone, like 99 percent of the world. Desmond could tell that Paola wanted to get over it, wanted it to be okay, but her real feelings were obvious in the way she answered Desmond's questions too slowly, or too quickly, or rejected his ideas with numb indifference.

Mary opened the door. "Luca will be down in five," she said. "Everything ready?"

"Yeah," Desmond nodded. "I was just coming to get our Everyday Bag." He held the leather duffel up for her approval. "Come on, I'll walk you downstairs. Luca can meet us."

Mary raised her eyebrows, but Desmond insisted.

"You can't treat him like he's 8. He may not be mentally caught up with his body, there's no way to account for the missing experience, but the chemistry is there. The boy's brain has changed. He's at the tail end of adolescence. And we all need to be aware of it." Desmond drew a breath before adding, "I trust Luca more than anyone in the world, including me and you, but I think we need to watch him around Paola."

Mary said, "I'm already on it."

They went downstairs, then outside. Everyone was inside their cars, seven in total, except Will, who was standing outside the final car waiting for Desmond, Mary, and Luca. Paola was already sitting in the back row. Mary and Desmond gave a light nod to John, sitting in the passenger seat of a town car in front.

"Isn't anyone else concerned that John showed up from nowhere?" Desmond asked. "After disappearing for months, right when we needed him most?"

It was said in a whisper, and only to Mary, but Will answered. "I am. And I'll bet my share of the garden, if we get one look at Honest John's Shangri-La, that there's something none of us are gonna like not too far away. He never did seem like much of a team player, and doesn't strike me as the type to cross a state for a heroic *I'm sorry.* But then again, maybe I'm wrong. Sure as shit hope I am." Will climbed inside the van. Desmond and Mary followed.

Like usual, Desmond felt he was only hearing the tip of Will's iceberg. And though Will obviously thought they should follow John wherever he was going, he wasn't happy about it.

Desmond and John had nearly come to blows, a heated argument in the aftermath of Jimmy's murder. Desmond had backed down, not because he didn't want to make John swallow every one of his teeth, but because the words coming from John's mouth seemed so cruel they were almost inhuman. It was as though he'd forgotten every social boundary, demolishing the dam of what society saw as acceptable.

Desmond figured it for undiluted grief and turned his cheek. John disappeared. An hour later, the bleakers began to breach the inn. Will led them all to the second floor where they barricaded the stairwell and waited for death. But by nightfall, every bleaker had disappeared. They never returned; neither did John.

John had run off to have a temper tantrum, leaving them to certain death, but was now suddenly interested in their welfare? It made no sense. And it didn't exactly seem like he was sorry; it seemed a lot more like he was turning a to-do into a to-did.

Desmond wasn't a guy who held grudges. And maybe the grudge he had for John was the first one he'd had in his life, but it was a grudge nonetheless. A grudge without an antidote. That self-centered asshole had taken off and left him to his fate, along with an old man, two children, a mom, and a murdered kid. *Fuck him.*

The way John had been unable to handle his anger, the way he'd practically melted his humanity, center stage for all the Drury Inn to see, Desmond wouldn't doubt it if he'd been the one responsible for Jimmy, even if the bleakers had done the act. And judging by the silences that sat between the sentences no one wanted to say, everyone else at the Drury thought the same thing. *Fuck him.*

Even if he'd pulled them out of the fire today, Desmond harbored a frying pan's worth of anger. But still, the rest of their new friends couldn't feel the same way, and Will was obviously on board, even if it was just to get them from point A to B. Desmond was enough of a team player to bunt so long as they needed him to. *Fuck him later, follow for now.*

"What are you thinking?" Mary asked.

"He's thinking that we're driving into a rising tide of certain bullshit, and we both know he's right," Will said.

Paola looked scared. Mary looked at Will, quietly pleading with him to be quiet.

"She's old enough to know," he said, "And help us when the time comes. Him, though," Will pointed out the window at Luca, quickly approaching the van, "I'm not sure where he is right now, other than his own world. So let's just play it cool, follow John to nirvana, and see what happens."

Everyone nodded. Luca opened the door, tossed his bag inside, then climbed onto the seat, swinging the door behind him.

"I think you might be surprised," Luca said. "I don't think we're driving into a trap at all. I think we're finally going where we're supposed to go. I think we're finally at the beginning."

Desmond stared at Luca, wondering how the hell he'd heard their conversation from so far away.

* * * *

CHAPTER 9
LUCA HARDING

The vehicles rolled in a procession down the highway; John's car led. The van carrying Will, Desmond, Mary, Paola, and Luca was in the rear. Everyone else, including Scott, who'd made a full recovery, was somewhere in the middle.

Luca felt kinda like a prisoner. They were in the back of a van that had big plates on the side, which Luca thought looked like armor. And the van was being driven by two strangers who both looked to John every time they were about to open their mouths.

Desmond looked mad; Mary looked worried; Will was staring out the window.

Paola's face wasn't as easy to read. They'd been driving for five or six miles and she hadn't said a word without prompting, and only delivered one-line answers whenever Luca asked her a question. She looked a little scared, but mostly confused. It probably had something to do with him looking like a grownup.

It was like the time when Luca's dad shaved his mustache. His father had worn a mustache since before he was born, so when Luca ran downstairs one morning last May and saw the fresh, pink skin above his dad's lip, he almost felt like his father was a stranger. Throughout the rest of that day, all of the next, and into most of the following week, Luca had a hard time looking his dad in the eye. It was difficult to find balance between what his brain told him to see what he actually did.

Luca figured Paola probably didn't *want to* ignore him, but didn't know what else to do. Which is why he wasn't altogether surprised, though totally happy, when she finally adjusted her seatbelt, turned to her left, and looked Luca in the eye.

"What's it like," she said, "you know, aging like that? It's gotta be weirder than weird, right? Are your insides like your outsides? I mean, you look all grown up, but you must still think like you used to. You would have to."

Luca leaned closer to Paola and spoke in a whisper, not wanting Will, Desmond, or Mary to hear him, not to mention the two drivers up front, though he was pretty sure everyone could hear every word anyway.

"I don't know," he shook his head. "My brain feels really busy. Lots of colors and noise. Like a big bucket of Legos being dumped out and refilled, over and over. They're all moving around in my head so much that I can't build anything. It's just really, really loud, and I can see all the different colors and shapes but I can't do anything with them because they won't stop moving. Some of those Legos are the ways I used to think, but now there are a bunch of new Legos. So, I guess I'm supposed to learn how to put the blocks together." He looked at Paola, then added, "Does that make sense?"

"I guess," she said, leaning in her seat. After a minute she looked back over.

"You talk different now, you know. Not like you used to at all. Well, except using Legos to reference things," she said with a smile. "But it's weird because you don't talk like you're supposed to, either."

"How am I supposed to talk?" Luca said, unable to hide his injured expression.

Paola's cheeks flushed. "I don't know," she said. "At least, not exactly. It just seems like you're not quite … " Paola swallowed, then fell silent, thinking a moment before opening her mouth again. "Remember in school how there were two playgrounds, one for the older kids and one for the younger kids? At least that's how it was in my school."

Luca nodded. "Yeah, the kindergartners have their own playground. First, second, and third all shared the playground with the swings and slides. Fourth and fifth got the playground with the tetherball poles and handball courts. We weren't allowed to play there, and the older graders always kicked us out when we tried. Sixth and seventh-graders went to the middle school next door.

"Okay," Paola said. "Well, it seems to me like half of you has moved to the bigger playground even though you're supposed to still be on the smaller one. And you can't play tetherball or foursquare because you've never been on the playground before and no one's told you the rules."

Luca felt like he was about to cry. While he'd always been sensitive, he felt especially so with all these new feelings rushing through his head.

Paola touched his shoulder then brushed his arm. It tickled. "Don't be sad," she said. "The same thing happened to me one time, at least sort of." She smiled. "Not that I aged overnight like you, or anything. You definitely have me beat there."

Paola laughed, and Luca felt happy enough to copy her smile.

"After my mom and dad first split up, I didn't see my dad for a long time. I'm pretty sure it was about three months, though it felt like forever. My mom was so mad she didn't even want to let my dad in the house. One time, she locked him outside in his underwear." Mary turned her head toward the back seat, but Paola just shrugged. "It's true," she said.

"Anyway, when he came back home to visit, there was this weird distance between us. And it wasn't just that he'd been gone, or that he knew he'd ruined things by cheating on my mom." Mary looked back again, but Paola just glared until she turned back around, then went on. "It was more that I had changed in that time. He didn't know how to look at me, and in a lot of ways, I wasn't the little girl from three months earlier. I could tell he wanted to cuddle me, and tickle me, and play with me just like before. But everything felt different to him. And he had missed all the things in between. Not just the school stuff like my fourth-grade graduation from lower school and my violin recital. Other stuff, too. Like finding out about Santa Claus and my mom buying me my first training bra."

Luca could feel himself turning red.

Mary kissed Desmond on the cheek, then turned back to Paola. "What really did it," she said, "Was when he saw the stack of books on your nightstand. In his eyes, you'd gone from *Harry Potter* to *Twilight* overnight. That made him lose it." She turned to Luca. "Luca, you're unbelievably special, and we all owe you a debt we can never repay. We may not understand what's happening to you, but we all know we owe you. Everything will be okay, and your insides and outsides will match soon enough."

Mary patted Luca on the knee and smiled. He smiled back.

The rest of the trip was mostly silent, though the air between Luca and Paola quickly thawed. They started exchanging stories and jokes like they had for the last three months, though there was a crackling current that had never been there before; a current that excited Luca.

The winter trees started fading from the landscape, and the passengers saw the first blossoms of pink and green dotting some of the branches outside the window. The driver turned to the passengers and said, "We're almost here. Another 10 minutes, maybe."

Exactly 10 minutes later, the line of cars drove through a guarded gate, then into a compound that made the house they'd come from look like Anna's *My Little Pony* Show Stable. There was a large farm, though Luca couldn't tell what they were growing, and a silo like the one back home. There were a couple of other buildings, too. A large one that looked like a garage, and another one that had a whole bunch of wires on top, along with something that looked like a flying saucer. Just past the gate, there were three large houses in a row, three stories each. A high brick wall that made Luca think of Humpty Dumpty encircled what the others had called "the compound."

John's car drove into the large garage, and all the cars followed. Luca felt butterflies flutter inside him as John stepped from his car and the other men followed. Luca looked up at the seat in front of him. Desmond's face was mad, Mary's was still worried. Luca took Paola's hand, then followed Desmond and Mary from the car.

They were met by a large group of strange-looking people on the other side of the garage. The group looked nothing like the soldiers. Paola leaned into Luca's ear and whispered, "I didn't know the special place was *Little House on the Prairie*."

There were four men and one boy, dressed in dark suits with hooks instead of buttons. Their pants had suspenders, like clowns, except not funny, just black. All their shirts were pretty colors. Light pastels that looked like Easter.

Their boots were brown and scuffed, and their hats had wide brims, made of black felt. The men all had beards, but no mustaches, and their hair was long enough to brush the base of their necks. The boy's hair wasn't quite as long, but looked like it was cut with a bowl on top.

There were two women as well, probably a mom and a daughter. They both wore long hair parted down the middle. The mom wore it in a tight bun, the girl in pigtails. Their dresses were solid blue and fell all the way to their ankles, and their shoes were a shiny black.

They stood in a semicircle and said, "We're well met to know you," one at a time.

John met them on the other side of the strangers. In a soft voice, he turned to his old friends from the Drury and said, "This is home now. You'll be safe here." He gestured toward the house in the middle. "Come inside, there's someone I want you all to meet. The man who saved my life, the man who helped me finally find the inner peace I've been seeking for so long."

Luca could feel Desmond getting angrier, but he followed him, just like Desmond followed John. As they approached the house, an old man stepped outside, then climbed down the front porch stairs, each step creaking loudly beneath his weight. The man wore a long, ivory-colored robe. Something terrible must have happened to him because the skin on his neck was bright red and really wrinkled. It looked like leftover ham. A mask covered the left side of his face.

"This, my friends," John said, "is The Prophet."

* * * *

CHAPTER 10
BRENT FOSTER

Black Island Research Facility
March 21

"Rise and shine, sleepy head," Michael teased, standing in the threshold of Brent's dorm-sized room.

"Fuck, what time is it?" Brent said, turning and looking at the clock. 5:15 a.m. His head was pounding. He'd been up too late, and drank a few too many beers in the dining hall when he got back from Jane's. Today was supposed to be his day off.

"Early, but the guys are getting ready early and a spot's opened up."

"Huh? A spot for what?"

"We're going into the city on an extraction run. Sanchez is sick, and I vouched for you."

"Extraction?"

"I don't know all the details, but they sent a team in last week to follow up on leads. Supposedly there was an infected sighting."

"I thought you all shot the infected on sight."

"Change in protocol, or so say the scientists. They want us to catch some live ones for observation. Only problem is we haven't seen too many, not in a while. Most everything we've spotted was either a full-on alien or an infected that was already dead. At any rate, a couple of our guys managed to trap one of the infected in an apartment building and need us to extract them."

"So, we're gonna fly back with one of those things?"

"We're bringing a second chopper with a cage, so *we* won't be. The good news is you get to meet Ed."

"Who's Ed?" Brent asked.

"Commander Edward Keenan, one of the best we've got. He came on a bit after I got here, but shit if he ain't the toughest sonofabitch I've seen. Dude is ALL business, and unlike some of the other captains I've seen in my years, actually gets out in the field and gets his hands dirty."

"Sounds like fun," Brent said as he sat up, his head still adjusting to the light that Michael turned on.

"He's not a ball-buster or anything. Barely talks at all, in fact. But hell if you can't learn something just by being next to the guy."

"What time we leaving?" Brent asked, not wanting to let Michael down.

"Oh-six-hundred sharp. So, grab a shower and get dressed and ready."

"Yeah," Brent said, as he stumbled off to the shower, hoping he'd make it through the day on little sleep.

**

They flew a Blackhawk, with four Guardsmen and two pilots, into the city. A second chopper, another Blackhawk with the cage, followed with six more Guardsmen, including pilots.

Captain Keenan was in charge of the mission, though he'd yet to say a word to the men, preferring stolid silence the entire flight. Keenan looked around 40 with a nearly shaved head and beard stubble. He appeared tough and fit, but world-weary and just as likely to take a long nap as he was to jump into a firefight.

"We're here," one of the two pilots called as they encircled an apartment building that was all too familiar to Brent – the building across the street from his old apartment; the one where he'd met the 215ers. Last time he'd seen the building, it was crawling with aliens.

The hairs on the back of his neck stood on end as a chill ran down his spine. To be so close to home, to be able to see his apartment, right across the street, gave him the surreal sensation of stepping back in time. That if he could simply step through time and space, he could somehow find his way back to his family.

Keenan stood and opened the door, then leaned out of the chopper, looking at the rooftop. "Okay, I've got a visual on Alpha Team. Set her down."

"Yes, sir," one of the pilots said as the chopper lifted, then straightened before slowly lowering.

On the rooftop, Keenan barked orders over the chopper's rotors.

"I want two of you, Schultz and Cooper, to stay behind. It's your job to protect the pilots and the chopper. You see something alien, shoot it before it touches the chopper. For those of you who haven't faced these things, remember your video training. Their movement is deceptively fast and unpredictable. Wait until you have a shot lined up *before* firing."

They met up with Sanchez and Turner of the Alpha Team just outside the rooftop doorway leading to the stairwell.

"We've got two infected trapped in the elevator on the ninth floor," Turner said to Keenan. "We dropped gas on them 15 minutes ago, so they should be out. We cleared most of the hostiles, but there's a few we missed, so be prepared to shoot."

"You got the gear?" Keenan asked Michael, who patted the big, black bag strapped to his back like camping gear.

"OK, let's do this," Keenan said, then stepped out of the morning and into darkness.

**

The emergency lights that once lit the hallways had burned out, so the men used lights attached to their rifles, which added to the claustrophobic feeling of the walls closing in around them as they navigated their way down the stairwell to the ninth floor. The sound of their boots echoed and carried the length of the stairwell, which was sure to draw the attention of aliens, were there any inside.

Once they reached the ninth floor, Keenan instructed Brent and Michael to stay behind and guard the stairwell door. One of the men took the backpack from Michael and carried it with his left hand, his rifle in the right as he and the remaining men headed down the hall toward the elevator, about 12 doors down.

"You okay?" Michael asked Brent. "You look sick."

"I used to live across the street."

"No shit?"

"Yeah. And I know it's crazy as fuck, but I feel like we just went over there, maybe Gina and Ben will be in the apartment waiting for me."

"You know that's not possible, right? We haven't run into anyone in a long time. The odds that anyone is left here are next to nothing."

"I know," Brent admitted, frustrated. "At least logically. Yet, being here, so close to home, it feels like I should at least *try* to go over there."

"No way Keenan's gonna let you do that. You'd be putting this whole operation, including all our men, at risk. So, unless you want us to leave you behind – and by the by, I'm not letting you do something that fucking stupid – you need to get your head in the right here, right now. Okay, buddy?"

Michael's voice was firmer than Brent had ever heard it, but still compassionate, showing that he was looking out for Brent's interests even if Brent was getting a bit loco.

"You're right," Brent said. Besides, Brent didn't think he could take another disappointment so soon after yesterday's helicopter ride over the dead city.

"FUCK!" someone screamed in the hallway. Gunfire exploded and echoed like thunder, followed by more gunfire and the unmistakable, unholy shrieks of the aliens.

"Shit!" Michael said, swinging the door all the way open and storming into the hall. As Michael lifted his rifle, dark arms and claws appeared in the gun's light moving swiftly, ripping, tearing, and shredding, blood splashing the wall behind him as Michael's cries faded into a gurgle. Michael's gun fell as the doorway faded to black, even as the sound of chaos travelled into the stairwell.

Brent's heart froze in his chest as he brought his gun and light up, illuminating the carnage. The alien deftly turned its slick, black head and opened its maw, shrieking and clicking.

For a moment that seemed to stretch into infinity, Brent froze, unable to move.

The alien dropped Michael's corpse to the ground, then turned, its body moving impossibly fluidly, raising its claws as it descended on Brent. His finger found the trigger and he squeezed off a burst of gunfire that sent the alien sprawling back against the wall.

The clip went silent but the chaos continued – more gunshots, screams, and alien shrieks. Worse, the unmistakable sound of more aliens approaching.

Fuck, fuck, fuck!

He struggled to pull the empty clip from the rifle and replace it with one of three more he had. The new magazine clicked into place just in time as another alien pushed through the door, held open by Michael's corpse-turned-doorstop.

Brent screamed as he fired into the alien, tearing its head to ribbons. Brent finished loading another clip as he reached Michael and ducked down to grab full clips from the man's belt, all the while trying to avoid looking at what was left of his body. Smoke poured through the hall just ahead of him; one of the men must've accidentally thrown a smoke grenade.

More screams and flashing lights echoed off the walls through smoke as Brent stepped into the hall, coughing as he aimed his rifle into the cloud of darkness, trying to make sense of the movement. It was impossible to grasp the scene; there was simply too much smoke, too many bodies moving, and too many gun lights dancing all over the place. Brent sank into the corner of the hallway, fear an electric current surging through his entire body, as he lifted his gun and held it shakily in front of him, waiting for anything to move toward him and hoping not to accidentally shoot another human.

Bodies continued to hit the ground until the gunshots finally fell silent.

Lights littered the ground, at least five of them, as the smoke began to dissipate.

Is everyone dead?

Brent's heart pounded in his chest as he strained to hear anything other than the ringing in his ears from the gunfire. His light shook up and down as his hand refused to stay steady, casting a shaky beam through the smoke.

Something moved ahead. He blinked his eyes and held the gun tighter, only to have it shake more dramatically, afraid to speak or even breathe.

"Identify yourself," a man's voice said as a shadow moved through the smoke, light aimed waist-high, scanning the hallway.

"Brent Foster," he said, his voice shaky as his hands.

"Anyone else?" the man said, stepping through and into view. It was Capt. Keenan, brow sweaty with a streak of blood across his left cheek, likely someone else's.

"Anyone else alive?" Keenan repeated.

Nobody answered.

"Jesus Christ," Keenan sighed.

Both radios crackled to life. "Beta Team, do you read?"

"Beta One," Keenan said, "We have massive casualties. Send someone from Delta Team in to help. Beta One out."

"How many casualties? Do we need the medic? Alpha One out."

"Almost everyone," Keenan said. "No medics are necessary. Beta One out."

As the smoke cleared, Keenan flashed his light across the hall to reveal the fallen comrades and alien corpses littering the narrow passage; blood, both red and black, smeared the walls, floors, and ceilings. There were at least six of the creatures from what Brent could see.

"Looks like a nest," Brent stammered.

"Or an ambush," Keenan countered as he located the Guardsman he was looking for and retrieved the black backpack from his body. "Come on; help me get these elevator doors open so we can see what the hell was worth killing all our men for."

Keenan dug inside the bag, brought out a pry bar, and slid it between the elevator doors at the center. Ed held his rifle in one hand and turned back to Brent, "I'm gonna stick this in and pull, which will trigger the pneumatic release and open the doors, either partially or all the way. But we won't be able to close them again. So, be ready to fire, but only if they come at us. We want to take these things alive if we can. Understand?"

"Yes, sir," Brent said, trying to sound more confident than he felt.

Keenan applied all his force to the pry bar, opening the doors about 60 percent. Keenan trained his light inside on the two infected bodies, face down in the darkness, seemingly asleep. *Hopefully, asleep.*

Brent thought of Joe and how dangerous he'd become once infected. How *inhuman.* Though he was sad Luis was dead, he was glad he didn't have to watch his friend devolve into a zombie-like creature.

"Friendly coming through," a man announced from the stairwell as he and a second Guardsman from the second chopper entered the hallway. "Jesus Christ," one of them uttered when he saw the bloodbath. Keenan pushed the doors the rest of the way open. Once the elevator doors were fully open, he instructed the two men to go inside and pull the bodies out.

Brent stepped back, gun ready, light shining into the elevator as his eyes kept watch for more aliens from either direction.

The Guardsmen pulled the first body out. Keenan dropped to the ground, quickly handcuffing the infected. He then tied a hobble restraint strap around the feet and connected it to the handcuffs, locking the infected's limbs behind them.

Keenan turned the body over to reveal the face. Instantly, Brent felt as if someone had punched him in the chest, knocking all the breath from his body.

No . . . it can't be.

He inched closer. The face was scarred, slightly dark, but there was no doubt it was her.

Gina!

He looked into the elevator and saw the smaller body, face down, wearing dirty, blue pajamas.

"Ben!" he cried out and ran inside the elevator, pushing past the Guardsmen.

Brent turned the boy over to expose the blue Stanley Train shirt covered in dirt, grime, and blood, then picked his son up and cradled him in his arms.

"Put him down!" one of the Guardsmen commanded, putting a hand on Brent's shoulder.

Brent turned. "This is my family!" he said.

Keenan held up a hand to tell the guard to stand down then turned to Brent.

"You can't kill them," Brent begged Keenan, tears streaming his cheeks as he stared at his son's face, scarred, a cruel mask of the child he once was. His eyes were closed, eyelids darkened. Nearly black. God only knew what his eyes looked like beneath the lids.

"Please," Brent begged. He looked up and found Keenan's eyes. "Please," he repeated. "We can't bring them back to Black Island."

* * * *

::EPISODE 8::
(SECOND EPISODE OF SEASON TWO)
"THE VANISHED"

PROLOGUE

Oct. 15
Kingsland, Alabama
2 a.m.

The Prophet had been waiting decades for this night.

The Dream would become reality, and a new world would be ushered unto the righteous. A world created by Him, free of the secular, the wretched, the sinful, and all the creeping evil that had slithered through the soul of this great nation and sunk its fangs of depravity into the good and the pure.

"Tonight, we celebrate Him, for He has come!" The Prophet raised his hands in the air as he looked upon the small sea of followers lining the first two pews of The Lord's One True Way Unity Church, planted deep enough in the Bible Belt to make certain the soil was rich without the taint that soured so much of the rest of the country, and, of course, the world.

The Prophet's following was small but loyal, made from mostly family members, of which there were 16, from himself to his youngest grandchild, 1-year-old Ellie Mae. He winked at Ellie Mae in the front row as she yawned another adorable yawn. Her mother — also his youngest daughter, Pam — smiled, her eyes brightened by the Truth.

The Prophet was glad they'd made it to the church tonight. Glad that they'd been able to overcome the obstacles that Satan had thrown in their way.

Pam's husband, Derek, had grown more confrontational over their differences of faith of late. Derek had made no secret that he was a Protestant. The Prophet was willing to let that slide, assuming the man would come around in his own time. But lately, Derek had drifted further from the flock. He began to question The Glorious Day that had been foretold to The Prophet by God Himself decades earlier. He was badmouthing the church, and The Prophet, to Pam. He began throwing the C-word around, calling their congregation a "cult." He even threatened to take Ellie May away from Pam and go off to Nebraska, where his family was from.

It was one thing for Derek to disagree within the church and attempt to sow his seeds of discontent among the parishioners. The Prophet might have even put up with it a bit longer, letting the young man make a fool of himself until he came around. But the straw that broke the camel's back came three nights ago when Derek plastered his face all over the TV, getting interviewed by one of those so-called journalists who'd taken to poking fun of The Prophet's Message whenever possible. As Oct. 15 neared, the sinners grew more bold in their mockery of The Prophet and of God, turning The Prophet into the punchline of late-night comedy routines. As The Day grew closer, it was more imperative than ever that The Family stick together.

Yet, Derek betrayed them at the worst possible time. He appeared in an interview on one of those "news" shows on MSNBC. Derek mocked the church, laughed at them, and questioned the sanity of The Prophet, telling the news host that he thought the church posed a danger to people and that he would likely be seeking a divorce and full custody of their child.

Fortunately, God saw fit to inspire Pam's older brothers, Elwin and Dwayne, to intercede, giving a nice, "friendly" talking-to to Derek. The boys had a way with words, and their fists, which made their daddy proud and helped him keep order in a world that sometimes forgot how to keep things straight. Tonight, Derek was still recovering from the boys' visit, which meant he wouldn't be here. Which was a shame, really. The Prophet didn't approve of Derek's background, nor his recent betrayal. But what kind of example would he be if he were not a forgiving man? Any who sought redemption would receive it.

If they sought it in time. Derek lost his opportunity. Tonight was The End and The Beginning, and Derek was on the wrong side of the fence.

Such a shame.

Missing tonight was to miss the Second Coming. To miss His Glorious Return. To be struck blind and dumb as the doors of Heaven itself were thrown open to the righteous among them.

Sorry, Derek, no room for Protestants.

But Pam and Ellie Mae, they would certainly be welcome.

And they'd all get to see Gladys again. She would be waiting.

The Prophet couldn't wait for Ellie Mae to meet her Grandma. Gladys succumbed to cancer two days before Ellie Mae blessed the world with her presence, a huge loss to the congregation and family alike. Gladys had been so anticipating Ellie Mae's birth. She had a lot of love in her heart. Even at the end, when the pain was enough to twist her face into a cruel mockery of the Good Lord's Everlasting

Love, Gladys always had a smile and open arms for her entire family, and all The Prophet's followers.

Oh, how he missed her.

But man was not meant to question His will. Nor was he meant to mourn those who entered the Kingdom of Heaven. For all who believed would be reunited in the coming Light of the Lord to spend Eternity in His Glory and Love. And that reunion was about to take place in minutes.

The Prophet looked at the clock, an old Western Electric that had set in the same spot for six decades, from back when this church had belonged to The Prophet's father – back before The Prophet had returned to Him. The clock read 2:06 a.m.

It was almost time.

The Prophet led the congregation in the Lord's Prayer, then began to deliver the sermon he'd been preparing for years. Though his back often hurt, and he was feeling every bit of his age most days, tonight he felt electric. He was without pain, and stronger than he'd felt in decades. His voice was an extension of this strength, strong and deep from his chest, in full bellow.

He spoke of Love, God, and family. Without those, you had nothing. You may have yourself a house, but without God, your house had no foundation. And as surely as Rome crumbled into the rubble of its own sin, your house would crumble, too.

Man had vanquished God from the world in the past few decades; had banished him as surely as God had banished Adam and Eve from Eden. But at least God banished Adam and Eden for their own good. Man did it with an arrogant sneer, and it would've surely been the death of them, if the Good Lord hadn't seen fit to save The Prophet and his flock.

"Foolish men thought this garden was theirs to banish Him from?!"

The congregation laughed.

The Prophet smiled.

2:12 a.m.

Almost time.

"Men are so certain of themselves. So arrogant."

"Amen," the congregation said. Little Ellie Mae said, "A-may."

"You can't throw God out of His Kingdom! Can you?!"

"No!" the congregation shouted.

"Hell no!" The Prophet said. "For He alone holds the keys! He alone determines the fate of all. He alone, Amen!"

"Amen!"

"Man tried to hide God from us. Tried to hide Heaven. Said they didn't exist and that they'd just go away like a bad dream. But you can't hide Heaven, can you? You can't deny the Lord and render him undone, can you?"

"No," they said.

"Because as long as there is Love - as long as there are men who aren't blind to His Love and able to hear his call - there is always a way. Amen!"

"Amen!"

"When God called me so many years ago, I was just an ordinary man. Blind to His Love. Deaf to His Truth. Arrogant! I was lost like a white hair in a lion's mane. But then . . . then I heard His voice call to me. Delivered a message to me. Showed me how foolish I was to turn my back on my father's church. That without family," he paused to look down the rows of his family, "without you, I was as far from Eden as man had ever been. He told me what I had to do. That I had to come home and make things right. To build this church back up to bring His word home and swing the doors to His kingdom open wide for us all, Amen!"

"Amen!"

"It is time, my family. It is time to open the door and welcome Him back into our world. Time to shake the arrogance and hubris of humanity to its core and remind them that not only is God alive, but that He has returned, Amen! And NO MAN can or shall close the doors to Him, ever again. Amen!"

"Amen!" the family cried, standing in a wave. Pam held Ellie Mae in her arms and gave her a kiss on the head. Pam's eyes were wet. Dwayne's wife was crying, too. Tears of joy. Tears of the joyous Love they'd know for eternity, no doubt.

The Prophet looked at his congregation: family, friends, and even a couple of strangers whom he'd never seen before tonight. His church had never been so full. All here to witness His return! The Prophet's heart swelled with joy.

"Are you ready to welcome Him back?"

"Yes!" they all echoed.

The Prophet retrieved the vial of black liquid. The vial *they'd* tried to keep from him. He lifted it above his head for all to see. The liquid glimmered in the light of the church. In the light of His Love.

A hush blanketed the room. You could hear their breaths caught in their throats, each and every one. They were viewing a gift from Him. The key to the kingdom. Many erupted into tears of joy.

Outside, thunder shattered the silence. One, two, several strikes, so loud they may have been tearing the sky apart above them. God had a way with dramatic entrances, The Prophet figured.

"Then let us open the doors to Heaven and welcome Him back into our world, Amen!"

"Amen!"

The Prophet opened the vial.

The door of the church flew open as the man burst in. The one who had tried to stop The Prophet from realizing God's Dream. The man screamed, "No!"

But he was too late.

The liquid boiled over, spilling out and onto The Prophet's hand, burning his flesh. He screamed, but his voice was drowned by the crash of thunder and flashes of light, brighter than anything he'd ever seen.

Then blackness.

**

The Prophet woke up coughing, vomiting smog from his lungs. Darkness and flames licked the world around him, and for a moment The Prophet was certain he'd woken in Hell rather than the Heaven he was promised. He cried out, "Why?"

But then he saw he wasn't in Hell, unless the Lake of Fire looked exactly like the ground outside his church. Rain started to fall, slowly at first, then hard and fast, smothering most of the fire as The Prophet lay there, helpless to do anything but watch as drool spilled from his gaping mouth and pooled onto the ground below.

He passed in and out of consciousness, drifting through an endless series of meandering thoughts, but always returning to the question: Who dragged him to safety? Someone had to have pulled him from the church. The Prophet had felt something, like *someone* was with him, but didn't see anyone and couldn't remember a thing.

He thought of the famous poem *Footsteps*.

Perhaps it was Him.

**

The Prophet woke to the morning light. His body was stiff, his face numb. He brought his hands to his face; it felt mottled and burned on the left side. However, and thankfully, it did not hurt to touch.

He looked around. *Where is Gladys? Where's my family?*

The Prophet was alone, sitting in the ashes of the church. He looked around. The rest of his compound was untouched. Only the church lay in cinders, struck and burned from the face of the planet, reduced to little more than a memory frosting the air over its charred foundation.

The Prophet stumbled to his feet and approached the blackened remains of the church he'd known all his life. It was as though a giant, or the Devil himself, had picked up the roof and tore off the walls, leaving nothing but the remains of the floor, pews, and several piles of smoldering remains he couldn't make out at first.

Then it hit him.

There were bodies.

The entire congregation had been reduced to cinders. He found the smallest of piles and thought of Ellie Mae, smiling at him.

The Prophet fell to the ground weeping.

"What have I done?"

* * * *

CHAPTER 1
BRENT FOSTER

Black Island, New York
Black Island Research Facility – Level 6
March 22, 2012
Morning

The woman and child behind the glass are not my family.

That was the thought Brent kept beating into his brain as he glared into the cavernous observation chamber behind God knows how much bulletproof, bombproof, and everything else-proof glass, here beneath the earth at the end of the world.

The glass was one-way, *thank God*. Brent couldn't imagine having to look into his family's new sets of alien eyes, or having them see him on the free side of the chamber. The cell reminded him of an enclosed room he'd once seen at a zoo where penguins were kept, except this cell had no pretense of a natural habitat. It was sterile, industrial, and lacked anything that could ever be accused of being a creature comfort. No cots and no toilets. Nothing but gray, concrete-looking walls, a row of drains in the floor, and ominous looking vents and holes in the ceiling. On the far side of the chamber was an oversized square door, which exited into another room Brent hadn't been cleared to enter.

This was Brent's first time this deep under the massive facility beneath Black Island. Civilian access was limited to the first level. The farther down, the higher clearance level needed to access it. The whole place reminded Brent of the interior of spaceships he'd seen on shows — industrial in color and style, sliding doors with retina and hand security panels, and the constant hum of electronics beneath the continuous rush of cold, sterile-smelling air into the facility. The room he was in was small, one of several that looked into the viewing chamber where his family was being held, though he could not see into those rooms through the one-way mirrored glass. He wondered how many other men were in identical chambers watching their wives and sons, and what those people had planned for them.

Gina and Ben paced back and forth like animals, slightly hunched, arms swinging loosely, heads tilted as if trying to constantly hear something just out of earshot. Both bodies were stripped of clothing, a final indignity, layered atop the alien infection that had already bleached them of much of their humanity. While their skin wasn't as dark as the alien skin, or as wet — and it didn't have what seemed like lights beneath the surface — it had definitely already altered from human form. Their skin was smooth, yet scarred in places, and slightly waxen. It was as if whatever infected them was slowly shedding the outer skin and replacing it with something else, not fully alien, but not fully human. Perhaps it was working with what biology allowed in its best approximation of the alien skin.

If he had any remaining rays of hope that his family could be saved, they were dimmed to a flicker five minutes earlier when Capt. Keenan brought Brent down to Level 6 and he'd gotten his first look at the haunting in Ben and Gina's eyes. The beautiful life that used to dance inside them was gone, replaced by dark, reptilian pupils; their eyes left as vacuums of humanity no different than those of the doorman, Joe, after he'd been infected.

"What are they going to do with them?" Brent asked.

"I'm not sure," Keenan said as if considering a tiny insect. "Observe them, of course. But beyond that, I don't know."

"They're gonna run tests, aren't they?"

"I imagine so."

Brent knew exactly what a battery of tests would mean. While he contemplated the certain death sentence for his family, he watched as his 3-year-old-son huddled close to Gina, eyes on the windows, as if at any moment one of them would crash in and something would storm inside to threaten them. Even though the boy's eyes were dark and alien, Brent recognized fear when he saw it, no matter the species.

The boy's fingers clung tighter to Gina, but her maternal instinct was apparently dead. She seemed to regard the child as a stranger, something she was reluctantly forced to share space with. Were Gina still *Gina*, she would have been shielding Ben in her arms, protecting him from any slings or arrows that might come his way. This thing that had been Gina simply allowed the child to be near, but offered no comfort, reassuring touch, or hint of humanity.

Brent's heart shattered yet again.

"I need to go inside. Please."

"I know what you're thinking, but they're not your family," Keenan said with zero emotion. Brent wondered what Keenan had done before the world went to hell. His bedside manner was shit, and Brent had a feeling he was catching him on a good day.

As if Keenan sensed Brent was looking for more and would get it even if he had to start asking, he said, "I don't know much, just a tiny bit I heard from one of the science geeks on Level 7. These aliens in the city are like parasites, you see. They infect people, kill their hosts, then play house in the shells. That's why what you see in that room is not your family. Your wife and son, as you knew them, are dead. The parasites are like hermit crabs crawling into a new home."

Brent turned back and saw his son shivering, clinging to Gina's leg.

"No," Brent said. "You can't see it. But I *can*. My son is still in there. I know it because I can fucking see it! And I don't want your scientists killing him. He's not dead! Look at him! Look how he's clinging to his mother. You think an alien, some damned hermit crab, would be doing that were it simply inhabiting a *shell?*"

Keenan stared at Gina and Ben, as if genuinely considering Brent's question. There was a look in his eye as if he were thinking about someone else, or remembering something. After a long minute, Keenan shook his head, as if casting the memories away, then turned back to Brent, eyes clear and focused again. "The last vestiges of humanity. Instincts. Nothing more."

"Bullshit!" Brent said. He ran a hand through his hair, swallowing a scream and speaking through clenched teeth. "I want to speak to whoever's in charge!"

"You know . . . "

"No!" Brent said, putting a finger up, pointing precariously close to Keenan's face. "Don't say it! I've done everything that's been asked of me. You all shot my friend. You took all our belongings, shaved us down, and brought us to this place where we have to do what we're told, when we're told, and never question authority. I never said a word. Never resisted. Did as ordered. Figured you all are the government, or what's left of it, anyway. Believed you'll make sure everything's okay. But I can't sit by while people I don't know make choices I have no say in about MY family, without even giving me the chance to speak!"

"I understand your frustration," Keenan said.

"The fuck you do!" Brent shot back and turned from Keenan, eyes back on the window, watching as Ben followed Gina to the far end of the room, huddling together in a corner.

"How can you understand this?" Brent said. "They don't have your family behind glass."

Brent wanted to get in Keenan's face, yell at him, push him, even if Keenan punched right back. It would be worth it if he could wake whatever humanity might still be inside the man. But he had to weigh his options carefully. Michael, his first and only friend outside of Jane, and the person who vouched for him to get the position as Guardsman, had been killed the day before. Right now Keenan was his closest thing to a friend in the Guard, and the only thing allowing him access to see Gina and Ben. If he pissed Keenan off, his access, as limited as it was, would be severed. He'd be left alone, topside, wondering every moment what was happening to his family.

"I'm sorry," he said to Keenan.

"I'll see what I can do," Keenan said. "But I can't make any promises."

"Thank you," Brent said, unable to move his eyes from the viewing window.

**

Later in the day, a stranger came to see Brent while he was sitting on his bed typing a report into his laptop about everything that happened in the city the day before.

"Hello, Mr. Foster. My name is Sullivan," a fresh-faced young man with wire-framed glasses said. "I'd like you to come with me. I think it's time the two of us had a talk."

Brent looked Mr. Sullivan over, then closed his laptop, stood, and shook his hand.

"It's nice to meet you," Brent said, nervous, then gestured toward the door. "After you."

Sullivan was silent the entire trip to the elevator. Brent stayed a step behind him, observing and absorbing everything from the length of his step to the thread count of his jacket. He had the gait of someone important, and the confident shoulders of someone in charge, but he wasn't a decision maker. He had the calm walk, but not the decisive step. Mr. Sullivan, Brent was sure, was the guy brought in to make sure things stayed calm; no rocking boats, and, most importantly, no one stepping out of line.

They took the elevator to Level 5, the administrative wing, another area Brent had never been to, even during his initial interview.

"This way, please," Sullivan said, guiding Brent along yet another sterile corridor that looked like so many of the others he'd been in.

They took a few more turns, Brent taking mental notes of the layout, just in case he ever needed to return. He did this constantly whenever he was brought new places in the facility. When he returned to his room in the evening, he'd draw maps, then study them, committing everything to memory, in case he was ever lost and needed to navigate his way out. Or, needed to break into a place he wasn't allowed. Though his family had only been imprisoned for one night, part of him was already preparing for the possibility of arranging an escape, even if the notion of breaking into, let alone *out of*, the facility seemed impossible.

Sullivan led Brent to a dead end where he stopped, pivoted to face a door on the left, then placed his hand on a pad beside it. The door whooshed open.

Sullivan's office was small and sparsely furnished. A chair, a wooden desk, and a Zen rock garden on the corner of his desk. Opposite the desk was a leather chair where Brent was offered a seat.

Sullivan sat behind the desk, opened a drawer, and slid out a tablet computer, which he placed in front of him on the desk. He left the screen black.

"Captain Keenan said you wanted to see me?" Sullivan began, not unfriendly.

"Are you in charge?"

"No, but let's just say I have every ear that matters. And, before you say you don't wish to speak to me, let me say that I am as close as anyone gets to those in charge. So, I urge you to share your concerns. Or," Sullivan smiled, "forever hold your peace."

Sullivan's voice was crisp, well-educated and slightly foreign, though Brent couldn't place the accent. Perhaps from the United Kingdom.

"I want to know what's going to be done with my family."

"You mean the infected that we picked up yesterday?"

"Yes," Brent replied, stifling a burst of loathing. "They're my wife and son."

"I'm sorry," Sullivan said, never breaking eye contact. "I understand how difficult this must be for you."

I doubt it.

"I want to know what's going to happen to them."

Sullivan paused, as if trying to decide how much he would share. "Do you know why Black Island Research Facility is here?"

"Just what you all told me when I arrived: a facility designed to monitor threats to the country and to proactively act against them when they arise, whatever that means."

"Good memory. Yes, that's the short-and-sweet version; the story we tell to the politicians who fund us, and the journalists," at this he winked at Brent, "whom we speak to. That's the public face of what we do. Naturally, there's more."

Naturally.

"Black Island is also one of four New Eden stations in the world," continued Sullivan. "A place to begin society anew, should our old society come to an end. These stations are responsible for repopulating the planet, making it hospitable again, something it is not even close to in its current state. It may surprise you that we don't know much about these aliens despite having captured a few living ones and having dissected many dead ones. We need to know as much as we can if we are to eradicate them from Earth and reclaim our planet."

"That's a noble endeavor, Mr. Sullivan. But don't skirt the question. What's going to happen to my family as you play hero and race to save the world? Are they to be experimented on as your guinea pigs?"

"Yes, Mr. Foster, more or less," Sullivan said, as matter-of-fact as Keenan had been earlier. "If these subjects were not your family, you'd want us to find out everything we could, wouldn't you? In order for science to progress, it must experiment. We're finding fewer and fewer survivors, fewer still who are infected."

"Maybe that's because your Guardsmen have itchy trigger fingers and don't hesitate to burn them alive," Brent said, the adrenaline building in his voice. "They even killed a good friend of mine who was willing to let them experiment on him! But they never even gave him a chance. Just shot him dead, no questions asked."

"Yes," Sullivan said, as academic as ever. "That is unfortunate. I believe we can agree that our initial recruits were a bit too eager, or perhaps a bit too frightened, after everything that happened. Once we learned what the Guardsmen were doing, we stepped in and put a stop to it, ordering all infected to be captured alive."

"Are there other infected alive here?" Brent asked.

"I'm not at liberty to discuss the finer details; I hope you'll understand. In fact, I'll also be requesting that you keep the details of your family's capture and the existence of any infected on this island to yourself. There's no need to start a panic." Sullivan leaned forward. "Can I trust you to do that, or will we need to have you remanded to the facility at all times? I'm sure that could prove a bit of a problem for your relationship with the teacher and her daughter."

Brent flinched. If that was a threat, it was the smoothest he'd ever been given. And most effective. He wondered just how carefully they were monitoring his activities. For all he knew, they had the whole island bugged.

"I won't say a word," Brent said, more than slightly defeated. "Like you said, no need to scare people. So, truly, what can you tell me about Gina and Ben? What's going to happen to them?"

"I'm afraid I can't say, truly. But you can be assured that our scientists will be as merciful as the situation allows. I'm not a scientist, nor do I even pretend to understand all the things they have to deal with it. But suffice it to say our team is one of the best in the world, if not *the* best that's left, and they are working for the good of mankind."

"Do you think they'll find a cure? Do you think they can cure Gina and Ben?" Brent asked, retreating into his vulnerabilities and feeling the fool for it to expose a lofty dream, only to be shot down by such a clinical man.

"I wouldn't insult you or dare to raise your hopes by speculating. I hope you'll understand. I will say that if there is such a thing as a cure, these *are* the people who *could* find it. I say *could*, not *will*. Obviously, time and availability of subjects comes into play, as does the basic uncertainty of science. I believe the best thing you can do for now is try and shift the way you think of the subjects. They're not your family, not anymore. Your wife and child are dead, their bodies are merely puppets for whatever species has infected them."

"No," Brent said sharply, abandoning his emotional retreat. "You didn't see my son."

"Actually, I did see the subjects."

"No, if you saw them, you wouldn't be saying my son is gone. There's some part of him in there. I see it in the way he acts, the way he clings to Gina. He's not gone. My son is not some fucking puppet!"

Sullivan stared at Brent for what seemed an eternity, giving Brent time to calm down and wonder if perhaps he'd been too forceful. He didn't want to appear as a threat that may go off the reservation. He needed to play the good boy or Black Island Research would do what governments do with any threat – eliminate him.

Finally, Sullivan looked down to his tablet, turned it on, navigated to a file on the desktop, and handed it to Brent.

"Please press play, Mr. Foster," Sullivan said, frost upon his words.

Brent took the tablet, which showed the frozen image of a woman in a chamber just like, if not the very same as, the one his family was in. She was clearly infected: eyes big and black, skin deteriorated significantly. She stood alone in the center of the room, the video shot from outside the observation window. Brent pressed a white triangle over the image bringing the video to life.

A figure in full white protective gear entered the chamber through one of the two doors on the far wall.

"Unlike the others, subject 10-0014 appears to be non-violent on Day Five," a woman's voice said. Judging from the echo, it was the voice of the woman in the white gear. The infected woman stood still, watching as the suited scientist moved closer.

"She seems to be responding positively to treatment with HZVT-816 Variant C. We've now given her six doses, spaced 12 hours apart. Her skin shows signs of minor healing; pigmentation seems to be returning to her body. I will now take a closer look at the subject's eyes."

As the scientist stepped closer to the infected, Brent's heart felt like it pounded twice as fast, doubling its beat in anticipation and dread of what was to come. Surely, there had to be a reason Sullivan was showing him this video. Was it to foster hope, or crush it?

The scientist turned on a flashlight and raised it to the infected woman's eye. The infected woman recoiled, mouth opened wide and jaw unhinged, and released an unholy shriek that echoed in the chamber and crackled on the tablet speakers.

The infected woman's hands seized the scientist by the helmet, pulling her closer. The scientist screamed, dropping the flashlight. Dozens of slippery black tendrils shot from the infected woman's mouth and pierced the faceplate of the scientist's helmet, goring through the thick plastic as blood splattered the insides and the scientist's screams ended in a choking gurgle.

A siren sounded in the video as the chamber suddenly erupted in bright flames from above, engulfing the entire screen.

Sullivan reached out and took the tablet from Brent, hit stop on the video, then spoke. "Burn Protocol. It's what we do when infection threatens to break free from the chambers. It's the only way to ensure that what we put inside doesn't get outside."

Brent stared in numb disbelief, "Why are you showing me this?"

"I need to disabuse you of the notion that the subjects in there are your family. The scientist in that video was named Lenora Paulson. The subject was her sister, Frankie. Like you, Lenora made the mistake of thinking her sister was still human. She thought that because the infected hadn't deteriorated at the same rate, wasn't aggressive, and still seemed to recognize Lenora that perhaps she wasn't lost. Lenora thought if she tried hard enough, she could cure her. As you can see, these infected, no matter how they appear, are no longer human. Your wife and child died. The sooner you accept that, the sooner you can begin to live again."

* * * *

CHAPTER 2
RYAN OLSON

Brookdale, Tennessee
Feb. 17
Morning

He dreamed of Mary again, waking up with a hard-on for the third morning in a row.

Ryan's hands wrapped around his cock, and he started to tug, imagining the swell of Mary's breasts and the blush of her nipples against the snow of her skin.

Fuck, I love her tits.

Ryan yanked faster.

Outside, a scream shattered the silence . . . and drained his erection. A gunshot followed, cracking the morning like thunder.

Ryan bolted up in bed, then ran to the window. He was on the seventh floor of an abandoned apartment. He stuck to apartments since they were easier to barricade, and preferred the upper floors because they gave him more leverage if the world went even further to hell down on the ground. The creatures didn't like to climb the fire escape ladders that were on many of the buildings, nor did they seem to have the patience or intellect to figure out how to move intricate barriers in the stairways and halls, which Ryan happened to excel at creating. Turns out stocking intricate displays on the end caps *did* serve some purpose, after all. So, as long as he was careful and built good traps, he was safe . . . from the monsters, for now.

He peered out the window and saw a young black kid racing down the street with two men chasing him.

"What the hell?" Ryan said as he tried to make sense of the scene below.

This was the first time he'd seen anybody, let alone three people at once, since the third day after the world flushed its people away. The first person had been a crazy guy pushing a shopping cart down the street outside Warson Woods. Ryan had asked the guy if he'd seen anyone else, but the guy yelled something about yellow cabs that made no sense to Ryan, so he left the stranger to wander aimlessly, knowing full well he would attract the wrong attention soon enough. The last person he saw was some weird guy later that day who seemed to be following Ryan from a long distance, but then vanished never to be seen again.

The men chasing the young black kid were wearing jackets with hoods, one red and the other blue. They appeared to be white, or light skinned, from the best Ryan could tell seven floors up. They also seemed slower and older. But guns were a great equalizer to speed. And the man in red was aiming a pistol at the kid.

The kid stopped in his tracks in the middle of the road, just beneath the awning of Ryan's borrowed apartment. Ryan cracked the window open so he could hear what they were saying. A crisp, cool breeze floated into the room, and on it, the voices from below.

"Give it back!" the man in the red jacket demanded.

"It ain't yours," the kid said, a voice that seemed younger than the kid's height. Judging by the rising crack in his voice, Ryan pegged him at about 13 or so.

"I ain't askin'," Red Jacket said, stepping closer, gun aimed directly at the teen.

Blue Jacket had no gun, but stepped forward to intimidate nonetheless. "Hand the shit over, kid. Now." he pressed.

The boy reached into his pocket and retrieved something too small for Ryan to see from his birds-eye perch. Red Jacket took the item, then pistol-whipped the kid hard upside the head, sending his six feet or so crashing down to the cement.

Ryan took both the thugs to be in their late teens, early 20s. Grown men picking on an unarmed kid.

Fucking pussies.

Ryan returned to the bed, retrieved the rifle he kept propped against the nightstand at all times, then went back to the window and scanned the street. The two men retreated back down the street while the boy sat on the ground, glaring at them, hand on his head where he'd been hit. He looked as if he was contemplating making a run at the men, but didn't know how to level the playing field without a gun. Ryan wondered why the boy hadn't been armed. It wasn't as if you needed a license to carry any longer, and there were no shortages of stores to get a weapon without a license, waiting period, or even cash.

Ryan opened the window the rest of the way and leaned out. "Psst, you okay?"

The boy snapped his head up, flinching. For a moment it looked like he was going to bolt. He tried to stand, but lost his balance and fell back on his ass.

"Hold on; I'll be right down," Ryan said, then turned and raced from his apartment, already dressed. Ryan always slept in sweats, a shirt, and sneakers because he never knew when he'd need to run next, or in which direction. It was best to be ready at all times. He may not have done the best job of preparing for many of life's slings before the world went away, but he'd become incredibly resourceful in the past few months.

He unlocked the wooden gate he'd just finished building, then eased his body past the stacked items that served as a barrier blocking the stairwell and ran down the stairs, two steps at a time.

The boy, in jeans and a green, long-sleeve jersey, looked even younger up close, despite his height. His eyes widened to softballs at the rifle.

"Don't worry; I'm not gonna shoot you," Ryan said soothingly. "What happened? What did those men take from you?"

"Medicine for my Gramps. I took it from the drug store down the street. I didn't know it was their drug store."

"It isn't," Ryan said, watching as the men turned the corner a block away, heading toward the drug store. "Were they in the drug store when you went in there?"

"No, they came out of the old Pizza Hut across the street. I didn't even see them until I came out and they told me to stop. That's when I took off running."

"What's the medicine for?" Ryan asked. "Is it important?"

"Yeah, it's his heart medicine. If he doesn't get it, he could die."

"Shit," exploded Ryan. "Okay, you wait here. I'm gonna go get your medicine back."

"You sure you wanna do that, mister?"

Ryan cocked a smile. "Not really, but that's not gonna stop me."

"Thank you," the boy said.

"My name is Ryan." He jerked his thumb at the building behind him. "Why don't you wait for me upstairs. I'm in apartment 720. Just lock the door. There's a handgun on the kitchen table if you need it. You know how to use a gun?"

"Um ... no, not really," the boy said, fumbling his eyes on his fingertips.

"OK. Don't sweat it. Just aim and fire, if you have to. The safety is already off, so don't mess with it unless you need it. OK?"

"Okay," the kid promised. "My name is Carmine."

"I'll be right back, Carmine."

Ryan raced down the street, slowing only when he reached the alley that had swallowed the jacketed thugs. The men were standing in front of the Pizza Hut shooting the shit.

"Here we go," Ryan said to himself, quickly closing the distance between them, rifle aimed at Red Jacket the entire time.

"Hey!" he yelled, startling the men. "You took something from a friend of mine," Ryan said.

Red Jacket reached into his pocket. Ryan shouted, "Don't move or I'll blow your fucking head off. I'm a Marine sniper, and I never miss!"

Ryan wasn't sure if his lie or tone of voice was convincing, but he gave his best *don't-fuck-with-me* look.

"What's your problem, man?" Blue Jacket asked. Up close, Ryan saw that both men were clearly over 30. Red Jacket was pale with freckles and bright-orange, curly hair that reminded Ryan of a giant pubic bush. Blue Jacket was a pudgy black guy who reminded Ryan of Ice Cube, if the rapper had a lazy eye, unibrow, and looked a bit slow.

"My problem is that you took something from my friend. And I want it back. Now."

"It ain't his," Red Jacket whined. "He stole it from our store."

"Your store?" Ryan asked, glancing at the sign over the store which read, Billings Pharmacy. "Which one of you is Billings?"

The two exchanged a glance, confused by the question.

"It's not your store," Ryan said. "You're just squatting until someone bigger and badder comes along to take it from you."

"Yeah?" Blue Jacket asked. "Is that you?"

"I don't give a shit about your drug store, asshole. Neither does my friend. He just needs some medicine for his grandpa."

"We ain't in the business of giving shit away," Red Jacket retorted.

"Do you even know what kind of medicine it is?" Ryan asked.

"Nah," Red Jacket said with a shrug. "Don't really care much, neither."

"It's heart medicine, dipshit. Do either of you need heart medicine?"

Ryan wasn't sure if they felt stupid or were just playing tough, but both men stared blankly at him.

"You going to give it to me or do I need to take it, and maybe the whole fucking store along with it?"

"Nah, you ain't got to do that," Red Jacket said, reaching into his pocket.

Ryan adjusted his aim on the rifle as if to say *don't even try it.*

Red Jacket pulled out a shrink-wrapped pack of six vials.

"Put it on top of the car," Ryan instructed, pointing to the Blue Volvo next to them.

Red Jacket was a good boy; he did exactly as he was told.

"Now, I'm gonna leave you boys to go about your business. Next time you see my friend, I suggest you keep walkin' because the thing about snipers is we're really good at not being seen. So, if I even see you lookin' at my friend wrong, I might just add you to the notches on my rifle. Hoo-rah!"

Ryan swiped the meds, slipped them into his sweatpants, and backed away in reverse, rifle aimed at the two ass clowns until he reached the alley corner and turned. He waited a moment to see if they'd give chase, but apparently these bullies were more bark than bite when facing anything bigger than a pup.

Ryan headed toward a home that hadn't been home long enough. His intervention today meant he'd made enemies and he'd have to move again; just when he was starting to like this place. Which was probably the kick in the ass he needed, anyway.

He'd never find Mary and Paola by staying put. He had to keep searching, even if that search was in vain.

* * * *

CHAPTER 3
MARY OLSON

Kingsland, Alabama
The Sanctuary
March 20
10:40 a.m.

"The Prophet?" Mary said, barely hiding her snicker.

Had John gone off the deep end, running off to do God-knows-what, following a so-called prophet? Prophet of what? *Apparently he hadn't foretold whatever the hell it was that had burned half his body,* Mary thought with a sting of guilt.

"He foresaw everything that happened," John said, eyes toward the sky and hands in the air, proudly singing the praises of his new best friend. Mary had never known John to be a religious or terribly excited man. Back in Warson Woods, the only thing he ever prattled on with unbridled enthusiasm about was Jenny, and how thrilled they were to be together. John always had a story about the latest thing they'd done, or were planning to do. It was nauseating, at times. But that was John and Jenny, and you put up with it.

Since Oct. 15, the old, effervescent John had vanished into a shell, replaced by a bitter drunk, pissed at the world and happy about nothing . . . until now.

The Prophet had ignited something in John's eyes and his spirit; that much was clear despite the mystery enveloping Mr. Godsend, which now enveloped them, too.

The Prophet hadn't budged since John's introduction; he just stood at the foot of the stairs watching, though observing was probably a word more fitting. While John was talking up the Prophet, most everyone's eyes were fixed on John. But The Prophet's eyes were fixed on everyone else, as if taking mental notes on how each of them responded to John's message.

"He saw it all, down to the day and time it would happen. That's why we're here," John said, warmth like honey on his voice. "The Sanctuary is more than the name of your new home, it's our purpose here as well." John waved his hands around the compound with enough pride to suggest he'd pounded the nails himself.

"How old is this place?" Desmond asked, moving his eyes from the three houses to the silo, then across to the hangar and back. "How many people are here?"

Will shot him a look, desperate for the guided tour from Animatronic John to be over. Although Desmond's face was turned from her, Mary was sure he could feel her glare.

"Oh, it's old," John said. "The land had been in his family for more than 100 years. It began with a simple house on farmland. Then The Prophet's grandfather built the church, which stood until Oct. 15. We're now home to more than 60 people, though there's room for you all should you decide to stay."

Mary took a step toward Desmond then grabbed his hand, squeezing it hard.

"The Prophet built The Sanctuary to prepare for the Glorious Day when Heaven would open its doors to its chosen few. He never asked to be a leader, never wanted it at all, but The Prophet is not just the son of The Father, Son, and Holy Spirit, he is the Son of The Inevitable, and there is no redirecting fate from eternity."

Mary squeezed harder, wishing the lecture would end soon. She felt as uncomfortable as the time her old friend, Susan, got married and became a Jehovah's Witness and started trying to sell Mary on her faith. Mary was on the fence with religion most times, but was never comfortable with the hard sell; especially when it came from someone she knew. This latest experience felt like that, but multiplied, as if John had also joined some multilevel marketing scheme and was trying to sell them on a "golden opportunity."

"God showed our Prophet the future. Gave him the vision and then the strength to see it in all its Glory, because only then could he lead the righteous to His Kingdom. Once he saw God, The Prophet knew his life's purpose. And as the Lord's Chosen, he bore the burden of choosing the path for everyone to follow – building the compound, gathering his flock, and waiting for the Glorious Day when Heaven would open its doors."

"You covered that," Desmond said.

John stopped speaking and turned to Desmond, considering him for a moment with undecided eyes, then opened his mouth to speak. Before he could say a word, The Prophet stepped forward and said, "Desmond, right?"

Desmond nodded. The Prophet moved faster than Desmond would have imagined, and was inches away almost immediately. "I understand how you're feeling right now," he said, "And I know that even as I'm talking, you're likely thinking, 'Well, who in the front door does he think he is?' Well, I'll tell you exactly who I am. I'm a man, no different from you, Desmond. I just saw something you didn't, something most couldn't, and not because I wanted to. And once I saw it, well, that something changed everything."

The Prophet started pacing, shaking his head earnestly side to side. "No, I didn't ask to see what the Good Lord saw fit to show me. And no, I can't say it's been an easy burden to bear. But I don't have a single regret. It's all a blessing, from the sky opening up and taking my family, my congregation, and little Ellie May, to the pox upon my face. And why do I feel these things are blessings?"

The Prophet paused for an answer he didn't expect, then dropped his voice to something just above a whisper. "Because I know my purpose. And when you know your purpose, everything else is *gooood.*"

His voice returned to its full bellow, "I'm here because while most men ignored God's voice, I *listened.* My congregation was welcomed into Heaven because they listened."

"I'm curious," Desmond said, sounding sincere, "Why did the rest of your congregation go to Heaven, but you were left behind? Doesn't seem like a very nice thing to do to one's messenger."

The Prophet smiled, "That's a great question, son, and one I must admit, I wondered about for a bit. After all, He had promised to reunite me with my wife. Yet, he took all but me. And I wondered, had I not been true enough to His Word? Had I strayed? What had I done to anger him so? But then I realized that perhaps God wasn't punishing me, but testing me. Could I, in the face of conflict, maintain my faith? Could I persevere? Could I still deliver His Word? Could I be a 10th of the man that Job was? Was I truly worthy to enter His Kingdom?"

The Prophet paused, and his pale-blue eyes met Desmond's. "I wasn't always a righteous man. I wasn't always a good man. And though He forgives, He does not always forget. I believe this is my final test. To show God what I am truly made of. That I am worthy. That I have repented and learned from all my youthful indiscretions. And that's why

I'm here, to do His work. To serve as His instrument until I have fulfilled my obligation to Him."

The Prophet turned to Mary. "I have seen terrible things. I saw you in my visions. You and your daughter, slaughtered by the very beasts that invaded your home this morning. God gave me this vision, worked through me and this church to intervene and save you all. To bring you here and offer you sanctuary from the Demons."

Demons?

The Prophet let the word sink in, then chewed on his lips and adjusted the mask that covered the left half of his face before continuing. "You see, while the Good Lord was smart enough to leave a man like me down here to help you, he isn't the only one with skin in this game. That black-backed Beelzebub downstairs is also playing for keeps. And much as I don't like to admit it, I think he might've outfoxed the Good Lord on this one. See, as capable as I might be at keeping you safe and spreading The Word, I am just a man. There is a war for this world and the souls left behind, and Satan has set his Demons against us, looking to claim us all."

Desmond waited until The Prophet turned his head, then caught his eye and said, in an uncharacteristic smirk, "These Demons, are they the ones who made all the bullet holes?"

The Prophet chuckled. "No, no. I wish. At least then I could blame it on pure evil rather than my own dirt-poor judgment. Even when God himself will take the time to speak with you, no one likes to be wrong. And I'm downright ashamed of some of what's happened on this here holy soil."

The Prophet held Desmond's eyes, then shook his head. "No, the bullet holes were my doing. On Oct. 15, after the Gates swung closed and left me alone without my flock, I needed help. Unfortunately, I'm a man of faith who put my faith in the wrong people in the immediate aftermath of His

124

Glory. There were survivors nearby. I took them in and gave them a job to do: to help me find someone. But they did things in their own way, and not in a way the Good Lord would approve of. They're all gone now, sizzling with the other sinners in The Lake of Fire. So no, we won't ever need to worry about them again. Besides," The Prophet waved his hand in the air, "it's not their fault really, the beginning of Limbo was awfully confusing with no one knowing what to expect. And men are men, after all; imperfect creatures full of sin, some more than others. Those unfortunate souls hadn't been here long enough to know their true virtues. They handled the situation real poorly, and we paid a dear price."

The Prophet shook his head. "But that's history now. We've cleaned house and scrubbed it good. The Demons stay outside, and we stay safe in here. With John's help," The Prophet pointed at John, thoroughly beaming, "only Good People are allowed into The Sanctuary."

"Who were you looking for?" Will asked, surprising Mary with his curiosity.

"Why, Brother John, of course. God told me to find him. And just when I'd nearly given up the search, he walked right through our front door. And John has proved me right; he's been such a guiding light since arriving here."

The Prophet slapped John on the back and added, "Why don't you introduce everyone, John?" Then he turned to the crowd of newcomers, "You're all welcome to stay as long as you like. John couldn't have said nicer things about you all, and I find myself awfully humbled to have you here with us at New Unity. Of course, you're under no obligation to stay. But it's good times and good people. And besides," he laughed, "There are no Demons in here!"

Most of the gunmen who helped out at the farm had already disappeared, but John introduced the remaining bystanders, starting with Eli, the oldest of the Amishlooking men, and Sarah, the woman. Sarah said hello in a voice that sounded thin enough to shatter. The round of introductions ended with Brother Rei, a disciple. John said his goodbyes, then told the group Brother Rei would lead them to their rooms.

Brother Rei looked young, no more than 25, but Mary would swear he was at least 10 years older judging by the short conversation on the way to housing, which quickly turned to Kurt Cobain after Desmond said, "Nice looking Nirvana." Rei steered the conversation to Cobain, but unless he was smelling Teen Spirit as a toddler, his story was off.

Rei turned to Luca, Scott, and Paola. "Children are in the second house," he said.

"What?" Mary and Paola cried in unison.

Rei smiled. "Oh, none of the children stay with their parents. Independence helps the children to grow up so much stronger. The Prophet knows you'll agree; independence has never been more important than it is right now."

Rei didn't raise his voice, though the generator in the background doubled its hum. Mary strained to listen, wondering if the generator was always running, and what that would cost the The Sanctuary in gas, and trips to get more.

Luca wore no expression; Paola looked angry. Mary hugged her, assuring her that everything would be okay and that Luca would look after her. Scott seemed content just to be alive after the morning's events. All three children said quiet goodbyes, then followed Sarah silently into the house.

"I'd like a room with Mary," Desmond said.

Rei turned and smiled, "Oh, we have a married couple?"

Mary laughed and shook her head.

"I'm sorry, but there can be no sinning in The Sanctuary," Rei said, "Women's quarters are in the third house." He bowed his head, gesturing toward the women's housing.

"That's ridiculous," Desmond said. "We're grown adults."

Desmond took a quiet step back and seemed like he would drop it, but then added, "Besides, we *are* married. Mary just didn't want anyone to know because Paola will get upset. She thinks her father's still alive." Desmond added a sneer to the ending. Mary wasn't sure if it was for her or Rei.

"I understand what you are doing," Rei said. "But even if you were married, your union would have taken place after Oct. 15 and is therefore unrecognized. I am quite sure The Prophet will be happy to marry you under his authority. Would you like me to make a request?" Rei smiled.

"No. Thank you," Desmond replied, his tone contradicting his verbal gratitude.

Rei said, "Sarah will take the children and get them settled. The Prophet would like the four of you to make yourselves at home for a short while. Everyone will meet back in the dining hall in an hour to break bread. One hour," Rei repeated, then bowed his head, took a step back, then turned around and headed toward the hangar.

"See you in an hour?" Mary said to Desmond, Will and Linc, though mostly to Desmond.

Will tapped his head. *Observe everything.*

Mary nodded, then headed up the stairs.

She immediately went to the window. Eli was bringing the men their bags. Just as he disappeared into the stairwell, the floorboards outside her room creaked, followed by a light knock on her door. "Miss?" said the timid voice.

Mary opened the door. "Sarah, hello."

"Where would you like me to set these?" Sarah pointed at the two bags by her feet. "There are another two downstairs."

Mary nodded, "Yes, may I help you with those?"

Sarah shook her head. "Oh, I wouldn't hear of it."

Mary wasn't surprised. "Thank you," she said, then pointed to the corner. "The corner will be fine."

Sarah brought the rest of Mary's belongings into the room while Mary washed up in the bathroom sink. When the door closed and Mary was alone again, she resumed her watch at the window.

There were three homes in the compound, plus a barn and silo. There was also the hangar and another smaller building, the purpose of which a mystery. New construction had been started on the farthest side of the compound, and though the building was far from finished, the giant cross hinted at what it would become. She was also fairly certain the houses had basements, which gave the compound plenty of square footage to hide acres of unknown.

The generator belched, causing Mary to wonder again about the gas situation and how difficult it was to keep the generator fueled.

Mary felt a sudden, and rather surprising, flutter of hope. Sure, The Prophet was delusional, but the compound *did* seem safe. And wasn't that what they were looking for – a place to grow their future and family? The world had changed, and humans were endangered. Wasn't it best to group together as closely as possible? The one thing that gave Mary the most hope was also the thing that made her most anxious: They had surrendered their guns, all of them. According to John, all guns were forbidden except in emergencies, or for the four main guards who kept watch. That had been The Prophet's law since whatever disaster had happened in the immediate aftermath of Oct. 15. And while that made the day-to-day safe, it also made the future terribly dangerous. What if the monsters broke through the compound's defenses? Were just four men with guns enough, or could they get to the rest of the supply before it was too late?

The hour passed quickly. Mary helped Sarah and her daughter, Rebecca, set six long tables, arranged in two longer rows of three, then went to the living room when people began to arrive. Desmond was waiting for her with Linc and Will. Paola, Luca, and Scott showed up a few seconds later. The group walked in a wide line to the table, the adults in a huddle and the children slightly behind.

"So?" Mary said.

"We're in a room together," Desmond whispered, "The three of us. Most rooms have three beds, doubles, nothing fancy. The third floor is off limits, reserved for The Prophet, John, and Rei."

"And there's something funny with Rei and John," Will added.

"You mean The Prophet and John?" Linc said.

"No," Will shook his head. "I mean Rei. Weird energy. Familiar. But unsure." Will was stumbling, tugging his month-old gray beard.

"You trying to say the dude's a bologna smoker?" Linc probed.

Will shot Linc a look. "No. And if I was, I wouldn't say it like that."

"Welcome," John declared as they arrived at the table.

Once everyone was sitting, The Prophet entered the house and took his place at the head of the table. When he arrived, everyone in the house stood silently, so Mary and the group played along, though not without a weird look or three passing between Will, Desmond, and herself. Linc gave an eye roll.

"Thank you for waiting," The Prophet said, "You may be seated."

As everyone sat down and their chairs squeaked into place on the wooden floor, The Prophet took the crystal wine glass brimming with a dark red in front of him. He raised it high, and the others joined, raising their smaller wine glasses, also filled with wine. The children appeared to have some sort of juice.

"Welcome to your first New Unity meal at The Sanctuary. We welcome you into our family."

* * * *

CHAPTER 4
PAOLA OLSON

Kingsland, Alabama
The Sanctuary
March 22
1:32 p.m.

Paola took another white plate from Rebecca and ran the small hand towel over the dish until it was dry, then placed it on the counter atop an identical stack.

The girls were on dish duty for the second day in a row, Paola's third at The Sanctuary. The kitchen was the largest Paola had ever seen, looking more like a restaurant than a house, even though the house was huge and even nicer than Desmond's back at Warson Woods. There were four deep stainless steel sinks and two faucets with hose attachments, which made washing dishes easy, but not as easy as a giant dishwasher would have been.

Yesterday, they'd been helped by Caitlin, who had taken the dishes to storage after Paola had dried them. Caitlin was on cleaning duty today, though.

"What's the deal with the dresses?" Paola asked in a whisper, finally working up the courage to ask what had been on her mind for two days.

Rebecca had just turned 13 a couple of weeks ago, yet she looked younger than Paola by at least a year. Perhaps, Paola thought, she looked young because of the way she was dressed, with her hair in a perfect ponytail and figure in a long, dark-blue dress that looked straight out of some puritanical catalog. All the girls wore the same style dress, though Paola was still wearing her jeans and T-shirts. She wondered how long until someone asked her to wear the uniform. Her mom had still not given permission for Paola to attend The Sanctuary's classes, just yet anyway. In fact, Paola wasn't even sure they'd be staying at Sanctuary, which might have been why nobody asked her to wear the ugly dress yet.

"What do you mean?" Rebecca asked, as if genuinely confused by the question.

"Why do you all wear these dresses?" Paola asked.

The girl looked down at her dress, then up at Paola, "The Prophet believes that it's best to dress modestly, lest we tempt the weakness in men."

"What?"

"Yes, The Prophet says men are easily confused by women's looks. It's a trick the Devil uses to confuse men, to lead them from the Lord's Path. So, it's our responsibility as women not to tempt them."

Paola had to bury the urge to laugh. The look on the girl's face reminded her of Paola's algebra teacher.

"So, if a guy hits on you, it's your fault because the way you're dressed?"

"Yes," Rebecca said, giving Paola's outfit an up-and-down look, but saying nothing.

"Wow," Paola said, "That's messed up."

"What do you mean?" Rebecca asked, face concerned; curious more than offended.

"You think it's a sin to have a guy look at you? Flirt with you?"

"Well, those things lead to other things. The Lord is clear on S-E-X before marriage."

Paola couldn't contain the laugh after the girl spelled out "sex." She felt as if she'd gone back in time to the '50s or something.

Rebecca turned away, red-faced, putting her attention back to the dishes in the sink.

"I'm sorry," Paola said, "I've never met someone so . . . religious before."

Rebecca handed Paola a plate, and said, "It's nothing I'm ashamed of."

"No, and I'm not saying you should be," Paola said awkwardly as she dried off the plate. "It's just, you know, different from what I'm used to."

A few moments of silence stretched between them, punctuated by the splashes of water and clinking of plates as Paola stacked them.

Finally, Rebecca spoke, though she kept her eyes on the plates in the sink, "Have you ever kissed a boy?"

Paola smiled, "Yes. Once in sixth grade. Tommy Volchek kissed me behind the bleachers in gym class."

"Just once?"

"Yeah, I thought he liked me, and would ask me to the dance. But after he kissed me, he got all weird, and stopped talking to me. I don't know why."

More silence. Then Rebecca asked, "What was it like?"

"It was weird at first, because it was, like, by surprise. At first, I pulled away. But then I kissed him back, and he put his tongue in my mouth. And *that* was weird, but it also made me tingly all over. Weird, but good. I kept wondering if I was doing it right, and was afraid that maybe he had more experience than me and that I was a bad kisser. Maybe I was; maybe that's why he didn't ask me to the dance. I dunno. What about you? Have you ever had a boyfriend?"

"Oh, heavens no," Rebecca said, flushing. "I didn't even know many boys before I came here. Mother home-schooled us."

"Us?" Paola asked.

"Yeah, me and my older sister, Alexis. She was 15."

"Was? What happened to her?"

"She vanished with everyone else," Rebecca said, her voice becoming unstable.

"I'm sorry."

"Don't be. The Prophet says she's in a better place, so maybe she's the lucky one."

Paola wanted to ask Rebecca more about her sister, but the girl had turned silent again, now moving onto the silverware in the sink. Paola decided to bring the conversation back to boys.

"Is there anyone here you like?" she asked.

"Don't be ridiculous," Rebecca said, avoiding eye contact. Her flushed face, however, gave her away.

Paola laughed, "Oh my God, you DO like someone, don't you? Who is it? Who?!"

"Shh," Rebecca said, turning to Paola and putting her wet finger against her lips and shushing her. "Don't be so loud!"

"Who?" Paola whispered, barely able to hide her huge smile. Finally, something juicy to talk about!

"Well, *maybe* there's someone," Rebecca said, eyes back on the dishes, trying to look as serious as possible.

"I knew it!" Paola shouted.

"Shhh!" Rebecca said again. "You don't have to tell the world!"

"Okay, okay," Paola said, whispering again. "Who is it? Have I met him?"

"Well, I'm sure you've met everyone here at mealtimes, but I don't know if you've talked to him. His name is Carl, he's the tall kid with dark, curly hair and really pretty blue eyes."

"Oh, I had seen him," Paola said with a smile. "He's cute."

A flash of jealousy flushed Rebecca's eyes, but she quickly turned back to the dishes.

"So," Paola asked, "What's the deal?"

"There is no *deal*. I just fancy him, is all."

"Has he asked you out?"

"Oh no, The Prophet doesn't allow courting."

"Doesn't allow it? What is he? Some kind of king or something? It's a free world, you can *court* whoever you want. I mean, maybe your mom can stop you, but that's it. I wouldn't let some 'prophet' tell me who I can and can't date."

Rebecca turned to Paola, a serious look in her eyes. "You mustn't say that to anyone else."

"What?" Paola asked. "Why not?"

"I like you, so I won't say anything. But some of the others here, they might tell on you, report you to one of the elders. And believe me, you don't want that."

"Why not?" Paola asked, suddenly nervous.

"Aren't you girls done yet?" a voice said from behind, shocking them both. Paola nearly dropped the glass she was drying, then caught it just before it hit the ground. She turned to see Sarah standing behind them both.

"Enough chit-chat, there's work to be done," Sarah said.

"Yes, Mother," Rebecca said, turning back to the dishes.

As Sarah left the kitchen, Paola thought about the change in Rebecca's mom. She'd been so timid and quiet when they'd met and in front of the others, but when speaking to her daughter, she wasn't timid at all. She was almost mean.

135

Paola wanted to continue the conversation, but could hear Sarah putting stuff away in the pantry room next to the kitchen, likely eavesdropping.

**

Paola waited all day to continue the conversation. She finally got her chance at bedtime. She shared a room with Rebecca. While the men's quarters were three beds to a room, less children in the Sanctuary meant the kids' rooms had two beds instead. That gave the girls plenty of privacy to continue their conversation.

But before Paola could get her first word out, Rebecca blurted a question that must've been prickling her mind for a while. "Is Luca your boyfriend?"

Paola was taken by surprise, not only by the question, but how much at a loss of words she was to explain Luca to anyone. "He's a friend," she finally managed to say after a moment's blankness, which was one way to put it.

"I've seen the way he looks at you, though. And you, him. There's something there, isn't there?"

"He's too young," Paola said.

Rebecca looked confused. Apparently, word of Luca's uniqueness had not yet spread to everyone at The Sanctuary, which was, perhaps, for the best. However, Paola didn't see the harm in sharing the information with Rebecca.

"He's only 8 years old!"

"What? He looks like he's twice that!"

"I know, I know," Paola said, then went into the story about how Luca had come to them at the Drury; how he'd saved her and, in the process, had aged. And then aged again when he saved Scott.

"I feel something special with him because he was in here," Paola said, pointing to her head. "He saved me, and we got to be good friends. I like him a lot. He's the sweetest kid. But I don't *like* like him."

She wasn't sure if she was convincing on that last part, either to Rebecca or herself.

Rebecca stared, "That is so weird. What did he do to heal you? It sounds like a miracle!"

"I don't know how it works. He doesn't either. He was as surprised as anyone when he did it."

"The Lord works in mysterious ways," Rebecca said, staring up at the ceiling, as if pondering His powers.

Paola stared, too, thinking not about the Lord, but rather, Luca. In the past two days, she'd hardly seen him at all, and she was surprised by how much she missed him. Perhaps it was just as well, though. Truth was, in his last transformation he'd gone from an awkward kid who looked close to her age to an older teen who was a hunk. If she'd just met him, she'd be all jelly inside just looking at him. But knowing him as she did made her feel weird, something between a crush and how a sister feels about a brother. The mix of the two feelings was confusing. She was half drawn to and half repulsed by Luca. She'd never been particularly good at hiding her feelings, and she didn't want either feeling leaking out to Luca. What was happening to him wasn't his fault, after all.

"He wants me to meet him," Rebecca said, seemingly out of the blue.

At first Paola thought she meant Luca. She asked, "Huh? Who wants to meet you?"

"Carl. He found me after dinner tonight, and said he wanted to meet me by the creek, where there's a rope swing. Have a picnic."

"Ooh, are you gonna go?"

"I don't know. My mother would kill me if she found out."

"Well, you've gotta make sure she doesn't find out," Paola said.

"I don't even know if that's possible in this place. There's guards all over, and everybody knows everybody's business."

"Well, he must think there's some way you two can sneak off if he's asking, right? Maybe he's in with the guards or something and has a plan?"

"You think?"

"He must have something in mind if he asked," Paola said.

Discussion quickly dimmed, and Paola was soon sound asleep and dreaming of Luca. Again.

* * * *

CHAPTER 5
BORICIO WOLFE

Dunn, Georgia
March 22
3:20 a.m.

Boricio slipped from the house and into the garage, quietly, but with just a fraction of his usual bounce. He didn't want anyone waking, but fuck them and the Apocalypse that made this shit a reality show if they wanted to stop him. Boricio eased the unfinished Z8 from the garage, quietly drove out and to the edge of the compound, then down a winding half mile where he finally pressed the pedal as far as it would go.

Hunting time.

It had been too long since he'd seen a fucker's head roll for the grease and grins of it. Sure, they'd taken care of the bikers nice and proper, but that was business. And there wasn't no pussy worth taking; well, not without causing a scene. Hopefully, a hunt would give him a nice store of pink meat. Given the slim pickings of late, Boricio was starting to worry he might never see another woman worth fucking. But the warehouse gave him hope that there were more out there, hiding and waiting to be found.

If he didn't get off soon, he might not be able to restrain himself from the pussy back home.

Watching Callie pirouette across the house in those tiny shorts, looking like the cover of *Low Rider*, transformed the hangout into the hard-on hotel. Ain't no way he was gonna be around that another 10 minutes without wanting to slam the Tampon Tunnel with the Boricio Express. And once the Boricio Express was booked, you could bet the ball sack and both balls in it that shit arrived on schedule.

Callie would like the Boricio Express just fine; the problem was that cock blocker, Charlie.

Boricio fucked like he cooked: better, spicier, and with thicker broth than any motherfucker within a 400-mile radius. Callie might not like it at first because it wasn't her idea. But if he forced her to start sucking at sundown, she'd be lapping up fourths by sunrise and panting for fifths – you could bet your ball sack and both balls in it. And it shouldn't fucking matter. Wasn't like Charlie was squirting his danglers in her dithers anyway. Chucky Cheese Dick had his feelings, sure, but that wasn't what kept Boricio's buttons in a row. This was about keeping, and maintaining, control of his team.

It was a dog-eat-dog world, and there ain't nothing a dog likes better than a heaping helping of pussy, whiskers or no. But pussy was hard to come by at the end of the world. And Boricio was a big dog; he'd bite the face off any other dog to keep his pussy in a high pile. But that was the same sorta shit that Bobby Big Boy had done to Charlie, and Boricio didn't want to schedule a rerun of that particular show. Boricio was smart enough to be the big dog who kept his puppies on patrol. Sometimes that meant letting the dogs feel like they had some power, and leaving things be.

Despite his occasional temper tantrums, Charlie had proven himself capable of playing for Team Boricio when he took care of that shit-pile stepfather of his. The kid was grinning like a drunk Mexican when he called Boricio in to see his handiwork. A thing of beauty what he'd done to Bob. Boricio hadn't done anything even approaching Charlie's level of artistry until his 21st kill.

It was a bitch restaurant reviewer who pissed him off. Took one bite of his best dish and declared it DOA without even swallowing. It was the last review she ever wrote. Boricio wouldn't have cared about the review itself. Fuck her. His shit was crème de la fuck-yeah, and he knew it. But she up and decided it wasn't worth her muffin before the spoon hit the fat of her mouth. Boricio found the first part of the review funny, laughing out loud at her dumb fuckery, but then he hit the last line: "The owners of L'aigle Noir must pay handsomely for the lines that circle the block. And at $20 a plate, they can afford it."

Fuck. Her.

Boricio waited six weeks. When he finally caught her, he made sure she swallowed. Four times in two hours. The bonus three were interest for her not taking a legitimate bite of his Chiliquelles de la Noche. It had been a long night with Miss Bitch Reviewer, but sweet enough to make the sudden move two states over worth it. It was the first time Boricio had ever gotten creative with his kills. And dammit, what was an artist such as himself without creativity?

Charlie, however, was like some kinda idiot savant when it came to creative killing, though. His first work was a goddamned masterpiece!

Boricio didn't know everything that had gone down in the room. And Charlie had refused to answer any questions, simply letting the work speak for itself. Boricio had no idea why Dumbfuck Charlie wouldn't want to talk about it; the fuck he knew whether the rookie was ashamed or perhaps frightened by what he'd done. If Boricio had demonstrated half the artistry the kid had on his first kill, he would've had the shit printed on a T-shirt and wore the fucker threadbare. Boy had a gift. Made Boricio proud, a feeling he wasn't sure he'd ever felt for another before.

Charlie had called Boricio into the room and shut the door so only Boricio would see what he'd done. He led him to the bed where Bob's hands and feet were tied to the black wrought iron bed posts. The man's arms and legs had been splayed apart as far as possible so he formed a giant X. The lower half of his nude body was covered beneath a blood-soaked down comforter.

Boricio walked around the bed, not touching a thing, admiring the boy's handiwork like an artist surveying the work of his protégé. Charlie watched the entire time, eyes on Boricio, as if waiting for a critique.

Bob's eyes were wide open in a permanent shocked expression, which made Boricio smile. *Didn't see this coming, did ya, Bob?* Bob's cheeks had been sliced open and hung like bloody fatty flaps over the sides of his face. On the right cheek, Charlie had used a nail-gun he'd found in the room to shoot a nail into the man's face. Since there was only one nail, Boricio figured the boy was simply experimenting and hadn't liked the result. The man's mouth was dark purple, puffy, and bloody, like ole Charlie had spent a fat hour hitting or cutting him in the same goddamn spot. He looked like a losing boxer at the end of the fight with a mouth full of gauze to soak up the blood.

Across Bobby's chest were more wounds with flesh peeled back, most probably given to Bob while he was still begging. His nipple had been cut off. Long wounds stretched from the man's wrists to his armpits where Charlie had cut him several times. Blood soaked the bed beneath him. Two pens had been jabbed into each side of the man's ribcage and left there.

Boricio looked at the comforter and up to Charlie, "May I?"

"Yes," Charlie said.

Boricio pulled the covers off Bob and beheld Charlie's masterstroke, the thing of beauty that assured Boricio that Charlie was a certifiably in-the-closet, 48-karat crazy ass motherfucker.

A pulpy stump sat in the middle of Bob's bloodied pubic forest where his cock had been.

Boricio looked up at Charlie and applauded, "Bravo, sir!"

Charlie looked like he was either about to burst out laughing or crying; Boricio wasn't sure which. His face looked queasy.

"Where did you . . . " Boricio had started to ask, then realized the reason that Bob's mouth was so puffy. "Oh. Wow. You made him eat his dick! That is . . . " Boricio said, pretending to wipe tears of joy from his eyes, "*That*, my boy, is a thing of fucking beauty!"

And then Charlie went and did something that shocked even Boricio; he sprayed his masterpiece with lighter fluid, lit a match, and set the fucker on fire.

"Don't you want to show the others?" Boricio had asked. "This is something to brag about!"

"No," Charlie said, "You're the only one who will know what I did here."

The way Charlie had said it was weird, and Boricio still hadn't figured out why the boy had shown him and nobody else. But he'd certainly earned himself a roster spot, and a top slot at that, on Team Boricio. If that meant Boricio would have to lay off Callie, then that's just what he'd have to do, for now, at least.

But he would need to fuck something. And soon.

**

Boricio had driven about 10 miles when he saw the impossible. The sudden shock caused the Z8 to suddenly fishtail. He quickly regained control, with a little help from some precision German engineering, then slapped the windshield and screamed, "That's some beer-battered bullshit!" He threw the BMW into reverse and tore back to where he'd seen the ghost.

But she was gone.

The woman.

The Christmas gift he'd killed on Oct. 14, and the very fucking one he saw at The Prophet's compound less than a week later. She was standing on the side of the road as if waiting for someone to pick her up. If it wasn't her, then the end of the world had just shit a Montezuma's Revenge worth of crazy on his face.

Fuck.

Boricio didn't like driving in the dark down Crazy Road.

But he kept driving, turning down every street and into every nearby neighborhood, searching for a trace of the woman or some clue to prove he wasn't going loco. Sick of the shit in his head, Boricio turned on the CD player to The Mummies, a band Adam liked – catchy swamp rock with every song hosting a double entendre.

A half hour later, Boricio was bobbing his head back and forth and mouthing the words in an attempt to stay awake. He'd been feeling tired a lot lately. He wasn't sure if he was getting bored from the changes to his lifestyle or if he was coming down with something. He rarely got sick, so the idea of catching something now didn't bother him too much. But there was only so much you could do when you were feeling dead-ass tired.

He pulled to the side of the road, killed the engine, and stepped from the BMW, feeling like he'd walked right off the map.

Boricio had no idea when he'd lost the highway; maybe it was a mile back, maybe it was 10. He had no idea where he was, and with the pitch black surrounding him, no clue how to figure it out. The GPS wasn't working, and there weren't any maps in the glove box. Boricio had been back and forth across the country, from Timbuktu to Fuck Your Mother, and his sense of direction was usually dead on. But right now he was a toddler in the mall and all the mommies were looking identical below the waist.

Boricio got back in the Z8 and leaned back to catch some shut eye.

He slept for a few minutes, maybe, when the shriek of a monster woke him. Life burst back into his eyes as his hand shot for his gun on pure reflex. But the threat was nowhere to be seen. He wasn't sure if the monster was in his dreams or nearby, but he was too damned tired to stick around and find out. He revved the engine, then roared onto the road, swinging a left at the first crossroads. He had nearly a full tank of gas and would just drive until he figured out where he was or found sunlight, when it would be easier to find his way back.

Daylight apparently wasn't too far off since Boricio crashed into it head first about an hour later, alongside an uncomfortably loud wave of déjà vu that ended in a row of houses that reminded him an awful lot of the ritzy-titsy homes up in Gulfport, Mississippi.

Boricio pulled the Z8 into a perfectly bricked horseshoe drive, and smiled. His smile grew bigger when he stepped inside the unlocked house.

The two-story house was posh, with eight bedrooms, six bathrooms, and three boat slips, two occupied. Same as most of the other rich houses Boricio had seen, this one was flush with alcohol, clothes, guns, jewelry, lots of pills, pounds of weed, loads of money, and shelves lined with food.

The living room was massive, with a pile of rich bitchy furniture pushed to one side. Eight bedrolls sat in a circle, each with a large bank of pillows, several bottles of water, and a medium-sized red bucket. The buckets had what looked and smelled like vomit. The air was thick, sour and weirdly familiar.

Two buckets lay on their side with scabs of black vomit crusting the lacquered hardwood floor. A red and white bedroll was in the center with wooden instruments, spirit sticks burned to a nub, and a large two-liter jug of sludge, filled to the top, with an empty shot glass sitting beside it on the floor. Boricio picked up the two-liter jug and shot glass, then went upstairs, found the master bedroom, and fell into the plush oversized bed. He filled the glass to the top, put it to his lips, then spilled the entire psychedelic mess down his throat.

For a few moments, he felt nothing. Then something moved in his guts.

Seconds later, vomit spewed from his mouth, and Boricio fell over, face down on the Egyptian cotton. He smiled. He felt lighter, stronger, better. He turned over, looking up where the ceiling had been. It was replaced by colors: swirling, spinning, dancing across his mind. But the colors weren't alone. They came loaded with memories, unpleasant ones, which started as whispers but were growing louder by the second, mixing into a chaotic mix of sound and visuals that threatened to swallow him whole.

He snarled, had to fight as thoughts piled on top of him, too many to sort, voices, images, and a million colors — *fuck, the colors* — as his body swayed back and forth in the waves, all the while his stomach lurching with each movement. The waves, the noise, and the colored memories rose in pitch, carrying him ever higher, impossibly high, as if into the sky above, though he could see nothing but the colors

146

and memories. He continued to rise and felt the rising fear of the inevitable drop that would come.

A childhood fear whispered into his mind: *Fall in your sleep, and hit the ground, you'll die in both worlds, and never be found.*

And then he fell.

But the fall wasn't long. It was instant. And instead of crashing to the ground, he simply stopped moving.

He woke face up in a dark, cold, slippery pit that was wet with the putrid scent of death. The only light came from above, but seemed so dim and far away as if to be thousands of feet from where he lay. He sat up and noticed a crow next to him, pulling at something in the ground.

A worm?

Then Boricio saw it wasn't worm, but rather the flesh from a corpse. One of thousands of tangled, naked bodies that lined every square inch of the pit around him, piled as high as he could see.

Jesus Christ.

Not one to stick around in hell-holes, Boricio grabbed a handful of corpse and started to climb towards the light. He climbed and climbed until sweat started to stew in his pores and coat his body. His muscles bulged and he felt inches from exhaustion, but after an hour, he was getting closer to the dim light above, which he could now make out as stars. As he drew closer, Boricio felt a gust of cool air and could see the grass swaying at the edges of the pit just yards away.

He continued to climb but lost his grip when three heads emerged from the grass. Then he heard a horrible scream from the sky above just as the corpses beneath him came to life, clawing, tearing, biting.

This shit is about as real as a pair of Beverly Hills tits, but fuck me in my starfish and hit me with a slap of hot yogurt if it don't feel exactly like the here-and-now.

The fingers kept clawing at Boricio, a thousand at once. For the first time in years, Boricio nearly screamed. But he didn't. He clawed back, kicked at limbs, and bit hands that brushed across his face, cursing and spitting out chunks of flesh as he bit them. He kept moving until he reached the lip, and clawed his way onto the soft, cold grass, hugging him like a blanket as it rolled in waves beneath the purple sky. The pit, with its corpses, moaned in defeat.

Boricio bathed in the light of the moon, so fat it filled much of the night sky, and laughed.

I'm alive!

A sharp cry from a wolf sliced through the air, followed by an echoing chorus.

It's a dog-eat-dog world, Boricio. How big is your bark?

The howls were getting closer, and the fuckers sounded hungry. Boricio rolled to his feet and stood up, opened his hands like claws, and steeled himself ready for whatever was about to come.

No pack of Motel Six for fleas motherfuckers is gonna take me down, you could bet your ball sack and both balls in it.

The howls fell silent as a fog rolled in, covering earth and sky alike.

Boricio, now blinded, titled his head to better hear his surroundings. The moaning from the pit stopped, leaving him in silence except for his heartbeat. He turned in the dark fog, waiting for anything from any side, his claws at the ready.

The fog receded, and two figures emerged into view. A tall woman stood beside a dog, a Husky with large, sad eyes that looked even larger and sadder beneath the bright light of the full moon.

The woman turned to the Husky and said, "It's a dog-eat-dog world, eh, Oggy Doggy?"

The Husky ignored the woman, but turned to Boricio and spoke, "Well fuck a duck, son, it looks like you just screwed the pooch!"

Boricio stared, knowing this was a bad trip and not sure how in the hell to respond.

Before he could speak, someone else appeared behind the pair. A small boy with big eyes. The boy studied Boricio, looking him over from head to toe, eyes narrowed in study. Finally he said, "Who are you, mister? Are you one of the voices?"

"I'm Boricio," he said. "Now, you wanna tell me what the hell you're doing out here smack dab in the middle of Fuck-All?"

"I'm lost," he said. "But I came from over there."

The boy pointed at the horizon, then down at the pit. "That's the middle."

Another voice, one deeper than the child's, chimed in, seemingly from the child's mouth, "The Center of Fuck-All."

"Where you from, you know, besides your mama's furbox?"

"Las Orillas."

"Where are your parents?"

"Everyone is gone."

The woman put her arm around the boy as the Husky lay down at his feet. The boy suddenly seemed to grow in a matter of seconds, shooting from a small boy to one old enough to have a few hairs on his balls.

Boricio stumbled backwards, then righted himself and returned forward. "None of this is real, right?"

The boy shook his head. "Everything is real, Mr. Boricio," he said.

The woman and dog nodded in agreement.

The woman then whispered something in the Husky's ear. He raised his snout in the air, stole a glance at the moon, then fell into a loud, 30-second howl. When he was finished, he winked, then fell back to a sleeping position at the boy's feet.

"Everything's real, Mr. Boricio," the boy repeated. He looked at the moon, and then the woman. She nodded and the boy said, "Sorry, Mr. Boricio, but I have to get going now."

"Wait," Boricio growled, "Who in the fuck are you?"

The boy smiled, now growing to around Charlie's age. In a grown man's voice, he said, "Sorry," he said, "My name is Luca. I've got to tell you something."

Another fog rolled in, and Boricio braced for the unknown, whether it be wolf, woman, dog, or child.

When the fog retreated, they were gone.

All of them, the corpses in the pit, too. The moon hung in the air another moment, but only long enough to widen and blanket the sky in the brightest white, bright enough to bleed beneath Boricio's closed lids.

Boricio opened his eyes and found himself in the forest, not too far off the highway, the BMW Z8 about 100 yards away.

Well, that was some beer-battered bullshit if ever I've tasted any.

Boricio got in the Z8 and keyed the ignition. As he found his way back to the familiar, and was heading home, he wondered what the hell Luca, real or not, was trying to tell him.

* * * *

CHAPTER 6
DESMOND ARMSTRONG

Kingsland, Alabama
The Sanctuary
March 23
9:06 a.m.

Desmond added another freshly-measured and cut two-by-four to the pile, wiped his brow, took a long gulp of icy water, then picked up another board. He rolled the tape measure to the appropriate spot and marked a wooden check with his pencil before placing the board into the path of the circular saw, paying just enough attention to the task at hand so as not to cut off a finger.

It had been four days since they arrived at The Sanctuary; each day of Desmond's newfound "freedom" had put him in a different part of the compound. Today, he was in the wood shop, helping with tasks for the construction of the new church. Though Desmond was decent enough with his hands, so far he had yet to be assigned a single task that a decent reward and a focused gorilla couldn't manage.

That was fine. He promised Will and Mary that he'd play nice, and he had. No reason not to see things out, so long as he kept his eyes and ears on full alert.

Luca seemed to love the place. That wasn't too surprising since everyone doted on him, at least in their weird, far-off way. It was as if everyone at the church all took the same personality-draining pills, which turned them into Stepford Wife-like clones. Plus, Luca was allowed to stay with the other children for learning time, despite his size. The Prophet didn't seem too shocked to learn that Luca would be celebrating his ninth birthday in another few weeks. Desmond figured that John had told The Prophet, whose real name nobody seemed to know, everything that had happened back at the Drury Inn.

Paola had taken to Sarah's daughter, Rebecca, who had just turned 13 two weeks ago. While Desmond wasn't buying the bond between Mary and Sarah just yet, Mary was playing a good game, side by side with Sarah during the daily chores of cooking, cleaning, and laundry. Will and Linc were doing their part, too, keeping their hands busy and noses down.

Scott, like Luca, seemed genuinely happy in his new environment, and particularly happy to be around girls his own age, judging from the awkward smiles and stolen glances Desmond had noticed.

While the others seemed ready to call this place home, Desmond wasn't so sure how long he could put up listening to a second-rate evangelist who just happened to have outlived the rest of the parasites. Mary was all he had in the world, along with Paola and Luca, of course. He'd be goddamned if he was going to be barred from their lives, seeing them only after breaking bread, where "The Good Lord's Word" was spread more than butter, or at random times when they had intersecting chores. He'd rather face bleakers and monsters and whatever else the Apocalypse had in store than be forced to surrender the most of himself.

But for now, he'd wait — coiled, at the ready — with his mouth shut and eyes open.

Each evening after dinner, Desmond and Will exchanged the day's tidings. Will had already confirmed that the third floor of the men's house was only for The Prophet, John, and Rei, and that there was no doubt something fishy between Rei and John. Will was also positive that the third floor housed the weapons; not just because it would make sense for The Prophet to want them nearby, but because the locked door at the top of the stairs was the first and last stop in between each of the soldier's shifts. Will was sure that's where weapons were picked up and dropped off. No one was packing unless they were on active duty.

Desmond wondered if The Prophet followed that particular part of The Word. God only knew what the man was packing under his weird-ass white robes.

There were four soldiers standing guard at all times throughout the compound: one per rooftop on each of the three homes and a fourth sitting in a booth beside the entrance gate. Each of the houses had a small, makeshift tower on its roof: a small room with a desk and chair, a Bible, and a 14-page stapled copy of The Word, which served as a neat summary of the New Unity's much longer dogma.

Linc was the only one of their crew so far who had been assigned guard duty. Will got the skinny from Linc, who passed it to Desmond. According to Linc, each tower had a floodlight and a switch. Flip the switch and every alarm in the compound started screaming.

Desmond looked up from his two-by-four as Will entered the workshop. He smiled at the old man's appearance, wondering what The Prophet really thought of him.

Will sported a wild look from the moment Desmond met him, with unevenly cut hair, shorn close, and a couple of days' worth of stubble. But lately, it appeared that grooming his hair or beard was the last thing on his mind.

Will's hair wasn't especially long, but it was much longer than anyone else's in the group, including Luca's, who had his overgrown locks trimmed just two days prior. And what it lacked in length it made up for in general wildness, jutting out from his head, thick tufts in every direction. The hair on his head made Will look untamed, but what really added to the old dog's feral appearance was his barbarous-looking beard. Will's beard was mostly white, but the black thatches that peppered his whiskers looked almost angry, the way they smothered the white around them. And the hairs were thick, like wire. Will had a habit of running his hands through his hair and tugging his beard when making a point, which happened most times he opened his mouth. It made him appear extra wild, along with the way his eyes would fade along with his voice as he fell deeper into thought.

Even Desmond would agree that Will was the smartest of the group, but he was also the looniest. And he seemed the most likely candidate to piss off the powers that be at The Sanctuary, something that Desmond was constantly preparing to defend, if needed.

"What's up?" Desmond said.

"You're wanted outside," Will replied. "They'd like us to go on a supply run."

Desmond raised his eyebrows. "A supply run? You mean they're letting us free range birdies out of the coop?"

Will laughed. "Apparently so. And Old Man Testament must be warming to us, too. We're supposed to report to the third floor to check out firearms."

Desmond's eyebrows lifted higher, the bewilderment on his face telling.

"I know," Will said. "Crazy. Seems I was right about the weapons being on the third floor, doesn't it?"

"I never question whether you're right or not," Desmond smiled. "I just wish you'd enlighten us more often."

Will ignored Desmond's comment; he just ran his hands through his hair, then tugged on his beard and said, "They're waiting, so head on up to the third floor and get a gun from Rei. And see if they'll give you something with a clip." Will held up an old fashioned revolver. "This is fine, but I'd prefer something faster in a fight."

Desmond nodded. "Anything else?"

Will shook his head. "No, not for now. Still trying to figure what in the hell is up between Rei and John. Can't get my finger anywhere near it."

"Not sure I even want to know," Desmond confessed. "This whole place makes me feel, I don't know, like I'm in a bad horror movie version of Catholic school."

Will's half laugh wasn't reassuring. Will pivoted and strolled toward the door only to stop halfway. He turned and said, "Remember, something with a clip if you can."

A minute later, Desmond was knocking on the locked door atop the third floor. "Brother Desmond," Rei said, opening the door, blocking access to the room beyond, his smile wide and scarily genuine.

Desmond returned a smile thin enough to see through and said, "Will told me to report for a firearm; he said we were going out on a supply run."

"Brother Will is correct," Rei said. "Please wait here."

Rei closed the door, locked it, then came back a minute later, unlocking and opening the door and handing Desmond a Colt Revolver, identical to Will's, along with one box of ammunition.

Desmond held the revolver in his hand. The weight felt good, great even, but it wasn't his gun, one he was very familiar with. "I'd like one of my own guns, something with a bit more power," he said.

"This is your gun, assigned by the New Unity. It's what's best."

"Look," Desmond tried taking a step forward, but Rei blocked the entrance with his body. "You all are holding onto a lot of my guns. I understand the need for safety, security, and all that, so I surrendered my arms like a good boy and haven't said *boo* since. But if you're sending me outside, and giving me a gun anyway, I see no reason why I can't have one of the guns I came in with."

There was a long moment of silence, then Rei shook his head sadly as though the answer was simple and Desmond was simply too dim to see it.

"Sometimes," he said, "you must accept things on faith. This is one of those things. New Unity knows what's best, for you and for us all, Brother Desmond. New Unity is your new home, and you must let us help you learn to trust. We're here to take care of you." He smiled again, sickly sweet, then placed both his hands around Desmond's right one, closing his fingers around the revolver. Rei leaned several inches closer to Desmond and said, "Be well, and travel safe, Brother Desmond. Please come back to us whole."

The door swung quietly closed in Desmond's face, followed quickly by the sound of the lock clicking into place. The situation wasn't worth pressing. Not now. So Desmond descended the stairs, his insides a volatile cocktail of defeat and fury.

Will was already in the back seat of the midnight-blue Sequoia when Desmond climbed inside. They were being chaperoned by two of the Sanctuary's soldiers, a loudmouth big guy named Paul and a near-mute skinny guy named Ricky. Flashes of Laurel and Hardy stormed in Desmond's mind.

"So, what sorts of supplies are we gathering?" Desmond asked to the front seat.

Paul was driving. He turned and said, "Food. There's a Costco not too far from here. It has everything we need."

"Why keep making trips?" Desmond shrugged. "Can't one of you big guys drive one of those 18-wheelers back to The Sanctuary? Seems like the smart thing to do would be loading one truck all at once, making just one trip to the old Big Box and back, and be done with it. But who am I to say, I never foresaw nothing worth foreseeing."

Desmond smiled, winking at Will, then leaned in his seat while Paul glared at him in the rearview, silent. Will kicked Desmond on the ankle, hard, a slight scowl on his face saying, *not now.*

Desmond figured they were getting close when a mile marker on the road promised civilization in four miles, but the sign was splattered with what looked like fresh blood, filling Desmond with a sudden wave of dread. He placed his hand over the revolver and said, "That sign look like that the last time you hit Costco?"

Paul said no, trying to sound tough, but his voice cracked through a gauze of panic.

A sudden, thick fear drowned the cabin as they took the highway exit and drove a couple of blocks to Costco's giant, nearly empty parking lot.

They proceeded to the front of the store and parked on the sidewalk.

They were about to get out of the truck when Ricky screamed "Demon!" a split second before the first one flew into the passenger side door with a jarring thud. The beast cracked the window, coating it with black blood, before it skittered away, hunched over like a wounded dog running away to lick its wounds.

Paul turned off the truck, his hand oddly calm.

"What the fuck are you doing?!" Desmond shouted. "Let's get the fuck out of here!"

Paul ignored him.

More of the monsters appeared, racing toward the truck, about 10 of them in total. They rammed into the truck at full speed just as the first one had done, cracking the windows and bashing in the doors. Desmond and Will took aim at the windows and held, waiting for one to breach. Desmond chanced a glance back to the front seat to see why Paul wasn't driving away. The queer reality he saw took a full second to register: The two men held hands in prayer, as still as statues.

Paul whispered fast: "In the name of the Good Lord and under the protection of The Prophet, His window to The Wasteland, I COMMAND every Demon that has followed me, was sent to me, or transferred to me, to depart my body now. In the name of the Good Lord and under the protection of The Prophet, His window to The Wasteland, I cover myself and all my property with the blood of Jesus. Demons as I sleep and Demons as I wake, I command you to stay away. Banish all evil thoughts from inside me. And as we step from this truck, I beg the Good Lord to build a Fiery Wall of Vengeance around us."

Paul released Ricky's hand, then turned to the back seat. "You ready?"

"Let's leave. We'll find another store," Desmond said.

"No, we fight. We have the Lord on our side; we do not back down from Satan's minions."

With that, he opened the door, stepped outside, and fired into one of the creatures.

Desmond turned to Will, shrugged his shoulders, opened the door, and joined in the firefight. Will followed.

Paul and Ricky were machines. Every bullet found its mark in a symphony of grisly screams, on a stage displaying a ballet of gore. Desmond and Will each managed to take down a creature or two each, though it was hard to tell for sure as Paul and Ricky seemed to put a shot in every one of the bastards. There were enough broken bodies to make a true count difficult, but Desmond guessed there to be enough body parts strewn about to account for 20 or so of the fiends.

When their last bullet casings clinked on the concrete, Paul and Ricky hopped back into the truck, leaving Desmond and Will standing outside confused.

"Are we canceling our shopping trip?" Desmond asked, following Paul and Ricky back inside the vehicle with Will behind.

Paul glared in the rearview. Ricky remained silent.

Will turned to Desmond and said, "Seems our righteous new friends have been taken by surprise. Those creatures were attacking in formation, which I'm guessing they haven't seen before. So, Paul up there has to swing back to The Sanctuary and make a full report. That sound about right, Paul?"

Desmond figured Paul would keep doing his Ricky impersonation, but instead, he snapped back.

"They're *Demons*, not creatures," Paul said. "They're Satan's minions, the very same that The Prophet has warned us about. You saw how The Good Lord protected us back there. You can't deny the truth."

"What I saw," Desmond said, voice cool, "was a couple of well-trained crack shots hitting every one of their marks with high-caliber automatic weapons. The Good Lord would've been looking out for me and Will a little more, too, at least if He saw fit to make sure we'd left The Sanctuary with better guns." Desmond couldn't help the last words ringing in a sneer.

They cancelled their shopping trip. The drive home was silent. Desmond could feel Will's burning disapproval, which was fine. It only echoed Desmond's own disapproval of allowing himself to be dragged down into the ridiculous emotions of the situation. He knew better than that. That's what he'd been doing for the last decade – working with people online and off, always making the compromise that would satisfy the majority. Now, here, he was acting like a petulant child. Junkie behavior, throwing tantrums when he didn't get what he wanted, which made sense since what he wanted more than anything right now was Mary.

Part of him wished that he'd never driven back to Warson Woods, but kept driving that morning of Oct. 15. Survival is a hell of a lot easier when it's a table for one. No one else to worry about. Nobody else to keep track of. Nobody else forcing him to act against his instincts by catering to the whims of a religious despot. Desmond had his own ideas of *sanctuary* and they had nothing to do with some archaic rules handed down by imaginary beings and interpreted by delusional at best, deceptive at worst, men.

Yet, as they drove back to the compound and swung into the hangar, he knew that such thinking was futile. He'd grown to love Mary and Paola, Luca too. And hell, he even loved Will, if only in the role of crazy uncle. So, he'd continue to play along until he thought of a better plan.

Desmond opened his door to the sounds of panic.

"What's happened?" Paul yelled to a passing guard. The man made a sharp detour then a beeline toward the hangar. His story was half out of his mouth before his legs stopped walking.

"Rebecca and Carl are missing. We can't find them anywhere. Last time anyone saw them was just after breakfast. We searched all the buildings of the compound without success. The Prophet says we should now start searching the woods."

The porch creaked across the way as John's feet hit the bottom stair. He crossed the courtyard, came into the hangar and slapped Desmond on the shoulder, handing him his holster with a Glock inside it. "Come on," he said. "We're going to find Rebecca and Carl."

John then turned to Paul, "Desmond and I are going to circle round to Dawn Creek Road and will search the woods on the north end. Lenny and Eli are gonna take the south end. We'll all meet up in the middle, okay?"

"Yes, Brother John," Paul said.

John turned, walked into the hangar and climbed into a silver Audi that looked so new, every mile on it had to have come after Oct. 15. John turned the key, and the Audi hummed to life. Desmond was surprised by the sudden turn of events, but understanding would have to wait. He nodded an *adios* to Will, then joined John in the Audi. John punched the accelerator, swung a right out of the hangar, and headed away from the compound, all while Desmond scanned the courtyard in search of Mary.

Desmond had already decided to bury the hatchet with John before they started talking. Whatever was happening at The Sanctuary wasn't John's fault. He was the symptom, not the disease. John was a good guy before Oct. 15 from what Desmond knew, even if he was a little annoying. And really, after losing your wife alongside the rest of the world, who wouldn't be looking for a few magic beans? You never knew what people were really going through until you were lacing up their boots. So, who was he to judge John for taking off and leaving them stranded? People did bad shit when they were at their lowest. Hell, Desmond had ruined the wedding of the one serious girlfriend he'd ever had. It didn't even make sense; he had been genuinely happy for her. But he drank too much and said a lot of stuff he shouldn't have said, at the wedding or anywhere else. He'd thought about it with redwood-thick regret maybe once a week since. And the end of the world hadn't stopped it. John had his own shit to think about, too. No one could argue; he saved them back at the house and brought them to where he thought they'd be safe. Even if he was misguided, John's intentions were probably good.

"I'm sorry," Desmond said, "about everything. Not just about lately since we came to The Sanctuary, but all of it. Back at the Drury. Hell, back on the bridge. I'm sorry."

John kept driving, and Desmond kept talking.

"It was hard, you know, after you left. Mary and the kids were scared out of their minds. And Jimmy . . . " Desmond had forgotten about Jimmy for a moment. He felt a cold chill run through his body and hoped John hadn't noticed his bristle. "It was all too much at once. Then you disappeared. And the next month, well, it was awful."

Desmond didn't want to dive into deeper detail; in fact, he wanted to leave the conversation right there and never pick it up again. Fortunately, John swung off the highway and into a thatch of woods on the right.

"Rebecca loves this patch of woods," John said, diverting the conversation. "Before last October, she used to live just on the other side." John pointed through the windshield, toward a rolling hill dotted with the first promise of spring. He decelerated, killed the engine, and stepped from the car.

Desmond followed, gun drawn. "You won't need that," John offered. "I can't feel a single Demon right now. We're safe." He cupped his hands next to his mouth and screamed. "Rebecca!"

He turned to Desmond. "No worries, Desmond. I understand how you feel." He held out his hand. Desmond shook it, and John said, "We're all trying to survive and make the most of this. Breathe in, breathe out, be merry."

They checked the surrounding woods and were all the way up the hill, ready to descend the backside, when Desmond's thoughts derailed. He'd heard that last expression from John before. But not from John. It was out of place coming from him, eerie even. Not just the words, but the tone. The echo was odd, and ominous. He felt like he was pulling splinters of thought while trying to place it.

They were at the top of the hill, looking at the horror on the other side when Desmond realized with a sick, slippery dread where he'd heard that expression before.

We're all trying to survive and make the most of this. Breathe in, breathe out, be merry.

That was something Jimmy had said.

* * * *

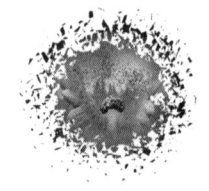

CHAPTER 7
RYAN OLSON

Brookdale, Tennessee
Feb. 17
Morning

"How long will this medicine last?" Ryan asked, inspecting the pills as they headed up the street toward Carmine's apartment in the opposite direction of the drug store. Ryan didn't want the kid walking back there alone with those ass clowns still out there. The more he thought about it, the more Ryan wished he'd shot the bastards when he had a chance. He pissed them off, so they'd likely want vengeance, against him or Carmine, or both.

"I think he takes one a day. There's 100 in each bottle, so a while." Carmine answered.

"How bad a shape is he in?"

"He's in a wheelchair; lost a leg to diabetes a few years back."

"Shit," Ryan said. "Does he have diabetes medicine?"

"Yeah, he's good on all that other stuff. I got those last week. Those men weren't there then. Or maybe they just didn't see me."

"Well, for future reference, I'd find another place to shop, okay?"

"Yeah, there's another drug store a few blocks the other way, but it's a bit farther and I like to keep as close to Gramps as possible. I'll go there next time, though."

"And maybe stick to homes and stuff for food, just to make sure you don't cross paths with those guys."

"Yeah," Carmine said as he continued to lead Ryan down another street.

"You see any monsters around here? Or any other people?" Ryan asked.

"You all are the first I've seen since November. But yeah, I see the monsters every now and then. I hide. They haven't seen me yet. I don't see them near as much as I used to, I don't think."

"What about your grandpa?"

"He don't leave the house, so as long as none of those things hears us or sees us, we're okay. What's your deal?" Carmine asked. "You from here?"

"No, I'm looking for my wife and daughter. Well, my ex-wife."

"Ah," Carmine said as if he'd been there, done that. "You heard from them at all?"

"No."

"How you know they're alive?"

"I don't," Ryan said. "Just a feeling."

"Do you know what happened? Where all the people went?" Carmine asked.

"Nope, no idea. What do you think happened?"

"I dunno. I ran into this dude a while back who said everyone was taken by the government. Some big, secret experiment going on."

"And they grabbed up everyone all at once?" Ryan said incredulously.

"I didn't say I *believed* him, just sharing what I heard," Carmine said, smiling. "Gramps thinks God took everyone. Said God got good 'n pissed off and rinsed the planet, but left some of us behind on accident."

"Some accident," Ryan said. "How does Gramps explain the monsters?"

"He ain't seen 'em yet. I told him a little bit, but I didn't want to scare him too much or he'd never let me out."

"So, what are you two gonna do? You gonna go somewhere? You got anyone else?"

"Not that I know of. My mom died when I was born. Don't know my Dad; he cut out shortly after. Gramps said he's an asshole and if God got rid of all the bad people, he surely got rid of my dad."

They turned another street, and Carmine pointed out a faded, peach-colored apartment building a block away, six stories and rundown before October, in all likelihood. A depressing-looking place, from the outside anyway.

As they reached the parking lot, a gunshot cracked and echoed off the buildings.

Ryan spun around and saw Red Jacket and Blue Jacket, both armed this time, aiming and firing.

"Duck!" Ryan screamed as he dropped behind a black pickup truck.

Carmine scrambled inside the apartment building. Ryan wished he'd not done that. Now the fuckers knew where he lived.

"Hey, Marine! You hiding? That ain't very brave!" Red Jacket shouted, suddenly ballsy and brave.

A spray of bullets slapped the surrounding metal. Ryan kept his head low. Blue Jacket made a beeline across the street, heading for the apartment, probably after Carmine.

Ryan swung into the clearing, hoping to tag Blue Jacket, but didn't have time to aim. In his periphery, he registered blood-colored movement as Red Jacket flew into view, about five car lengths ahead, then settled behind a blue Buick, taking aim at him. Ryan twisted and fired at Red Jacket, missing by a mile, then rolled out of the way as Red Jacket fired, his shot spitting up asphalt where it struck the road five yards behind Ryan.

Ryan rolled to a spot between a sedan and a truck, and paused.

Blue Jacket laughed, turning away from the apartment's entrance where Carmine had gone, his attention now on Ryan as he eyed the street in search of him. Ryan was across the street, insulated by a row of cars on Blue Jacket's side, and his own.

"You see that, Jessie?" Blue Jacket called. "You ever see a Marine who shot like a drunk retard before?"

Red Jacket returned the laugh, then said, "Maybe he meant he's a cook for the Marines."

Ryan crawled behind a truck, staying low, pretty sure neither man knew exactly where he was. They were fishing with their insults, hoping he'd bite, but it wouldn't be long before they found him. He had to put some distance between himself and Red Jacket before Blue Jacket flanked him from behind and had him trapped.

The going was slow, but Ryan stayed low. Both men were too close for him to peek his head up. On the other side of the street, he heard a patter of 20 or so footsteps. Ryan finally risked a peak and saw Blue Jacket jogging north, likely looking to flank him from behind.

He could hear Red Jacket's footsteps approaching, maybe two cars ahead. *They're getting closer.* Ryan squeezed under the truck, praying he'd fit. Somehow, he did, just barely.

He held his breath. It was game over if either of the Jackets knew where he was.

"Hey, Marine?" Red Jacket called. "You're not calling your mommy to cry, are ya?"

Ryan wanted to yell any one of the seven smart answers in his head, but swallowed every one. He heard Blue Jacket a second before he saw him coming from behind. There was no way to get a shot off, though. Blue Jacket retreated a step, suddenly unsure, as though he felt Ryan was near even though he couldn't see him.

If Blue Jacket retreated completely, Ryan would lose his chance. He glanced back and saw that Red Jacket had crossed the street, putting a bit more distance between them. That gave him the opening he needed to strike. Ryan slid his rifle up, took careful aim at Blue Jacket's gut, and squeezed the trigger.

The bullet's scream was punctuated with one from Blue Jacket as he fell to the ground. As he fell, Ryan took a second shot, this one zeroed in on the man's face. Direct hit.

Ryan rolled free from under the truck, then raced around the side and searched for Red Jacket, who had vanished from sight.

Or not.

Red Jacket popped up at Ryan's 2 o'clock and fired, but missed.

Ryan returned fire, hitting Red Jacket in the shoulder, a few inches from where Ryan was aiming. Red Jacket dropped his gun, screaming in agony, and fell to the ground behind an ancient, powder-blue Honda.

Ryan raced across the street to finish Red Jacket off once and for all.

As he reached the curb, he landed awkwardly, twisting his ankle, and fell hard to the ground.

"Fuck!" Ryan cried out, as Red Jacket stood up, cackling like a hyena. The man's injury couldn't have been too bad.

Judging from the small amount of blood, Ryan figured he must've grazed the man, who then overplayed his injury to lure Ryan over.

Ryan struggled to locate his rifle, which ejected from his grasp in the tumble. *Where? Where? There!* He wormed a foot to his left, retrieved the rifle, and flipped onto his back in one fluid motion. He already knew he was down to his last round. No second chances. No misses.

He instantly found his target a dozen yards away and took aim.

Red Jacket's smiling eyes went from *fuck you* to *fuck me.* He looked down, searching for his pistol. Not seeing it, he glared at Ryan, then ducked between the cars and ran off, disappearing into a maze of alleys.

Great.

Ryan picked himself up gingerly, dusted himself off, then limped toward the apartment building, calling for Carmine and unsure of what awaited him inside.

* * * *

CHAPTER 8
BRENT FOSTER

Black Island, New York
Black Island Research Facility
March 22, 2012
5:01 p.m.

The phone rang again, the third time in 10 minutes. Brent didn't bother to answer.

If it were Guardsmen on the other end, they'd simply come to his dorm and get him. So it had to be Jane. And the last thing he needed to do right now was deal with distractions. He needed to keep his head clear, a task impossible enough with the world missing, but now it felt hopeless. The scenes he saw the other night, along with his adulterous guilt, presented a near fatal distraction from what he needed to concentrate on most: a solid plan to save Gina and Ben.

The phone blared again only to fall silent after the sixth ring.

Sitting at the table in his room, doubling as desk and dining area, Brent used a black rolling ball pen to sketch the new areas of the facility's map into his small, black journal, one of few items he owned, which he got from the commissary a month earlier. As he drew, ideas for an escape plan began to take root in his head. The toughest part would be gaining access to Level 6. There was no way he'd be able to pass the security devices. Hacking into complex computer systems might work in the movies. But in reality, most people could barely remember their banking security questions, let alone crack passwords or infiltrate complicated firewalls.

He'd have to be resourceful. And ruthless. He knew what that meant ...

A hostage.

He'd need to force whoever was in charge to provide him access to Level 6, then access the chamber, and then permit him to escape with Gina and Ben. It was a plan fat on assumptions. For one, would Black Island Research ever allow one hostage's life to outweigh the safety of the entire facility? That seemed doubtful unless he could find, and get to, a valuable enough target. Yet, even after months on the island and now working for the Guardsmen, he still had no idea who the hell was in charge. Whoever it was had gone through great trouble to keep themselves and the scientists insulated from everyone else. While such lengths seemed mysterious and almost conspiratorial to Brent, they were also perfectly logical.

That was how you set up governments. You put the leader at a safe distance from the people. You didn't allow the president and the vice president to travel together for fear that some lunatic with a gun and nothing to lose might try to change history with bullets. And when the world went to hell, and people turned desperate and savage, the leader had to be at a safe distance, perhaps even veiled in secrecy, to steer clear of danger.

That meant Brent wouldn't have access to anyone too high profile. And anyone beneath a leader might be expendable. The moment he stepped into the chamber with his hostage, someone might seal the doors and execute a burn protocol, killing them both and the threat of an escape. Perhaps he could get to Ed Keenan, or maybe Sullivan. Both seemed to have value to the Island. Ed would be the tougher of the two to catch by surprise. Sullivan might be easier, but there was something Brent didn't trust about the man. He was too calm, too sure of himself, too used to wielding power. Sullivan definitely seemed like someone you didn't fuck with.

Brent stared at the page for what seemed an eternity, waiting as if in prayer for an answer to bleed through the ink. Though he had been a features writer at the paper, there were times he had to write about complex subjects he knew little about. That's when he'd break out the sketch pad and map out what he knew, what he needed to know. He'd work at it, hard, immersing himself in the subject until the fog lifted and the answers showed themselves.

But that wasn't happening now. The longer Brent stared at his map, the more holes he found in his plan. The biggest of which was his wife. What if Gina went full-on monster and attacked him? Hell, what if Ben did, too? What would he do? What could he do? Would he defend himself against a 3-year-old by bashing his son's skull in or shooting him dead? Brent doubted he could bring himself to ever choose his own life over his son's, even if it was a husk of his son with a monster inside. When it came right down to it, he would allow his wife or son to kill him rather than fight back.

Another fear, and perhaps the most realistic: What if he failed to even get to the chamber? He'd be shot for sure, or worse, excommunicated back to the ravaged wastelands of the outside world. No power, dwindling supplies, nuclear hotspots, bandits (he'd heard stories of from some of the other Guardsmen), and aliens.

He had to admit it: Black Island was, for all its limitations and restrictions, an oasis in a sea of chaos.

The more Brent considered his half-cocked plan, quarter-cocked more like, the more he resigned himself to the knowledge that he was at the mercy of Black Island. As was his family. He thought about what he'd told Luis so many months ago, how Black Island might be able to cure him. Brent wondered if they *could* cure the infection, or if the people who were bitten were already dead. The real question, Brent supposed, was whether the scientists were acting to find a cure or find a way to simply eradicate the cause. What motive would they have to synthesize a cure unless one of their own had been infected?

Wait, that's it!

If he could infect someone else on the island, someone too valuable to lose, those in charge would be have to be compelled to accelerate work on a cure. Right?

But again, there was the problem of determining who, if anyone, on the island held that sort of value. If there were such a person, what were the odds Brent could get to them? And how would he even begin to go about infecting them? Could he lure them to the chamber? Or was there another, better way?

Could he somehow inject them with the blood of the creatures? Perhaps the blood of the infected would work just as well. Shit, could the virus, or whatever it was, be introduced via the blood at all?

Even if it could, Brent shook his head, there was still the problem of access.

Despite this plan's flagrant flaws, the idea of infection seemed more likely to be pulled off when compared to a brute force, smash-and-grab approach, even if that likelihood was minimal. Brent scribbled at the bottom of the page:

Who to infect? WHO?

Brent needed a break. He dropped his pen on the page and watched it roll to the edge of the table, then stood, went to his pantry, slipped the journal inside a baggie and then slid the baggie into a canister of rolled oats. He placed the canister on the shelf next to two other identical canisters.

The phone rang again.

Perhaps he would see Jane, after all. Last night, he told her he wasn't feeling well. And he'd yet to tell her about what happened in the city. Had yet to tell her that his wife and son were still alive.

**

Though dinner was full of awkward adult moments, Brent was able to maintain playful conversation with Emily.

"Aren't you gonna have some more green beans?" the girl teased playfully, pointing to his plate, still heaped with his original serving of the vegetables, though he'd just piled second helpings of grilled chicken, instant potatoes, and gravy. This was an inside joke between the two of them. During a prior dinner, she noticed he hadn't eaten all his green beans on two separate occasions, and asked if he liked them. He lied and said yes, so he wouldn't offend Jane. However, on a third night, a night when Emily was missing her dad and feeling withdrawn, Brent waited until Jane left the table to get something from the kitchen, and scooped up some green beans from his plate and put them on the girl's.

Her expression was priceless, mouth wide open in shock which turned to a smile. "Hey! I thought you . . . "

"Shh," he whispered, holding a finger to his lips. "Truth is, I hate the things. Can you help me out and finish them?"

174

Emily laughed and said, "Sure!" then stabbed the remaining green beans onto her fork and began to eat them. When Jane returned from the kitchen with a pitcher of tea, Emily got a case of the giggles that wouldn't go away, which of course, made Brent fall into his own fit of laughter.

Now, as he dug into his chicken and gravy, Emily repeated the question, "Aren't you gonna have some more green beans?" with a huge grin on her face.

Jane pretended Brent hadn't told her about the little joke and feigned ignorance, "Yeah, Brent, don't you like my green beans?"

Brent cast a sideways glance at Emily, who was trying to keep the giggles inside.

"Sure," Brent said, overly animated, "I LOVE your green beans! In fact, I think I'll have a whole lot more!"

Jane handed him the bowl and Brent ladled a heaping spoonful onto his plate. "One scoop," he said, then got another, and another. "Two servings. Three. Should I have even more?"

He scooped more onto his plate, smiling at Emily.

"I'm gonna start some coffee," Jane said, finding an excuse to leave the table.

"OK, I'm just gonna finish up all these green beans."

"You do that," she said, laughing on her way out of the room.

Brent scooped a fifth spoonful of green beans onto this plate and then looked at Emily with a huge grin and said, "I hope you're hungry!"

He scraped the whole pile of green beans onto her plate, smiling.

"Hey! I don't want all those!"

Just then, Jane came back into the room and sat back down, and noticed Brent's green beans were all gone. "Wow, you really DO love them!"

"Yeah, and Emily was so jealous, she decided to have a bunch of 'em, too."

Emily looked at her plate with an exaggerated frown, which only made Brent laugh harder. He reached over, then took her plate and scooped half the green beans onto his. "Okay, I'll help you," he said.

She giggled again, and they both dug into their green beans. Even though Brent had to hide his distaste, the laughs were totally worth it.

**

A while later, Brent asked Emily if she'd like him to read her a story before bedtime. She ran into her room as he and Jane sat beside one another on the sofa. He flashed back to their last moment alone on the sofa and flushed.

Emily ran back and hopped up on his lap, holding a book, "Can you read this one?"

He took the book, turned it over, saw Stanley Train smiling back, and thought of Ben, scared, clinging to a mother who no longer recognized him in the chamber on Level 6. It was all Brent could do not to disappear down the rabbit hole of thought that would surely reduce him to tears. He smiled and said, "Sure, I'll read *Stanley Train Saves the Day.*"

As he read the book aloud, one he'd read to Ben countless times before, he thought back to the many nights he stayed up with Ben, rocking him to sleep, reading to him, and the last time he'd simply lain next to him in bed as his son's breath rose and fell like a sleeping angel beside him.

Brent started to cough, trying to hold back the tears, and excused himself to go into the kitchen to get a drink.

Instead of water, he chose a bottle of beer from Jane's fridge. It tasted like shit, but it would help. Despite his best efforts, his eyes were still full of water.

Jane appeared behind him, "Are you okay?" she whispered. Her eyes were concerned, but also scared, he thought. She probably didn't want the mistake of the other night to ruin their friendship. Or perhaps, she liked him a lot more than she'd let on earlier, and was afraid of rejection.

He wanted to tell her the truth — that his family was still alive. She deserved to know. But he also wanted to tell her because he needed someone who could advise him, someone who might help him from making the biggest mistake of his life. But Sullivan had warned him not to tell a soul. And while he trusted Jane as much as almost anyone he'd ever known, and certainly as much as anyone he knew now, he didn't want to put her at risk. Nor did he want to make her feel guilty about what had happened between them.

For now, he had to keep the secret.

"I can't talk about it," he said. "It's not about us, though. Something at work."

He took another few sips, returned Jane's thin smile, the headed back to the couch to finish the tale of the brave train who saved the day.

**

After Emily went to bed, Brent said he had to leave, saying that tomorrow promised to be a long day. The goodbye was as awkward as a high school first date; he didn't know whether to hug her, kiss her, or leave her with a peck on the cheek. Prior to the other night, they usually hugged their farewell for the evening, as you would with any good friend or family member. Brent went with the hug, which felt deep, and lingered longer than expected, each holding onto the embrace as if it might be their last together.

**

Brent stopped by the dining hall to get another beer, which he popped open and sipped on his way to the elevator. He'd finish the beer, hit the sack, and pray he'd be able to sleep without dreams of Gina and Ben tormenting him. As the elevator descended, he found himself thinking back on dinner, laughing with Emily, reading to her, then hugging Jane goodbye. He was torn between the world he couldn't give up on and the world he couldn't allow himself to have.

As long as there was hope that he could save his family, he had to try. Even if that meant risking his life, or happiness with another.

The elevator door slid open, and he began walking to his room, beer in hand, tumbling the plan again in his head. There was something there; he could feel it as if it were just beneath the ice, ready for discovery if only he struck the right center. He was inches from the missing ingredient that would make the plan come together perfectly. Perhaps another half hour scribbling in his journal would help put some plan into shape.

He fumbled in his pocket, found the keycard, and slid it into the door's handle. The door clicked open, and he stumbled into the dark.

Only it wasn't dark. A dim light over his dining table was on. Beneath it, sat Keenan, reading Brent's journal.

"So, who you gonna infect?" Keenan said, accusing eyes looking up from the pages.

The beer bottle smashed against the ground, shattering before Brent even realized he'd dropped it.

Brent stumbled back, and slipped, falling to the ground in the beer.

Keenan was up in seconds, lightning-quick for a guy in his 40s.

"Don't move," Keenan said, training his gun on Brent before Brent could even consider his next move.

Keenan reached down with his left hand, patting Brent down, then offered the hand to help him up.

"We need to talk," Keenan said simply.

" ... "

"Mr. Foster, we need to talk, now." Keenan repeated with added mettle, hand still extended.

Brent remained frozen on the floor, dumbstruck. *How the fuck did he find the journal? SHIT! But he didn't shoot me? Why the hell not? And why didn't he haul me away to be condemned to some unfathomable misery at the hands of Sullivan?*

"Um ... OK," Brent stammered, his voice betraying his every weakness. He slowly extended his left arm and took Keenan's left hand in his own. Keenan clamped down and yanked up with the force of an ox, sling-shotting Brent into a full and upright position. After Brent checked to make sure his fingers were still intact, he followed Keenan to the table, ignoring the spilled beer, broken glass, and his freshly soaked pants.

Brent sat. Keenan stood, gun still on Brent. "What the hell are you thinking?"

"What?" Brent said, offering a ridiculous ruse.

"Don't dick around. I want to know what you're gonna do. Now. Or I go to the brass with this, and you'll be reunited with your family quicker than you think."

Brent had never considered that as an option for how Black Island Research might get rid of him. Hell, they could probably use more infected "subjects."

"I don't know what I was thinking," Brent confessed. "I was trying to figure out a way to get my family out of there. I wasn't *planning* to infect anyone. Well, not seriously, anyway. I was just writing down different ways I might be able to get to my family and get them out of here."

Keenan sat down and placed the gun on the table between them. Close enough to dare Brent to make a play, but far enough to ensure Keenan would have it in his hands and trained on Brent in seconds.

"Get them out of here?" Keenan said, shaking his head, as if it was the damnedest thing he'd ever heard. "And then what? Where you gonna go? Who can help you? And what the hell are you gonna do, keep your family in a cage somewhere? How long you gonna do that before you shoot them and then yourself in the head?"

"I don't know," Brent said sheepishly, staring at the floor, embarrassed and ashamed, like a scolded child who'd not thought out the very obvious consequences of a very stupid plan. "What am I supposed to do, though? Give up? They're my family. You fight for your family. You never give up. It's what you're supposed to do. Right?"

Keenan stared at him for a long time as silence grew a thick skin between them.

"I need to tell you something that can't leave this room, which is bugged, by the way."

"Bugged?" Brent said, surprised.

"Yeah," Keenan said, holding up a black box with a red light. "But right now, they're not hearing shit." Keenan leaned forward. "What I'm about to tell you must stay between us. OK?"

This is either going to be incredibly good or impossibly bad.

"OK."

"That's not your family down there."

"What?" Brent asked, more skeptical than surprised, wondering if Keenan was about to rattle off the whole, 'they used to be your family and now they're aliens' routine, though something told him he wasn't.

"Let me ask you a question, Brent. What happened on October 15?"

"What do you mean?"

"Just answer the question. What happened on October 15?"

"Everyone disappeared," Brent said as nonchalantly as if commenting on grass growing. "Well, everyone but us."

"No," Keenan said. "They didn't vanish . . . We did."

* * * *

::EPISODE 9::
(THIRD EPISODE OF SEASON TWO)
"SNOWFALL"

CHAPTER 1
REBECCA SNOW

May 13
Five months BEFORE the world went away . . .

Rebecca didn't remember falling asleep, but now her eyes were slowly blinking as she gazed around her room and tried to pull herself from the frayed edges of her expiring dream.

The moon hung fat in the window, bathing her room in a milky luminescence. She looked at her alarm clock: 10:14 p.m.

It was the same dream she'd been having for two weeks now, though this one felt clearer. Usually, Mother was blurred in the dream. This time she was clearer, closer, almost there. She was angry, like she sometimes was in real life, with fire in her eyes and a sting in her slap. Mother didn't hit her in the dream, but she probably would have if Rebecca hadn't woken up when she did. The last thing she remembered was Mother's blur fading as she came closer into view, dragging Alexis behind her, Mother's long fingers coiled inside her sister's soft, blonde hair.

Rebecca had been waking up each morning, remembering the end of the dream with Mother still a blur. And each morning, Rebecca felt a weird sense of dread.

She shook away the stupid fear that came from the stupid dream, then left the bed to answer the bladder telling her to hit the bathroom. Her small feet hit the wood floor, and carried her from the room and down the hallway to the bathroom. She peed what felt like a gallon, then headed back toward her room, stopping by the blackened crack at Alexis' room.

Alexis was 15 years old, three years older than Rebecca, and always in trouble. Rebecca used to hate it when Alexis was in trouble, since sisters were supposed to stick together and all. But Alexis had been getting in an awful lot of trouble lately, pretty much all the time. Mother spent a lot of time yelling at Alexis because Alexis was bad, and did a lot of the bad stuff that girls did when they got older and stopped caring about doing right by God. Rebecca wished Alexis would remember to do right by God more often, but figured it was just as well, since the stuff she did usually made Rebecca look good. Rebecca had been treated like the ugly duckling for most of her life, including by their mother, for her red hair, pale skin, and freckles, while Alexis was treated like the beautiful princess. It was different now, and she enjoyed the positive attention, even if it came at the expense of her sister. Rebecca occasionally felt a tiny twinge of guilt for feeling this way, but it wasn't like she was *forcing* Alexis to be bad. Alexis made her choices, and if those choices happened to make Rebecca look good in comparison, was that really so bad?

Rebecca peeked inside her sister's room. She couldn't hear or see much of anything. There was a lump beneath the blankets, but Alexis wasn't snoring. And Alexis *always* snored. Rebecca sensed something was off, so she widened the crack and crept inside.

Alexis had been acting awfully weird all through last night's dinner, and a few hours before that. *Could she be sick, or, oh my gosh!, on drugs?* Rebecca took a tentative step forward and perked her ears, but still heard nothing but silence. *Weird.* Her final few steps toward the bed took nearly a minute, since she was being extra careful not to make a sound. If her sister rolled over and saw her, there would be a *huge* fight!

As she drew closer, she realized that the lump beneath the blanket was too short to be Alexis. With that, she rushed the rest of the distance to the bed and pulled back the covers to give light to the lie that a row of pillows created.

Alexis was gone.

Mother was going to be really angry; she was going to completely lose her temper. Alexis was going to be in more trouble than she'd ever been in before. She had asked, no, begged Mother, to go to a dance at the community center tonight. Mother said no, of course, since dancing with boys was a sin and Alexis was obviously already running around with too many sinful thoughts inside her head as it was. She certainly didn't need to be in a room full of boys whose bodies were practically made of sinful thoughts.

Alexis hated living in the sticks like they did, hated being home-schooled even more. Dances, and the few other events held at the community center, were really the only chances she ever had to meet people her own age and socialize. Rebecca understood that, even felt some of the same feelings herself, but that was still no reason to lie to Mother. Alexis was going to be in big, big trouble. And while her mother could be a bit too strict at times, acts this defiant deserved whatever punishment her mother served up.

Like Mother always said, "Nothing separates a child from God like the evils of their own will. It is a parent's job to ensure that their child stays on the righteous path."

Rebecca left Alexis' room in a fraction of the time she took to enter and ran toward Mother's. She would be mad at Rebecca for waking her, but madder if she didn't. Even though Rebecca fell asleep too early to know for sure, she figured Mother must have gone to bed not too long after since tomorrow her mother had the morning shift at the diner. She'd been going in extra early ever since Lydia got pregnant. Trucks started rolling in right around 6, which meant Mother had to have her apron on no later than 5:30. A half hour drive to get there, and another half hour to get ready and paint the tired from her eyes, meant she was getting up at 4:30 sharp each morning.

Rebecca opened Mother's door to a deafening snore. She approached her mother's sleeping body, reconsidering every step. *Maybe I should just go back to bed.* But darn it, Alexis *deserved* to get caught, and Rebecca deserved some of Mother's appreciation, and attention. Whenever Alexis was in "big trouble," Mother spent more time with Rebecca for some reason. Maybe they would even make another rag doll to go with the Raggedy Susie they made in November.

OK, I'll tell her. But how should I put it so Mother doesn't get too mad right away, or mad at me?

Rebecca tapped her mother's shoulder, waited for her to turn, then let loose all at once with everything in her head, "Mother, wake up! Alexis snuck out of the house, and I think, though I'm not certain, that she snuck off to the dance even though you told her not to go!"

Mother was awake on contact of the first word. She offered a quick look at Rebecca with full moon eyes and silent understanding, then launched out of bed and over to her dresser. She opened the bottom drawer, yanked out the first item she saw, and pulled the ragged camel-colored sweater over her bony frame. Then she dashed into the kitchen where she grabbed her keys from the hook, her pack of Pall Malls, then yelled back at Rebecca, standing in the threshold. "You're not staying here alone. Get in the car. We're going to get your sister."

Rebecca climbed into the old El Camino she thought once belonged to her dad, though she wasn't really sure since Mother had never really answered the question and her memories of him were too old to sort. They drove the first few minutes in silence, Mother's anger frosting the windows as her cigarette smoke filled the cabin. The cigarettes made Mother look old. Though the woman looked young for her age, and had beautiful, blonde hair like Alexis, there was something about when she smoked that made her look old. Old and sad, which made Rebecca sad.

She wished things could be like they used to be. But over the past few years, something had changed, made her mother so serious and quick to anger. It must have been big and bad, maybe scary, too. Rebecca wanted to ask her mom what was wrong, so many times, but truth was, she was afraid the answer might be her. It seemed Mother was disappointed in her. She wasn't sure why. She listened and behaved so much better than Alexis. She even tried to do things that she knew would help her Mother, like get her coffee cup ready before she went to bed, and put coffee in the filter, and other little things like that to make her mother's life easier, and a little happier. But most times it seemed like her mother hardly noticed these things and only saw the bad things that Rebecca did.

Rebecca finally broke the silence. "I can't believe Alexis would sneak out of the house," she said, shaking her head. "This is just like the stuff you're always warning her about. Things would be a lot better if she would just listen. She's probably with that Ronnie Hendricks." Rebecca glanced at Mother, checking for approval, but Mother's eyes were fixed ahead, mouth sucking on the cigarette with a scowl.

"Ronnie is a bad kid," Rebecca went on, trying not to hide her discomfort of the smoke. It was too cold to roll the windows down, so she'd just have to suck it up. "I think he probably sins a whole bunch, too. Once I saw him smoking behind the A&W. He had a whole pack of Camels, but the box was nearly empty, so he probably smokes a bunch."

Mother didn't respond to Rebecca's accusation, or anything else she said for the remaining 15 minutes to the community center. But her face stayed angry, all the way until she pulled into the community center parking lot, parked right in front of the entrance, then turned to Rebecca and said, "You need to quit your brown-nosing, young lady. And I mean now. Open this door or move an inch before I get back, and you'll be in just as much trouble as your sister."

Mother didn't wait for Rebecca to respond, just ducked from the car, slammed the door behind her, and marched toward the community center doors in her pajama bottoms and a sweater. Alexis would die of embarrassment before she even had a chance to be punished.

Even though Mother was acting mad at her, Rebecca knew it was really because she was so mad at Alexis, who was probably sinning all over the place. Rebecca hated that Alexis always got in trouble, even if she sometimes told on her. She hoped maybe this time her punishment would be so serious that it would put an end to her sister's sinning. They had their differences, but that didn't mean Rebecca wanted her sister to burn for eternity in The Lake of Fire. And like Mother said, Alexis' soul was definitely at risk. Ronnie was a sinner for sure, but just because he was willing to sell his soul to the Devil didn't mean he had to take her sister's, too.

Rebecca's thoughts were shattered by sudden shrieks from Alexis, growing louder as Mother dragged her by the hair toward the Camino.

"AHHHH, MOTHER! That HURTS!" she screamed. Mother's fist was curled inside Alexis' hair. *The DREAM!* A dreadful chill charged through Rebecca's every nerve. *No, this can't be happening.*

"I will NOT raise a harlot!" her mother screamed, cigarette dangling out of her mouth as she shoved Alexis forward.

Alexis was as red as the county fire truck, and getting redder as the small huddle of kids, mostly boys, laughed and pointed at Alexis as she was dragged toward the Camino. Rebecca felt a small but undeniably sharp pain, a stabbing wound slipping into her guilt.

Mother opened the passenger door, shoved Alexis inside so hard that the girl's head hit the outside of the door with a loud thud, which made her cry out even louder as she fell into the seat next to Rebecca.

Mother walked to her side of the car, climbed inside, started the car, then peeled out from the lot.

A long minute of silence smothered them before Alexis turned to Rebecca and hissed through tears, "What are you smiling at, brat?"

"I ... I wasn't," Rebecca said truthfully.

Mother snapped toward Alexis. She looked so mad, Rebecca was sure she was about to slap Alexis across the side of the face. Rebecca felt the usual fear growing fat. She didn't mind if Alexis got in trouble, but she didn't want the hitting to start.

She quietly prayed that it wouldn't, and was glad when it didn't.

"You should thank your sister," Mother said. "She's looking out for your soul." With that, she snapped her attention back to the road.

"You *told on me?* I can't believe it, you little BITCH! You are so dead."

Mother reached across and backhanded Alexis across the face, her elbow hitting Rebecca along the way. Mother didn't allow swears.

"If Rebecca hadn't told me when she did, Good Lord knows what would have happened to you tonight."

"Nothing would have happened to me, Mother!" Alexis glared, defiant. "The problem isn't me, it's that you don't trust me."

Rebecca waited for Mother's hand to redden her sister's face again and prayed it wouldn't.

"Of course, I don't trust you," Mother said. "Nothing separates a child from God like the evils of their own will. And I know exactly where your will would like to lie. Any sort of sinning could have happened tonight. You could have done drugs, or worse, you could have gotten knocked up."

"Like you did?"

The back of Mother's hand found the side of Alexis's face again, but harder, the slap a thunderclap within the Camino's interior. Rebecca could tell that her sister wanted to scream, but muffled her cry. With her left hand steady on the wheel, Mother let her hand fly once more to underline her point, more violent and practiced than the prior strike.

Rebecca turned her watering eyes away from her sister, and stared at the road ahead, wondering when the evils of her own will might separate her from God, and Mother.

* * * *

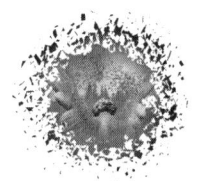

CHAPTER 2
DESMOND ARMSTRONG

Kingsland, Alabama
In the woods near The Sanctuary
March 25
11:11 a.m.

"We're all trying to survive and make the most of this. *Breathe in, breathe out, be merry.*"

Desmond hated Jimmy's words falling from John's mouth. It was an unnerving he couldn't pinpoint. And he HATED being unnerved.

Those words had been playing on infinite repeat in Desmond's head as they crunched through the carpet of drying leaves in search of Rebecca and Carl. The pair had marched through the forest and over the hill looking for the two missing children, but there was still no sign.

Desmond kept the gun in his waistband. He didn't trust his trigger finger, or the man up ahead making it itchy.

Desmond couldn't explain why he thought Jimmy's words in John's mouth sounded so wrong, and felt so ominous. They just did, like some sort of weird impression more than a mimic. People picked up idioms and expressions all the time. And Jimmy and John had been neighbors for years, not to mention all that time they'd spent side by side at the Drury, back in the beginning of the end of the world. So, it would be natural for John to adopt Jimmy's telltale expression, right? Maybe it was even intentional – John using Jimmy's phrase to show Desmond he was relaxed. Maybe he was trying to put him at ease as they searched for the missing children, alone in the woods crawling with unknowns and, possibly, "Demons."

Or maybe he was just trying to repair old wounds.

Or maybe not.

Desmond wished it felt right, but it didn't. And he couldn't ignore it. He had thrived in life via his sharp instincts. It was difficult, if not downright impossible, to shake the vibe that something was *off*.

"Are Rebecca and Carl an item?" Desmond asked, trying to ease the tension, even if it was only in his head. "I mean, I know they're both a bit young, especially Rebecca, but do you happen to know if the two of them are sweet on one another?"

John turned back to Desmond and frowned. It wasn't an accusing frown, so much as surprise by the audacity of the suggestion. "No, of course not. That sort of behavior is forbidden at The Sanctuary. The Prophet would be terribly upset if something like that were to happen."

"But they're kids," Desmond said. "Kids are going to do what kids are going to do. Thousands of years of evolution aren't going to change that innate drive just because The Prophet wants to keep everyone tucked in their beds with God in their hearts. It has nothing to do with the end of the world, that's just the way people are wired. And kids, well, you remember puberty, right? Kids don't care what grown-ups say. They're gonna try and get away with whatever they can. Least that's the way it was for me, my friends, and everyone I knew."

John shook his head and set his jaw. "It is *our* duty as The Chosen adults to hold kids in our charge to a higher standard. The old way went to Hell because the adults who knew better didn't." He raised his hand in the air. "Maybe everyone is burning in the Lake of Fire because they didn't hold themselves and their children to a standard as high as ours. Is it so inconceivable that this happened because of our soft morality and bottomless capacity for sin?"

Desmond wasn't sure what he should say, but figured nothing was best. He was creeped beyond belief and in mild shock that John bought into all the Bible thumping. He bought the bullshit wholesale. He and John may not have gotten along before, but Desmond figured him for a sharp guy, and was surprised by his clear lack of judgment of basic human nature. Then again, if John had lost his grip on sanity, then maybe that would explain the weird vibe he was giving off.

And if there's any place to lose one's sanity, it's back at The Loony Farm.

If John needed to clutch the Bible to get him through the night, who was Desmond to scoff? You didn't tell an alcoholic that the 12 steps were bullshit if they were working for them. It was a matter of belief. John needed to believe, too. He had lost Jenny, and the rest of the world. He didn't have the strength to survive without something. *That's gotta be it; it's his crutch.* And Desmond wasn't the kind of guy to kick away one's crutch, even if he didn't see a need for it. He was a guy, however, that would fight back if you tried to push your crutch on him.

Yet, that's exactly what Desmond was having to do at The Sanctuary; sit on his hands and bite his tongue while playing out the role he'd been cast into. He wasn't sure how much longer he could keep a smile on his face before he snapped and spoke out. If it were just him, Desmond would have *maybe* followed John to The Sanctuary, then left about five seconds after the so-called "Prophet" started passing out the Kool-Aid.

But Desmond wasn't alone. He had a new family: Mary and Paola and Luca and Will, plus Linc and Scott. And while he couldn't tell what was going on in the back of Will's mind, the rest of the group obviously felt safe, at least safer than they had. If they didn't mind the heaping bullshits of dogma, not to mention the prison-like rules, so be it. He would eat shit and smile when he swallowed, at least a little while longer, or until a better opportunity came along.

"Up here," John called. Desmond recalibrated his senses, turned and saw John pointing toward the wide and tall opening of a cave. A dozen paces later Desmond was standing beside John, looking into the darkness.

"Think they went inside?" Desmond asked.

John shrugged. "No way of knowing. Can't think of a reason *not* to go inside and look. Can you?"

John glared at Desmond, almost accusingly. Desmond shook his head and stepped past John, into the permanent night of the cave. Desmond wanted to mend fences, so he played along. While John seemed a bit wacky, he didn't seem like a threat. John wasn't the most masculine of men, and his prowess with a gun seemed ineffectual enough that if he went postal, Desmond would be able to protect himself with little difficulty.

"I've got the light," John said, flicking his Coleman flashlight to life and stepping in front of Desmond. He bounced the beam around the cave's interior, highlighting the dingy gray of the rocky walls, plastered in damp moss and a wretched scent. Something slick squished beneath their feet, maybe molding leaves blown in from outside. But probably not, Desmond figured. It felt 20 degrees colder inside the cave than a step outside, and it seemed to grow colder with each echoing step.

"How deep do you think it goes?" Desmond asked.

John stopped.

"Not sure," John said, kneeling and shining his light into a wide fissure. "See that?" Desmond didn't, so he kneeled, too. John kneeled another few inches forward lowering the light's path to something Desmond couldn't see.

Desmond said, "I don't . . ."

John's flashlight went dark and the pair was plunged into darkness.

Something moved behind them. Something that sounded large.

Desmond threw his hand in front of him to feel for John, but it fell through air. He stood, swallowing panic.

"JOHN!"

His call echoed and caromed across the walls of the cave and came back to mock him. Desmond called again, but heard nothing as he reached out, moving forward.

He pulled his pistol from his waistband and slipped his itchy finger over the trigger as he stepped forward, trying to retrace his path back to the mouth of the cave.

Something moved again, this time closer.

"John!" he cried out.

His cry was answered by the sound of clicking, echoing against the cave walls.

* * * *

CHAPTER 3
EDWARD KEENAN

Black Island, New York
March 22, 2012
8:58 p.m.

"What?! What do you mean *we're* the ones who vanished?" Brent asked, his eyes staring at Ed as if he'd just told him the moon wasn't real.

"What were you doing at 2:15 a.m. on October 15?"

"Sleeping. I woke up sometime in the morning, and my wife and son were gone."

"Right. But it wasn't they who vanished. It was you. You, me, and everyone else you've met on this island."

"What are you talking about? We didn't go anywhere." Brent said, his exasperation clearly rising.

"You know how you've felt *off* since the vanishings?" Ed asked. "Like the world around you isn't quite right?"

"Well, yeah, but look around. It's not like things are exactly *normal.*"

"More than that. Deeper. Anything unusual, about the world itself? Something slightly off – like the feeling you get if someone's been in your house when you weren't home, or when you're trying to remember something but can't, or even déjà vu? It's like all of that, but different."

Ed waited for a response.

"What are you saying?" Brent finally asked.

"I know this is going to sound crazy, but considering all we've seen, please just hear me out. *This* isn't our Earth. It looks the same, feels the same, and has a lot of the same history, but this is not our world. It's a parallel world, and on October 15, something happened here that killed millions in an instant. That same something pulled us over from our Earth to this one. You, me, and everyone you've met on the island so far are all from our world, snatched over at the exact instant that The Vanishing happened here."

"Wait a second. So people here, on this other Earth, vanished, too?" Brent said, "I'm confused."

"Millions died in an instant, all at once. We've seen their corpses. But there's a hell of a lot more people that vanished. They went somewhere; maybe to our planet, or maybe taken away by some giant spaceship; who knows?"

"So, what does this have to do with Gina and Ben?" Brent asked, his eyes scared and confused as he tried to work out what Ed was saying. If he even believed Ed.

"The Gina and Ben who are on Level 6, the infected people we found, they're from this world, not ours. Everyone we've found who is still alive from this world are also infected with this alien parasite; the same aliens we've encountered. They've infected all who remained here."

"I know my wife and son when I see them!" Brent said, eyes red with emotion and struggling to hold back the tears.

"Yes, but they're not *your* wife and son; they may look the same, sound the same, and maybe even have the same histories, but they're alternate versions of your Gina and Ben, or what we're calling parallels."

Brent shook his head, "No, this is all crazy *Twilight Zone* shit. You're either insane or fucking with me."

"All the things you've seen since October – the dead bodies, the aliens, the weird weather – and you choose to close your mind now?"

"Listen, I love science fiction. I get the idea of alternate worlds as a concept, but the reality of it is impossible. To suggest there's millions of different realities based on each action we take, branching and spinning off new worlds, that's all bullshit theory, not fact."

Ed sighed. He wasn't sure why, but he thought Brent would be easier to convince. "I'm not saying there's all these different worlds, different versions of us, and all that. I don't know what there is. Hell, the scientists here don't even have a grasp, so far as I can tell. All I know is that there are two Earths in question; two versions of us all. I met my parallel when I got here. He's one of the scientists, hell of a lot smarter than I am, so obviously this isn't an exact duplicate of our world. But it's as real as you and me sitting here, and that broken beer bottle you dropped that's stinking up the room."

Brent sighed with a slight shake of his head, then a gentle nod.

He's getting it. Just a bit more convincing.

"OK, let's say you're telling the truth, or the truth as you see it, anyway. How do you know that Ben and Gina didn't come over here with me? That they aren't my family?"

"There are slight chromosomal differences, the scientists said, between our two peoples. Like I said, I'm not a scientist, and I didn't understand what they told me about that. Something about their people being slightly different, maybe more evolved, but whatever it is, they know the difference. And they tested the woman and child on Level 6. They're not yours."

Brent looked like he was staring at a crossword puzzle perfect but for a missing word. He was close to being won over; he just needed the last piece.

"Trust me."

Brent ran his hands through his hair so hard, Ed couldn't tell if he were trying to pull his hair out or keep his brains in. He looked up at Ed a few times. Ed kept silent, allowing Brent time to finish processing the information.

"So, if they're not my family, *where* is my family? Are they still alive?"

Good man. Now we're moving in the right direction.

"I presume they're still on our Earth, and *probably* alive, though I can't be sure. Nobody here knows much about what happened, why it happened, or how we were all brought over. Well, someone here might know, but they didn't tell me."

Brent stared straight ahead, at Ed, but not really. He looked exactly like Ed expected a man to look who'd been told that his wife and son, practically given up for as dead, were really alive. *Maybe.*

Finally, after several minutes, Brent found his next question. "Why did they tell you any of this? Why not tell everyone?"

"There are very few who know. Very few. I'm the only one from our world who knows. Well, now I'm the only other one from our world. I ask you this: Why does the government ever lie to its people? Two reasons, to maintain control and to maintain safety. In this case, both."

"How the hell would knowing we're on another planet, dimension, whatever, change how we act?"

"The less the others know, the better. Black Island Research Facility is attempting to figure out what happened, how to defeat the aliens, and repopulate the planet. If everyone suddenly thought this world wasn't theirs, they might just storm the palace, so to speak, demanding to be sent back. There's something to be said for keeping people in the dark about some things."

"I still don't get why they told you."

"Because on our Earth I was one of the people who worked in the shadows, keeping the government's secrets. I was good at my job. They need me."

"So, why are you telling me?" Brent asked.

"Because I need you. I need you to help me do something. Michael was going to help me, but he's dead now. You're the only one I can trust."

"What do you mean?"

"I'll explain more tomorrow. Let's just say that I'm not willingly working for them. They've got my daughter, and possibly someone else I care about."

Brent stared, shocked. "They're holding them hostage?"

"Something like that. An insurance policy so that I do what they need me to do, something only I can do."

"What's that?" Brent asked.

"Find someone from our world. Someone who may hold the key to many of these mysteries."

"Who?"

"A man named Boricio Wolfe. And you're gonna help me find him."

* * * *

202

CHAPTER 4
RYAN OLSON

Brookdale, Tennessee
Feb. 17
Late morning

"You okay?" Carmine asked as Ryan limped into the mammoth apartment building.

"Twisted my ankle, but I'll live," Ryan said, making his way through the front door, which was battered and blue, with peeling paint and a giant window where someone had thoughtfully drawn a giant penis in thick, black marker. Below that, what looked to be a gang sign. "I didn't think you'd make it," Carmine said. "Come on; I'll introduce you to Gramps."

The hallways were dark, except for the dim light bleeding from the windows at either end of each hall, providing just enough light for Ryan to see the shithole in all its glory. There were two kinds of public housing: buildings where the residents worked to keep things repaired and as nice as possible, and then there was this — housing so decrepit and uncared for that you could sink a year's worth of renovation and 10,000 gallons of paint into it, and it would still look ghetto. Even in the dark, the walls stank of oppression and decay. Toys, sacks of trash, and discarded furniture littered the hall, as if the residents couldn't be bothered to take their trash to the dumpsters. The hallway smelled like rotting food. Ryan hoped it was food, at least. Then again, everything was food to something nowadays.

Ryan choked back his belittling comments on the place. It wasn't the kid's fault he lived in a slum, and Ryan certainly wasn't going to judge him or make him feel shitty. They reached the far end of the hall, and Carmine fished a flashlight from his pocket and clicked it on, then pushed through the doorway.

"We're on the fifth floor," he said, almost apologetically.

"The higher you are, the less likely you'll have to deal with those monsters, at least that's what I've found," Ryan said.

The stairwell was mercifully trash-free. The last thing Ryan needed was to trip and fall down the stairs. The notion of doctors died when the world turned out its lights on humanity. He figured his ankle would be okay in a day or so, but hoped he wouldn't have to run anytime soon.

Be careful what you hope for; you'll tempt that cruel bitch, fate.

"So one of 'em got away?" Carmine asked.

"Yeah," Ryan sighed as they made it to the second floor.

"Think he'll come back? Think he'll bring others?"

"I dunno," Ryan said. "But I think if there were others, they would have probably brought them this time. Unfortunately, he saw where you went. So, if he does come back, you and your grandpa are sitting targets."

"So, what should we do?"

"Well, the way I see it, you've got two choices. You either move, or prepare to defend yourselves. That means learning how to use the gun I gave you."

"Gramps doesn't much like guns."

"Well, Gramps needs to recognize that the world has changed. If you're not armed, you're at the mercy of man and monster, alike."

Carmine laughed, "Gramps still thinks he's tough. A few months ago, we were at the park, and some crackhead came up with a gun and told Gramps to hand over his wallet. Gramps told the guy he had exactly 10 seconds to leave, or he'd whoop his ass so bad his mama wouldn't even recognize his ugly face."

Ryan laughed, "What happened?"

"The crackhead just stared at him for a long time, and I was *sure* he was gonna just shoot us right there on the spot. But then he just backed off. Said something like, 'It ain't even worth it' or something. Gramps used to be a semi-pro boxer and taught for years when he got back from the war. He never got too well known, but he'd taught a lot of the great boxers in the day. So, he's kinda close to being a local celebrity. Maybe the dude recognized him or something. But, like you said, things have changed. People now, they don't care who you are or what your rep is."

"No, they don't," Ryan said, as he considered a third possible solution to their predicament. He could track Red Jacket down and finish the job. He'd have to wait until his ankle was better, and hope Red Jacket didn't come back before then. But if he could find the bastard, he could make sure Carmine and his grandpa would be safe, from one asshole, anyway.

"Fifth floor," Carmine said, as he pushed through the squeaky doorway and into the hall, lit by large, grimy windows at either end. Ryan followed the boy to the fourth door on the left, noting that the hallway was in far better condition than the first floor. Gramps probably didn't put up with trashy neighbors, Ryan guessed, liking the old brawler before they even met.

Carmine knocked on the door twice, waited, then twice again, and said, "It's me, Gramps," before sliding his keys into the deadbolt. He turned to Ryan, "Wait here, a sec, and leave the gun in the hall, okay?"

"OK," Ryan said, leaning his rifle against the wall.

"I've got company," Carmine said as he entered the apartment, and placed the flashlight on a small end table beside the front door. "He saved me from some punks who tried to jack your meds. Is it alright if he comes in?"

From his spot in the doorway, Ryan could see into the small apartment, well-lit by open windows in the living room. Though the apartment was small, and looked as if it had been decorated in the '70s, it was immaculate, orderly, and well-preserved.

Gramps wheeled into view, emerging from a bedroom in the back of the apartment. The man was stocky, bald, and looked like he was in his early 60s. He was wearing powder-blue dress pants that hung loosely over where the bottom of the man's left leg had once been, and a dark-blue polo shirt. He looked like he was about to head to the park for a Sunday stroll, but his face was stone-cold serious.

Gramps eyed Ryan up and down, "Why'd you bring a stranger here?" he asked Carmine, though his eyes never left Ryan. Though the man had no weapon, his stare was intimidating, as if he might leap right out of the chair and kick your ass, even if you had a weapon.

Ryan rolled his shoulders forward slightly, trying to appear less of a threat. He considered saying something, but kept his mouth shut and let the boy talk.

"He was walking me home when these two men came at me with guns. They followed us here and shot at us."

"Yeah," Gramps said, "I heard the racket outside. So, where is it?"

"Huh?" Carmine asked.

"Where's this man's gun? I heard three guns."

"Out in the hallway, sir," Ryan said.

"Get it," Gramps said.

Ryan turned, heart in his throat, uncertain what the man intended to do. He retrieved the rifle, returned to the room, and handed it to Gramps.

"A Nosler, eh? Good gun," Gramps said, turning the rifle over in his hands before handing it back. For a man who didn't like guns, he had no trouble making out the make and model.

"I'm not all that familiar with them, myself," Ryan explained. "I picked it up from an abandoned house for protection. Did some practice shooting; got decent."

Gramps stared at Ryan for a moment, as if somehow reading the man's mind, making sure he was, in fact, safe. Though he felt absurd, Ryan tried to think nice thoughts, and not at all about the robbery at his store, just in case the man *could* read minds. Of course, trying *not* to think about the robbery gone south, or the dead bodies, only made them clearer in his mind's eye. He hoped like hell his smile covered the sick feeling of remembering Clarissa's body, dead eyes staring up at him.

"Thank you for looking out for Carmine," Gramps said, holding out his giant hand, "Name is Joe Turner."

"You're welcome, Mr. Turner, my name is Ryan Olson," he said, shaking the man's surprisingly soft hand.

"Carmine said a lot of nice things about you," Ryan said, trying to be nice without kissing the man's ass too much. Guys like Joe couldn't stand a sycophant.

Joe ignored the compliment, asked Carmine to shut the door, and invited Ryan to have a seat in the living room. Carmine handed Joe the medicine, which Joe looked at, then thanked the boy before asking Carmine to bring it to the kitchen and put it in the medicine cabinet. Ryan leaned the rifle against the wall beside the door and limped to the couch, trying to stay in front of Joe at all times, figuring a man in a wheelchair would be extra jumpy about strangers being out of his line of sight.

"So, where you staying at?" Joe asked.

"Over by the drug store, but I'm originally from Missouri."

"Missouri? What brings you 'round here?"

"I'm looking for my wife and daughter, hoping they're still alive."

"They were gone when you woke up?" Carmine asked.

"I dunno, well, I mean, my ex-wife, we're divorced. We don't live together. But I went to their house as soon as I realized what happened. But nobody was there. I noticed stuff was scattered all over, though, and found a list Mary, my ex, had written, listing a whole bunch of stuff that wasn't in the house. My guess is they're alive and that they packed a bunch of stuff, and took off. I have no idea where they went, though."

"So, you're just wandering around, looking?" Joe asked.

"Started out doing that, but lately, I've stayed put, kinda losing hope," Ryan admitted. "So, what are your plans? Are you staying here?"

"Got somewhere better?" Joe said smiling.

"Wish I could say I did. You two, and those punks that came after your grandson, are the first people I've seen since October."

"Where all you been?"

"Missouri, Kentucky, Arkansas, and here, so far. I was going to head down to Alabama next, maybe."

"What made you choose those places?"

"I dunno, trying to stick to areas Mary might have gone, places she knew people, without going too far."

Joe stared at Ryan, again as if he were reading his thoughts. "There's something you're not saying."

Ryan glanced at Carmine, who smiled. "Gramps has a way of seeing the things you ain't sayin'."

Ryan looked at Joe, "This is gonna sound weird, but basically, I'm following hunches and these weird dreams I'm having. They were stronger a few months back, something calling me south. They stopped around the time I got here. So, I just stayed put, thinking maybe I was supposed to wait here. I know, it's weird, but right now, weird's all I've got to go on."

"Not weird at all," Joe said. "God works in mysterious ways. Maybe He is showing you the way."

Ryan didn't bother debating the man on theology. If religion was all the man had to hold, who was Ryan to take it away or question it? So, he nodded and said, "Maybe."

"Or maybe God meant for you to save me," Carmine offered.

"Well, I'm glad I was useful to someone," Ryan said, as he stared out the window, wondering how long until Red Jacket came back seeking vengeance.

**

Ryan stayed for dinner, which Carmine cooked with a portable gas stove. They had tomato soup and old crackers. They were on the stale side, but it was good to have hot food for a change. Ryan had been existing solely on a diet of chips, cold, canned meats, and warm cans of soda.

After dinner, Ryan asked what the bathroom situation was. He wasn't surprised to find it was more or less the same as his. They used buckets, dumped outside daily. Water had stopped flowing a week or so after the Vanishings, so they'd been using bottled water ever since.

Ryan felt weird using someone else's bucket to do his business, but this was the new reality, and there was no place for shyness over bodily functions in the world anymore. He made his way into the bathroom, lit by a small window that looked out onto the street behind them, squatted, and pissed and shit. He grabbed some squares of toilet paper and wiped, dropping it all in the bucket.

Now, what? Do I bring the bucket out, or leave it and expect someone else to clean up my mess?

Until now, he'd been on his own, so piss and shit bucket etiquette questions weren't something he'd given much thought to. He washed his hands using water from a gallon, which sat on a shelf behind him, and a blue bar of soap on the sink. He dried his hands on a towel hanging on the door, then opened the door gingerly, carrying the bucket awkwardly and painfully aware of the smell of his own waste.

"Where should I bring this?"

Ryan got his answer, took care of the bucket, then came back in the apartment. "How bad you hurt?" Joe asked, giving him the eye.

"Hurts when I walk, but I'll live," Ryan said. "Probably be better in the morning, or maybe the day after that."

"Why don't you stay the night? I'd hate to send you out and have something happen and you can't run."

"Oh, I don't know," Ryan said, "I don't want to put you out."

"Nonsense, you wouldn't even be hurt if you hadn't helped my boy."

"Thank you," Ryan said.

"Besides, we might need your help if that thug comes back lookin' for trouble."

* * * *

CHAPTER 5
CHARLIE WILKENS

Dunn, Georgia
March 24
6:20 a.m.

It was only in the quiet moments when Charlie felt he could see the world as it truly was. He lay in bed watching the morning sun spill through the window and creep across Callie's soft cheeks. Though he lay beside her, and both were in their underwear and T-shirts, he may as well have been sleeping outside. Charlie was still in the "friend zone."

He'd gotten used to being consigned to the role of friend, and most times was cool with it. Having Callie as a friend was better than not having her in his life. She was, in fact, one of the closest friends he'd ever had. But times like this, lying close enough to smell her, wanting so much to touch her, to hold her, to kiss her — times like this were tough as hell.

She said it was "better this way." Things were too complicated in the world now to get involved. Better for her, maybe. But not for him. He wondered if things were normal, if the world hadn't vanished, if she'd feel any different? Would she even talk to someone like him? She was as geeky as he was, liking all the same TV shows, books, and comics. Hell, she even drew him a killer version of *The Maxx*. But she was still a hot girl. And social law said girls like her didn't go for guys like him, even if it *were* the end of the world.

But he'd be damned if someone like Vic would get her.

Vic had been eying Callie like a dog looking at an abandoned burger left on the table. The worst part was the asshole didn't even have the decency to hide his ogling from Charlie. It was as if he was daring Charlie to say something. Even though Charlie wasn't really with Callie, Vic didn't know that. So, to ogle her was a clear "fuck you" to Charlie as far as he was concerned. Last week, the fucker even licked his lips when Callie was bending over outside. Charlie pretended not to see the bald steroid case, because if Vic knew he'd seen, and Charlie had done nothing, it would've made him look weak. Vic was as much a bully as Bob, with a nose fine-tuned to sniffing out pussies ripe for torment.

Charlie hoped the little scene last night might finally give Vic pause before fucking with Charlie overtly. Putting a knife in the one-eyed biker who killed Jeremy must've earned him *some* respect. Judging from Adam's stunned expression and Boricio's smile, he knew he'd at least impressed them. Vic grinned, but Charlie couldn't read what inspired the smile. Had Charlie finally done something to impress the man, or was he smiling in mockery, judging Charlie's kill as that of a pussy?

He wasn't sure what Callie had thought either.

He didn't even look at her after he'd killed the man. He stormed from the room, and went outside to clear his head. She followed a few minutes later, finding him on the side of the house. She approached cautiously, as if suddenly afraid.

He could barely look her in the eyes, though he wasn't sure why. Maybe it was shame, or maybe he was afraid he'd puke once he really thought about what he'd done. He killed a man. Another man. Bob was one thing. Bob had earned Charlie's rage and hate with years of abuse, treating his mom like shit, raping Callie, and then saying the shit he did about Charlie's dad. *Nobody* said shit about his dad. But killing the biker had been different. He'd taken no joy from it. Worse, he instantly regretted the decision. He had to go outside to try and push the thoughts from his head, before they began a forever loop in his mind's movie reel.

Callie stepped closer, meeting his eyes. She hugged him, burying her face into his chest. She didn't say a word. She simply hugged him. And he hugged her. And then he broke down, crying.

"It's okay," she said, over and over, whispering to him as she hugged him so hard, he wondered who needed the hug more.

Callie had been acting weird lately. Sad, and almost needy at times. Usually, she was either tough talking, brash, and funny, or light-hearted and friendly, sharing stories of her childhood. But lately, she spent a lot of time staring at thoughts just out of focus. Sometimes, she looked like she wanted to cry. And when they slept together, she'd snuggle up closely to him, pulling his arm around her, though never once pushing it into more romantic areas. It was as close to a romantic bond as he'd ever had, yet he didn't dare attempt to breach the line.

Sometimes, he wondered if she was finally falling for him. But he was too damned afraid to make another move and have a repeat of the awkwardness that followed his first attempt to ask her out.

They remained outside for a while, neither saying much and not really needing to. Sometimes, just being close to someone is enough. They went to bed a bit after that, lying together, her in his arms. They stayed that same way all through the night.

Now, as the golden light of morning caressed her skin, he had to fight the urge, and his morning wood, to follow the sun's touch on her skin.

He closed his eyes, flashing back over the past few months, wondering where it all was leading. Not just he and Callie, but what he was doing with Boricio and crew, and whether or not his place had permanence. Would he be better off trying to go it alone, or just he and Callie, assuming she'd come with him? Boricio was no saint, and maybe the world's biggest dick, but at the same time he seemed to have a respect for Charlie that no man since his dad had given him. He was like a cool uncle, in a way. But he sensed there was a side to Boricio that was pitch-black; a side he didn't allow the others to see but Charlie was certain was there. A savage side hungry to break free from its chains.

When Charlie thought back about all the time spent with Boricio, all the daring shit and all the big words, he still found himself confronted with a frightening question: What did they really know about Boricio?

What had he done before he showed up as a prisoner of The Prophet with him and Adam? From the best Charlie could tell, Boricio had been a cook, a mechanic, and a debt collector of some sort at one point, though Charlie wasn't sure if that meant the kind who cashed in on legitimate debts, or something more sinister. Charlie suspected the latter, and could see Boricio being a mobster henchman, but only for a while. Boricio liked to fly solo, that much was clear. Charlie figured Boricio had grown up on the streets, pretty much doing whatever he needed to do in order to survive. If that included grifting, strong-arm robbery, or seducing women with money, so be it. Boricio was all about getting his. And Team Boricio was only a team so far as it continued to serve the captain's needs. The players, themselves, seemed expendable.

Expendable.

The past few months saw a flux of team members; a wanderer picked up there, a casualty from monster or bandit there. The deaths didn't faze Boricio one bit; he hadn't stopped to mourn their losses for a second. In fact, Charlie wasn't even sure Boricio was capable of mourning, or feeling much, really. But there were times when Boricio would say something nice or inspirational to him and Adam; moments when Boricio actually seemed to care about them, perhaps felt some responsibility for taking care of them. Charlie wondered if this was the real Boricio he was seeing in those moments, or if it was simply another mask worn by the man to manipulate them to stick with him.

If he or Adam were to die tomorrow, would Boricio even care?

As Charlie pondered the thought, he felt foolish, and almost like a child, wondering if Boricio was *really his friend.* These were the sort of thoughts the *Old Charlie* used to obsess about, always wondering if people liked him, always wanting to avoid things that might offend or anger someone. The kinds of thoughts that had made him such a loser, and a target. The kinds of thoughts that attracted bullies and thugs like Vic. And Bob. The kinds of thoughts that kept him from living life.

Times like now, as he lay in the morning stillness, more or less alone with his thoughts and the new day dawning outside, he felt hate.

Hate for Old Charlie, who had let others control his life. Hate for the fears that ruled his existence. Hate for every cowardly choice he'd ever made. Hate for every bully who exploited his kindness. And hate for never striking back at those bullies.

Life was too short to live in constant fear.

He was tired of being Old Charlie.

He was tired of pretending to be some different, manlier Charlie.

Now, as the morning sun rose outside and his wood rose in his shorts, he decided, is the time to become New Charlie, for real.

If there was one thing he had learned from Boricio, it was that he didn't *have* to be a pussy. He didn't *have* to take it. He could fight back.

He could kill.

He could do whatever it took to survive. Because now, more than ever, weakness and fear were qualities that would kill him, and possibly Callie.

The world had been wiped clean, so had Charlie's slate.

It was time to reinvent himself.

To the New Charlie.

He imagined himself toasting an invisible glass of champagne.

He took initiative last night, by killing the biker who killed Jeremy. He'd done something positive, which made him strong in the eyes of the others. He would build on that today. Do something decisive. Take charge. Step into his new self.

He would kill the Old, Weak Charlie once and for all.

* * * *

CHAPTER 6
MARY OLSON

Kingsland, Alabama
The Sanctuary
March 23
Morning

Mary was sipping a tall glass of tepid water, letting her last swallow sit in her mouth as she leaned against the bar talking to Will. John and Desmond had left The Sanctuary an hour earlier to look for Rebecca and Carl.

The mood was humid, everyone waiting for word, while trying to go about the day. The children were still in class; Mary and Will were taking a largely unnoticed break from their chores.

"I don't know," Mary said, shaking her head. "It doesn't feel right. And I *know* how much Desmond hates it. I can feel him biting his tongue, and practically hear the million and one things he isn't saying. It's exhausting, and we're not even living together."

"Yeah," Will shook his head, "dude isn't half as subtle as he thinks he is."

"What do you think?" She tried pinning Will to an answer like the hundred times she'd failed before. "Are we safe?"

Will nodded. "Sure, we're safe. At least as safe as we would be out there," he jerked his thumb toward the wall. "Truthfully, I think safe got swallowed by a tar pit."

Mary got it a second before Will said, "You know, like the dinosaurs, safe doesn't exist anymore."

She felt stupid for giving him long enough to explain.

"There are guards, high walls and weapons, and all the food we need. And besides," Will said, "if they wanted us dead, we'd be in the dirt. So yeah, I expect we're safe, to a degree anyway."

"But what about The Prophet, and all the weird, cultish stuff? Doesn't it bother you at all?"

Will gave Mary an old man's tired chuckle, friendly enough to say he cared, but with an edge of exhaustion that also said he was sick of being asked the same question in 35 different versions 35 times a day.

"Not sure what else to say," he shook his head. "One man's church is another man's cult. Can't say I care for it. And yeah, it bothers me, but not enough to do anything. It bothers me, all of it. But not as much as whatever's on the other side of that wall, and not enough to leave. And even if it did, I probably wouldn't. The dreams tell me to stay and I do what they tell me."

Will crossed his arms across his chest. Mary thought he may as well have said *harrumph.*

"How can you let a dream tell you what to do?"

Will stared for a while, maybe a full 10 seconds before he said, "Dreams are how I found Luca, and what led me to you, right? Or am I missing something?"

"Alright," she said. "I'll buy the dreams, and whatever strings you let them pull. But why are you so damned vague about them?" Mary was surprised at her sudden welling anger, frothing forth from months' worth of pent-up frustration for Will and his obvious secrets and cranky grandpa muttering. "Why can't you just tell us whatever it is you won't tell us? Don't you think we should know? Don't you think we *deserve* to know?"

Will's voice softened against the intensity of Mary's. "I know you're nervous, Desmond, too. I get it, and I want everyone safe. I promise, no hesitation when it's time to move on. We'll leave the second it's a good idea. But until then, I can't say anything, and it's not because I *want* to stay hushed. It's because my dreams keep telling me to shut the hell up and I'm too smart to stay stupid. Every time I've been stupid enough to ignore what I'm told not to do, I've suffered. People I dreamed about suffered. So, I have to sit tight and let things play out, and hope there's a moment I can influence things in a positive way."

Will's eyes grew big and held Mary's. "Let's presume for a moment that there is something out there. I'm not calling it God, just something that's aware of us. And it's watching me right now, has been for a while. Wants to make damned sure I don't say anything I shouldn't. It'll punish us all if I speak. My next promise is that I won't let that happen," he smiled. "I'm not positive about the something that may or may not be God watching me thing, but the punishment part's a guarantee. Trust me. I've tried to intervene before. It never ends well."

A door slammed behind them announcing the end of classes. Before Mary could respond, Scott and Luca started walking toward them. Luca was the first to speak, trying on a new version of a slower paced, deeper toned adult voice.

"Hi," he said. "What's everyone talking about?"

"Hey, Luca," Will said, slapping him on the back. "Afternoon," he nodded at Scott.

"We were just talking about Rebecca and Carl," Mary said.

"What about them?" Scott said.

"Is everything okay?" Luca raised.

Will raised his eyebrows and Mary looked behind her. "They didn't tell you?" he said. They both shook their heads.

Mary said, "Rebecca and Carl disappeared. No one knows where they went. John and Desmond left The Sanctuary to see if they could find them, and we've been searching here." Will gestured toward Mary. "At least we were until Mary wanted an early lunch and a break from the garden."

"That's my mom, always the slacker," Paola said, approaching them. Since she wasn't in classes yet (if Mary was even going to allow her to enroll), she was working laundry duty today, folding clothes for the residents of The Sanctuary. "What did I miss?" she asked, coming to stand beside her mom.

"I thought they'd asked everyone; nobody asked any of you?" Mary said bewildered. "Rebecca and Carl are gone, and no one knows where they went." Paola's face flashed with something Mary had seen a million times before, then her nose twitched. Paola knew something, and Mary needed to know. "Paola, dear, what do you know?"

"Um ... well ... I didn't really think she would do it," Paola said, shaking her head. Her voice sped up and so did her hands. "She seemed so afraid to do something like that, I didn't really think she would do it. But I guess she did if she's missing." Before Mary could press Paola into telling her what that meant, she continued, "Rebecca told me she was thinking about sneaking into the woods by her old house for a picnic with Carl."

Will and Mary exchanged a look. Will broke the instant silence, "You need to go find Sarah."

Mary nodded and launched from her seat like a geyser just as Luca asked if anyone needed any help. Mary shook her head and said maybe later, then darted toward the middle house.

She walked fast, anxious to tell Sarah the good news, imagining how worried Rebecca's mother must be, probably beyond hysterics. Mary could only imagine how she would be feeling or what she would want to do in the same situation. Mothers will do anything and everything to protect their child. Mothers with missing offspring must go through some unimaginable torment.

Mary found Sarah sitting with another of the women, Rosemary, just inside the kitchen area.

"We think we know where Rebecca is," Mary said. Sarah looked up at Mary, her eyes red and watery.

"Yes?"

Mary cleared her throat, sure that the news would be a relief to Sarah but unsure if it would frighten her, too. Rebecca had gone off the reservation, literally. Who knows how this holier-than-though bunch will react to that. "Paola told me Rebecca said she was thinking of having a picnic with Carl, over in the woods by your old house. That's close, right? It should be easy enough to find them. I'm sure they're safe."

An awkward silence expanded between them for a few seconds.

Sarah stood up, and her face went from that of a worried mother, to the stern face of an angry spinster.

"Thank you for informing me. I am sorry to hear my daughter has shamed The Sanctuary. I'll inform Brother Rei so he can pray for her soul and send someone to get her."

Holier-than-though indeed. Poor Rebecca, and Carl.

Sarah turned back to Rosemary, who put a hand on her shoulder and whispered something, while Mary stood alone with her shock. She had an inkling Sarah's reaction might involve some scorn. But complete and total disdain? No ounce of relief? No hint of a smile? Just anger? Rebecca had always seemed so nice and calm. Mary knew she was a bit high-strung, but she'd never seen the kind of righteous anger that flashed just now.

Once she gathered herself, Mary returned to her huddle with Will and the others, who'd moved to the front porch. They watched as Sarah, Rei, and Rosemary stormed over to the garden where The Prophet was sitting by himself in prayer. Though they couldn't hear the group, they could feel the anger coming from them.

"Sorry," Paola shook her head, "I shouldn't have said anything."

"Yes, you should have," Mary pulled Paola close and wrapped her arms around her. "You were perfect."

* * * *

CHAPTER 7
DESMOND ARMSTRONG

"JOHN!"

Still nothing.

The clicking cut through the dark, bounced across the walls of the cave and boomeranged back. Desmond swallowed, then held his breath when he thought his swallow might have been too loud. The squish beneath his foot from earlier was now moving on its own, at least it felt that way in the freezing fear of the pitch-black cave.

The clicking came closer.

Can these fuckers see in the dark?

Desmond swam in the darkness, waving his hands slowly and awkwardly through the air, one tentative step at a time, searching for wall or John, and hoping not to find a monster. Between the clicking and being rendered virtually blind, Desmond had nothing to hold onto and everything to fear. No matter where he turned, his hands met air. And no matter where he turned, the clicking moved closer, as if it were just out of reach, watching him — waiting to strike.

Desmond stopped moving completely, but that didn't help.

Click ... click ... click ...

It can see me. I know it. Fuck!

Closer and closer, louder and louder, a single click and decibel at a time.

When the clicking was close enough for Desmond to hear the squish of its wet skin, he turned himself into a statue, holding his breath as the world around him heaved and sighed. In and out, in and out, Desmond drew and released shallow breaths.

His body tensed, Desmond felt a sudden boiling hatred for John.

Desmond would survive this. He would kill the monsters and find his way out. Then he would kill the traitor. Desmond took silent aim at the clicking, no longer worried about his itchy trigger finger, eager to use it in fact, and thankful for the darkness that made accidents easy.

John had betrayed him, lured him into a cave to get swallowed by death. He had probably been mocking him with all that insincere hokum about The Prophet and The Word. Desmond didn't know what kind of mind fuck or game John was playing, but he would pay for it all, and with interest, for this and for leaving them stranded last October.

Desmond inched forward, but his foot found a wrong step, followed by a second that made the first look graceful. He fell forward, hard, trying to catch himself with the balls of his palms. He missed, landing with the point of his chin instead. His gun didn't go off but landed and bounced with a clatter into the darkness and out of sight.

SHIT!

Desmond felt around for the gun but found nothing, the ground cold, wet, and sticky to the touch.

That's when he stood and the panic got mean.

Something brushed his arm and the clicking screamed in his ear, like an army of aluminum cockroaches. Piss flooded the front of his pants, rolling down Desmond's leg. Desmond fell to the ground, searching frantically for the gun. The weird lights beneath the creatures' skin pulsed and faded, never "on" long enough for Desmond to get a bead on exactly where they were. Desmond wondered if they'd evolved a way to turn their lights off when hunting.

The clicking intensified, and he felt the thing next to him, surely ready to strike.

Desmond's hands were everywhere, but the gun wasn't. And the clicking was now loud enough to be the last thing he ever heard. Without his gun, Desmond was dead. The clicking promised just seconds of breath. Desmond inhaled and prepared to die, just as invisible hands found him in the darkness.

The hand over his mouth made him choke on his panic. He fought hard to keep the whimper inside, and wasn't sure if John's sudden whisper in his ear made things worse. "Shh, they'll hear you," he said.

John's left hand dragged Desmond to the back wall of the cave, slowly, a half step at a time, none of them tentative. Desmond could feel John's right hand, holding the gun in front of them, sweeping back and forth, probing the darkness for "demons." When they reached the wall, John released Desmond and took a step to the side, still silent.

Desmond's heartbeat was thunder in the cave. The clicking grew indecisive, suddenly flying this way and that, in and out of earshot like a bad connection. Just when the clicking sounded like it had receded, it was suddenly on top of them. Desmond lost it and finally screamed. John didn't. He opened fire, nearly making them deaf five times in short succession.

Then silence, save for Desmond's pounding heart, which he swore echoed back to him off the cave walls. John's flashlight returned from the dead, momentarily blinding Desmond's sight. He squinted in agony to make sense of the scene. After a few more seconds, his eyes better adjusted, the full carnage came into view: two fallen monsters lay still, their bodies oozing goo and cast in an artificial glow. The lights in their skin pulsed slowly and faded.

Desmond listened for more clicking, but after hearing nothing but the ringing in his ears for a minute, he exploded at John. "What the hell?!" he shouted.

John said nothing, which he was clearly good at. Desmond spotted his gun under the dawn of John's light, then knelt to retrieve it. "Why didn't you answer me?"

"Because I didn't want to die." John waited half a minute, maybe he wanted to let it sink in, or maybe he thought Desmond would want a turn to speak. Or maybe he didn't think he needed to explain himself further. He finally said, "My light died, then I heard the Demons. Soon as I heard their clicking, I closed my mouth so I wouldn't draw any attention. That's when you started getting loud and moving around and generally letting the Demons know where the party was. Naturally, that's when they started closing in. I couldn't exactly yell at you to stop moving, so I just kept hoping you would. Only break we got was when you fell, and then only for a moment."

John could have mentioned the piss, since there was no hiding the scent of ammonia mingling with the ancient sour inside the cave. Or he could have mentioned Desmond's scream, or anything else really. He had saved his life after all. Desmond felt a wave of guilt as he realized he'd cast John as Judas in his head just a few minutes earlier, ready to end his life.

"Sorry."

John said, "Don't worry about it. Just ... "

The sudden crackle from John's radio finished his sentence.

It was Lenny, one of the soldiers at The Sanctuary. "Brother John? We found 'em."

John lifted the receiver to his lips. "Where were they?"

A crackle of static, then, "They were down by the river if you can believe it. Having a picnic."

"Are they in custody?"

Another crackle, then, "Yes, sir. Brother Eli and I are headed back with them now."

"Thanks, Lenny," John said, "See you back at The Sanctuary."

They never finished their conversation. John said, "They're safe. It's time to get back." He stepped past Desmond, then left the cave and headed back over the hill toward the Audi. Desmond followed close behind, a chill accompanying the crunch of every leaf.

* * * *

CHAPTER 8
REBECCA SNOW

The white Suburban drove through the front gates of The Sanctuary, then pulled into the courtyard. The driver's side door opened and Lenny, the man Rebecca overheard Desmond call an "all-purpose grunt," opened the back door. Rebecca and Carl stepped from the vehicle, heads hung, and were met by Eli who got out from the passenger side, then led them across The Sanctuary courtyard to the site of the unfinished church. A group of watchers was waiting and working, including some of the new people: the man-boy Luca, Paola and her mother, Mary, and the weird old guy, Will.

Mary smiled at her, but she could tell it was a fake smile masking sadness, like there were words she couldn't say. Paola's mom seemed so nice, not like Mother at all.

Mother had been terrifying for a while, especially when they were alone. Rebecca couldn't imagine how Mother was going to respond to her getting caught on a picnic with Carl, but she was terrified. Mother would give her a beating for sure, and might make her do the starving secret, where she was only allowed to eat if someone was watching. Otherwise, she had to spit out most of her food for a week. That's what she made her do the last time, when she asked if God was wrong for leaving them behind.

Whatever happened, it was going to be terrible. While Rebecca wasn't afraid Mother would kill her, she was pretty sure she'd make her wish she was dead. Mother was almost always quiet in front of others, particularly the men, whom you were supposed to always obey. But behind closed doors her hiss was loud and her fangs sank deep.

Rebecca trembled with every step, doing everything she could to keep her knees from knocking. Carl walked beside her. Rebecca could feel her hand drawn to his, could feel herself wanting to take it. Could feel him wanting it, too. But she ignored the feeling and kept walking forward, both arms dangling limp at her side. Their picnic had been so magical before the men showed up. She'd never met anyone so interested in what she had to say, and who seemed to find her so pretty.

Mother was crossing the courtyard from the far end, approaching Eli and the juvenile outlaws. Her walk was steady and chin straight, eyes sailing straight through Rebecca on their way to Eli.

Mother stood a few feet from them. "I'm so sorry," she said to Eli, her voice barely above a whisper.

There were a few dozen eyes on Rebecca, but they felt like a million. In addition to her friend Paola and all the other "new people" watching her, Rebecca could feel the judging eyes from Brother Rei, standing at the edge of the onlookers, eyes moving from Mother to the open book in the palm of his hand.

Brother Rei took a step forward and opened his mousey mouth. "You realize The Prophet will have no choice but to hold court and declare judgment, don't you?"

Mother nodded.

Brother Rei held the book open for Mother, then led her eyes to where he wanted them to go with his finger. He cast a disapproving glance at Carl then turned his stare to Rebecca. Mother didn't need to see whatever Brother Rei had in the book. Rebecca thought The Prophet and Mother seemed to share a brain. Most of the time when The Prophet was speaking, Rebecca thought it sounded just like Mother, only fancier. She knew the Book of The Sanctuary Law as well as any of them.

"Of course, Brother Rei," Mother said. "I completely understand. The Prophet has my full support. What is done is done, and whatever is needed to right the ship before it sinks is fine with me. The child's soul must be saved." Mother was still looking at Brother Rei, but directing her words at Rebecca when she said, "She made her bed; she deserves to lie in it and sleep beneath the soiled covers."

Mother finally turned to Rebecca and pressed her fingers into her cheeks, not hard enough to hurt, but hard enough to let Rebecca know there was another round coming later, behind closed doors, hidden from the curious eyes of the congregation. She pursed her lips and hissed, "I will not raise another harlot."

She released Rebecca's face with a jerking motion and pinch, then turned to Carl. Her voice grew louder and she said, "You will both face the consequences." Then, almost at a yell and with her finger just an inch from his face, she said, "*You* should know better. How old are you?"

"Fifteen, ma'am," Carl said, eyes in the dirt.

"What did you do to my daughter?"

"Nothing, ma'am."

"Don't lie to me," Mother growled. "Did you take her virginity?"

Carl looked up, visibly shocked. Rebecca cried out, "Mother!" embarrassed and afraid for Carl.

"No, ma'am," he shook his head. "It was nothing like that. We just sat down for a picnic, that was all."

"I told you not to lie to me!" Spit flew from Mother's mouth. She was losing her temper publicly, for the first time since arriving at Sanctuary.

"It's okay, Sarah," Brother Rei said, placing a soothing hand on her shoulder, his beady eyes glistening with secret pleasure. "All is well and as it should be according to The Good Lord's Plan. You need not worry about a thing. We'll take it from here. Brother Paul," he said, turning to the man in robes behind him. "Please take the boy to the stockade immediately. I will be in to question him shortly."

"No!" Rebecca cried. No one responded out loud, though Paola looked like she was going to cry, and Mary looked like she wanted to pull Rebecca into a hug. Luca's eyes were pointed right at her, but it looked like they were focused on something she couldn't see, off in "Luca land," as some of the kids had commented behind his back. The soldiers all looked mad at her. The old man just looked mad.

Brother Rei turned to Mother. "Clearly, young Rebecca cannot be trusted, so we'll be moving her from the girls' quarters back to her lodging with you. That way you can keep an eye on her. If that's okay, of course," he lowered his head and waited for Mother to respond. Rebecca decided she hated Brother Rei.

"Of course," Mother said, and turned to the crowd, though Rebecca could tell her words were meant mostly for the newcomers. "I apologize that my daughter caused all of this trouble, and for bringing shame to The Sanctuary."

The old man, Will, said, "No trouble at all, ma'am. We're just happy she was found safe. No harm done." Rebecca didn't miss the glance Will gave Brother Rei after the "no harm done" comment.

Mother gave Will a dirty look disguised inside a quiet stare, then shoved Rebecca into the first step toward their lodging, hand tight around the girl's neck as she pushed her forward. It wasn't until they were on the other side of the front door when Mother's fingers twisted inside Rebecca's hair and she yanked them at the root.

"You will get every bit of what's coming to you, child," she said. "And praise be to The Good Lord for making it happen. Thanks to His Glory, there's hope for you yet."

"Yes, Mother, thank the Lord."

* * * *

CHAPTER 9
DESMOND ARMSTRONG

Desmond and John traveled back to The Sanctuary in near-silence. Desmond wasn't much in the mood for conversation. Thankfully, John's one-word answers to his sparse comments obliged. When they finally returned, the dust had already settled on the situation, and everyone had resumed their regularly scheduled stations.

John parked the Audi in the hangar, and both men stepped from the car. John held his hand out to Desmond. "I'm going to see Rei," he said. "I'll take your firearm to him now and save you the trip."

Desmond nodded, pulled the gun from his waistband, and handed it to John.

"You coming to lunch?"

John nodded. "See you there for sure."

Will and Mary were digging in the dirt, each filling their own basket with ripe tomatoes. Desmond approached them from behind, then leaned to a squat and whispered. "These people are freaks. We need to get out of here, like yesterday."

Will set a tomato at the bottom of the basket, then looked up at Desmond. "You got somewhere better for us to go?"

Desmond wore the same defeated look he always got when Will made his usual, single-sentence argument. He stood, deciding to say nothing about John's overwhelming creepiness, or the two monsters they left lying in the cave. Desmond pivoted his gaze across the courtyard, along the short row of three houses, then over to the communication tower, and hangar, before looking over everything a second time and kneeling back down.

"So, what happened with the kids?"

Will and Mary took turns telling Desmond what happened. Will's story focused on Rei, Mary's on Sarah.

"Where's Carl at now?" Desmond asked.

Will pointed to a set of double doors leading to a basement beneath the third house. "Looks like that's where they keep the sinners," he said.

Desmond shook his head, then threw a rock from the garden toward the dust of the courtyard. "It's bad enough we ended up shacking at the bullshit factory, but it's a crying shame we have to pick their tomatoes, too."

Mary looked hurt, Will didn't even look up. A door slammed in the distance, instantly attracting Desmond's eyes away from his friends to the possible threats approaching from behind.

John and Rei were a few feet away and smiling. John held his smile as Rei opened his mouth. "Brother Desmond, Brother Will, we thought it would be a good idea if you came and witnessed the hearing."

Desmond didn't say anything since *fuck you* probably wouldn't have done much good, and might have put Will and Mary, and maybe the rest of their crew, in danger. Desmond didn't care about himself, but he wasn't willing to put anyone he cared about in jeopardy, at least not intentionally.

John stepped into Desmond's silence. "If you're going to be a part of The Sanctuary, you must know how our justice system works and see it in action."

I have a pretty good idea, Desmond thought, but said, "What makes you think I'm gonna like what I see?"

"Nothing," John shook his head. "I don't think you'll like it at all, actually. Which is exactly why you need to see it. If you want to live here, you must understand our law."

He didn't wait for Desmond to answer, simply cut through the courtyard a few steps behind Rei, expecting that Desmond, and whoever decided to join him, would follow.

**

Every stair creaked on the way down to the otherwise silent basement. The right side of the room looked like a carpenter's workstation with hunks of painted wood, finishing tools, and an abandoned construction project, which filled the space with the scent of pine. The left side reminded Desmond of a dungeon.

Carl was on the left side, strapped to the wall like a medieval torture victim. Will and Desmond paused in the doorway, as though their bodies refused to push them further inside. John and Rei entered in perfect step, stopping just three feet from Carl's tortured face.

The boy was silent, though his eyes said plenty. A bead of sweat fled his forehead and spilled to the cement to punctuate his terror.

John took a step back and crossed his arms, watching. Rei took a step forward and started to pace, waving his hands in the air. "You know how God feels about liars, right?"

The way the kid flinched a second early, Desmond figured Rei's act was a routine. Brother Rei's palm met the side of the child's face, sending Carl's head reeling to the side. Carl righted his head and looked back at Rei. Rei smiled and tucked Carl's damp hair behind his ear with a smile.

He turned his back to Carl and started to pace. "I'm going to ask you to tell me what happened again." He turned back to Carl. "And this time, I pray you have the sense to tell me the Good Lord's truth. Now, Carl, what happened between you and the girl?"

"Nothing, like I said. I asked her if she would have a picnic with me. She said yes, and we went near the river by her old house. That's it."

"Yet, you knew this was forbidden at The Sanctuary, did you not?"

At first Carl said nothing, but then he started nodding his head. "Yes, yes I did, sir. I'm sorry, really I am. I just wanted a moment with her, away from all this. I didn't mean nothing by it."

"It's okay," Rei's voice softened. "Who could blame you after all?"

Carl looked confused, but hopeful. Rei continued. "She's a pretty girl, isn't she?"

Carl nodded.

Rei continued, "Fair skinned, long, beautiful red hair, and budding breasts. Who wouldn't want to touch? Obviously, the girl seduced you. You had no choice. You only took the apple because it was so freely handed to you."

Carl was still confused, but it looked like he was starting to figure it out. He shook his head and said, "No, I'm the one who asked her. Rebecca's real shy; she won't even ask me if I'm thirsty half the time."

Rei attempted a laugh, though Desmond thought it sounded more like a weasel choking. He leaned in closer, "Come now, Carl, you can tell me the truth." He gestured to the dungeon's new visitors. "We're all friends here. And your friends want you to come down from there as soon as possible." He placed a hand on top of Carl's restraints, then allowed his fingers to run down Carl's arm. "Really, it makes sense to end this sooner rather than later, don't you agree?"

Rei turned to Will and Desmond. They were silent. John nodded.

"I'll be honest," Rei took Carl's eyes. "I've no stomach for this. I want it to be over as soon as possible. I want to get you out of those restraints and outside to the long table filled with good people, people who can't wait to see you back, and know you're safe. It's easy to get there. All you have to do is tell me the truth."

Rei waited a beat to speak, then said, "I've known girls like Rebecca my entire life. There used to be millions, until The Lord thinned the herd a bit. Now they're scarce. You'll know these girls in your life, too. Whores pretending to be godly girls, doing their siren's duty by distracting you from God's Good Grace."

"It isn't like that." Carl's head was pointed at the floor, shaking.

"Well, that truly is a shame." Rei looked so profoundly disappointed, Desmond half believed he was. "Have you read The Book of The Sanctuary Law? A rhetorical question, of course, as it's required reading of all students. But have you *really* read it? Have you taken these laws to heart?"

"Of course," Carl said.

"Then you clearly understand the brand of justice The Prophet will be forced to bring on you if you're found guilty." Brother Rei leaned in close. "If you did indeed seduce this child, you will be stoned to death."

Desmond felt a chill run down his spine. He looked to Will, who stared straight ahead, attempting to avoid emotion. Then Desmond saw that John was watching him, likely gauging his reaction. Desmond pretended not to notice John's gaze.

"Nothing happened. Nothing!" Carl said, the treble in his voice rising.

Desmond was chewing on his lip, doing everything possible to keep his brain from sending his body into motion. Will's plastic glare said: *Don't be stupid. Sit tight.*

Why in the hell would John bring him down to see this? What was he expecting to think? Did he want him to get the hell out of there? Was he testing him? Did it have anything to do with Mary? Was John trying to get to her by getting Desmond to leave?

As if on cue, John smiled.

Creepy fuck.

Rei continued his pacing routine in front of the boy, stretching each minute to the length of painful. He finally stopped pacing in front of Carl, waiting for the boy to meet his eyes. He said, "If everything is as you say, you have nothing to worry about. The Prophet can see innocence as clearly as the daylight. But I would like to help you improve your odds, to give you another chance. Because God forbid, if you're found guilty ... I'm afraid you'll have to face his full wrath. Not The Prophet's, mind you; he is but a humble servant of The Almighty. You will indeed be punished, and it will be according to The Word."

Rei cleared his throat and softened his voice. "I suggest you start telling the truth and stop protecting the whore. Tell us it was her idea. Tell us how she seduced you. How she practically pulled you inside of her. Tell us you couldn't help yourself, you are only a fragile, young man, after all. A young man with wants and needs that Satan loves to exploit. You're not yet equipped to deal with these slings and arrows and the Eves that are everywhere. Tell us how you fought off her advances. Tell us you did everything you could to steer clear of the shadows and remain faithful to The Word."

Desmond could see Carl starting to break, and was digging his fingernails into his palm to keep himself from beating Rei to a pulp and releasing Carl from his shackles. If John wasn't standing a foot away with a gun, he probably would have - damn the consequences.

"Do it for both of you," Rei whispered, dripping the final sweet drop of his own seduction into the boy's ear. "The punishment for girls is far less strict than it is for men. You will be helping both of you by admitting the truth. The Prophet is a great man, a loving man. He'll be looking for any excuse to show mercy on the child. Give him one, Carl. Allow God's grace to spare your life."

Desmond was glad he didn't have his gun. If he did, he'd probably empty it into Brother Weasel before he could finish his brainwashing.

"Let's get you down from there." Rei ran his hands across Carl's shackles. "Tell us, is that what happened? Did Rebecca seduce you?"

The perverse smile that spread across Rei's lips just before his final question caused Desmond to make a vow inside his head. Given the chance, he'd kill Rei. John, too. Not just for making him watch, but for playing his part.

Carl started to cry, then nodded. From behind a torrent of fresh tears he said, "Yes, yes, that's exactly what happened. The picnic was all her idea. I only said yes because she was trying to seduce me and I didn't know no better. And that's the honest truth."

"Thank you, Carl," Rei said, eyes now turning to Desmond and Will. "The truth shall set ye free."

* * * *

CHAPTER 10
BRENT FOSTER

The next night . . .

For the first time in months, Brent was smiling. He could hardly contain himself. His joy at the thought that Gina and Ben might still be alive was more than he could sort. A part of him had given up and died. Its resurrection was unfamiliar, but wonderful.

And while Keenan hadn't said much about why he needed help searching for Boricio, or why he didn't just start the hunt with any of Black Island's other more qualified Guardsmen, Brent couldn't help but think that Keenan had a plan.

And Keenan's plan might actually bring him home.

Keenan hadn't said it in so many words, had even talked Brent down when he asked if it might be possible to return to their world. But there was something in his eyes. Keenan didn't have to say a thing, Brent could see it clearly — Keenan believed he could get them home. Unfortunately, Keenan had to leave before giving Brent additional details.

He promised that he'd fill him in more tomorrow, when they'd leave Black Island and start their search. Until then, Brent had to keep his mouth shut, even when he thought he was alone. Continue acting normal. Every home on the island was monitored, and if they knew what he knew, it could endanger him and Keenan.

Brent was practically giddy, so it was some surprise to Jane when she opened her door to find him smiling like a fool. "What's got you so happy, and . . . " she glanced down at her watch, which read 4:05 p.m. "So early?"

"Just happy to see you," he said. Jane welcomed him in, then closed the door. "Got out of work early today."

Emily, with cute pigtails and turquoise bows to match her T-shirt, ran toward him and hopped into his arms, yelling "Mr. Brent!" He scooped the 6-year-old into a giant hug, and she planted a big kiss on his cheek. He noticed the scent of strawberry.

She giggled, and said, "I just gave you a strawberry kiss!"

"Huh?" Brent said.

"She found some strawberry lip balm," Jane explained. "You'd think she found a pony, the way she's carrying on."

"Yeah, Ben used to get excited about the littlest things," Brent said. "To be so young, and have such simple things bring you so much happiness."

"I haven't even started dinner," Jane said, glancing toward the kitchen.

"Good," Brent said, "I can help. We can all cook together."

"*You* can cook?" A surprised look arched Emily's eyebrows.

Brent laughed as he carried the girl into the kitchen. "Yeah, of course I can cook!"

"I thought only mommies cooked."

Jane laughed. "Mike didn't like to cook, so she figured no daddies cooked."

"What can you cook?" Emily asked.

"I dunno, let's see what you have." He sat the girl on the kitchen counter, then turned to their pantry. "So, um, let's see . . . I can make, um . . . snakes and meatballs."

"Snakes?!" Emily screeched, "Eeeew!"

"You don't like snakes? I thought all kids like snakes."

She giggled. "G-R-O-S-S, gross!"

Brent laughed. He loved the girl's goofiness. It reminded him a lot of how Ben was, or would be with a few years and a lot more language added to his personality.

"OK, no snakes. Let's see. Um, oh, I've got it, how about some boiled worm stew? Do you like that?"

Emily stuck out her tongue, "Yuck!"

"OK, one last try, and then I give up," Brent said, pretending to look high and low in the pantry. "Well, you have a whole jar of blueberry bumblebees! I bet those would make a great pie! Who doesn't love blueberry bumblebee pie?"

"I don't want you to cook," she said, her voice completely serious, as if he'd make her eat every disgusting dish he listed.

Brent and Jane laughed at her frown.

"OK, how about spaghetti, then? You like spaghetti?"

"Normal spaghetti?" she asked.

"Yes, normal spaghetti. No worms, or anything!"

Yeah!" she said enthusiastically, "Can I help?"

"If your mom says okay."

"OK," Jane said. "And if you're really good, I'll let you help clean the dishes, too."

"OK!" Emily said, not getting the joke.

"That's good, because daddies aren't so good at cleaning dishes," Brent said with a wink at Jane.

"That's okay," Emily said, in all seriousness. "I'm sure there are other things you can do well."

Brent laughed from somewhere deep in his belly.

"What?" she said, not understanding why he was laughing.

"You're so cute," he said, kissing her on the forehead.

**

As they ate dinner, and Emily and Jane talked about the day's events, Brent's earlier smile began to dull with the realization that he had to soon tell them he'd be leaving in the morning, and would gone for a week or so. Though he wasn't sure why, it surprised him how much he expected to miss Jane and Emily, how much they'd come to mean to him in the months since fate set them all together. Their dinner routine was one of the few things he had left to look forward to. And now he was going to have to tell them he might not be back for a couple of weeks. Hell, he might not make it back *at all,* if things went bad out in the world, or if this Boricio guy didn't want to be found.

How do I tell them?

Finally, mouth full of pasta, he decided to simply say it. "I've got some bad news," he said, regretting his choice of words even as they were leaving his mouth. "I'm going on a mission with one of the other men, and I'll be gone from the island for a week or so."

"What?" Jane said, her eyes big and watering with concern.

"What do you mean?" Emily asked immediately, worry furrowing her brow.

"I can't say much about it, and I'm not sure where we're going, but they need us to go on a run and I'll probably be gone a week, two at most."

"Two weeks?!" Emily cried, making a sad face.

"Is it dangerous?" Jane asked.

"No, not at all," Brent said, even though he was sure it probably would be. "Just a routine mission, everything will be fine. Believe me, if it were dangerous, they'd be sending more people. Not like they don't have tougher guys than me in the Guard."

"I don't want you to go," Emily said, now in full pout.

Brent felt uncomfortable, not knowing what to say, and wishing he'd thought out his messaging better before making his announcement. He should have known Emily would be upset.

"I don't want to lose another Daddy," Emily said.

Brent glanced at Jane, and felt his heart breaking.

He slid his chair closer and hugged Emily. "Don't worry, nothing will to happen to me. I swear."

"How do you know?"

"Because I know everything, except maybe how to make good spaghetti," he said, trying to make her smile, but she wasn't playing ball.

Brent wondered if he should tell the girl and her mother that her real daddy might still be alive. Wouldn't that ease the pain of Brent leaving? Wouldn't that make them a little less sad?

Before the thought took root, the smarter side of him shut it down.

Don't you dare give these people false hope! Even if her daddy is alive, even if Gina and Ben are alive, there's no guarantee anyone will get off this planet! Keep your mouth shut!

As Emily wrapped her arms tight around his neck, Brent looked at Jane, and saw that look in her eyes again. That mixture of sadness and strong feelings for him. Even if they weren't dating or together, there was a strong bond between them, some sort of love forged in sadness and tragedy. And these days, that kind of love was all there was. But this wasn't his family. And as long as Gina and Ben might still be out there waiting for him, he had to do whatever it took to get back. He couldn't afford to feel love for a new family.

It was in that moment Brent considered something he should've thought about last night or earlier today. If Gina and Ben *were* still alive on his Earth, what happened after Oct. 15? Did they wake up to find him gone with no idea where he went? Did they think something happened to him? That he'd been killed? Maybe they thought he just got up and walked out on them as so many parents did these days.

It killed him to picture Gina and Ben wondering where he was, wondering why he didn't love them enough to stay.

And then another idea surfaced, one that sent a chill through his core. What if the Brent of this world took his place over there? Maybe that Brent didn't even know he was in another world. Or worse, maybe he sensed something was wrong, but didn't know what it was. What if the Other Brent snapped and did something to harm Gina and Ben?

Every second he remained on this planet was another second of possible pain in the lives of those he loved most. He had to get back to Earth, no matter what he had to do, or who tried to stop him. He would do anything. Kill anyone who tried to stop him.

Because that's what you do for family.

* * * *

CHAPTER 11
REBECCA SNOW

It was standing room only in the New Unity Church, temporarily located on the bottom floor of the women's housing. The Prophet would have preferred to hold the hearing in his newly finished church, as he explained with apology while everyone shuffled inside, but construction was running behind and this would have to do.

Everyone was there, old people and new, all standing together. The Prophet was sitting at the head of a long table in the front of the room, their best attempt at recreating a judge's chambers. Brother Rei was sitting to his left, John to his right, both dressed in thin, white robes. Even with half his face concealed by the mask, The Prophet looked serious, sitting at the head of the table and stroking his chin for several minutes before finally opening his mouth and casting his eyes from Rebecca, who stood along the far wall, alone, to the onlookers, then back, with pain in his pupils, as though the burden of his duty was too much to bear.

Finally, he cleared his throat and stood to address the room. The already silent room grew so still that Rebecca wondered if some of the congregation had stopped breathing completely. She looked over at Mother, who may as well have been carved from rock. Her eyes weren't moving, and she didn't even have the usual twitch at the edges of her mouth. Her expression was indifference, if she wore any at all.

"Please bring the corrupted forward." The Prophet waved his hand toward the door, and Brother Eli ushered Carl inside, and then to the front of the room. Carl stood in front of The Prophet, who held his hands wide, as though offering the audience a giant embrace. He said, "Please, son, tell us what happened. And remember, The Good Lord always sees a way to reward the virtuous, and there is nothing more virtuous than looking into the eyes of honesty and speaking openly without flinching. Now, tell us what happened."

Carl kept his head straight and his voice steady. "Rebecca seduced me. She knew I was weak and so she took advantage, tried to get me alone so she could corrupt me with her wicked ways." He stole a quick glance at Rebecca, then added, his voice shaky this time, "Not really her fault. She has the Devil inside her, like all women do."

Rebecca couldn't believe what she was hearing, couldn't believe what was happening. Her ears were burning, her face was crimson, and her stomach was at a rolling boil. She felt like she was about to throw up or cry. Maybe both. She shouted out in protest, "He's lying!" but her words were drowned by The Prophet.

"Silence!" he commanded, though the kind, patient look still covered his face.

Rebecca shrank back. The Prophet continued, meeting Carl's eyes. "You must pay for your sins," he said. "You may have been led down the dark path by the Devil himself, and though you merely bit the beautiful apple that was set in your palm, we learn through punishment what not to do, just as we learn the steps to Heaven by following the Word. I'm afraid I'm going to have to give you two weeks in the Sin Box. That should afford you plenty of time to think about the corruption you allowed to infiltrate your heart and reaffirm your vows to The Lord Almighty so it never happens again. It shouldn't be too tough to manage that in two weeks." The Prophet smiled. "The Good Lord did make the entire world in half that time, after all."

Carl said nothing, so Brother Eli led him to the back of the room. The coward didn't look at Rebecca once. She glared at him, her heart broken. He was the first nice boy she'd allowed to get close to her. And he betrayed her.

Is this God's punishment for my wicked thoughts?

The Prophet said, "Please, come forth, Rebecca."

She walked slowly to the front of the room and faced The Prophet, trying to stop her tears. "And what do you say in your defense?" The Prophet narrowed his eyes and she glanced to the ground.

"That's not how it happened at all," she said, her voice cracking, tears waiting to gush from behind their gossamer-thin wall. "Carl asked me if I would meet him for a picnic. He seemed nice, like the kind of guy you could trust."

She did everything she could not to turn and shoot him a look. "So, I said yes. But I shouldn't have left The Sanctuary. That was wrong." She looked down, caught her breath, then looked back, this time meeting The Prophet's eyes. "But what he's saying happened, didn't. He asked me to meet him, and I said okay." She turned to Mother, and the congregation. "I'm sorry I didn't tell you where we were going."

The Prophet flashed an almost imperceptible glance at Brother Rei, though Rebecca caught it and felt fear flutter through her body. Brother Rei stood from his seat and looked at Rebecca. "Are you saying that Carl is lying?" he asked, his voice soft and almost soothing.

Rebecca was silent.

Brother Rei continued. "We cannot tolerate liars, Rebecca. That is a violation of the Good Lord's Word. Truth is power, and nothing is more powerful than The Truth. Let me ask you again. If you're saying Carl is lying, tell us now. Because if he is, he'll be spending his two weeks inside the hole healing from a freshly removed tongue."

Panic bleached Carl's face, but no words escaped his lips. Rebecca wanted to blurt out that of course Carl was lying. He had to save himself after all, didn't he, but the thought of Carl missing his tongue was enough to keep her silent. Like Rebecca, Carl had seen Brother Rei make good on his threats enough times to know they never lay idle.

Rebecca looked down, her head heavy with despair and fear. She shook her head, knowing she had no other choice. "No, it happened just like you said. Please forgive me."

Brother Rei smiled, then sat. The Prophet stood up and came around to Rebecca's side of the table, stopping just inches away. He rolled his voice in honey before using it again. His smile wide, The Prophet said, "Listen, child, I know you've been tricked by The Dark Lord himself. Satan is a slippery snake capable of slithering just about anywhere, fooling Eve herself. And he likes to slither in those places where it's easiest to get to. And believe me, it's never easier than when you're young and haven't learned to recognize the Devil in all his sinister forms. I was once young like you, believe it or not." The Prophet held his belly and chuckled, then waited for the congregation to return his laugh. They did. Of course, they did.

He pulled a handkerchief from his pocket, wiped it across his brow, then said, "I've half a mind to overlook this incident, maybe even more than half, seeing as how you are so young and it was awfully easy for the Devil to get to you. But spare the rod and spoil the child. So, I'm afraid we simply cannot afford such leniency now, when He is watching our every move, judging to see who shall enter His Kingdom."

The Prophet raised his hands and looked at the sky. "Rules are in place for a reason, and I can't turn my back on punishment entirely, unless I'm willing to surrender to the chaos of Hades below." He chuckled again. "But if I'm willing to do that, well I may as well swing the gates wide open and pour some lemonade for the Demons." He stared into Rebecca's eyes. "However, since you are so young, I will defer to your mother in this matter. Allow her to choose your punishment. Either the one provided by our laws, or something of her own design."

He turned his eyes toward Mother. "Please come forward, Sarah," he said.

Sarah made herself a statue before The Prophet, still not meeting Rebecca's eyes. He looked solemn before he swallowed, replacing his grim expression with an apologetic half smile. "Your daughter has broken one of The Sanctuary's unbreakable rules, and has thus brought shame to us all and called into question your fitness as a parent. Worse, she has degraded the character and threatened the soul of one of our fine, young men, and through her actions invited the Demons to knock on our door."

The Prophet narrowed his eyes at Sarah. "Now, I may be the humble servant of The Good Lord up in Heaven, but even the mouthpiece of God doesn't get the right to claim judgment over a child so young. Rebecca is the spawn of your womb, Sarah, so I must ask you: Shall we overlook this sin and allow you to administer her punishment? Or should she be punished according to The Word, so we can set her as subject to the strength of the Law, showing Satan that he cannot use our children as vessels to poison our well?"

Rebecca looked at her mother, but Mother would not meet her eyes. Rebecca cried out, "Mother, PLEASE!"

Mother stared at The Prophet, ignoring her pleas.

"Punish the sinner," she said, an icicle coring her voice, eyes fixed on The Prophet's. "Punish the sinner now, while there is still time to save her soul, before she joins her sister in The Lake of Fire."

Rebecca cried out, then turned to The Prophet. There were a few punishments he could choose to administer, she knew. Though none were deadly, all terrified her.

"Okay," The Prophet said, then exhaled a giant sigh. He shook his head as though it pained him to say what he had to say next, but then said it like it was a Sunday morning sermon anyway. "The Sanctuary hereby states that Rebecca will be punished in accordance with The Word and those rules written within. She shall spend one week in the Box of Shame and have all of the locks upon her head removed effective immediately and permanently, so she may no longer seduce the men of The Sanctuary."

"What?" Rebecca was no longer crying. She was screaming, and about to run for the door. But Brother Rei was too fast. He was already on his feet, as were Brothers John and Eli, each on one side of Rebecca, holding one of her arms tight, and hurting her. Brother Rei took a step forward and met Rebecca's eyes, then produced a pair of oversized black handled shears seemingly from nowhere, and held them in front of her face.

"Please, don't struggle," Brother Rei said, smiling as if he would enjoy nothing more than a struggle. He stepped closer. "I would hate to slip and slit your throat. Be still, and this will all be over soon."

Brother Rei seemed to enjoy every one of the five minutes it took him to shear Rebecca's hair to nothing more than a few ragged patches. She cried the entire time, unable to look at any of the congregation. When he was finished, he set the shears on the long table and let Rebecca fall to the floor, sobbing over the high pile of dirty hair and salty tears.

She felt like an ugly, wretched sinner with the eyes of the world upon her, judging.

**

May 14, last year
Five months BEFORE the Events of Oct. 15
12:15 a.m.

Rebecca had her butt on the toilet and her head in the sink. Guilt had slithered its way through her stomach, then sent her into the bathroom where she lost everything from both ends. No one woke to the sound of her suffering, which was just as well. She sat in her silence and sick, thinking about everything that happened between Alexis and Mother outside the community center.

Rebecca crept back to her room and slipped under the covers, but tossed and turned for another hour or so, crying to herself in whispers and whimpers, "I'm so sorry," she kept crying, her words meant for Alexis, though her sister was a room away.

Finally, she kicked the covers past her knees and swung her feet to the floor. Maybe Alexis was up, too. Maybe she could tell her she was sorry. That would probably make the bad feelings go away so she could finally get to sleep.

Rebecca left her room and crept down the hallway. Her sister's door was closed, so Rebecca opened it a crack and peeked inside. Alexis was wide awake. "Come in," she said.

"I'm so sorry," Rebecca spaced the three words evenly to keep herself from crying.

Alexis didn't say anything for a while, then her teeth defied the darkness with a sudden flash of white. "It's okay," she said. "I get it. I used to be there, too."

"What do you mean?"

Alexis flicked the light on her nightstand, and the dim bulb wrapped the room in its yellowy glow. "Mom's not who you think she is," Alexis said. "Though I totally get why you can't see it now, but believe me, you will."

Rebecca didn't say anything, so Alexis kept talking. "And there's nothing wrong with Robbie. He's a nice guy. You'd like him, too, if you got to know him. Everyone in his family smokes, that doesn't make him a bad guy. He gets straight A's, you know."

"Would Mother like him?"

Alexis shook her head. "Mom wouldn't like anyone except maybe Jesus, and even then she'd probably say I couldn't date him until I was 18, and only if he shaved. I haven't done anything with Robbie, and he hasn't even asked me to. We just danced, and had two kisses is all. But I really, really like him."

"Why do you like him so much?"

"Because, when Robbie looks at me I don't feel like Alexis, the home-schooled freaky girl who has no friends, and who will live and die in this Podunk town. For at least a few minutes, I'm special. Like there's a whole world out there, waiting for me to find it. I feel free and happy. So happy, it almost feels weird. I feel guilty whenever I'm happy, but I know in my heart that's *not* how I'm supposed to feel, despite what Mother says. It's not what God would want."

Alexis pulled her sister's hands into hers, then leaned forward so she could see her clearer through the flickering shadows. "Someday, you'll see Mother for who she is. I can't make it happen faster than it's supposed to happen, but I can promise you it will. I don't know how or when, or even with who, but I know I'm getting out of here someday. The sooner the better. When I'm gone, I won't be able to look out for you anymore. I need you to promise me you won't let this town, or Mother, trap you. Can you do that?"

Rebecca was unsure, but she nodded anyway.

"And I need you to promise me you'll be careful with Mother, too. Can you do that?"

Rebecca was unsure but she nodded anyway.

"I forgive you," Alexis said, squeezing Rebecca's hands tighter. "And I love you. Everything will be okay."

Rebecca lay beside her sister. "I need to go," she said. "I shouldn't be here in the morning when Mother comes to check."

Alexis pet the top of Rebecca's head. "Sshhh ... " she said. "Mother only has the power you give her. Never any more than that."

Rebecca returned to her room. Though she still felt horrible, she now felt something else — a connection to her sister she'd never had before. And with that connection, she fell asleep with a faint smile, remembering how much she loved her.

* * * *

CHAPTER 12
CHARLIE WILKENS

Abrams, Georgia
March 22
1:14 p.m.

Charlie leaned against the metal railing of the overpass, focusing the binoculars on the Walmart just off the highway. They were about an hour north of home, and from what he could tell, the parking lot looked empty of monsters and men.

"I don't see anything," he said to Callie, Adam, and Vic, who stood behind him, each looking through their own sets of binoculars, except Vic, who was staring through the scope on his rifle.

"Me either," Callie said. "Front doors and windows are intact, no signs of looting, and no monsters. Looks good. I think we hit the jackpot."

"Would like to hit *your* jackpot," Vic said with a grin and a wink.

Charlie turned to him, "What did you just say?"

Vic looked at him, and chuckled, "You steppin' up to me, boy? Might wanna reconsider, seeing as how Boricio ain't here to watch your back."

"I don't need anyone to watch shit," Charlie said, stepping forward.

Vic stepped forward, puffing his massive chest, standing almost a foot taller than Charlie and outweighing him by at least 80 pounds of muscle. His face was inches away, eyes boring into Charlie's, hot, alcohol-laced breath steaming his face.

"You think you can take me, boy?"

Charlie's knee was shaking, and he prayed like hell that nobody would notice, especially Callie.

"Come on, guys," Callie said, stepping toward them both, "we're a team, right? Let's get into that store. It looks like it's gonna storm bad."

As if on cue, dark clouds choked all but a sliver of the sun, and the temperature seemed to drop another 10 degrees, turning an already cold morning icy.

Charlie didn't dare break his gaze with Vic. Though the man was huge, psychotic, and had a rifle in his hand, Charlie had something Vic didn't — years of pent-up rage, aimed at guys exactly like Vic. He also had a switchblade in his pocket, one he'd lifted a couple months back and had never let anyone see him holding. He didn't think he'd be quick or agile enough to lunge at Vic with a blade, but if he had Vic down, and Vic didn't know he had it, the element of surprise would be on Charlie's side.

As seconds of silence passed, Charlie started to doubt that his pent-up rage, or his tiny knife, were nearly as useful as they had seemed just moments ago. When it came down to it, he'd never won a fight; he barely ever landed a punch before getting his ass handed right back. No way he could take on a Professional Asshole like Vic in a straight-up match. Fucking with Vic, out here on the highway, almost an hour from home, was a mistake. But he couldn't back down. Too much was on the line.

Vic leaned forward so quickly, Charlie nearly fell backward trying to avoid him. As Charlie caught his balance, Vic laughed his hoarse smoker's laugh, "Oh shit, you shoulda seen your face. Goddamn, boy, you crack me up."

Charlie glared, not sure if Vic were further insulting him, giving him an out, or backing off in a way that made it seem like he were just fucking with Charlie. That was something Bob would've done. Whatever the case, Charlie glanced at Callie, and she had that face that said: *No, not now.*

"Dude, you need to take it easy. That's how guys talk, bro. Callie didn't take offense, did ya, babe?"

Callie smiled, saying "No, Vic" in such a way that didn't show her disgust for the guy, yet didn't encourage more comments. Though she often spoke her mind, and could dish insults with the best of them, she also had an uncanny ability to get out of tricky situations with her words. Charlie admired her diplomacy, always managing to keep everyone friendly, at least to her. It was the opposite of Charlie's uncanny ability to alienate and make an enemy of anyone.

"It's all good," she said.

"We square?" Vic asked Charlie. Though he was smiling, there was a glimmer in his eye, barely hiding his desire to fuck with Charlie some more.

"Yeah," Charlie said, taking the opportunity to save face.

"Then, let's get rollin'," Vic said, climbing back into the cab of the moving truck. "Let's fill this fucker up."

"I dunno," Adam said, as they all got in. "Aren't we close to The Prophet's place? You think this could be a trap? Hard to believe there's a store so close to them that they haven't hit yet."

Adam had a point. They'd seen The Prophet's people a couple of times at stores they intended to hit. It was Adam who'd recognized one of the men, a guy named John. Big dude. While the Prophet's men didn't travel in large numbers, there was no doubt they were more experienced with guns, and that was a fight that neither Charlie, Adam, nor Jeremy wanted. Fortunately, Vic hadn't been with them the few times when they had run into the Prophet's men, so they'd been able to sneak away without a confrontation. But now that Jeremy was dead, Vic was coming with them, and Charlie doubted Vic would ever back down or avoid a fight. The steroid case thought he was invincible, and would cross the street just to find a fight to prove it.

"Trap or not, I don't give a shit," Vic said, finality in his voice. "We're running low on supplies, and we're going in there and taking whatever's there, no matter whose turf this is."

"OK," Charlie said. Though Old Charlie would have been reluctant to go along with Vic's plan, New Charlie was a man of action, particularly if there didn't seem to be much danger. He'd already backed down once this morning, so he would need to do something brave to make up for it, otherwise he'd feel even shittier the next time his head hit the pillow, and he had to lie in the lingering Friend Zone with the fat of his boner.

** **

As they drove into the Walmart parking lot, the clouds continued their war on the sun, now shrouding it completely in gloom.

They hopped from the cabin, and Charlie immediately noticed that the temperature had dropped again, another 10 degrees at least. The wind started to howl, blowing his hair into his eyes.

"That's weird," Adam said, looking up.

Their eyes went to the sky and saw what Adam had already seen. The clouds weren't just moving fast. They were ... forming into something. In the distance, they heard what sounded like a train gathering velocity and volume.

"What the fuck is that?" Vic asked.

The clouds swirled and churned, blacker than clouds had any right to be. There were some weird storms and clouds after the world vanished, but Charlie hadn't seen anything like this. The clouds looked like snakes slithering and weaving in and out of one another, spreading across the sky and racing toward them. The snakes began to reach down, forming into an inverted triangle, reaching down to touch the tree\ line about a quarter mile on the other end of the highway.

No, not a triangle. A funnel.

"Shit!" Charlie said, "It's a tornado!"

"Get in the truck," Vic said.

"No, it's going too fast; get in the store!" Callie said, and began to run to the front doors, which were closed since the store's power was out. She forced the doors open and called out, "Come on!"

Charlie, Vic, and Adam couldn't tear their eyes away from the scene. As the funnel hit the ground, it grew wider, and objects began to get caught in the vortex of swirling darkness and destruction, then sucked into the ceiling of the churning abyss above.

The wind around them howled louder, sounding more like wolves than wind. "Come on!" Charlie shouted, leading the way into the store as Vic and Adam followed. Charlie pulled the doors shut once they all crossed the threshold.

"We supposed to get in a doorway or something?" Adam asked, looking around the store in a half daze.

"Find something heavy to get under," Charlie suggested, though he wasn't certain of the what-to-do-in-a-tornado advice he'd heard, and ignored, a few dozen times in his life.

The wind outside intensified, whistling loudly as it found its way into the store through vents in the ceiling. Rain began to pelt the windows, doors, and roof. Something slammed hard into the doors, cracking, but not breaking the glass, and was whisked away by the wind again before Charlie could see what it was.

The howling grew louder as the concussion of a train thundered through the store.

The four of them looked at one another, no one saying a word.

The sound grew so loud, it hurt to hear it.

"Do you hear that?" Callie asked, her head tilted to the side.

"Who can't? This twister shit is fuckin' loud!" Vic said.

"No, no. Not the train sound, or the howling! It's ... it's something else!" Callie shouted.

Charlie adjusted the frequency of his ears and heard something just above the sound of the howling storm. It was barely there, like the faint crackle and static of a distant radio. But it was familiar, too familiar, in a very unnerving way. Charlie couldn't put his finger on what made the sound so familiar, but it made his flesh pimple with goose bumps and jolted his heart rate into overdrive.

The mysterious sound grew louder, like the storm outside. Then the light bulb went off.

Oh my god! Oh my fucking god!

"What *is* that?" Adam cried, his face perplexed with confusion and dread.

"It sounds like . . . " Callie began.

"CLICKING!" Charlie finished. "The monsters!"

"What the fuck?" Vic said, aiming his rifle at the windows, toward the unseen enemy lurking in the storm.

Something slammed into one of the windows, shattering it as if it had been blasted by a bazooka. Vic trained his scope at the impact site and squeezed off a round that sailed straight through the new opening into the raging whirlwind of rain and debris outside. No kill. No hit. Nothing. Instead, the air pressure vacuum created by the blown-out window channeled flying chunks of glass, dirt, rocks, and other wreckage directly down upon them. The onslaught of winged shrapnel tore at Charlie's face and eyes, scratching him like a demon-possessed razor with a million blades. The rain joined the debris in drenching him from head to foot. "Find cover!" he bellowed as he pulled his shirt over this face and dove behind a foodstuff display stand.

After a few moments' reprieve, he pulled his shirt down and looked around, searching for Callie. But shrapnel found his eyes again instantly, stinging his sight and sending him to the ground, wiping his lenses through his shirt as another explosion of glass triggered behind him. Shards of glass and wind lashed his back, and threw him forward into an overturned shopping cart, knocking the wind from his body. Charlie gulped at the air, trying to catch his breath, crawling over the cart and along the ground, body soaked in rain and blood and wracked in pain as if a hundred hammers and knives had struck him.

The storm howled louder as torrents swept into the store with the force of thunder. His eyes closed, he could only hear the damage, but it sounded like the world was being ripped apart. Shopping carts clanged into shelving; shelves fell like dominoes; objects slammed into the front of the store, and all about the interior walls. Charlie felt like he was the unwitting passenger in a hellish amusement park ride, locked into a death chamber where he couldn't see where the danger was coming from because it was coming from *everywhere*. He cried out for Callie, but his cry was more of an animalistic wail than an assembly of words.

Please, make it stop!

He stopped in his tracks and balled up on the ground, trying to shrink his moving target. The wind and water, however, had other plans and propelled him forward, sliding him into the dark rain of debris at the velocity of a steep water slide. He didn't travel far before colliding with something hard, banging his shoulder and hip into an eruption of pain.

He choked on a scream as his shirt slid from his face and water went into his open mouth. The wind and clicking grew louder as another sound emerged from the chaos.

Metal crunching.

Charlie wiped at his eyes, spit out the water, and felt himself slipping again, carried by the wind and river of water now pouring into the store. The sound of metal crunching amplified. He closed his eyes as he tumbled and slid deeper into the store, slamming into overturned shelves and clothing racks, each banging and bruising him, until he stopped with a hard thud, slamming back first into a solid structure midway through the store, a wall, door, or, maybe a changing room station.

The chaos crescendoed: the storm at its most violent, the whistle of wind at its most menacing, the clicking of god-knows-what terrors close at hand, and the sound of crunching metal deafening. He held tight to the wall and door behind him, and managed to stand and look up, searching for the source of the crunching metal.

That's when he saw it, dark tendrils of storm cloud that looked so solid they could be the curling fingers of some ungodly tornado beast, reaching into a tear in the roof and peeling back the top of the store like the tin of a sardine can.

As the roof tore away in chunks of charred sky, the swirling darkness gathered the debris into itself, feeding itself. Charlie stared in horror as the dark storm sucked items up from the store and swallowed them upward into itself like some kind of unholy vacuum from hell.

"Callie!!" screamed Charlie.

More debris slammed his body from all sides, making his struggle to hold onto the door with one hand while pulling his drenched shirt over his face with the other near-impossible. The moment his shirt was over his face, his fingers were yanked from the door. He flew backward and slammed headfirst into something solid and unmoving.

The last thing he felt was his body flying up and into the terrible storm.

**

Charlie woke up choking, gasping for air, face down in a cold puddle of mud. He turned over, afraid to open his eyes and see whatever was left of the store and his companions.

He was soaked to the bone, battered, and his mouth filled with the copper of blood. Around him was nothing but silence, save for a gentle breeze, which seemed a comical cousin to the hell they'd just faced.

There was a comfort in the darkness of keeping his eyes closed. Something urged him to just go to sleep . . . *surrender.*

No more pain.

No more suffering.

No more bullying, ever again.

No more life in a world of monsters.

Just let go and succumb to the everlasting peace.

The peace seemed so real in his head that a smile cracked his face. His first genuine smile in as long as he could remember. His body felt as if it were rocking gently back and forth in an ocean without a care in the world. He felt that if he kept his eyes closed, and allowed his body to float, it would eventually drift into the everlasting peace that the darkness promised.

So easy. That's it. Just let go.

He wanted to more than anything he'd ever wanted in his life. Let go. The smile on his face spread and he began to cry, at the thought of everlasting happiness.

Not a care in the world.

Just let go.

He thought of his dad, flashing back to a time when he was really young, sitting with his dad on the couch as he read him a story. Something about a train. A smiling, happy train. He remembered looking up to his dad with such awe. This man was His Daddy! Daddies lived forever. They didn't die. They didn't leave you.

Daddy.

Tears streamed from Charlie's eyes.

Let go, son. I'm here. Be with me. We're waiting.

"Dad?" he cried.

"Hello?" a man's cracked voice called out. Not in the darkness, but in the real world, where Charlie lay in a puddle of mud.

"Charlie? Is that you?" It was Vic. He sounded bad.

No, don't go, Charlie. Stay. Close your eyes. Come back to us.

If Vic were alive, though, perhaps Callie was, too.

Charlie turned away from the calm sea of ghosts and sat up, pain pinching his ribs, chest, back, and head simultaneously. He opened his eyes to the blinding, white light of what was left of the morning. Assuming it was still morning. He had no idea how long he'd been out.

His eyes adjusted to the milky-gray fog hanging thick around him. Wisps of gray thinned, allowing him to see maybe 40 yards in any direction. That's when he saw that the ground beneath him was all dirt and mud. No grass. No vegetation. No asphalt. No debris, even, as if the storm had lifted the top layer from the ground and delivered it to hell. He looked around, trying to see beyond the fog, but could find nothing to indicate where he'd been dropped. He assumed if Vic was close by, they couldn't be too far from the store, and maybe Callie and Adam.

"Vic?" he called out as he stood up, triggering an injection of pain throughout his body. He was banged up, but nothing that would keep him from walking.

"Cha-Charlie?" the man said, from somewhere in the fog. His voice sounded pained, but there was something else there, too. Joy that Charlie was there. That he wasn't alone. So Vic *did* need others.

"Is anyone else with you?" Charlie called out as he stepped toward the direction of Vic's voice. "Have you seen Callie or Adam?"

"No, I ain't seen nothin'," Vic said. "Please, help me."

Charlie saw Vic on the ground, sitting up, but holding his left forearm, bleeding onto the man's pants.

"You okay?" Charlie asked as he stepped forward.

Vic looked up, the giant, bald steroid case suddenly seemed fragile, eyes worried. "Something cut me, but I think I'll be okay. I need to find something to stop the bleeding. You got a knife or something? Can you cut my shirt, tie it around my wound?"

The knife.

Charlie reached into his pocket, felt the blade and pulled it out. "You think that'll work?"

"Yeah," Vic said, "I've had worse than this. We'll just need to get home or find a place with equipment, and I'll show you how to stitch this up."

"Stitches?" Charlie said, "I don't know how to do stitches!"

"Don't be such a pussy, man. Just cut my shirt before I bleed out, okay?"

"Yeah," Charlie said as he walked behind Vic and leaned down, looking at where the man's shirt ended and his massive biceps began.

What would Old Charlie do?

Fuck that; what will New Charlie do?

He pushed the small button on the knife, and the blade popped out with an inviting click.

"Come on, man, hurry! I'm gonna bleed out," Vic said, turning back and looking up at Charlie.

Charlie dropped to a knee, grabbed Vic under the chin with his left hand, and twisted Vic's head back, exposing his neck.

Vic tried to escape, but he was too late.

Charlie dug the blade deep into the man's Adam's apple, and then jerked the blade sideways, as hot blood shot all over his hand.

"Wha . . . " was all Vic could manage as he slumped forward clutching the blade.

Charlie let go, stood up, and stepped back, afraid he'd not mortally wounded the man - that Vic would pull the blade out, stand up, and come after him like some kinda Terminator or something.

Oh shit, what did I do?!

Vic pulled the blade out, choking up blood, then looked up to Charlie, eyes filled with anger and confusion.

He tried to say something but all that fell from his mouth was more blood.

Then Vic stopped moving.

Charlie leaned down, grabbed his blade, and wiped the blood off on the dead man's shirt. He wanted to say something like *fuck you, take that you steroid fuck,* or any of the other million, rage-filled thoughts running through his head. But instead, he said nothing. He was simply taking out the trash.

You didn't do victory dances for taking out the trash.

266

Something screamed out in the distance, veiled by the fog.

Callie!

And then another sound. A truck.

Charlie's heart pounded hard in his chest as adrenaline coursed through his system, pushing him forward despite the aches and invisible path before him.

"No!" she cried.

"Callie!" he screamed, not caring if whatever she was scared of heard him. "Callie!"

Another scream, and then the truck revved its engine and took off.

Fuck this fog!

Then silence.

"Callie!"

Charlie raced further forward through the fog as the truck's engine faded into the distance, direction unknown. As he ran forward, the ground unveiled itself, 30 yards at a time through the fog. He prayed he wouldn't find her dead on the ground.

"Callie!" he cried again, as something took form in the fog ahead.

He raced forward, blindly, hand on his blade and heart in his throat, dread coursing through him.

"Charlie?" a voice said from the shadows ahead.

Adam!

Charlie closed the distance and found Adam stumbling toward him, just as bruised and bloodied as Charlie.

"What happened?" Charlie asked.

"They took Callie!"

* * * *

CHAPTER 13
RYAN OLSON

Brookdale, Tennessee
Feb. 17
Nighttime

Ryan woke to an explosion of loud, yet muffled music, which seemed to be drifting in from a nearby apartment.

"What the ... ?" he bolted up in his sleeping bag, momentarily disoriented, feeling around for his rifle, then finding it on the floor beside him in the darkness. He pulled it toward him and slipped his finger over the trigger.

"What is that?" Carmine whispered, stepping into the room, though Ryan could barely see him in the dim light bleeding from the moon.

"What's going on?" Joe called out, way too loud. The clank of his wheelchair clattered across the apartment. Both his voice and noises were loud, even above the riot of the music.

There was a second explosion of music, this time from another nearby apartment. "Stereos!" Ryan said, as he realized with sick dread what was happening.

"What's going on?" Joe said, wheeling himself into the living room.

"Shh," Ryan said, moving in a crouch toward the windows, then peering out at the parking lot below. Sure enough, the music had achieved the desired effect. No fewer than six of the creatures were moving toward the apartment building, targeting the source of the music.

Red Jacket, you sonofabitch!

"He's luring them here," Ryan explained to Carmine, who ran to the window and gasped.

"Who's leading what here?" Joe asked, annoyed and nervous. Maybe afraid, but unwilling to show it in front of his grandson.

"The thug we ran into earlier; the one who got away. I think he came back here and is using the music to lure the monsters to us."

"Monsters?" Joe asked.

That's when Ryan caught Carmine staring at him, trying to throw him a look he wasn't catching. He remembered too late that the boy had not told his gramps of the real danger lurking out there.

Shit.

"There's something I didn't tell you, Gramps," Carmine said, his voice on the verge of breaking. "There are monsters out there." He gestured out the window. "Big, black things that look like aliens or something, with lights under their skin and giant teeth and claws."

Joe laughed, but only until he realized no one else was.

"Wait . . . you're serious?"

Carmine nodded.

"I want you both to go in Joe's room and lock the door," Ryan said. "Don't make a peep!"

"What are you gonna do?" Joe asked.

"We've got two problems: the monsters and whoever turned on the radios. I need to take care of the latter first, then try to lure the monsters away."

"No," Joe said, "You two go. You can run, get away. Go to the roof, bar the door or something."

"No, Gramps, we're not leaving you!" Carmine said.

Ryan stared at the man. Wheelchair or not, this man had balls of steel, willing to sacrifice himself to save his grandson.

Ryan hoped it wouldn't come to that. "I've got a plan," he said, lying like a motherfucker. If he had a plan, his brain had better inform his body what the hell it was. "Go in there. Lock the door. Move the bed to block it, if you can do it quickly. And then stay quiet. You still have the gun I gave you, Carmine?"

Joe's eyes widened, but he didn't protest.

"Yeah, I put it in my room," Carmine said.

"Good. Give it to Joe."

"Remember," Ryan said, "Not a peep."

"Be careful," Joe said. He and Carmine retreated to his room.

Ryan confirmed his rifle was loaded, then slid a box of bullets into his pocket and approached the front door at a creep, hoping like hell Red Jacket wasn't on the other side, waiting to take him out. Ryan figured his odds were good; Red Jacket probably wouldn't hang around too long after rolling out the sonic red carpet for the monsters. Odds are he either holed up in another apartment on one of the higher levels, or he'd gone to the roof. If he were really quick, and had a car, he might have already made it back downstairs and took off to who knows where before the place was overrun.

Pussy. Couldn't fight his own fight, had to get the monsters to do it for him.

Ryan held his breath, forced himself to step into the hall, then let out his breath at the silence of no shots fired. The sound of music, loud rock he didn't recognize, came from either direction: two different sources, two different songs blasting.

Though his ankle was still mostly fire, he limped as quickly as he could to the apartment nearest the stairway. He tried the doorknob. Surprisingly, it wasn't locked. If Ryan were baiting this trap, he would've locked the door to delay entry. Give the monsters more time to find them.

Inside the room, Ryan found a large boom box sitting on top of the dining room table, with a front panel lit up in bright blue. He searched desperately for the off button in the darkness, but with the bright light of the display screen, it was hard to see details of the buttons on top of the device.

"Fuck!" he yelled, turning the radio around with one hand, while the other stayed on the rifle, "Where the hell is it?"

He found the button, small and lit green, on the top, where he should've seen it before, and pressed down hard. The light, and music died, but music from the other end of the hall continued to scream.

He limped into the hall, praying none of the monsters had made it up the stairs yet. They didn't seem terribly bright or fast in his limited experience with them, so he hoped he had another few minutes to throw them off his trail. The hall clear, Ryan pushed himself as fast as he could to the second apartment, then turned the knob. Also unlocked. He slipped into the dark, scanning the darkness for the radio. Judging from the sound, it was in one of the bedrooms. He navigated past furniture toward the back of the apartment, and stumbled into the creeping feeling that he wasn't alone.

He turned and saw a shadow among shadows, flickering in the kitchen. Though he couldn't make out the man's features, he knew who it was. Red Jacket. Waiting.

Ryan raised his rifle — too late.

Red Jacket fired his pistol, the gunshot thundering over the sound of the music.

Ryan stumbled back, then fell against the wall feeling as if someone had hit him in the gut with a baseball bat.

So, this is what it feels like to be shot.

The man stepped from the kitchen, into the scant light seeping through the windows, and aimed his gun at Ryan. "Shoulda left well enough alone, Soldier Boy."

Ryan tried to raise his rifle, but realized too late that his hands were empty. He'd dropped his weapon when the bullet hit. The pain in his gut spread like fire, and he felt dizzy and nauseous, making movement difficult, if not impossible. He wasn't sure if this is what it was like when your body went into shock, but he prayed he would stay conscious. If he closed his eyes, he'd never open them again.

Move, damn it! You can't die like this!

But he couldn't.

Red Jacket leaned down, grabbed the rifle, then went into the back of the apartment and silenced the stereo. Ryan waited in the silence, listening, unable to turn around, waiting for Red Jacket to reappear and finish him off.

Time slowed to a crawl, and Ryan thought of Mary and Paola. He flashed back to the night of his daughter's birth. How scared he'd been, waiting in the emergency room. Mary's water broke seven weeks before Paola was due. They raced to the hospital, Ryan driving like a bat out of hell, pushing his Chevy to 110, fully anticipating a police chase or accident to give their story a different ending, but far too afraid not to drive like a stunt car driver.

The surgeons waited almost 16 hours before deciding they'd have to do a C-section. They said it was routine, but there was "always a chance," however small, that something could go wrong. As Ryan waited in the hallway outside of the operating room while they prepped Mary for surgery, he grew more fearful that something bad would happen — that he'd lose the baby, Mary, or both. He'd never felt more helpless. He tried to tell himself surgeons performed these procedures all the time, and that things almost never went wrong, but nothing gave him comfort.

It was nothing short of a miracle when things *didn't* go wrong, and they handed him his beautiful baby girl. In that moment, every fear and reservation he'd had since Mary said she was pregnant vanished in the purity of his newborn child. Ryan had thought he'd known what love was, but had never known anything like what swelled his heart in that moment.

The pain numbed as Ryan continued to wait for Red Jacket to show himself. He wanted to get up, but his limbs refused to obey.

Instead, he thought more about Paola. And Mary. And all the pain he'd caused them with his affair. He wasn't sure where it had all gone wrong, or why. And now, as his world was about to end, it didn't matter. All he had was regret. He thought again of Paola, and the first time Mary saw her child. She was out of it during the procedure. So she had to wait until the nurse came to Mary's recovery room a couple hours later. The look in Mary's eyes, the happiness and joy, that moment when things weren't perfect, but were so damned right, that moment would be the one he'd cling to as the icy cold of death came to greet him.

Red Jacket finally stepped back into view. Ryan saw only the man's boots and jeans; he was dead enough already to be unable to look up.

The man stood in front of him, quiet. Ryan wondered why he wasn't saying anything. Was he toying with him? Was he thinking of some fucking cheesy movie line like the kind a monologuing villain might give before dispatching the hero?

But then Ryan realized he couldn't even hear the man's breathing. Or his own.

It was as if someone had wrapped gauze around his head. The few sounds that made it through were muffled. For all he knew, Red Jacket was reciting the Declaration of Independence and encoring it with *Born in the U.S.A.*

Ryan couldn't believe it. He was dying.

No last-minute reprieve. No rescue.

This is it.

Suddenly, Red Jacket's legs were gone. Snatched in an instant.

Ryan heard screams – muffled shrieks – and gunfire.

His heart raced as he strained to move and see what was happening. But the connection between his brain and body was severed.

The monsters had gotten into the room, that much he knew. Beyond that, everything was darkness and muffled chaos.

Please God, please don't . . .

More screams, and then something grabbed Ryan's legs and pulled. He slumped from the wall and onto the ground, looking up at the ceiling.

And then it appeared over him, the monster.

Oh God.

Ryan closed his eyes, pictured Mary's bright eyes, so happy and filled with joy. So full of love. So full of ... life.

And then pain.

I love you, girls.

Ryan's body shut down as the darkness swallowed him.

**

Ryan woke to a cool, wet rag dousing his head.

He opened his eyes, and the brightness blinded him. Carmine's face swam into focus as his eyes adjusted to the light.

He was lying on Joe's couch.

"He's awake, Gramps!" the boy said, as excited as a child on Christmas morning.

Ryan tried to move, but his body was still racked with pain. His stomach, back, and neck felt as if they'd been crushed in a giant compressor that stopped just short of breaking every bone in his upper body.

"I thought you was never gonna wake," Joe said, wheeling himself next to Carmine.

"What happened?" Ryan said, nervous and scanning for his rifle, remembering his last moments, as chaos erupted around him.

"You're safe now," Joe said. "That thug is dead and so are the monsters."

"How? Who?" Ryan asked, voice cracked and thin, throat raw.

"Get him some water, will you, Carmine?"

"OK, Gramps," Carmine said, and went into the kitchen.

"I know you told us to stay put, but when a fighter hears all hell breaking loose, he don't hide."

Ryan smiled. *Balls of steel.*

"There were two of them. Not sure where the rest went, but only two made it up the stairs, and we were able to take 'em out. They'd already killed the thug who shot you."

"Thank you," Ryan said as Carmine returned with a bottle of water and brought it to Ryan's lips. Ryan took a sip, nearly choked, causing water to dribble down his chin, then took another sip. The water soothed his throat and felt like the best liquid ever sipped.

"Thank you for saving Carmine," Joe said.

Ryan downed more water, surprised how thirsty he was.

"How long was I out?"

"Five days," Carmine said.

FIVE DAYS?!

"You was in bad shape," Joe said.

"How did you guys heal me?" Ryan asked, reaching to his gut to feel where he'd been shot. The skin was tender, but smooth, hair missing from the area. No stitches or open wound.

"We didn't. Your wounds healed on their own. Like a miracle," Joe said.

Ryan didn't know what to say. Though his body was achy, the pain wasn't nearly as bad as it had been. He tried to sit, and though groggy and stiff, he managed.

"The Lord must've been looking out for you," Joe said. "I never seen a gunshot wound heal that quickly. And the bite wounds are almost all gone, too."

Bite wounds?

* * * *

::EPISODE 10::
(FOURTH EPISODE OF SEASON TWO)
"COLD FRONT"

CHAPTER 1
CALLIE THOMPSON

Abrams, Georgia
March 22
Afternoon

When Callie was small, she used to watch *The Wizard of Oz* with a heavy heart beneath a blanket of sadness, wishing she could be swept away by a tornado, then delivered to a fantastical world with talking scarecrows and tin men with hearts of gold. Instead, her first tornado delivered her to hell.

She woke face down in the mud, body aching, scratches up and down her arms and face, raked by the flying debris. She scrambled around in search of her gun, but found nothing but mud. Her arms were lacerated with fresh cuts. Everything was gone — the store, the parking lot, the trees, and everything else as far as she could see. It was as if God himself had reached down, scooped up the top layer of earth, and tossed it into the heavens.

There was an awful, ashen nothing smothering the world in every direction.

"Charlie! Adam! Vic!"

Where are they?

She wondered if they'd landed safe as she had, or if they'd been torn to pieces inside the belly of the twister or carried God knows how high, before being flung violently to their deaths.

Her cry brought nothing but a windy silence punctuated by the beating of her own heart. The ground beneath her was a mixture of dirt, mud, and the few remaining roots of vegetation. She could vaguely make out small mountains of debris in the distance, probably the remains of the store and every bit of surrounding life. Her eyes strained to find bodies among the tall piles, but a thick fog rolled in from the west and blanketed the world from all sides, imprisoning her vision beneath a gauze of white.

Then, all of a sudden, her stomach inverted and her terror thickened at the sound behind her. In that instant, Callie went from feeling like a single speck on an infinite landscape of nothing to a walking bull's eye, targeted by an unseen enemy.

Click, click, click.

The sound echoed, scurrying in every direction. She turned, scanning the inscrutable for any signs of the creatures, but could see nothing.

She'd heard the clicking in the thick of the tornado, too, though she saw no evidence of the creatures anywhere from within the storm's angry eye. But the storm itself seemed almost alive, sentient in its precision and utter destruction, like it was looking for them. It had certainly found them; maybe the fog had come to finish the job.

"Charlie!" she cried again, as wisps of white fog swirled around her, like cold fingers on her crawling skin.

A shiver ran through her, and she balled her fists, tensing at every shadow, real and imagined. She was a blind woman entering an arena and waiting for arrows to pierce her from all sides. She wanted to call out again, but each time she spoke, it seemed as though the fog sensed it and thickened to strangle her words.

"Charlie!" she called again, damn the consequences.

Nothing.

Then, the fog seemed to part in the distance, opening the curtain to reveal a hint of a structure. *Is that the store? Another building?* Positive identification was too hard as the fog further dimmed her vision and perception of distance. She continued to inch toward the shape, hoping to find Charlie, Adam, or hell, she'd even settle for Vic.

Click, click, click.

The noise now sounded like it was coming from behind, so Callie accelerated her pace, moving faster toward the shape in the fog. It loomed impossibly tall as she drew closer. She squinted her eyes, trying to pull sense from the inscrutable.

I don't remember passing anything that tall. Is it a radio tower?

Radio towers were so commonplace in the urban landscape, they almost blended into the background unless you were looking directly at them. But this shape seemed too solid for a radio tower. She moved faster still, out of curiosity as much as an instinct to evade death and desire to find her companions, until the shape's truth was finally unveiled.

Oh my God!

It was a tower, alright, but not manmade. Now she knew where all the debris had gone. Cars, shards of building, trees, grass, glass, windows, rock, power lines, and everything else were all twisted together, impossibly woven into a giant tower as wide as a shopping center and so tall it vanished into the fog overhead.

It was 20 stories if it was an inch.

Icy talons slithered around her soul and slowed her heart's beat to a snare of terror. Whatever had done this, whether it was nature or supernatural, was powerful, and there was no doubt it was indeed sentient. It knew exactly what it was doing.

This kind of organization couldn't happen by accident. It *had* to be by design.

**

Callie wasn't sure how long she stared at the tower. Her internal clock, which had been pretty damned accurate most of her life, was haywire. And the fog wasn't helping.

She called for Charlie and the others a few more times, continuously moving toward where she thought the highway had to be. Soon, another shadow appeared, and this time, lights came along with it. Truck lights, approaching, maybe 40 yards away.

Charlie?

She waved her hands frantically and called out his name, though she couldn't be certain the driver could see her in the blanket of murk.

The vehicle, which she could now tell was a van, slowed. The driver had seen her. As it got closer, she realized it wasn't Charlie, Adam, or Vic.

Her heart raced as she wondered what to do. If this gang were the bikers they'd run into, she was a dead girl walking.

Click, click, click.

Shit! I have to get out of here!

The van — black, with blacked-out windows — looked like it meant business. She stepped aside as it pulled up and she was facing the blacked-out passenger window. Callie waited for it to roll down, heart in her throat, fists balled, and feet ready to turn and run in an instant. Instead, the side panel door burst open, and two men in black paramilitary gear with giant, black goggles covering the intent of their eyes hopped from the van, darting toward her, rifles in hand.

She turned and dashed into the fog as fast as she could, ignoring the threat of monsters.

The truck revved behind her, though she didn't dare turn to see where it was going. It was angling to head her off, she figured. She got maybe another 10 yards before something struck her in the back of the legs. She tried to jump, but instead, the hard object, a black wooden club like police carried, tangled her legs and sent her sprawling into the cold mud.

Callie flipped over, pain shooting through her legs, and grabbed the club, then rose to her feet, ready to swing. She was too late. She saw the Taser seconds before its wires found her chest, sending an agonizing jolt through her body.

She cried out and crumpled to the ground. Seconds later, the van pulled up, and the two commandos threw her unceremoniously inside the back. As the door swung closed and the van drove away, she swore she could hear Charlie screaming her name.

"Who the hell are you?" Callie shouted as one of the men twisted her arms behind her, restraining them with some kind of wire she couldn't see. The binding chewed hard into her wrists.

"Ow!" she screamed, kicking at the man in front of her, catching him in the crotch.

He screamed, cocked his arm back, and swung hard. His punch landed in her chest, forcefully knocking the wind from her body.

As she gasped for air, the man behind her slid a rag over her face. The funny scent made her feel woozy on contact. As Callie slipped into the inescapable surrender of nothing, she spied a patch on the arm of her attacker's jacket, which answered her question as to who the hell these people were.

The patch read, *Black Mountain Research Facility.*

* * * *

CHAPTER 2
CHARLIE WILKENS

Abrams, Georgia
March 22
Afternoon

"Who took her?!" Charlie screamed at Adam.

"I don't know. A black van and men in black."

"Why didn't you *do* something?" Charlie screamed, pushing Adam hard. "Why didn't you stop them?!"

"With what?!" Adam cried, holding out his empty, gunless hands. "They had all kinds of weapons. Big ones. They looked like military."

"Military?"

"Yeah, or SWAT, or something. They had tons of equipment, all over them. They looked deadly serious."

Charlie stared into the fog, as if he might somehow divine answers from the nothingness surrounding them. There weren't any answers, but there *was* something else in the fog.

He heard it seconds before the shadow passed them.

Click, click, click, click.

"Shh!" he said to Adam, scouring the ground for anything Adam could use as a weapon. Finding nothing, Charlie flicked open his knife, then pivoted in circles, trying to discern where the monster was.

Click, click, click.

The shadow, with the weird illumination beneath its skin, moved past them again, this time closer.

Is it toying with us?

Adam drew closer, eyes wide and full of terror. He balled his fists, as if he could somehow conquer the creatures with his knuckles alone.

Click, click, click.

Movement again, then nothing. The fog thickened around them, as if it and the monster were partners in crime.

"I'm scared," Adam wheezed.

Movement again. Adam screamed and jumped back, holding his bleeding left arm. The cut wasn't deep, but it looked nasty.

Charlie spun around, knife poised to strike. "Come on, you fucker!" he screamed.

Click, click, click

Charlie spun around, but it had disappeared again into the mist.

Adam looked up, eyes tearing, "It hurts so bad."

"Stop crying!" Charlie said, annoyed. They didn't have time for crying. Or weakness. He felt bad that Adam was hurt, but there was nothing Charlie could do, except what he was doing: waiting for a chance to strike back.

Click, click, click.

Charlie turned again as the creature flashed by, colliding into him hard. The knife slipped from Charlie's hand and fell to the ground.

Click, click, click.

The creature scurried toward the fallen blade.

Charlie couldn't afford to lose his only weapon. He screamed and dove to the cold, muddy ground, launching himself into the creature and sending it veering off course. Miraculously, Charlie wound up next to his knife. He grabbed it just as the creature recovered itself, stood and shrieked, opening its mouth wide to reveal its rows of horribly jagged teeth, like the charred maw of an alien wolf.

The creature leaped up, at least 10 feet high, then fell on top of Charlie hard, raising a clawed hand.

Charlie thrust his knife up quickly into the creature's androgynous crotch. The creature unleashed an ear-piercing scream and collapsed to the ground, twitching. Adrenaline coursing his every vein, Charlie rolled over, hopped onto the creature's slick, wet body, and brought his blade down into its chest, head, and eyes with repeated ferocity.

"Die! Die! Die!" he screamed as the creature's black blood spurted from the holes Charlie peppered in its flesh. He kept stabbing until the creature was nothing more than a mangled, shuddering mess.

"I think it's dead," Adam said, approaching Charlie cautiously, tail between his legs. Charlie was sick of Adam's dead weight and scared puppy routine. He was pissed and wanted to lash out at something, and right now; kicking a scared puppy seemed like a great idea. He fought the urge, got up, and started walking away before he took out his rage on Adam.

"Where you going?" Adam called, but Charlie ignored him, walking into the fog with no idea where the hell he was headed.

**

Charlie found the highway, or where the highway had been before the tornado tore it to nothing. The fog was still soup-thick; he couldn't see far enough to figure which way was which, so he simply started walking along the broken path of where the highway had been, hoping it would lead them back to Boricio HQ. Adam was following him, though at a distance, likely afraid to get too close and rekindle the fire of Charlie's anger.

After 20 minutes, the road appeared, in chunks of asphalt at first, then the full road. Ten minutes later, Charlie saw a sign indicating he was traveling south, which was the right direction. The fog had cleared, replaced by a light-gray sky. Soon, the lightest drizzle of snow started to descend from the heavens.

If there is still a heaven.

Shivering and damp from the storm, Charlie continued forward, hoping to locate a usable vehicle. And soon. He kept walking, freezing, teeth chattering, with every muscle in his body on fire. He'd been surviving on anger alone, but that anger wouldn't carry him much farther. They had to be at least 60 miles away from HQ, if not more. No way he'd make it that far in his present condition. And if he was going to save Callie, he had to get back. Boricio would know what to do. Boricio always had an answer.

He'd find the fuckers who took Callie. They'd regret fucking with Team Boricio.

His mind erupted with images of the unholy hell Boricio would rain down upon them. Charlie couldn't help but smile.

**

Time eventually lost all bearing. It seemed like forever since he'd seen any sign of civilization. The snow was falling harder, and was nearly as thick as the fog had been, his visibility compromised yet again.

We have to find a car. Soon.

The thought of "we" caused Charlie to turn around, and look back for Adam. But Adam was gone.

Fuck him. Better off without him slowing me down.

Charlie pivoted back and kept walking.

Just as he did, he saw something in the distance, maybe a car in the road. His languishing heart found traction and sped up, as did his feet, fueled by fresh hope. When he reached the car, an old maroon Caddie, he nearly screamed in joy. He looked back for Adam on impulse, to tell him the good news, but Adam still wasn't there.

Oh well.

He opened the car door and found keys in the ignition.

Yes!

He turned the key.

Nothing.

Shit!

He turned it again.

Still nothing.

Yes, the keys had been in the ignition, but the car had also been left on, meaning it ran dry of gas and exhausted its battery long ago.

"Fuck!" he screamed as he slammed his fists against the steering wheel.

Instant pain from fist to shoulder was the prize for his loss of control. Anger wasn't going to magically turn the engine, nor keep him warm in the constricting cocoon of white death. Outside, the snowstorm had become a howling blizzard, reducing the world to a thick wall of white.

Like the fog, but freezing.

He was exhausted, in pain, and trembling. Abandoning the shelter of the car to confront the cold kiss of the storm was suicide. So he hunkered down and waited. He hoped Adam was smart enough to find him and get out of the cold, too. But he was too exhausted to worry about Adam.

Charlie reclined the front seat, leaned his head against the headrest, and closed his eyes. *Maybe just a few winks.*

As he drifted off, memories of a movie where the hero was fighting sleep in the cold flashed behind his eyes. There was danger there, something about if he fell asleep, he would never wake up.

Don't fall asleep, or you won't save Callie.

Charlie opened his eyes, trying to shake himself free from the seduction of sleep. But within minutes, his eyelids grew heavy again.

Just a few minutes . . .

Charlie closed his eyes, tired of fighting, and surrendered.

* * * *

CHAPTER 3
MARY OLSON

Kingsland, Alabama
The Sanctuary
March 24
9:06 a.m.

Mary sat on the toilet, holding her stomach. She hoped she wasn't coming down with something. Aside from the occasional bout of sniffles, she almost never got sick. There was nothing like a boiling stomach, rolling in anger and making you too stupid to think straight. She needed to be stronger than ever, not struck by the lightning of an oncoming virus. She didn't dare consider what the flu might do to her body now that modern medicine was a memory.

Maybe it wasn't the flu, but stress. Stress could certainly tear a body in two. And she'd had more than her share recently, with what had happened to poor Rebecca and all. It was awful, punishing an innocent girl like she was Devil's seed, shearing her hair to nothing and locking her in a wooden box for a little more than being a normal 13-year-old girl. The end of the world didn't entitle anyone to forget human decency, compassion, and fairness. Such predatory behavior was vicious, befitting of wolves, not people. And those who allowed it to happen without a word of protest? Sheep.

As awful as all of it was, Mary had the hardest time with the part played by the girl's mother, Sarah. Not only had Sarah done nothing to stop it, she'd fueled the fire and fanned the flames. What sort of mother would do that? If that had been Paola, The Prophet would've needed Rei and every other "brother" in the compound to keep her nails from clawing the color from his face. Sarah had practically issued the directive to lock her daughter away.

Punish the sinner. Punish the sinner now, while there is still time to save her soul, before she joins her sister in The Lake of Fire.

The cruelty of Sarah's words was a ragged blade digging into her spine. Mary shuddered, continuing to rock back and forth on the toilet in a self-embrace.

Mary was so enraged, she wasn't sure whether it was the sick in her stomach or the sick in her soul that had driven her from the lunch table and into the bathroom for the first time that day. This was the second. The space in the middle had been spent outside in the garden with Desmond and Will.

**

The garden was at the back of the property, behind the hangar, a favorite spot for the three grown-ups in their group. While Linc was technically part of their group, he'd been steadily spending more time with the members of the church, which left Mary feeling like Desmond and Will were the only adults she could truly count on here.

The garden had two long stone benches. The trio always sat on one, Desmond and Will on either side with Mary in the middle, huddled close together to ensure their chatter didn't carry too far.

"You should've seen it, Mary," Desmond whispered. "It was some fucked up shit, the way they got their 'confession.' If I was a kid like Carl, getting tortured by a pious dickhead like Rei, I would've confessed to stealing the Lindbergh baby!" He shook his head. "Rei's every word was insidiously chosen to led the boy down a series of feelings and then fed him the answers they wanted from him. Carl didn't stand a chance. It was expert manipulation and mind control!"

"What did he say?" Mary asked. "Rei, I mean. Not Carl."

Desmond gritted his teeth. "I remember it word for word: *'Do it for both of you. The punishment for girls is far less strict than it will be for you. You will be helping both of you by admitting the truth. The Prophet is a great man, a loving man. He'll be looking for any excuse to show mercy on the child. Give him one, Carl. Allow God's grace to spare your life.'* I'm telling you both, if I'd had my gun I might've emptied it on 'Brother' Rei. Maybe John, too."

Will whistled as Desmond finished his eerie impression of Rei. "Des is right. I thought I was gonna have to pull him back."

"What did Carl say?" Mary asked Desmond.

"The only thing he knew that would get the shackles off his wrists. Rei didn't really give him a choice; he told Carl to admit that Rebecca seduced him. You should've seen that asshole's smile, like a pedophile clown at a kid's birthday party. Carl started crying, saying that, *'Yeah, that's exactly how it happened, the picnic was all Rebecca's idea,'* and adding that he only agreed because the devil made him do it. He finished with, 'and that's the honest truth.' Rei just kept on smiling his pedoclown smile, then signed his masterpiece with, 'The truth shall set ye free.' The 'ye' made me want to crack his skull. John was just sitting there watching the farce play out, enjoying every moment. Worse, he was watching me watch them! I don't know if this was some kind of power play by John, a 'look what we can do if you step out of line,' or if he honestly felt that I needed to see how 'justice' was handled here." Desmond shook his head, teeth gritted, stewing.

"I don't mean to piss in the pool," Will said, "but is it possible Rei was actually *looking out* for Carl? Carl could have been sentenced to death for taking Rebecca into the woods. And since all the courthouses are empty, there isn't anyone gonna stop them here. If Carl pleaded guilty to a lesser charge, his life was spared, like copping to manslaughter instead of murder. You do a little time, but don't get the needle. I'm not saying it's right; I'm saying that's the way it is. We may not like the pews, but that's where we're sitting."

"What sort of fucked up religion kills kids for being kids?" retorted Desmond.

Mary didn't think Desmond was really hunting for an answer. She said, "I think we should leave The Sanctuary. We're not safe here, not anymore. I want to go now, before it's too late. What if someone misinterprets Luca and Paola holding hands or something?"

She rubbed her hand along Desmond's shoulder, then turned to Will. "Do you *really* want to wait until something happens to one of ours before deciding to leave? We've felt unsettled since the day we arrived here, and we're only sinking deeper. So, why are we staying? What are we afraid of? The monsters out there? I'm starting to think that maybe they're not as bad as the ones in here. At least they click, letting you know when they're coming."

Will sighed, then sagged on the back of the stone bench and tugged on his beard. He was tugging for nearly a full minute while everyone gave him the quiet to think, then he swung his right ankle atop his left knee and leaned in toward Mary. "Look, Mary, I hear ya. And if you wanna leave tomorrow, I'll tip my hat and say toodaloo to this place along with you. But I think it'd be wrong. I think we'd be in more danger than we are now. But hell, that's like sprinkling salt on a salt lick and saying it's saltier. We're in danger no matter what we do. But I think we should stay. Better to stay with the devil you know, or can at least understand, than the devil you don't, which is the bleakers. Even so, you wanna go, I'll go right along with you, and make sure the kids know I think it's the best idea ever."

Desmond said, "Why don't you just tell her 'no.' That would be better than the, *sure you can do it if you want us all dead* speech."

"I said it like I meant it," Will replied, resuming the tugging on his beard. "What we're seeing behind these walls is easier to understand than whatever's out there," he nodded toward the gate. "I may not know what all this means, but something is telling me this isn't where we're supposed to go, but it is where we're supposed to wait. Someone's been letting me look on things from up high for a while now. I figure, if someone's kind enough to show me things I need to see before I need to see them, I'm a damned fool to turn my eyes."

"I don't care about your dreams," Mary said, bluntly. There was no time for sparing Will's feelings when her child's life might be in danger. "Not anymore. I want out. I want to feel safe! The world's full of monsters, but that doesn't mean I have to sleep in their house. I don't want to raise my child, or Luca, anywhere near these wackos."

"*Religious* wackos," Desmond added.

"Just because you don't understand something, doesn't make it wacko," Will said. "Religion isn't evil just on account of it being religion."

"You're a man of science, Will." Desmond shook his head. "You don't believe in the religious shit these people are peddling, do you? And who the hell is this guy to claim himself 'The Prophet?'"

"I don't think science and religion are mutually exclusive. I don't have to believe in a big man with a long beard to see that there's order in the chaos, that there *could be* an architect of creation. And if someone, or something, whether it be God or something else, is revealing the future to me in my dreams, then maybe the same thing is true for The Prophet. Maybe his world is dictated by things he's seen, or whoever made certain he saw them."

Will stood from the bench and started pacing, like he usually did after sitting for more than five minutes straight. "Let's give God a rest from the conversation. This isn't about Him. Let's agree, at least for the length of this conversation, that there's more to life than the physical existence we're living in right now. Let's say there's an underlying reality where energy, and maybe consciousness, can give birth to particles and matter. If that's true, it would mean you could basically push yourself into forever."

Mary stared blankly at Will, not sure where he was going with this.

Will turned from Desmond to her and said, "I'll melt some ice in the theory so it's easier to drink. Has Paola ever played video games?"

"Sure," Mary said.

"She have a favorite?"

"Yeah, she loved the Zelda games."

Will said, "That's Nintendo, right? With the elf kid in green with the big sword, right?" The memory of the game made Mary smile. She nodded, then Will went on. "Someone, or a group of people, thought up the game. Then it existed, right? I mean, sure, you had coders and artists and everyone else who made it reality, but it didn't exist until it did, and it was the idea that made it happen. Once that world is built, it's there forever. Now, I'm not some old man off his rocker who thinks *Toy Story* is a docudrama; I'm merely trying to draw an analogy. What if we can *create* worlds to inhabit? What if we are doing so right now, and we don't even realize it?"

"That's a weak analogy," rebuffed Desmond. "Even if it comes close to explaining an afterlife, which is what I think you're getting at, it doesn't come anywhere near an explanation for the fairytales and illusion of organized religion."

"Sure, my beliefs may be fed by a longing to fly past my death," Will conceded, "but that right there is the place where science and I split for a while. Science likes to give a finger to faith because it's only looking for truth. But that's forgetting the fact that faith is an egg until a new truth hatches. Name one scientific discovery that didn't start with an unsubstantiated belief. Wasn't too long ago when an atom couldn't be split."

Mary said, "And Pluto used to be a planet."

"That it did." Will laughed, then continued. "Maybe space and distance are only illusions. It's just the way things look to us since we can't see, or fathom, the larger construct that is reality. It's like how the colorblind can never know the true of a red. People claiming to know God might know there's *something* out there, because they feel it, like breath in the air. And maybe religion is the only name they've got for it, so they sculpt it in their own image, with their own prejudices and laws and such, but it's something to believe in. It may be a light year from the truth, but it's the closest they know. If science can't accept that religion might be more than fairytales and magic tricks, well, that's its own shortcoming. Or was. I'm keeping an open mind, though. I've seen too much, been through too much, not to. I don't know what's guiding me, but I know what happens when I start to doubt it or fail to heed the warnings."

Desmond said, "Listen, I respect your mind, Will. You and I agree on a lot of things, and I appreciate all you've done for us. But we need to start thinking more logically and less superstitiously. Mary is right; we need to get the hell out of here ASAP."

"That's not what I'm doing at all," started Will. But Desmond didn't let him finish.

"You talk about science, and offer respect for scientific research. But right now you sound like a man of faith, not science; a man of faith who doesn't subject his irrational beliefs to the same scrutiny he would a controlled experiment or peer review. That's all fine, as long as you're not trying to convince me there's science behind your dreams."

"There's science behind everything," parleyed Will.

"Forget science then," Desmond's voice was showing his impatience. "Why are you looking for something outside your physical existence in the first place? Do you know something about physical limits that we don't? Why do you need more than physical reality? Fire, water, glass; wind, rain and snow; human touch, laughter, sex. The physical world is all around us; don't you think that's magic enough already? Aren't the millions of years of evolution, countless species in an impossible number of variations, and the inarguable intelligence of man enough for you?"

"Sure they are," Will smiled, "but that doesn't mean there isn't a whole helluva lot more."

Now Mary was standing, her stomach turning again, a cold sweat on her brow. "I'm sure you two could argue forever, but we need to make up our minds, do we stay here or do we ... "

That was when John appeared from nowhere. "You're not thinking of leaving now, are you?" he said, quickly approaching the bench until he was standing a few feet from the group. "The Prophet has let you into his home. I can't imagine he would take kindly to your sudden departure."

John smiled, and after a few seconds, he nodded, then walked off in the other direction.

**

Mary wasn't sure if it had been John's sudden appearance or something else that had sent her scurrying up the stairs and into the bathroom, but that's where she'd been sitting since, sick as a dog.

* * * *

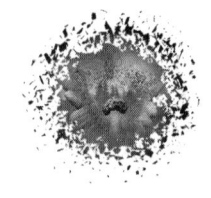

CHAPTER 4
EDWARD KEENAN

Ed glanced over at Brent Foster sitting shotgun next to him as they sped toward Georgia in a world without speed limits, hunting a man named Boricio.

Did I choose the right ally in Brent? Does he have what it takes to see this through 'til the end?

Brent's lack of combat training didn't exactly make him the kind of guy you'd want beside you in the field. But he was passionate, almost impossibly so. And there was something about him that made Ed trust him immediately, even if Brent *were* contemplating some sort of attack against him or someone else high ranking at Black Island.

Who could blame him? He was willing to do whatever he needed to protect his family, even if they'd been reduced to zombies. And protecting them was tantamount to suicide. Ed could understand, if not respect, that sort of foolish dedication.

As one desolate town piled on top of another, Brent grew uncharacteristically quiet. He was probably lost in thoughts, perhaps dealing with feelings of guilt over giving up on the creatures that were parallels of his wife and son. Though they were alternate versions of his family, he clearly felt for them. But they weren't his true family, and they couldn't be saved. The scientists at Black Island Research Facility were conducting their secret experiments, something the Ed Keenan of this world – his parallel – told him was for the greater good. When the government said something was for "the greater good," it usually meant someone was going to die. That was the way of the world, a reality Ed was no stranger to. He'd participated in many dubious acts, ostensibly for the greater good. He'd believed in his missions and government, until they turned on him.

Had that also been for the greater good?

Ed tried not to dwell on a past that would only serve to pull him from his present mission, a mission for the greater good, of course.

Finally, Brent broke a few hours of silence. "So, Captain, what is it about this Boricio guy that has you so charged up?"

"I don't know, and call me Ed. None of this captain shit when we're not on base."

"Okay, Ed. So, there's got to be something special about him, right? Do they think he knows what happened? Or that he's behind it? Or even that he has some kind of cure for the infected?"

"They didn't tell me much. They gave me a picture; how the hell they got that, I don't know, unless he's a parallel of someone here. But I know they want to get to him before Black Mountain finds him."

"Black *Mountain*?" Brent asked. "Like Black Island?"

"Yes and no. They started out the same. But it seems the group in Georgia went rogue. We're not even sure they're still here or that there are any survivors. But if they're alive, there's an excellent chance they're looking for Boricio, too."

"And they couldn't tell you why?" Brent asked as if he didn't believe Ed.

"Is it so hard to believe they only tell me what I need to know?"

"You seem like the type who would insist on needing to know *everything*."

Ed smiled, "Fair enough. And you're right. But in this case, the details are sensitive. Even if I did know, I wouldn't tell you. Suffice it to say, they want this guy, so we need to find him first and convince him to come back with us. What happens after that, I don't know."

Brent was quiet a while longer, then asked, "Have you seen your daughter?"

A grenade of emotion detonated within Ed's every ounce of being.

"No. They showed me pictures, but I don't know where they have her or the other girl, Teagan."

"The one with the baby?"

"If the baby lived, yes."

"I haven't seen any babies on the island," Brent said. "And I don't remember Jane telling me about having to watch any."

"Like I said, I don't know. They're keeping mum."

"Why tell you about your daughter's status, but not the other girl?"

"My guess is something bad happened and they don't want to upset me."

"You think she's dead?"

Ed looked at Brent, "You sure are chatty."

"Sorry," Brent said, "I just like to know what's going on, what's at stake."

After a few moments, Brent spoke again, "I gotta ask you something that's been gnawing at me since the other night, when you went all parallel universe on me: Why did you pick me?"

"I told you. Michael is dead. I need someone I can trust. Though, Michael was a hell of a lot less chatty."

"Yeah, but you hardly know me. And this *is* a Black Island-sanctioned mission, right? If that's the case, why not just take any of the other men who are surely more equipped to get your back? What are we *really* doing here?"

Ed looked at Brent and grinned, "Anyone ever tell you that you ask too many questions?"

"Every day at my old job," Brent said, smiling back. "So, is that an evasion or the opening to an answer?"

Maybe this guy has better field sense than I thought; he can sure smell out answers.

"Here's the deal," Ed drummed his thumbs on the steering wheel. "I can't trust everyone on Black Island. I knew Michael was clean, but I have my suspicions about others. They have a mole, someone working in the interests of Black Mountain. Maybe even a few people; I'm not sure. I can't go into the how's and why's, but I'm fairly certain the place has been compromised. And the mole may even be among the original six."

"Original six?" Brent asked.

"There is a room in Black Island that seems to have been spared whatever happened on October 15. I'm thinking there's a reason for that, and it might not be a good reason. Six people from this world survived, including my parallel, Sullivan, and four scientists. I have reason to believe that one or more of them are complicit in the events of October 15, and I'm not sure they want us to succeed in finding Boricio. This mission is critical; I need at least one other person with no connections to anyone. And I have a good feeling about you."

"Good feeling?" Brent asked suspiciously.

"OK, I've been watching you, and so far, you *seem* clean. Well, clean for a journalist, anyway."

Brent laughed.

They drove a while longer, the weather growing uglier with every mile. They drove through a few patches of rain and were now getting some snow, which slicked the empty roads. This was the first snow Ed had seen all season, and so late in winter, too. There were a few people at Black Island researching weather patterns; he'd even seen video of a bizarre tornado, bigger by far than anything ever captured on camera. It grabbed an entire city, then threw it down in a stack of debris as though it were cleaning a house and sweeping dust into a corner. Weird shit. Ed found himself wondering if the weird storms were an extension of the aliens in some way. He hoped not. If the storms *were* an alien creation, God help the humans who tried to survive them.

Brent had been quiet a while. Ed looked over to see that he'd fallen asleep, his head on the passenger window.

Would he have gone through with his crazy plan if I hadn't intervened? Would he have been able to infect someone as he intended? And, God, what would the consequences have been?

Ed supposed it didn't matter. The people in charge wouldn't have let Brent leave with two infected people, no matter whom he had as a hostage. Ed had played out extraction scenarios in his head a hundred times, imagining how he'd rescue his daughter. It wasn't feasible; a facility like Black Island had too many fail-safes to allow someone to slip in and out without harm. And while Ed might be able to defeat the security, and even reach to his daughter, he doubted he could escape in a manner that wouldn't put her at mortal risk.

And risking Jade wasn't an option. She'd already suffered enough from the curse of being his daughter.

The way he figured it, they had no reason to harm her; there was nothing to gain in pissing him off by hurting her, especially when they allowed so many civilians to live on the island unmolested. Plus, their stated goal of trying to rebuild society seemed genuine enough, at least on the face of it. But that meant they would have to do everything that needed to be done to protect that goal, no matter who was in their way. So, Ed would play ball. He'd worked for worse people, after all.

His parallel, the other Keenan, said his daughter would remain safe. Ed trusted him with that much. Keenan 2 had lived a slightly different life, a daughterless one, and Ed figured that though she was not his flesh and blood, that there may be some sort of connection which would keep her safe for a little while, anyway. Ed knew that Keenan 2 wasn't the puppet master. Second in command, maybe. But not in charge. Someone else was pulling the strings behind the scenes, isolated from everyone and everything, using Keenan 2 as an intermediary. As Ed continued driving through a world growing whiter, he wondered if he'd ever find out who was really the man behind the curtain at Black Island.

Is there a seventh person?

**

They reached the east coast of Georgia by nightfall. They arrived by way of Interstate 95, though there were several times when they had to find a detour around some obstruction, one of the many new travel norms of their brave new world.

Ed decided to locate a hotel to stay at for the night. They'd need a solid night's rest before searching for Boricio in the morning. He had a feeling they'd need every watt of energy their bodies could produce, especially if they came across anyone from Black Mountain. He found a newer-looking Holiday Inn off the highway, which looked nice and alien-free. The hotel was a free-standing building at the end of a shopping plaza that included a few restaurants, a Home Depot, a department store, a small grocery store chain he'd never heard of, and four different banks. He chuckled at the plethora of banks in this world as well as his own.

He cut the lights as he pulled into the hotel's parking lot, which was 60 percent full from the guests who involuntarily checked out on Oct. 15, then waited 10 minutes to scout the scene for any aliens. None showed.

They grabbed their gear and headed inside. On instinct, he began securing the perimeter, once inside. He locked the lobby's glass double doors. He checked the side doors and confirmed they couldn't be opened from the outside without a key card (which wouldn't work anyway without electricity), then headed up seven flights of stairs, banging their rifles and shouting the entire time, to attract anything that might be inside the hotel to come out now, rather than later when they weren't prepared.

All the noise was for naught; the hotel was a ghost town.

They found a room with two queen beds and a small kitchen suite. Ed drew the drapes and lit a few of the small, battery-operated lanterns he'd brought, placing them along the floor in the bathroom to cast just enough light into the main room so that they could see without broadcasting their location beyond the thick hotel curtains.

"Hope you like canned pasta," Ed mused, opening a duffel bag and tossing Brent a can of spaghetti and meatballs.

"You didn't bring a hotplate or anything?" Brent asked.

"We don't want to cook anything; that would attract attention."

"Ah," Brent said, pulling the tab on his can. Ed handed him a plastic fork, and they dug into their dinners.

"Not exactly Jane's cooking, but surprisingly not horrible." Brent said.

Ed sat on the floor, scooping food from his can, ignoring Brent's many attempts to start a conversation. He never understood why people wanted to talk while they were eating. He put up with it from his family, since he figured that's what he was expected to do. But that didn't mean he'd put up with other people doing it. People talking during dinner may as well have been fingernails on a chalkboard.

"What's the worst thing you ever had to eat?" Brent continued, deaf and blind to Ed's uncommunicative posture.

"I ate a spider once, does that count?" Ed said, hoping to end the conversation.

"What the hell?" Brent said, nearly spitting out his food. "Really?"

Ed couldn't help but laugh.

"You've gotta do what you've gotta do. It wasn't terrible. They're not as bad as people say. Well, until I realized it was pregnant. Oh, what a mess that was. Little baby spiders spilling out all over the place. Kinda looked like wet, dark pieces of pasta, actually."

"Stop!" Brent said, looking like he might vomit.

Ed smiled. *Good, now I can eat in peace.*

He shoved a meatball into his mouth as Brent dipped his uneaten forkful of pasta back into the can.

**

Sleep took them by 10 p.m. Ed didn't bother structuring night shifts as he didn't anticipate any problems, none at least that he couldn't handle with an open bag of ammunition at his bedside.

Once asleep, he dreamed he was in a field of tall grass that stretched to forever. The voice he'd been dreaming of was back. Brent was also there, walking beside him, looking down at a map.

"You're close," the voice said.

"Who's that?" Brent asked.

"You can hear it?" Ed said, surprised.

"Yeah, who is that?"

307

"If you can hear it, you don't need to ask," Ed said, not intending to be cryptic, though it wasn't like he was the one choosing his words. The voice was speaking through him.

Brent looked back down at his map. "I see it here."

Ed stared at the map, too, which looked like one of those old treasure maps you used to see in movies and comic books, with a big, red X.

"Uh-oh," Brent said. "It knows we're here."

Ed looked at him, confused. Was the voice now speaking through Brent? Who, or what, was "it?"

Overhead, the sky grew instantly black, darkness spreading like spilled ink in clear water, canvassing the world. Wind and rain were on sudden assault everywhere around them, whipping the long blades of grass against their faces in stinging lashes. The wind howled like a scattered pack of wounded animals, crying at once from every direction.

Ed closed his eyes, lifting an arm to cover his face, pushing through the grass.

"Keep going!" he shouted to Brent, as they pushed blindly into the thrashing sea.

The assault ended as suddenly as it began, though the darkness still churned overhead. When Ed gazed around, Brent was gone. He turned, searching, and called out, "Brent!"

And then he heard the sound of a child singing. He couldn't tell if the voice was that of a boy or girl. The melody sounded like a religious hymn, though he couldn't make out the words.

He continued forward until he spotted a church steeple peeking over the grass.

"Brent?!"

Nothing but the child's singing, coming from the church. He was close enough to determine the tune – *Jesus Loves Me* – but was still too far to decipher the words.

He raced forward and came out into a clearing in front of a church, standing before a barracks-neat row of three houses in the background. In front of the church were six giant wooden crosses. The child, in a white robe, was knelt down singing in front of one of the crosses.

Oh my god, someone's nailed to it.

Ed moved closer as the child's singing continued.

"The Darkness loves me! This I know,
for The Prophet tells me so."

His slowed his gate as he locked onto the bulging dead eyes of the man on the cross.

Brent.

Brent had been crucified, nailed in place through his hands and shins. His limp mouth hung agape, tongue savagely removed. Dried blood had pooled in the stubble upon his chin. He smelled of death. A crude mark had been etched into the flesh of his chest. Ed stepped closer to make it out. It was a number, 9.

"Little ones to Him belong;
They are weak but He is strong."

And then the singing stopped.

* * * *

CHAPTER 5
LUCA HARDING

Kingsland, Alabama
The Sanctuary
March 24
11:07 a.m.

Everything had been weird since yesterday.

Mary, Will, and Desmond weren't talking with the others too much. They seemed angry at Rebecca's mom and The Prophet.

Luca wanted to be angry at the people for punishing Rebecca, cutting all her hair off and making her cry. And he *was* angry, at first. But then he began to pick up on all the feelings of the people like radio signals and realized that things weren't as simple as he'd first thought.

When he focused in these frequencies, he learned that some of the people were mad at Rebecca and Carl, but most were afraid for them. That meant they were acting out of fear, not anger. And while Rebecca's mom, Sarah, seemed angriest of all, she wasn't really. She was actually the most afraid, convinced her daughter was going to hell and thus doing what she believed was right. Luca's radar was intercepting more than just sensory feelings, though. He was sometimes catching snippets of actual dialogue. At first, he thought he was overhearing bits of conversations. But no one was ever talking. That could only mean one of two things:

I'm hearing their inner thoughts, or maybe the voices that normally speak to me are now communicating via other people's voices in some attempt to trick me.

After morning class, Luca and Scott headed to the church for their construction shifts. They weren't old or skilled enough to be trusted with the hard work, so they spent most of their time prepping work areas and cleaning up for the men who were building the church. Most of the time, they sat back, watching, and talked to one another. Scott was nice and told funny jokes, though not as funny as Jimmy's had been.

Scott was like a PG-13 version of Jimmy, which was okay, and he might have seemed funnier if Luca were still 8. But his own thoughts felt more grown-up than they used to. Things he once thought were funny he now found silly, even babyish. But his thoughts still didn't feel as grown up as his outside had become, though he really wasn't certain what being an adult felt like. Luca felt trapped between child and adult, ping-ponging between the two. As weird as it was to him, he was sure it was weirder for those around him. Paola and Scott were still talking to him like he was a little kid, when they talked to him at all.

Scott was telling one of his corny jokes, something about a llama walking into a bar. Even though he wanted to listen, Luca kept sensing his attention pulled toward the Box of Shame.

The box was wooden and shaped like an outhouse Luca once saw outside the Miller's house back home a year ago.

When he asked his dad what it was, he followed the answer by wondering out loud why construction workers would ever want to poop outside. "Because sometimes you just have to go," his father exclaimed. Luca started telling his mom that if Anna didn't get out of the bathroom soon, he was gonna use the Miller's outhouse across the street. Fortunately, it had never come to that, which was a good thing since his dad said that outhouses smelled like the worst parts of the zoo.

The Box of Shame looked just like an outhouse, except there was a huge wooden bar across the door that kept it from opening. There were two small holes at the top of the front and one larger hole at the bottom where Luca had seen Rebecca's mom slide some water in and take a bowl from. Luca assumed the bowl was where the girl was forced to use the bathroom, which made the Box of Shame more like an outhouse than by just its appearance.

"You want to join us later?" Scott asked, "We're going on a store run, me and a couple of the guys. I bet if I ask, they'd let you go, even though you're still technically a kid."

"*You?*" Luca said, not meaning to sound so surprised, but also slightly annoyed that Scott felt it necessary to *again* point out that Luca wasn't yet a man, despite his appearances.

"Yeah, why not me?" Scott said.

"Well, isn't it dangerous?"

"I can handle myself," Scott said, sounding offended that Luca would think, let alone suggest, otherwise.

"Yeah, but you're still healing from the other day," Luca said, trying to delicately point out that Scott would be dead if Luca hadn't saved him — exchanging years of his youth to do so — and now he was gonna risk his life again? Had Luca's sacrifice meant nothing to Scott? For all Luca knew, he'd never get those years back.

Scott stared at the church, like he was searching for a change of subject. Luca returned his attention to the box and its occupant, locked away in punishment.

"She'll be okay," Scott said, catching what held Luca's attention. "It's cool outside and they've got guards out all hours, so I doubt the monsters will get to her."

"How many days is she going to be locked in there?" Luca asked.

"A whole week," Scott said. "I can't even imagine being locked in a room that long, let alone a box."

"Me, either," Luca said. "I bet she's scared."

"I'll bet she won't run off with a boy again," Scott said with a laugh.

Luca looked at him, "What? Are you saying she deserves this?"

Scott matched Luca's sudden flash of intensity with his own look of nervous fear.

"I'm just saying, well, she knew the rules, right? I mean, if they did it to Paola, that would be one thing. We're new here. But Rebecca's a religious girl. She's been here a while. And she knows what's expected of her. She made her choice."

"So, she deserved to be put in a box and have her hair cut off?" Luca asked, surprised at how accepting Scott was of the punishment, even while the rest of their group was clearly distressed.

"I'm not saying that," Scott said, laughing nervously.

'Stop looking at me like that, freak.'

Luca heard the thought in Scott's head, no different than if the teen had said it.

"Is that how you act to someone who saved your life? Call them a freak?" Luca snapped at Scott.

"What?! I didn't call you ... " Scott froze as realization crept across his face, bleaching his skin along the way.

'You heard me?'

313

Luca turned away, suddenly afraid, not wanting to reveal his new gift and accidentally push himself further from the group. Luca walked away, quickly.

Scott either said or thought, '*What's going on?*' as Luca picked up his pace and headed toward the Quiet Spot at the back of the property, behind the hangar, where there were two stone benches and a small garden where the grown-ups liked to sit and talk in whispers and hushes.

As Luca passed the Box of Shame, he heard Rebecca cry.

"Help me," she said.

Luca couldn't be sure if she'd spoken the words or thought them. He turned and saw several people, including Scott, watching him. He didn't dare draw more attention, so he turned back and kept walking, ignoring the girl's plea. More thoughts flooded his brain from different voices he didn't recognize, likely coming from the men at the church:

'*What a freak.*'

'*I wonder what he's doing?*'

'*Definitely weird. I think the Devil's inside him.*'

As he put the corner of the hangar between himself and the crew working on the church, he broke into a run, racing toward the Quiet Spot, eager to have his head to himself. As he rounded the corner, he saw someone else sitting in the Quiet Spot.

John.

"Hello, Luca," he said. John was sitting on one of the benches, Brother Rei standing beside him, their conversation severed.

Luca froze.

John was definitely different from how he'd been at the Drury Inn, though Luca couldn't put his finger on exactly *what* that difference was. It wasn't like they'd spent that much time together before John left the Drury after Jimmy's death. Besides, most people had changed in the past few months, even if Luca's evolution had been the most evident after he saved Paola and Scott.

Even if everyone was different, John's difference was the only one that felt so wrong.

While the others seemed wary of Luca, John seemed intrigued and not scared in the least. If anything, John made Luca nervous, as did Brother Rei, who looked like a frightful rat with his beady dark eyes, large nose, and almost non-existent chin. "Hello, Brother John and Brother Rei," Luca said, his eyes finding interest at his feet.

"Everything okay?" John asked.

"Yeah," Luca said, less than convincingly.

"Have a seat," John said, waving his hand at the bench beside him.

Luca sat, unable to meet John's stare. Even though Luca was closer in height to the adults, he still felt like a child and found it hard to look them in the eyes.

"Are you upset about Rebecca?" John asked.

"Yeah," Luca admitted. He didn't mind telling John so much, but was a bit nervous to speak in front of Brother Rei.

"Doesn't seem fair, does it?" John said.

Luca looked up, met John's eyes. "You feel the same?"

"It doesn't matter how I feel," John said. "This is our new home. We must abide by the rules of The Sanctuary and The Prophet."

Luca nodded slowly, mostly so he wouldn't get in trouble, then asked, "Why do they call him The Prophet?"

"You haven't heard the story?" Brother Rei said, as though surprised. "It's an interesting tale, one of the best. The Prophet was given a vision of what would happen on October 15, years before it came to pass. God spoke to him in his dreams, told him to get his people ready, to prepare them to enter His Kingdom."

"Do you believe him?" Luca asked, wondering only after if maybe he should've kept his mouth shut.

"Didn't Will say he dreamed of the day, also?" John said.

"Well, yeah."

"And you believe him, right?" John asked.

"Yes," Luca said. "That's how he found me. His dreams."

"Ah, yes," John said. "And did Will say that God spoke to him in these dreams?"

"Well, um, no, I don't think so. I mean, he didn't mention God."

"Interesting," Brother Rei said, stepping close enough to Luca to keep him uncomfortable. "Will dreamed of this day, yet did nothing to help anyone?"

"I don't know. I mean, he helped *me*."

"And yet God didn't speak to him?" Brother Rei asked.

"I don't think so. Why?"

"Well," Brother Rei said, "If your friend had these visions, and *God* didn't provide them, perhaps someone else did. Perhaps the Devil has his ear?"

Luca felt a chill run through him as Brother Rei glared down at him, almost accusingly. Luca looked to John for relief, but John's face wore a weird smile that seemed inappropriate for the moment.

"How long have you known Will?" Brother Rei asked.

"Will is nice!" Luca cried. "He risked his life to save me, and to save Paola. He didn't have to do any of the things he's done."

"Exactly," Brother Rei said, and folded his arms across his narrow chest. He looked up at the sky, then back down to Luca. "Makes me wonder what his game is."

Luca stood. "I have to use the restroom," he said, not waiting for anyone to give him permission to leave. "I'll see you around."

Luca made it six steps when Brother Rei called out, "Brother Luca."

Luca turned, "Yes?"

Brother Rei looked even more like a rat when he smiled. "Let's keep this little chat just between the three of us, okay?"

Luca looked at John, who was still wearing the same simple smile, as if he wasn't really even there. Luca nodded, "Yes, sir."

"Good," Brother Rei said. "I'd hate to see you in the box next to the whore."

* * * *

CHAPTER 6
BORICIO WOLFE

Dunn, Georgia
March 24
4:15 a.m.

Boricio woke up in a gummy, groggy, gallon and a half of what-in-the-fuck.

He had busted into another one of them rich bitch homes, and found a handful of pills scattered across the kitchen counter. Since it wasn't The Matrix, and Boricio didn't have to pick red *or* blue, he scooped the entire mess in his pocket, then popped five of each into his mouth, cracked the lid from one of the house's million bottles of water, and swallowed the pills with a swish.

He had a nice five minutes or so where the world was normal. Then it started dancing the FuckedUP Boogaloo, studded and sequined in about a thousand fucked up colors. Things went from black to white, to Skittles, then back to black. The resulting drug-induced psychedelic coma had left him out for hours.

He figured it was a night later when he woke, maybe two. Either way, he needed to high-tail his ass back to base. The boys would be waiting on him, he was sure, so was more surprised than a date with a tranny when he arrived to find everyone gone, save for Harry who was in the garage, hunched over the engine of a Green Honda Element they'd picked up recently.

"The fuck you mean ain't nobody here?" Boricio said. "It's the middle of the night, where'd they go?"

Harry wiped his brow. "They left a while ago. Haven't heard a peep since. Sorry, Boss."

Boricio was furious. He growled, "Stay the fuck put. I'm going out," then headed back to his car. He turned, and growled, "I mean it. I'm gonna be kill-a-bitch pissed if I have to leave here looking for any more ex-members of Team Boricio."

"I'm not planning on going nowhere, Boss," Harry said. He nodded, then got back to the engine work.

Boricio would've kicked him hard for ending the conversation early, but figured it wasn't worth injuring the hand that fed the Boriciomobile. So he muttered something Harry couldn't hear, then headed outside to the Z8. He'd find Charles in Charge, and everyone he was in charge of, and deal with each of them accordingly, saving Callie for last.

Nobody, and I mean nobody, gives Boricio the old adios. I say when it's sayonara, and there ain't no one this side of the sun gonna tell me when I'm finished with their sky. Fuck every one of 'em. I find them and something's gone wrong that wasn't none of their fault, well then circle gets the fucking square and we're even as the number two. But I find out they surrendered their spot on Team Boricio, Boricio will cut their scalps and wear them as a necklace.

Boricio cranked *The Mummies* and whipped the Z8 to 110 mph.

It felt great to be out on the prowl. Truth was, ole Boricio felt better in flight than out of it, his nose in the air and hairs up on end, the taste of prey teasing his mouth.

The thought of prey in his mouth smeared a smile across it, then put a thick on his dick as he thought about a prime piece of prey he once had named Pepper, a Puerto Rican chica who had actually been quite tasty and not spicy at all. Boricio sunk his teeth into her two years earlier when the both of them were nice and drunk and she wasn't expecting a thing, least of all the flood of blood soaking the bed just a few seconds after Boricio filled her with white honey. She was still shaking from all the shudders he'd sent into her body with his few final thrusts that she didn't realize it was a knife he'd slipped in her gut right there at the end, at least not until she was swimming in the crimson bath.

Boricio eased on the gas and started rubbing his cock through his jeans.

There hadn't been a struggle. Her eyes just went from wide to not even there. Boricio had to leave town the next morning since he'd made things so messy. He was usually cleaner than he'd been that day, but Boricio was never at his best when hungry, and it had been far too long between snacks.

Control was the golden key to never getting caught, and Boricio knew himself well enough to fuck his worse habits in their ass, as long as he made the time to do it. So he kept himself on a tight schedule and vowed to never go hungry again. And he hadn't, at least not until the world went away and left him with nothing to fuck.

Soon as he found the Merry Band of Fuck-Alls, Boricio would maybe take Maid Marian Callie in a room with no windows and make her do every unladylike thing he could think of. He had the rest of the drive to imagine the specifics, but he could already guarantee it involved his pecker, her face, and a happy fucking ending. He wouldn't kill her, of course; that would be bad for business. But he'd spent enough time laying off, pretending that Charlie was hitting that. She had to be craving some cock by now.

Boricio slapped the steering wheel, suddenly pissed, thinking about the day he shat away after sucking down those trippy pills and dreaming again about some *Damien Omen*-looking kid that creeped him the fuck out.

Blind with rage and cruising near Mach 1, it was a miracle Boricio saw the curly Q of white smoke snaking on the dark horizon, but there was no doubt about what he saw. Boricio flipped a bitch and shot the Boriciomobile back toward the belching chimney.

It probably wasn't Charlie, or any of the Merry Band of Fuck-Alls, but it might be better. There was a 50/50 shot that whoever put the smoke in the chimney was wearing a furbox between her legs, and that made her ripe to make Boricio's acquaintance. And considering there might be more than one person in a house with a fire, Boricio figured his odds were even better than that.

There'd probably be at least one bitch good looking enough for Boricio to get on down and pray to the divine scar, fill her with milk, then drop her in the trunk and take her home for seconds. Shit, she could be homely as a mud fence, that wouldn't matter much these days. Ole Boricio would simply make her face the other way. He could still barrel down Boscoe Boulevard, splatter her sphincter, then leave her in a heap and hit the road. Maybe even leave her breathing, in case he wanted to swing that way again.

He pulled the Boriciomobile to the edge of a clearing, then took his binoculars from the passenger seat and pointed them toward the massive house sitting squat in the middle of nowhere. Boricio never could make sense of why people lived in those sorts of huge ass houses, in the capital of nothing, far enough from everything to be Ma and Pa Kettle hunting for their meals, but with marble and granite and Dom Perignon. Who delivered the Dom out to the middle of Fuck-All?

He stared through the binoculars for a long while, unmoving and seeing nothing. There was a massive window looking half a mile wide running along the front of the house, so Boricio figured it was a matter of time before someone would walk in front of it. He was right. And when he finally saw what he wanted to see, Boricio wanted to whoop and holler at a Christmas come early.

Standing in front of the half mile window was a Holy Trinity of fuck yeah: two girls and one guy, all of 'em purty. One to cut; two to fuck. Boricio wondered whether he'd start with the brunette or the sandy blonde, then figured he must've been an awful good boy all year for Santa to give him two to choose from.

Boricio tossed the binoculars on the passenger seat, exited the Z8, then peeled the shirt from his body and dropped it in the dirt, kicking it around on the ground and dragging it across the dirty sludge with his feet. His freshly dirtied shirt was now half frozen, sending a chill and a shudder through Boricio's body when he put it back on.

Perfect.

His guise ready, he headed toward the house, whistling *Here Comes Santa Claus*.

**

He knocked, then waited a long five minutes, perking his ears, though he couldn't hear a thing on the other side, especially from behind his own chattering teeth. Then a faint, metallic click strummed his ears. *A gun?* He figured as much and was instantly proven right. A sharp order blasted through the door, still muffled but clearly coming from the guy. Then the door opened, barely. The girls must have been standing behind it because Boricio could hear them breathing. Could smell them.

The guy was the only one Boricio could see, though he couldn't get a clear view with the rifle aimed right between his eyes. "Who are you?" the man shouted. The way his forehead was beaded and neck veins twitching, there was no way he'd ever pulled the trigger on a beating heart before.

Boricio raised his hands slowly.

"Sorry, Sir," he said, teeth still chattering. "I've been walking for days. You're the first person I seen in I don't even know how long." Boricio scrunched his face, then said, "Since the second week of January, I guess, when Billy stopped breathing on account of it being so cold."

Boricio's hands went higher in the air. "I don't mean no trouble at all, Sir. I know there ain't nothing more important than staying safe. And I don't mean to intrude. It's just that, well, I saw the fire and thought maybe you'd spare some help for a fellow survivor. I don't need much, maybe just a can of meat if you have it. Anything to take away the burn in my belly. Again, I don't need much," Boricio shook his head, even managed to force a rumble from his stomach. "I was hunting my own food, but then I ran out of bullets and now I've lost both my gun and my knife. I've got nothing, not even a jacket." Boricio shivered.

Would-be Rambo said, "How'd you 'lose' your weapons?"

"Didn't lose them so much as had them taken by the guy who killed my friend, Frank. It was just the both of us after Billy passed. We lasted about a month, up until last week when this guy, called himself Boricio, came from nowhere. Killed Frank like it was nothing. Never saw no one move like that. He told me I could live since I looked too pathetic to die. Then he took my gun and knife and left me for dead. That was two days ago, and I can't see my way. Been wandering in circles since." Boricio gave a hopeful smile. "Maybe you could see to help me with a way out of the woods along with that can of meat?" He lowered his hands, then held one out for the man with the gun. "My name is Tom, by the way, Tom Westin."

The gun was still between Boricio's eyes, but the asshole's hand was already getting heavy. "Jenna, I got my gun on him. I'm gonna need you to make sure he's clean."

Boricio shook his head and laughed. "I'm afraid I'm far from clean, been a long stretch since I felt a hot shower. I'm sure I'm ripe and sorry all over the place for that, but you're welcome to get as close as you need, to make sure I'm safe."

Jenna, the brunette, appeared from behind the doorway. She looked good behind the binoculars, but goddammit if she didn't look a heaping helping of tasty pussy salad standing just a few feet away.

Jenna frisked him up and down; Boricio apologized for his smell, which she said was nothing at all and that he smelled a whole lot better than she would if she hadn't cleaned herself in that long. There was a chirpy laugh from behind the door, followed by a "That's the truth!"

The rifle slowly fell from between Boricio's eyes until it was pointed at the hardwood floor. Its handler said, "I'm Jesse," then held his hand out for Boricio. "It's good to meet you, Tom." He opened the door wider to the sandy blonde standing on the other side. "This is Tanya."

"Nice to meet you," Tanya said.

Boricio smiled. "Thanks so much. It's good to finally see someone else. I worked construction before all this. I'm used to good folks, great conversation, and constant noise. The quiet's been killing me."

"Well come on in," Jesse said. "We'll get you cleaned up, and fill your belly with a lot more than a can of meat."

Too fucking easy.

Boricio was careful to keep the saunter from his step, entering the oversized living room with shoulders hunched, which was how he'd stay until it was time to make the layup.

It was a bad time to be stupid, people being an endangered species and all.

"I'm glad you're hungry," Jenna said. "It's my turn to cook, and I make amazing pasta."

"That's all you make," Tanya said.

Jenna led Boricio upstairs and to a bathroom where he could clean up, then showed him to a room where he was welcome to stay "at least for the night." There was a closet of clean men's clothes about Boricio's size. Jenna told him to help himself, then headed back downstairs. He was upstairs for a while, trying to glean as much information as he could, which amounted to approximately dick. But he figured he'd have plenty of time to dig later after the fuckforall. Once clean, Boricio went downstairs where Jenna led him to the kitchen table, sat him down, and started fattening him up immediately.

The bitch wasn't kidding; her pasta was a fat plate of fuck-yeah. He could've made better, though maybe not anymore considering ingredients were scarce. It wasn't like fresh tomatoes or cream were falling from the sky. Considering it was winter at the end of the world, the sauce was damn fantastic, but Boricio wished she hadn't used whatever 21 Season Salute had shit the sauce, since he tasted a touch of anise, and it clearly wasn't right for the dish. He was considering asking where the taste of anise was coming from, but Boricio figured it wasn't the sort of thing a guy like "Tom Westin" would wonder.

"This is the best thing I've had since my grandparent's 50th wedding anniversary last August. I really can't thank you enough," Boricio said, gobbling pasta and thinking of a half dozen or so ways he could show his appreciation, though there wasn't really much variety. Everything he thought of had some sort of sticky ending.

Then again, Boricio could always use more able bodied men on Team Boricio. But Jesse didn't seem like much of a hunter given his shitastic instincts to let some rogue like Tom Westin in the front door, so Boricio would have to end his days here. Plus, Boricio had had enough disappointment with his team making piss-poor decisions lately. *No more minor leaguers on Team Boricio!*

Fortunately for Boricio's mood, Jenna didn't seem too cautious at all. She wanted what Tom Westin had in his pants, and Boricio could smell it. He could've had her, even before his shower, but Boricio knew she'd be much tastier later, after Jesse was out of the way.

"How long have you been here?" Boricio asked between mouthfuls.

"Since the beginning," Jesse said. "Third week of October."

"Did you all know each other before then?"

Jesse shook his head. "No. We met at a community center, about 20 miles north of here. We waited a day. Then, when it was just us, we figured we should find a place to stay. Tanya knew about this place, and sure enough it was empty. We loaded the place with as many supplies as we could find, including 1,000 or so boxes of Barillo for Jenna. We stay mostly inside, though we've gone out looking every Saturday to see if there's anything out there worth seeing."

"You seen any of them monsters?" Boricio wondered if the version of the afraid face he was wearing looked as funny as he imagined it might.

"A couple of times when we were patrolling, but we stayed in the car and they've never come near. And they've stayed away from here entirely, least as far as I know."

How about that, they're living all Gilligan's Island in the middle of the woods. Well, it's time to rewrite the scene – get rid of the Professor so I can make a sweet tasting sandwich with Ginger and Mary Ann.

Boricio only pretended to get excited about the after dinner game of Monopoly, but then found himself genuinely enjoying it, the way Jenna kept flashing her smile, hinting she had something under the table, getting slick just for him, not to mention he ended up with Park Place on his second trip around the board, then Boardwalk just two times after that.

Sometime around midnight, Tanya said she was tired and urged Jenna to follow her. Boricio said he was tuckered, too, but would like to spend a few more minutes getting to know Jesse. The two girls disappeared upstairs, Jenna winking at Boricio on the way out. Once the guys were alone, Boricio took advantage of the twitch he'd noticed on Jesse all afternoon. Dude was a smoker, but the ladies probably didn't like it in the house, and his pussy lips were just fat enough to make him listen to every fucking word they said.

"Hey, man," Boricio said, "you wouldn't happen to have any smokes in this place, would ya? I ran out a while back, and have been jonesin' all day."

Jesse smiled. "Sure thing, happy you asked." He led Boricio outside, then handed him a pack of Marlboro Reds as soon as they were on the other side of the door. "Keep the pack," he said. "I have more than you'd believe." He laughed, lighting his cigarette, then holding the flame for Boricio.

The air was frigid, but not freezing. Boricio liked it. He took a long drag, then blew a large cloud into the wintry air. They talked about a bunch of bullshit that made Boricio wanna punch stuff for nearly 15 minutes. Finally, after two cigarettes each, things started getting good. "So, you fuck either one of them yet?" Boricio said.

Jesse's mouth was open a while, maybe half a minute before he said, "No. That's not the sort of relationship we have."

"That's not the sort of relationship we have," Boricio said in a perfect mockery of Tom immolating Jesse. Then he went

ahead and dropped Tom altogether so Boricio could come out to play. "The fuck sort of man lives with two fine ass pieces of pink pussy like that and don't do nothing about it? I was staring at Jenna all through dinner, wondering how her little eraser nipples were gonna taste as I pulled 'em in my teeth. You've had a half year to find out, and probably haven't done shit but fill every sock in your drawer. It's a crying fucking shame," Boricio took another long drag, then smiled at Jesse's whatthefuck expression, and waited. Jesse kept right on saying nothing, so Boricio said, "You know I'm fucking with you, right?"

Jesse broke into a nervous laughter. But Boricio never joined him so when the laughter died, Jesse was left trembling. Boricio stood between Jesse, and the doorway, blocking his way back into the house.

"So, which one of them pussies you think would taste better?" Boricio asked, friendly as could be. "My money's on Jenna, but you never know. Them quiet bitches are hellcats in bed half the time." He laughed, then added, "Ask me how I know."

Boricio slapped Jesse on the shoulder. "You've gotta stop being a bitch, Jesse. It's as simple as that. You keep being a bitch and the only thing you'll ever get to glazing is your first and oldest girlfriend, Rosy Palms. Haven't you noticed – it's the end of the world? Bitches have dropped their standards, man. You don't need a lobster dinner when you can fill the pantry with Capt'n Crunch. Now," Boricio whispered in Jesse's ear, "I'm going upstairs to fuck Jenna. I'll let you know how it is. I suggest you go for Tanya. She's mousy, but I guaran-fucking-tee she knows how to squeak."

Boricio reared his head back and squeaked loudly, "Squeeeeaak, Squeeeeaak!"

Jesse said nothing, staring at Boricio as if he'd just shit in the punch bowl.

"You don't want her?" Boricio asked, "I understand. No reason I can't have both. I'm just trying to be a gentleman."

Boricio turned toward the door, thinking he might actually let Jesse live if the dude had fun and played ball. Boricio's hand was on the doorknob when Jesse's sack got fuller, finally giving Boricio an excuse to make shit a whole lot more fun.

Jesse said, "I can't let you do that."

Boricio laughed. "*Let me?* I'm sorry; I wasn't aware I'd asked. Boricio don't wait for anyone to *let him* do shit."

Boricio punched Jesse in his throat, murdering speech, then swept his feet out from under him. Jesse fell hard to the snowy ground, the back of his head whiplashing into the stone walkway but not hard enough to knock him out. That meant more time for Boricio with his new plaything. Boricio crushed the heel of his boot into Jesse's gut, hard. That left Jesse twitching like an epileptic. Boricio strolled to the bricked-in grill, full saunter, and pulled a large fork from a magnetic strip on the side. He sidled back to Jesse, then made a fountain of blood with a set of holes in his neck.

Jesse tried to scream, but Boricio shoved the man's own fingers in his mouth until he was gagging, vomit trickling through the gaps. Next, he stabbed the fork into the pansy's other wrist and arm in four locations, effectively crippling the fucker so he couldn't hit Boricio with his free arm.

Jesse's eyes went wide and white, as he desperately struggled to break free. Boricio brought the fork down again and again, stabbing the man in each eye. The pain was so intense, Jesse bit down hard on his fingers, and kicked with his knees and legs, trying to get Boricio off of him. Boricio dropped the fork and pinched the man's nose, cutting off his last source of air, until he stopped moving.

Boricio was sporting a helluva throbber, and figured he'd take care of that before dealing with Jesse's body, so he charged back inside and took the stairs, two at a time. Tanya's room was on the right so he went there first. Jenna was a sure thing, but Boricio wasn't sure about Tanya. He'd love nothing more than to bring the full set back to the compound, but if she was a fighter, he'd settle for one.

Boricio opened the door to a thundering snore. Tanya was buried beneath the covers, rising and falling in time with her snoring. He closed the door then crossed the hall, passing the stairs on his way to Jenna's room.

There was a slight squeak as the door swung open, but it was dead silent inside. No snoring, no drawn breathing. Only the stillness of nothing. Boricio crept closer to the bed as his eyes adjusted to the dark.

Just as Jenna's shape started to form, she said, "I've been waiting for you. What took you so long?" Her voice was breathy and Boricio's hairy hot dog was begging to get buried in a bun. He slipped into bed and shoved his mouth on hers.

Jenna kissed Boricio hard and spun herself on top of his body. She was hot and wet, Boricio could feel it and smell it. He closed his eyes and waited. She could do whatever she wanted. Girls who had waited a long time were always extra juicy, and they knew exactly what they wanted to do.

Boricio leaned back and closed his eyes, ready for Jenna's opening act. That's when he felt the blade at his throat.

"Who the fuck are you?" Jenna said.

Well, FUCK me.

Boricio edged back against the headboard as Jenna nudged the knife deeper in his flesh. He felt a trickle of blood drizzle down to his collarbone, and registered a rare moment of fear.

"Who the fuck are you?" she repeated.

Boricio tried to speak, but he had to swallow, which made his Adam's Apple nick the knife. Jenna pulled it a centimeter back and said, "Last chance. Who. The fuck. Are you?"

Boricio had no idea what Jenna had heard, and the throb in his cock was shooting through his body and making it impossible to think clear. He said, "Name's Boricio."

"What do you want?"

"Nothing you don't wanna give me, sweetie." He smiled. Jenna made him pay with a gash across his neck. Boricio didn't cry out, though he wanted to, figuring the cut wasn't that deep since he wasn't gushing from the new seam.

"I know what happened," Boricio said. "In October. I know why things went crazy. And I'll tell you everything. But it's hard to think with that shit at my throat. So, do you mind?"

Jenna moved the blade back an inch, keeping it trained on Boricio's jugular. "Spill it," she said.

An inch was enough for Boricio. His hand flew to her throat. Jenna dropped the knife to grab for breath, fingers at her throat as Boricio's brought the fallen blade to the side of her face.

"Well, how about that," he said mockingly.

Jenna was dangerous, no doubt, so Boricio sank the knife into her belly while slapping his other hand over her mouth to muffle her cry. He watched her bleed, pissed that he'd barely enjoyed the kill, and still had a rager to satisfy.

He'd take care of that in a minute, hopefully in between Tanya's titties. Soon as Jenna's heart stopped, Boricio went down the hallway to Tanya's room, cock throbbing with every step. He opened the door to an empty room, no snores coming from the vacant bed.

Fuck! Are these bitches psychic or something?

Boricio stormed from the room and searched the house in a hard-on rage, but didn't find dick.

Where the FUCK did she go?

His cock couldn't wait.

He went back into Jenna's room, spread her legs, and slipped his cock inside her. She was still warm, and wet. He pumped, staring into her dead eyes, still filled with her final gaze of fear.

Seconds later, he exploded inside her, spilling every ounce of his seed.

"Oh fuck, yeah," he sighed, collapsing on top of Jenna's body, embracing her, not at all caring about the blood. He'd wash that off later.

"Why'd you have to go and do that, baby?" he whispered to her in the dark, caressing her face. "Hot as hell and deadly, what a combination. We coulda been something. We coulda been unstoppable."

He decided to sleep with his arm around Jenna's corpse, hoping that Tanya would be crazy enough to come back and try to fuck with him. Just thinking about it made him hard again. He fell asleep happy, a thick on his dick and a smile on his face.

* * * *

CHAPTER 7
CHARLIE WILKENS

Charlie woke to the sound of fire crackling, warmth bleeding across his blanketed body. He was wearing sweats and a shirt which he didn't recognize. The scratches on his arms had been cleaned, and scarred over. A roaring fireplace greeted his eyes as he rubbed the sleep from them. He was in a dark living room, in what appeared to be a cabin. Across from him lay Adam, his eyes barely open, until he noticed that Charlie was awake.

Adam sat up, a huge smile on his face, like a kid waking up to Christmas presents, "You're awake!"

Charlie eased himself up, his head pounding, and muscles achy, but otherwise feeling okay. "Yeah . . . Where are we? What happened?"

"A cabin I found."

"How did we get here?"

"I found you in a car, asleep. Your skin was blue, and you wouldn't wake up. I figured you for dead at first. But I found a weak pulse. So, I carried you until I found a car with some life still in it, then drove until I found this place."

"You carried me?" Charlie said, stunned, but also feeling guilty for practically wishing Adam dead.

"Yeah. Not far though. There was another car close from where you were. How are you feeling?"

"Okay," Charlie said, "A bit out of it, but alive."

"I got this, too," Adam said, holding up a shotgun. "And a whole bag of 'em, in case anyone shows up."

"Did ya get ammo, too?"

"Of course, duh," Adam said with a grin. Then, just like that, the glow in his face was gone. "I'm ... I'm sorry about Callie."

Adam's eyes were sad and mopey, all apologies.

"Don't worry," Charlie said, calling on his best reassuring voice. "We'll find her. And it wasn't your fault. There's nothing you could've done without a gun, except maybe get taken, too. Or killed."

"I wish it were me instead of her," Adam said. "I mean, she's a girl. God only knows what they'll do to her."

"She's a tough girl," Charlie said. "And if they were government people like you said, then they're probably not gonna kill or rape her or anything."

"So, why do you think they took her?" Adam asked.

"I have no idea," Charlie said. "But when Boricio finds out, he's gonna wage a goddamned holy war against them, don't ya think?"

"Oh yeah," Adam said. And then after a long pause, he asked, "Do you think Vic made it out of the storm?"

Charlie flashed back to the asshole's shocked face, eyes the size of softballs, the instant before he slit his throat.

Could Adam have seen me do it? Is he testing me, checking to see if I'll tell the truth?

Adam was likely too far away to have seen him do it, but maybe he had. The thought invited a chill back into his body despite the roaring fire. That left him with only one possible reply ...

"I killed him," Charlie said, flatly, watching Adam's face to gauge his reaction.

Adam's eyes expanded like a balloon for a moment. "Good. He was a dick."

Charlie laughed, laughed so hard it hurt his ribs, more relieved than amused.

Adam caught the laughter bug and started howling, too.

When the embers of laughter died, Adam said, "Though, it would've been good to have his help getting Callie back."

"Yeah, probably, but I think Boricio is an army all his own, right? We don't need Vic. The guy was a ticking time bomb. If he didn't make a move on us, he might have made one on Boricio. Guys like him aren't loyal, not like you and me."

"Thanks," Adam said, smiling sheepishly.

"How long was I out?" Charlie asked.

"More than a day. I was worried you weren't going to wake up. I got you some clothes from another house. I hope they'll work."

"A Day? Shit! We need to get going. How far are we from the compound?"

"About a half hour by car, I think," Adam said.

"OK, let's go."

**

They arrived at the compound just before dawn. The house was dark. Charlie flicked the lights to signal whoever was on watch, *if* anyone was. There were only two others left in their group, Boricio and Harry, the stoner mechanic who rarely did guard duty at night because he couldn't be trusted not to get wasted or doze off.

Charlie honked the horn and flashed the signal again.

Moments later, the front door opened and Harry came running to the gate, flashlight bobbing up and down as he ran. Charlie noticed with displeasure that Harry wasn't even armed.

"Charlie, is that you?"

"Who else would it be?" Charlie said, annoyed as he stuck his head from the Honda so Harry could see.

"Shit, man, Boricio was wondering where you all were! He took off a while ago looking for you."

"Fuuuuck!" Charlie said as he pulled the car inside the gate.

"Don't lock it," Charlie said to Harry, "We're gonna head back out. We need to get supplies, then find Boricio. Do you have something gassed and ready?"

"Yeah," Harry said in his drawl, "Got the F-150 gassed and ready to go if you want it. Where's Vic?"

"Vic was held up," Charlie said. "We're gonna get some shit from inside. We'll meet you in the garage in five minutes, okay?"

"Alright," Harry said with a smile. He took the Honda as Charlie and Adam darted to the house.

"What are we getting?" Adam asked. "I got a whole bag of guns in the car."

Charlie grabbed a flashlight from just inside the front door, clicked it on and headed upstairs to his room, Adam on his heels.

Charlie pulled out the bottom drawer of his dresser, reached his hand into the back, found what he was looking for, then pulled it out.

"What is it?" Adam said, stepping closer.

Charlie pulled out a small wooden cross that Callie had carved for him two months ago. He'd hidden it not out of shame, but because it was his most valued possession – the first gift anyone had made for him since he was a child.

"A cross," Charlie said as he slipped out of his borrowed clothes.

"I didn't know you were Christian," Adam said.

"I'm not, well, not much, anyway," Charlie said, as he slipped into his jeans, T-shirt, black jacket, and sneakers, then slipped the cross into his jacket pocket. "Callie made it for me. For luck."

Adam went to his room and changed into some fresh clothes, then they dashed downstairs and headed out the door. Charlie froze in his tracks, heart flatlining, at the sight of a red Mustang just inside the gate, parked with its lights off. The F-150 was running idle in front of the garage, lights illuminating the inside of the empty Mustang. Shadows came from within the garage. Someone was with Harry. "Who's that in garage?" Adam asked. "Is Boricio back?"

"I don't know," Charlie said, a nervous chill slithering through his gut, as they moved toward the garage

The bag of weapons in the car punctuated Charlie's thoughts; he wished he'd thought to bring a gun with him into the house. And he never thought to ask Adam where his knife went after Adam saved him. He looked at Adam, who was also unarmed.

Shit.

They approached the garage with practiced caution.

His ever sense in alert mode, Charlie nearly jumped out his skin when Harry came bolting into view. "Hey guys, guess who's back!" the mechanic said with a smile.

Charlie felt a swell of hope rise in his heart.

Boricio's back. Time to go get Callie, right now!

Except, it wasn't Boricio.

Seconds after Harry spoke, something black pierced him from behind, ripping through his back and out his stomach, followed by a river of gore.

Harry's eyes widened, his smile a memory, as he looked down and saw the dark, glistening alien hand which was twisted into a large blade jutting from his stomach as his guts spilled onto the ground. The blade retracted, and Harry fell to the ground as the owner of the dark alien blade stepped out of the shadows, a smile on his face and a scar across his neck.

"Hello, boys! Miss me?" said Vic.

* * * *

CHAPTER 8
EDWARD KEENAN

When Ed awoke, the morning sun was bleeding through a sliver of the slightly parted curtains, and Brent was gone.

He grabbed his Remington 870, and was on his feet in seconds. He was already dressed; all he needed was his tactical vest, which he quickly slipped on and fastened. Fully armed, he approached the hotel room door like a ghost, silently opening it and slipping into the hallway. Brent was at the end of the corridor staring out the window.

"What you looking at?" Ed asked, surprising Brent, who looked pale.

"Come look," Brent said, keeping his voice low, and waving his hand in a "come here" motion.

Ed jogged to the end of the hall and joined Brent at the window. Someone was in the parking lot. Not just one someone, but several someones — three men and one woman, walking between the cars, searching for something. They were identically dressed — camouflage pants, shirts, jackets, hunting gear. Each carried a hunting rifle and had a backpack strapped to their back. They were a serious bunch, but not military.

"Are they Black Mountain?" Brent asked.

"No, just civilians, probably looking for supplies or a place to stay."

"What do we do?"

"We wait. As long as they don't touch our van, we let them pass."

"And if they don't pass? If they come in here?"

"Then they've got a problem," Ed said.

"I don't think they're looking for supplies," Brent said. "I think they're looking for someone."

Ed watched as one of the men squatted and peered beneath a truck, his rifle muzzle leading the way.

"You know; I think you're right. The question is who?"

"They're looking for me," a scared voice said from behind, jolting both Ed and Brent.

Ed spun, gun aimed, and saw a young boy, maybe 12, eyes wide and scared, teetering toward terrified. The boy was dressed in jeans, a red T-shirt, and dark-blue jacket. *No gun.* With his big, blue eyes, mop of brown hair, and dirty face, he didn't *seem* much of a threat, but Ed kept his gun on the kid just the same.

"Please, don't let them find me," the boy said, voice raspy.

"Who are they?" Ed asked.

"I don't know. I woke up yesterday and they'd killed the man I was living with. I tried to hide, but they saw me, and now they're after me."

"Why?" Brent asked.

"I don't know, and I don't know what they want." The boy was on the verge of tears.

Ed lowered his gun, then looked back down to the parking lot, but didn't see them anymore. *Where are they?*

Seconds later, breaking glass answered the question.

"They're inside," Ed said to Brent, who already had his pistol ready.

"Hide in here. Do not leave until we come get you, okay?" Ed said, ushering the boy into the room at the end of the hall, not the room they were in. He didn't trust the boy enough to put him in a room with their supplies and weapons.

Ed closed the door with the boy inside, then turned to Brent. "You ready?"

"Ready for what? Are we gonna shoot them?"

"You want to talk it out over canned spaghetti?" Ed asked.

"I'd like to know what's going on before we shoot them; maybe it's a misunderstanding."

Ed stared at Brent hard, "We are not *really* having this conversation, are we? I don't need to convince you of the threat these people pose, do I?"

Brent looked chagrined, "No."

"Good. Follow my lead and don't shoot until I do."

Ed ducked into their room, grabbed a couple of grenades from his weapons bag and attached them to his vest. Then they slowly approached the stairwell. He doubted he'd need explosives with these people, but you could never afford to underestimate an unknown enemy. He would have waited in the hall to ambush them, but the door leading into the stairwell had a window, stripping the element of surprise.

Ed eased the door open and they stepped into the stairwell, which was lit by daylight from the skylight on the roof. The stairwell was empty, which meant the people were probably still circling the lower floors. Brent didn't say a word, watching Ed and waiting for cues.

A door opened in the stairwell, two floors down.

"We know you're in here, you little fucker!" a man shouted, voice fat with anger.

Ed put a hand up, telling Brent to stay put as a single set of footsteps echoed up the stairwell. They stopped one landing beneath, then opened the door and went through.

"Let's go," Ed mouthed, and they descended the stairs quickly. When they reached the sixth floor, Ed peered through the door's window and saw the man stepping into the first room across the hall.

"Open the door, *softly*," he told Brent.

Brent did as instructed and stepped into the hall, his shotgun lowered at an angle. As Ed reached the door, the hinge behind him squeaked. The man spun around, but was too late. Ed fired, sending a round of buckshot into the man's chest. He fell to the ground, killed in an instant.

Ed slipped another shell into the gun and turned back to Brent, "Good chance the rest of them gonna be coming up those stairs. Stay behind me; watch my back."

"OK," Brent said as Ed went down the stairs. One of the men came into the stairwell, looked up, and rushed a shot. A miss. Ed returned fire, a hit, shearing the man's head off in one shot. Ed kept moving, not missing a step, flying down the remainder of the stairs, over the corpse, and into the hallway beyond, searching. Nobody. They were likely still downstairs. He ducked back into the stairwell, looked down, saw movement on the bottom floor, and took aim.

Whoever was down there, moved back quickly out of the way.

"We don't want any trouble," a woman's voice said. "We just want the kid."

"Why?" Ed asked. "What's he to you?"

"None of your business."

"Wrong answer."

The woman didn't return a verbal shot, but Ed was pretty sure she was still there.

"What do you want with the kid?!" Ed shouted down the stairwell.

"He's got something that don't belong to him," the woman shouted back.

"What is it?!"

"Just give us the damned kid, and we'll be on our way!" the woman said.

"Well, there's two less of you now, so I say you leave right now before you join your friends!"

The woman screamed in frustration, though Ed wasn't sure she'd said a word.

"Ed?" Brent said from behind, at the top of the landing. His voice sounded off.

Ed turned and saw why. One of the men had a pistol to Brent's head and bloodshot eyes aimed at Ed. "Put your gun down," he said with something between a grin and a scared grimace.

Ed raised his shotgun, and stepped forward. "No, you put your gun down and I'll let you live."

The man pressed his pistol into Brent's temple and Brent cringed. "I'll shoot him," the man said.

"And I'll shoot you," Ed said, voice calm as he took another step forward. There were about 10 steps between him and the man. "You've got, what, a .38 Special? I've got a Remington with double ought buckshot. Do you really think you'll get me before I get you?"

Ed took two more steps. The man's eyes were darting between Ed and Brent.

"Last chance," Ed said. "I know you don't want to do this. Step away and I'll let you and your friend leave alive."

Something in the man's eyes changed, and Ed knew he'd seen the light. He said, "Okay," and pulled the pistol away from Brent's head and put it on the ground.

Brent stepped away, quickly, letting out a deep sigh, then maneuvered behind Ed.

Ed's shotgun roared again, striking the man in the chest and sending him to the ground.

Brent screamed in shock, "What the hell?!"

"We've got one more," Ed said, then pivoted and yelled down the stairwell, "Better run; you're on your own!"

The lower door slammed shut. Ed raced down the stairs, hit the first floor, and saw the woman running across the parking lot toward the truck they'd come in.

Ed sprinted outside. The woman slid into the driver's seat of the pickup, fired the engine, and hit the gas. Instead of fleeing, she came at him.

He raised the shotgun and fired twice. The first round shattered the window; the second shattered the woman. Blood painted the inside of the cab as the truck veered and slammed into a car to Ed's right. The woman's body crashed into the horn. Ed moved quickly to shove the woman aside before the horn alerted every alien within earshot to the open buffet at the Holiday Inn. The horn now silent, Ed turned back to the hotel's entrance, where Brent was standing with eyes wide open, staring past Ed into the distance.

Ed turned around to see a half dozen aliens across the parking lot, near one of the banks, now gathering together and running toward the hotel.

Ed started back to the truck.

"No," Brent said, "What about the kid?"

"Fuck!" Ed said, slamming on his brakes. He turned on his heels and raced back inside the hotel.

"Go! Go! Go!" Ed said, racing up the stairs, hoping like hell the aliens would lose track of him and give up. Brent was winded by the fifth floor. Ed passed him, saying, "Hurry up! I'm not waiting for you!"

They made it to the seventh floor, and went to the end of the hall where they'd told the kid to wait. "Go get him," Ed said, "I'm gonna get some ammo."

A few seconds later, before Ed even reached their room, Brent called out, "He's not in here!"

Shit!

Ed knew then what he was about to find in their room, though the realization wouldn't lessen the sting. He opened the door, spent a half-second looking inside, then left. He marched down the hallway back to Brent, anger fueling his every step. "The kid took our shit."

As if on cue, the sound of more glass breaking erupted downstairs.

The aliens were coming.

* * * *

CHAPTER 9
MARY OLSON

After dinner, Mary pulled Desmond to the side. "We have to go." Her eyes were bolted on his, and her fingers dug into his arm.

"As soon as we can," he said. "But nothing has changed. We have to stick with what we all agreed." They *had* agreed. John's eyes and ears were all over them. They'd wait and talk things over when they had more time alone. But right now, rash action would get them killed.

They should be able to leave whenever they wanted; it wasn't as though they were prisoners. But you never knew how far crazy would go to preserve itself, and The Sanctuary had crazy on discount.

"What do we have to lose?" Mary asked. "What are they going to do? Stop us at the gate? We're not prisoners. We don't even have to take the vehicle we came in. We can leave on foot; we'll find another car in no time. It's dangerous here, Desmond. I can feel it."

Desmond started to make an argument about the end of winter, and the snowstorm that felt like it was coming.

But he didn't get more than a sentence deep before one of The Sanctuary's residents, Estelle, broke the conversation.

"Sister Mary," she said, "The Prophet would like to see you. He's at the church construction site. He said he needs you as soon as possible, but not to inconvenience you. Finish what you're doing and join him as soon as you can." Estelle smiled, then curtsied and left.

Desmond raised his eyebrows. "What do you think *that's* all about?"

Mary shook her head. "I've no idea. But if I had to bet, I'd say John ratted us out."

"I'm coming with you."

"No," Mary said. "I don't think that's a good idea. Just be aware, and I'll catch you up as soon as I can."

"I don't like it," Desmond insisted. "The Prophet could do something horrible to you and I wouldn't be able to stop him. I won't even know what's going on."

Mary said, "I'm not Rebecca, or Sarah. If The Prophet tries something, anything at all, believe me, everyone in The Sanctuary is gonna know. I'll take that old man out quicker than you can say 'Hallelujah!'"

Desmond laughed, a broken cackle, but genuine. He said, "I'll be here, waiting," then pulled Mary into a hug. "I love you," he said.

"I love you, too."

Mary left Desmond with a lingering kiss at the edge of his mouth, then headed toward the church. She saw The Prophet standing by a tall pile of wood, hands folded in front of him, eyes scanning the wall of The Sanctuary. He turned his nose to the gray sky when Mary was just a few feet away. "Looks like it's gonna snow tonight."

"Not yet, it's too warm," Mary said. "It'll probably just rain."

The Prophet shook his head, "I say it's gonna drop a good 20 degrees. I imagine we'll be looking at a world that's white as an angel feather by morning." He found Mary's eyes. "Of course, I couldn't be more excited. I love it when it snows, the way it looks like God is giving the world a brand new chance."

Mary wanted to look away, but couldn't. The Prophet held her eyes like slaves. "That's what I wanted to talk to you about, Mary. Starting over. We're here waiting for the Gates to open. That means we're waiting here to keep the Devil from winning. That's why I'm rebuilding the Church." The Prophet gestured toward the structure behind him, which was coming along quickly; a frame and roof were already in place. "It's a testament to my faith in Him. I'm here because The Good Lord needs me. As much as I long to walk through those gates and greet the God who gives us breath, to see my loved ones, including my sweet Ellie Mae, I know I've got souls to save and a Devil to beat before I do."

"Now, Mary," The Prophet put his hand on her shoulder, "I know you have some legitimate concerns about the way we go about following The Word here at The Sanctuary. I appreciate those concerns, and want nothing more than to answer each and every one, take care of them here and now. While we good people and humble servants are here at New Unity waiting for the Gates to open, we need good people like you and your friends to wait right along with us. The Demons have claimed enough souls already, thank you very much. The Devil doesn't like what we're doing. He is building an army. I can feel it as sure as you can feel Paola's love. If you're out there in the troubled world beyond our walls, Satan will claim you."

The Prophet's voice lowered to a rumble of warning, and he withdrew his hand, yet moved closer to her. "We have something special here, Mary. Something the Demons can't breach. This truly is a Sanctuary. I know the punishment for that Rebecca seemed about as harsh as the sharp side of a wallop, and I do apologize for the dull weight of the required lesson. But it's imperative we keep our children from the Devil, now more than ever, and not just from the minions beyond these walls." He leaned in closer. "We must protect them from the whispers within them as well."

Mary kept her voice steady. "I'm not sure I believe in the Devil," she said. "At least, not like you do. The kids weren't doing anything wrong. Not really. Just the sort of stuff that kids do. No, they shouldn't have snuck out. And they shouldn't have made everyone worry. And on a practical level, we shouldn't have spent our resources and risked our people to chase them down and bring them back. But I don't believe it was 'evil,' or 'the Devil's' handiwork. It was a harmless picnic, prompted by an innocent crush."

"No, Mary," The Prophet looked down, as though the weight of her decaying faith was too heavy for him to hold his head to the heavens. "There is no such thing as innocence; not anymore. Not now in our second Age of Conscience. Do you know what the Age of Conscience is, Mary?"

Mary shook her head. The Prophet said he'd be happy to tell her if she cared to hear the story, almost as though she was being given a choice.

"A long time ago there was a Garden, and in that Garden the first sin was committed. Once man sinned, God no longer saw him as innocent. And once man was no longer innocent, the Good Lord had to appeal to his conscience. This was called 'The Age of Conscience,' and lasted until after the flood. During The Age of Conscience, man was tested on his own conscience – that is, to his knowledge of what was right or wrong. Needless to say," The Prophet chuckled and wiped his eyes, "man didn't do so well on that test. Not until after the flood."

His chuckle died, and his voice grew grave. "Don't you see Mary; this is our new 'after the flood.' God will judge us on how we govern ourselves in the days right after the flood. While we sit and wait, patient for the Gates to swing back open and lead us on the road toward the Glory of Forever, He is watching every single thing we do."

Mary was losing her patience. She wanted to run away from The Sanctuary, as far and as fast as she could, not stay a moment longer at Bible school. "You don't have to believe in the Devil, Mary, and you don't have to acknowledge the Demons who walk before you, even though they're the very Demons you've seen so many times with your own pretty eyes. But I do fear, Sister Mary, that if you cannot see the Demons swimming around us, or believe in the Devil hiding behind the gnarled shadows of everything we do, then Lucifer himself may have you fooled, too."

Mary was seething. She wanted to tell The Prophet where he could step off with all his condescending bullshit. He had no idea who she was, or what she believed. Nor did anyone behind the walls of The Sanctuary, which was populated by people who wanted protection from the madness outside, and were willing to believe, or pretend to believe, whatever they needed to in order to remain safe, or enjoy some illusion of safety. Brother Rei was crazy enough to believe every word he said, and Sarah, too, apparently. But who knew how many people behind the walls of The Sanctuary were simply choosing one monster over another?

Mary said nothing.

The Prophet said, "We've allowed you to stay here, in the safety of The Sanctuary, as a courtesy to Brother John. But it is now time you fell in line with our way of living. You can have a good life here, Mary. So could Paola and that miracle of a child, Luca. But to do so you must break bread at our table, and not just during mealtimes. You are the only citizens of Sanctuary not required to participate, take the oath, or be a part of The Church. I have tolerated it, for you know not what you do."

The Prophet shook his head and saddened his eyes, letting Mary know how truly sorry he was. "But I cannot allow you and yours to spread a cancer of doubt and sinful thoughts throughout my flock. You are a good, strong woman, Mary. I see the way you love your daughter. I see the way you care for young Luca, and the way you carry his heavy burden as though it were your own. There is a place here at The Sanctuary for a strong woman such as yourself. A safe place. But your group must choose. If you stay, you must live as we do; follow our rules and practice our faith. That means all of you. Do you understand what I'm saying?"

Mary didn't know what else to do, so she simply nodded.

The Prophet's hand was back on her shoulder. "I'll give you three days to think about it. I urge you to take your time and think it over. Consider your safety, and the lives of your family and friends. Think what might happen to Luca and Paola. You are not prisoners here, Mary. You are free to leave whenever you wish. Pick any car you'd like, and drive right out of here whenever you want. I won't do a thing to stop you. But I will weep a flood's worth of tears once you're gone, Mary. Because I have seen what's slithering through the black beyond those gates, and I will grieve knowing you're on the road to a fiery hell, and taking innocent children with you."

Mary nodded, still not knowing what to do, and thanked The Prophet for his valuable counsel. She was about to return to Desmond and let him know she was safe, even though The Prophet was every bit as crazy as they thought he was, when Brother Rei and John suddenly appeared. John nodded at Mary, then whispered something to The Prophet.

"You'll have to excuse me, Sister Mary," The Prophet said, then stepped to the side while Brother Rei stood staring at Mary.

The Prophet's face went paler than the mask that covered half of it, as he mopped his brow several times throughout the brief exchange. He finally turned to Mary and said, "It looks like we had a tragedy today. Outside The Sanctuary, of course. Brother Scott and Brother Eli are no longer with us. Both struck dead by the Demons. They were out on a run with Brothers Paul and James when the Demons attacked without warning, taking the warm breath of God right along with them."

John added, "The Demons used the store as a trap. They were waiting for our men when they got there, hiding the entire time. They only struck when they had the full advantage. It was a perfectly plotted ambush."

Mary stood there, silent, and in shock.

Scott was dead. He was still just a child, and he was murdered by the monsters. Just as Jimmy had been. The Prophet, as misguided as he was, had been right about one thing: This place was the only sanctuary she'd seen that the monsters had yet to breach.

"The Demons are growing stronger," Brother Rei said.

"No one is a firmer believer in the power of prayer than The Devil; not that he practices it, but because he suffers from it. I suggest we close our eyes and pray that we are able to preserve the safety behind the walls of The Sanctuary The Good Lord has seen fit to give us."

He took Mary's left hand, and Brother Rei took her right. They closed their eyes and lowered their heads as Mary stood and pretended to pray along with them, even though every fiber inside her wanted to run.

**

Mary picked at her dinner, which was an hour and a half later than usual, shuffling the potatoes around on her plate and scooping small forkfuls into her mouth, just enough so she wouldn't appear unappreciative of all the Good Lord had given them. She chewed with no pleasure and swallowed with less, each bite counting the minutes until she could speak with Desmond and Will again.

After dinner, the three of them gathered in the garden, where they spoke in swift whispers. Mary updated them, then shook her head. "I just don't know anymore. It's not that I think this place is safe, because I don't. And The Prophet's little talk designed to make me feel safer only made me want to run farther and faster. But I can't ignore what's happening outside. It sounds like it's getting worse, and I'm not sure we can handle it out there alone."

Will said, "We shouldn't forget, we'd all be dead right now if it weren't for the people here at The Sanctuary. Before John and his crew came in like The Cavalry, I was taking shots from the top of a silo with a few bullets to go and an army of crazy bleakers flooding through the gates."

Mary looked at Desmond, who was clearly swallowing his every other thought. It was tough to argue with the truth of Will's words, and Desmond dared not. Not now.

Mary said, "Scott didn't have to die. That is tragic and unnecessary. And I could never live with myself if something we could've prevented happens to Paola or Luca, or either one of you guys."

Desmond looked at Mary. "Will you be able to forgive yourself if The Prophet shaves Paola's hair and throws her in a box?" Mary wasn't sure if Desmond meant his words to sound as icy as they had, but she must have looked upset because he immediately said, "I'm sorry."

Mary didn't say anything, but she slipped her hand into Desmond's. Will said, "I'm with you, Mary. I'd never forgive myself either, and I'm the one pushing hardest to stay. So, I say we sleep on it. You said His Holy Worship has given us three days to decide, so I say we take three days to decide. Let's hit the hay and talk in the morning. The walls have ears and right now they're likely tuned to our conversation.

Early to bed, early to rise; we've a funeral in the morning, a wretched surprise."

"Thank you, Dr. Seuss," Desmond said.

The trio said good night. Mary returned to her room and tucked Paola in for the night before slipping beneath the stiff sheets of her hard bed, where she tossed and turned for hours, thinking about everything from Desmond to escape.

Everything felt wretched, and none of it right. They were all in grave danger if they left. She knew it like she knew that water was wet. Yet as certain as she was, she had no idea what to do. How long could they live at The Sanctuary before the cult came to punish one of them for some imagined sin?

And then there was the guilt, lying in bed with a dull ache between her legs, wanting nothing more than to have Desmond fill it. They'd not managed to sneak off a single time together, and as sad as it was to admit, they were both afraid of what would happen if they were caught. Mary was too goddamned old to feel like she was in high school, and she shouldn't have to bury her needs. She was wet and hungry, lying face down, filled with guilt for thinking about Desmond inside her, even though young Scott, barely old enough to scrape a razor on his face, would be six feet under in just a few hours.

Mary felt a chill imagining The Prophet's sermon, talking about how Scott could finally feel the Glory of strolling through the Gates to meet the Good Lord, after "bravely fighting off the evils of the approaching Demons" in his few final minutes.

When she finally fell asleep, Desmond disappeared, her mind filled by Ryan instead. He was lying still, as a young, black boy and an old, black man in a wheelchair hovered above, wiping a cloth across his face. He slowly opened his eyes to the bright light pouring in from the open windows. "He's awake, Gramps!" the boy said.

Ryan looked like he could barely move. "I thought you was never gonna wake," the old man said.

"What happened?" Ryan said, barely coherent.

The old man said he was safe and that the monsters were gone. Ryan was confused, asking questions and barely comprehending the answers. They hydrated him with water and told him again that he was safe, said he'd been out for five days after the monsters had bitten him. His eyes fluttered shut, and his breathing collapsed. His head fell back against the pillow.

That's when he saw Mary.

Ryan said. "Is that really you? I've been searching for you everywhere"

"You have?"

"Of course," he said. "I've been looking for you and Paola for months."

Something swam inside Mary's head, telling her she'd been in a similar spot many times before. "Is this real?" she asked. "Are you really still alive? I know I'm dreaming, but are you dreaming, too?"

"I was going to ask you the same thing," he said. Ryan smiled the same smile that had brought her to her knees more times than she could count. He met her eyes. "Are you and Paola really alive? I was almost out of hope."

"We are," Mary said. And though she didn't know why she said it, or even where it came from, she added, "Look for the broken cross. You'll know it when you see the stone walls. We need you to get here before the monsters attack."

Ryan turned to dust before she wandered through another series of dreams, not one of which she later remembered. When she woke the next morning, she had thoughts of Ryan at the front of her mind, like she often did, but didn't remember anything beyond that he'd been in her dreams.

She was awake for less than a minute when a queasy feeling rolled through her belly again, and sent her racing to the toilet. She made it just in time, as she vomited mostly fluids into the toilet.

Mary had felt that same feeling once before, 13 years earlier. The last time she had wanted dill pickles and green olives for 10 weeks straight.

There was life growing inside her, whether The Prophet would like it or not.

* * * *

CHAPTER 10
LUCA HARDING

Kingsland, Alabama
The Sanctuary
March 24
10:29 p.m.

Luca stared out the window at The Box of Shame, thinking about Rebecca and feeling the empty inside him that reminded him too much of the Terrible Scary. Scott had been killed by the monsters today, or the Demons, as everyone here called them, so Luca was alone in the room, trying not to feel sad. But it wasn't working.

He washed his face, brushed his teeth, missed his family, then got back into bed with his face to the wall. He lay like that for 15 minutes, before he couldn't stand to stare at the flickering shadows of tree branches on his wall any longer. He flipped to his other side so he could stare out the window at The Box of Shame, standing alone beneath the moonlight, illuminated by a thin shaft of silver raining from the sky like a spotlight on the girl's sadness.

I'm sorry you got put inside there, Luca thought. *It wasn't fair.*

Luca had become used to the voices in his head, but until earlier that day, he wasn't used to people answering back. But there was no mistaking the voice in his head this time. Rebecca said, "*Are you really there?*"

Luca thought, "*Yes, I'm upstairs in my room. I'm looking at the box right now, and I can feel that you're sad. Are you scared?*"

"Yes," Rebecca thought. "*It's really cold in here, and I'm hungry and lonely and I don't know what's going to happen to me. I heard bad stuff happened today. Is it true that someone died?*"

"*Some of the men went out on a run and were attacked by monsters. Scott died. So did Eli. They are going to have a funeral for both of them tomorrow.*"

"*Oh my God,*" Rebecca thought. "*Scott was your friend, wasn't he?*"

"*Yeah,*" Luca thought.

"*I'm so sorry.*"

"Me, too," Luca said. "*For Eli. Did you know him well?*"

"Yeah," she said, quiet for a full minute.

"*You're wondering what would happen if the monsters came inside The Sanctuary, aren't you?*" Luca thought. "*You're wondering if you would be safe, or if everyone would run and leave you behind?*"

Luca could feel Rebecca nodding.

"*I'm so cold. I keep wondering what's going to happen to me in here. I'm afraid it's going to be something really bad. Even if the monsters don't get me, I'll starve to death because no one will be here to put bread through the window.*"

"*I'll make sure you're safe.*"

"*How?*"

"*I don't know yet,*" Luca thought, "*But I'm going to sleep now, and that's where I do all my best thinking. It's where I meet all the voices who tell me everything I need to know.*"

"*Who are they? What do they say?*"

"*I dunno who they are. They say all sorts of things,*" Luca thought.

"*How do you know they're telling the truth?*"

"*Because I'm sleeping. The voices always tell the truth when I'm sleeping. I think because over there, they don't know how to lie. That's why I get more confused in the daytime sometimes than I do when I'm sleeping. When I'm sleeping, it's only the voices talking. In the daytime, I can hear all the other people, too. It's too much; I can't hear the voices that aren't people.*"

"*Huh?*" Rebecca said.

"*It'll make sense soon,*" Luca said. "*Are you still cold?*"

"Yes," she said.

"*I've got an idea,*" Luca said, and closed his eyes, imagining himself floating out of his body. He floated over his bed, looking down at himself, this older version of him that still seemed so different than how he visualized himself.

He looked outside the window, floated toward it, and dissolved through the wall.

It worked!

"*What?*" Rebecca asked.

"*Hold on.*"

Luca floated out into the night air; he could feel its coldness on his skin. He looked above the house and saw the guard sitting in the box on top of the roof. The man was smoking a cigarette, staring at, and through, Luca's ghost-self.

"*He can't see me.*"

"*Who can't see you?*" Rebecca asked.

"*The guard. He can't see me.*"

"*What are you doing? Are you outside?*"

"*I'm here.*"

"*Where? I can't see you.*"

"*Close your eyes.*"

Suddenly, Rebecca appeared, or a ghost-version of her, coming through the box and floating above it, looking around wide-eyed. Her bald head had small patches where Brother Rei hadn't gotten all the hair. She looked sickly, like those kids in the sad commercials Luca always saw on TV, and it made him sad for her.

"What did you do?" she asked, using her mouth instead of her mind. Luca turned to see if the guard had heard her. He hadn't.

"I don't know," he said, "This is the first time I've ever done this."

"Can he see us? Is this real?"

"I don't think he can see us," Luca said. "And I'm not sure if this is real, or that it matters."

"Take my hand; I want to show you something," he said.

Rebecca reached out and as their hands touched, a spark shot between their fingers. She pulled back, but only for a second before reaching out again.

Luca closed his hand around hers. Her hand was ice cold. He thought warm thoughts, and the girl smiled, feeling the heat.

"How?" she asked, looking down at her hand, then back up at him.

"Watch this," he said, pulling her up into the sky, both of them floating over the trees, and then even higher.

She pulled herself closer to him, as if she might fall if he let go.

Luca felt her coldness thaw against his chest, and he felt happy.

"Can we fall?" she asked.

"I don't think so," he said. "Let's go somewhere."

"Where?" she asked, looking at him, confused.

"There," he said, pointing to a nearby mountaintop, which glowed in a weird orange light.

They floated fast through the falling snow. Below them, in the middle of all the snow, was a circle of greenery and vibrant flowers, a place untouched by the winter. And in that grass, a wooden swing set with red seats, even nicer than the one he'd sat on with Paola.

They landed softly, and he let go of her, though reluctantly. They were surrounded by thousands of lightning bugs, which kept a respectable distance away from them, as if solely there to provide light for them.

"What is this?" she asked, walking in a circle around the swing set, staring at it as if it were made of magical candy. She looked at the lightning bugs with a smile that lit up her face.

"A swing," Luca said, with a smile.

"No, I mean this place," she said with a smile. "Is this real?"

"Are you warm?" he asked, taking a seat.

"Yes," she said.

"That's all that matters then," he said, kicking his feet out and setting the swing into motion. The swing's chains squeaked and the set moved slightly up and down with each motion. Rebecca took the opposite seat and kicked her feet out too with a big laugh.

"This is so weird!" she said. "You did this, all of this, didn't you?"

"I dunno," Luca said, not wanting to call attention to the things that made him different. "Let's just swing."

**

Luca wasn't sure how long they'd been swinging, but it seemed like a good while. She told him about her sister, Alexis, and how her mother hadn't always been so mean, or scared.

Luca talked about his family, Will, and a lot about Dog Vader. He got sad talking about Dog Vader, so he changed the subject to the rest of his friends.

"Is she your girlfriend?" Rebecca asked of Paola. "She's soooo pretty."

"No," Luca said, feeling weird talking about Paola with another girl. Luca looked up at the sky, noting how the stars looked a bit different than usual, though he wasn't sure how. Perhaps he had dreamed them into being, as well.

Looking at Rebecca, as she told her story, Luca felt incredibly sad for her. She'd been through so much, and he wanted to make her happy. But what could he do? If he tried to get her out of the box, the people would surely further punish her, and him. He tried to remember how his dad made his mom happy, and then an idea came to him.

"Hold on a second," he said, hopping off the swing.

He walked past the lightning bugs and into the snow, towards the trees which surrounded them, and thought a rose bush into being. The bush sprouted from the snow, pushing up, and growing within seconds, sprouting perfectly red flowers.

He picked one and then thought the thorns away, and they were gone.

He walked back to the swing holding the flower, and outstretched his hand, "Here. I know it's not much, but at least you can be happy here. For now."

She hopped off the swing, and stared at the flower, tears in her eyes, a smile on her face. "It's the most beautiful thing I've ever seen! Nobody has ever given me flowers before."

They stood awkwardly, like two young teens who didn't know what to do or say next. He wondered if he should hug her, when she leaned forward and hugged him.

Her hug was warm and felt so good and so real, he never wanted the moment to end.

Luca felt butterflies stirring in his belly, and giddy.

Suddenly, his arms were empty.

Luca opened his eyes, and she was gone.

"Rebecca?"

She didn't respond.

The lightning bugs scattered all at once, looking like a million candles flying apart and flickering out, casting the world into darkness.

Snow began to fall down upon the protected haven and cover the ground with increasing speed as if making up for lost time.

The swings vanished.

Someone was watching him.

At first, Luca couldn't tell who it was, but he saw a shadow in the snow, about 20 feet away. Luca had to get closer and closer, until he could almost smell him – the man from a few nights before. The Dark Man; the Man in the Middle, standing behind the rose bush.

The Man in the Middle should have scared him. Luca was pretty sure he was born inside of the Terrible Scary. But for the first time, Luca wasn't really afraid at all.

The Man in the Middle was wearing all black – pants, shirt, and a big, long coat like he'd seen cowboys wearing on TV. He was holding something in his black gloved hands, but it wasn't until Luca was standing a few feet away that he could see what it was – a large red rose, but different than the one he had picked for Rebecca, which was now gone, with her.

The rose looked like it had a million petals, and its deep color looked like blood against all the white of the surrounding snow. When Luca was only a few feet away, he could hear The Man in the Middle saying, "She loves me, she loves me not," as he pulled petals from the bud, then released them to the wind where they fluttered slowly into the flurry, then floated to the carpeted snow like droplets of blood.

"It's you," The Man in the Middle said.

"Do you have a rose for me?" Luca said, even though the question made no sense to him, like one of those things that happened in dreams. It was as if he was following someone else's script, even though the words came from his mouth.

"Of course." The Man in the Middle reached behind his back and produced a second red rose, with even more petals and none of them picked.

"Thank you," Luca said. He took the rose and started to pick the petals, one by one, adding fresh drops of blood to the new fallen snow. He said, "She loves me, she loves me not," just like The Man in the Middle.

They picked their petals together in silence, the cold wind stinging their cheeks, neither one afraid. Luca was about to leave to look for Rebecca when he said, "You're sharing the snow right now with all of us, right?"

The Man in the Middle looked down at Luca, and said, "She loves me not."

* * * *

CHAPTER 11
BORICIO WOLFE

In the woods
March 25
Early morning

Boricio stared through the binoculars, watching the snow cover the sloping roofs of the houses below, the place his gut told him that his team had gone to. There were no signs of Charlie, Adam, Vic, or Callie. But it made sense that they'd be down there. It was warm and looked like the safest place Boricio had seen in a while. If they were making a break from Team Boricio, this seemed like the best bet for the four of them.

He almost couldn't blame them for leaving. But he was pissed as a motherfucker that they hadn't thought to come get him. And to come *here*, of all places? To the enemy camp?

What, do they think they're too good for me? They don't want Boricio socializing with their new friends?

Either way, the trip wouldn't be a waste. Even if Chucky Fuckup wasn't down there letting Adam give him the old reach around, since Callie wouldn't, the odds were solid that Boricio would find something to fuck, even if not Callie. Now that he'd had a taste of fresh pussy, or not so fresh in Jenna's case, he was like a fatso off his diet.

Boricio tossed the binoculars into his backpack, then wrapped a scarf around his neck and pulled a wool hat over his head, just past his ears. He turned the pistol around in his hand, taking a long while to drop it in the trunk, along with the bag full of weapons, he would come back to get later.

He tossed his keys into a hole in a nearby tree, and covered the Z8 with a white tarp, where it was concealed well enough behind a thick wall of trees.

Boricio trudged through the snow toward the compound, until he found the road that led to the wrought iron gates in the distance. Every step thickened the new feeling inside him, a feeling he didn't know but liked a whole fuck of a lot. It was like walking into a dream, wide awake.

He'd been watching the place for hours, and hadn't seen one person he recognized. He hoped they wouldn't recognize him, either. And if they did, oh well. He'd gotten out of there once before.

Boricio reached the entrance to the compound and stood in front of the gate, staring at the letters carved into the stone wall: "The Sanctuary."

Even with the bitter wind biting the skin from his face, Boricio couldn't help but laugh out loud.

Ain't no sanctuary in the world with enough solace to save it from Boricio.

* * * *

::EPISODE 11::
(FIFTH EPISODE OF SEASON TWO)
"THE LOOPHOLE"

CHAPTER 1
"JOHN"

Kingsland, Alabama
The Sanctuary
March 25
9:06 a.m.

"It's coming."

The creature that was once John started its morning as it had each day, meditating in the middle of the manmade room, sucking in the soured air and reaching beyond the gates to speak with the best parts of him - the parts that crawled through the forest, waited in the mountains, and lingered in the shadows beyond The Sanctuary.

John smiled wide at the long awaited message, finally delivered by fraying fragments of his self, lingering in the shadows and oozing like oil over his thoughts.

"It's coming."

John was growing stronger by the day, and his new strength was making the old patience even more restless. He could end these humans in a flood of fury, before they had time to blink in disbelief. The man who called himself "The Prophet" believed them all safe, here in their laughably named "Sanctuary." This man was foolish enough to think that his "God" would somehow keep his congregation safe inside a self-proclaimed holy land.

The Prophet's holy land was hollow. The only thing keeping his congregation safe was *It*, or *John* as *It* was named in this mortal disguise. The humans would breathe their soured air as long as *John* allowed it, and not one second longer. The Prophet's archaic god had nothing to do with their safety, but everything to do with how easy it was going to be for *John* to slaughter all his little lambs at once.

For now, the human gathering served *John* well, fencing them inside, too blind to see the bars that their "protection" had built around them, too thick to bend or break. *He* allowed it, encouraged it, fostered the illusion of safety by having his legions of darkness strike hardest whenever doubt about the The Sanctuary's safety began to bleed through its walls.

Yesterday, he had to kill two. Today, he might need to kill another. *John* could sense the doubt threading itself through the seams of the woman, Mary, and her flock.

He should have killed them all back at the hotel, should never have allowed their strength to build, even if it was only a whisper compared to his inevitable scream.

But he couldn't kill them all, not then and not now. Not without damaging his connection to Luca. And that was something he simply couldn't afford to do. The boy was more than powerful, he was preordained.

Luca would soon play a large role in the inevitable. He simply needed a little encouragement, a nudge in the right direction. The Prophet gave *John* the breadcrumbs to lay, which made it easy for Luca to follow him precisely where he wanted him - here, behind the walls of The Sanctuary, sharing the soured air with his pompous flock.

Things were starting to settle into place, the pieces finally fitting together. It would happen soon — the event he'd been made for; the event that would unite his scattered parts and fraying fragments into the fabric of the future.

John could feel the grand design like these humans felt hunger. *He* was born from the past, was the core of the present, and the only thing the future cared about. Because *John* was all that mattered to the universe, *he* knew things the humans never could, things they were not designed to see.

How could they expect to stare into the infinite when they couldn't even smell the sour of the air?

John could see his true purpose forming in the shadows around him, slowly taking shape – crawling through the forest, waiting in the mountains, and lingering in the shadows while *he* waited behind the walls of The Sanctuary, preparing to strike.

His communication with the creatures these people called demons, monsters, and bleakers had grown stronger over the months. *John* was able to command them no different than he commanded his hand to pick up a drink, or his arm to bring it to his lips. The creatures were an extension of him, a deadly appendage, but they had grown dangerously restless, craving more strength in their numbers. They were gathering together in the world outside The Sanctuary, infesting new hosts, and spreading like wildfire through a bed of broken branches.

The Prophet had started the fire; he had been tricked into opening the vial and setting this life free – this life that feasted on death; this life that would erase the old.

The pieces were settling into place — until this morning.

Until *John* sensed the *thing* in the woods, watching them.

It was human, but not like the others. It was something more. Something *John* felt he should comprehend, but didn't, couldn't, even though he clawed inside his mind searching for the answer. Though the answer laid hidden, *he* had no more time to search. That *something* was standing in the snow, waiting at the gates of his death camp. That much *John* knew for certain.

A knock on his door confirmed what he knew.

"Brother John," Brother Rei called from the other side of the door, "We have a visitor."

John stood, allowing the morning sun to warm his nude shell, then slipped into his pants and shirt, then a robe over both. Humans felt the need to wear so many clothes, almost as if the layers could disguise the lies inside them.

John opened the door and saw the red fear brewing in Brother Rei's eyes, "He's still outside the gate; Brother Linc hasn't let him in yet. The man just showed up out of the blue this morning, saying something about God calling him here. I don't like the look of him."

John walked past Brother Rei, then descended downstairs, out the front door, and over to the wrought iron gate, where Brothers Linc and Ed stood guard with their rifles. The *thing* John had sensed stood calm behind the gate; this man who was not quite a man. The voices had said *it* was coming. Was this *it*? Was this the *thing* that would usher in the darkness?

"Hello, brother, my name is John. What brings you to The Sanctuary?"

"God sent me," the man said. The lie was revolting. But it was a different stench from the delusion the rest of The Sanctuary's willing prisoners had been telling themselves about a so-called God who cared about them. The "man" at the gate held no such illusions. He was smart enough to use God as the golden key to gain access. The question was, why?

Was he what *John* had been waiting for? Or was he another obstacle?

Though *John* wasn't quite ready for someone to jeopardize what he'd so carefully built, perhaps this was exactly how it was supposed to be. *He* never questioned the voices. They'd yet to steer him wrong.

"And who might you be, Brother?" *John* asked.

"The name's Boricio," he said with such boldness that it seemed he were waiting for applause.

"Welcome to The Sanctuary, Brother Boricio," John said, his plastic grin upon his face, then directed the men to let Boricio inside. "You've arrived on a rather unfortunate day. We're having a funeral."

"That is most unfortunate, indeed," Boricio agreed without a whiff of agreement, stepping through the gate and into The Sanctuary.

John bristled. Another piece of the puzzle had slid into place, but he had no idea who the piece belonged to.

And the voices weren't telling.

* * * *

CHAPTER 2
WILL BISHOP

Fort Lauderdale, Florida
Nov. 10, 1995
8:40 p.m.

Will sat behind the counter at Hidden Wonders, one of the last decent bookstores downtown, staring at the calendar on the wall. He couldn't believe tomorrow was a year to the day since he found the loophole.

For the four months prior, Will had been dreaming of Sam's accident happening on Nov. 11, last year. He couldn't tell Sam, of course. For one, Sam would think he was crazy. For two, fate — or whatever it was that pulled the strings, yet also tormented Will with glimpses into the future — didn't appreciate mortals like Will trying to intervene.

Will spent months searching for a loophole — a way to save Sam, without telling him what was going to happen. According to the dreams, which always had the same ending, no matter how they started, Sam was injured badly in a car accident. He was struck by a drunk driver at 2:15 p.m. on

374

his return trip to the bookstore they owned together. Sam would cross the street three blocks away and be in the path of an out-of-control car that drove straight into a restaurant and struck three diners, killing two of them instantly. As a result of the accident, Sam would wind up being a paraplegic, spending the rest of his years in almost constant pain and misery.

Considering Sam never missed a day of work, and would never take time off on a whim, no matter how compelling Will might make the whim sound, he would have to get creative if he expected to get Sam away from the bookstore and into a safe place.

Will ran through a hundred ideas, but none seemed like they would work, at least not without raising suspicion. With Sam, suspicion led to reservation, and reservation was often a brick wall between them.

He tried to order pizza for lunch, convince Sam to dine in. But Sam was a man of routine and only broke it when forced. He did the same things, day in and day out. Ate at the same diner every day for as long as they'd owned the bookstore. He was obsessive-compulsive about everything, and a break in routine was disaster in his personal world. Every day, Sam left Hidden Wonders at 12:30 p.m. on his way to the bank for their daily deposit. He ate lunch at the diner next to the bank, where he scribbled in his notebook, working on a novel he'd been writing every day for as long as they'd known one another.

A rhythm like clockwork.

So, Will would have to get creative if he were to successfully meddle with time.

Just before lunch, Will *accidentally* locked Sam in the storage room while he was counting the daily receipts and preparing the deposit. They had two locks on the door, one that locked and opened from the inside and another that locked and opened from the outside. That was how the door had been installed, for reasons only the last tenant knew. It was odd, but nothing Will or Sam ever bothered to change considering the million and one other things that needed their attention. There were always more things to fix than money to fix them. And besides, what were the odds one of them would actually get locked into the room from the outside? While parts of the city had gone to hell, their section of downtown had remained relatively safe.

Will managed to clear the storage room of any screwdrivers or tools Sam could use to open the door ahead of time. Sam didn't seem savvy enough to know how to use a credit card to slide the lock open, so Will's plan had a shot of success. Five minutes after Sam went inside, Will locked the door, then broke the key off inside.

Sam was pissed, especially when Will told him the locksmith said it would be several hours before he could get to the store and free him.

"Can't you get some pliers and turn it or something?" Sam asked from the other side of the door, sounding desperate, even though he'd only just discovered his predicament.

"No, it's jammed good," Will said.

"Why did you even lock it?!"

"I dunno, I saw some shady looking people walking by, like they were casing the place or something, and I wanted to make sure you were secure."

"Are they still out there?" Sam said, now sounding worried for Will, which turned up the flame under Will's guilt.

"No, they got on the bus. Just sit tight; the locksmith will probably be here sooner than he said. He wants to under-promise so he can over-deliver. Good business, right?"

"What the hell am I supposed to do until then? I already did the deposits and books."

"I dunno, maybe you can do some organizing while you're in there." Will laughed. Though Sam was obsessive about many things, organization of the storage room wasn't one of them, a source of minor bickering between them for years.

"Nice try," Sam said. "I'll find something to read. *That* shouldn't be a problem."

Will laughed, then went back to the counter up front, happy he'd managed to find a loophole, and hoping it would work. His past experiences at finding loopholes had always blown up in his face, though. But the other times, he'd tried direct methods of intervention, trying to tackle a problem head-on. Locking Sam in a room seemed less direct. He wasn't trying to stop the accident, but trying to keep Sam from being there. Perhaps fate wouldn't notice such an indirect method of interference.

Perhaps.

Shortly after 2 o'clock, Will heard the sirens of racing ambulances and police cars. Something had happened, right on schedule. And Will was safe and sound.

After 3 p.m., the locksmith freed a grateful Sam from the storage room. The way Sam carried on, and his level of gratitude, you'd think he'd been a prisoner of war and not a man who'd been subject to a minor inconvenience. Will teased him mercilessly, then called Wong's and had them deliver chicken fried rice and veggies, and convinced Sam to do the deposit later. He could have a late lunch in the storage room, and write in there.

"Fine," Sam said, reluctantly breaking routine for the first time in years.

Later that day, they heard from one of their customers about a horrible accident two blocks away. A drunk driver had driven straight into the window of Tony's Pizza just after 2 p.m. He killed two diners inside the restaurant.

"Wow," Will said to Sam, "You walk by there every day around that time."

"I know. Some luck I got locked in the back room, eh?"

Will smiled. *Lucky indeed.*

Will worried a little that something would happen to Sam in the days or weeks after that. But his fear eventually dimmed when no new dream warnings haunted his sleep. Will had found a loophole. And after that, the prophetic dreams had stopped, and he no longer woke filled with dread. Life had become, for the first time in decades, normal.

But now, a year later, while one stress was gone from his life, another remained – the bookstore.

He needed to convince Sam to sell it while they still could walk away with something other than debt. Will would be 50 next year, and didn't need this sort of uncertainty hanging like a pregnant cloud above his head.

"We should stop the bleeding now," he told Sam a hundred times, if not a thousand, after the new café/bookstore opened just down the street. The new bookstore was gigantic: two stories with music listening stations, comfy love seats and sofas sprinkled throughout the store. Bookstores were supposed to be intimate, but this new behemoth was as intimate as a whorehouse with its trendy café serving overpriced coffee and baked goods while hipster music piped through a premium speaker system, sending subtle messaging to their customers that they were in the perfect place to sit back, relax, and eventually buy anything from the books on the shelves to the board games on the end caps.

Hidden Wonders was the antithesis of the giant store – a narrow hole-in-the-wall packed to the rafters with an inventory that was half used books, and almost half titles that had never harbored hope of hitting a bestseller's list. It looked like an old and messy closet compared to these new spacious bookstores. Will knew there was no way in hell they had a chance to compete. He thought people wanted small, intimate, and friendly. But the numbers didn't lie. People *said* they wanted stores like Hidden Wonders, yet their actions told the truth – they preferred corporate-defined trendy, bargain-priced books, and overpriced snacks. Will found it funny that people balked at paying retail price for a book, something that a writer poured his or her heart and soul into, and which you could only find in specific shops, yet they gladly paid premium prices on coffee, something so readily available and at much cheaper prices.

He and Sam had the conversation again after lunch. Will suggested they sell the shop to Sam's usual eye roll and sigh that said, *not this again*, without having to say it at all.

There was an investor looking at the property. No, it wouldn't be a bookstore anymore, but they could get out with a small profit, if they were smart enough to act soon. The investor wasn't stupid; it wouldn't be long before he could read the writing written all over the wall. The offer would vanish, and Will would be back to wishing for another opportunity. Hidden Wonders' days were numbered, and the investor's offer was generous, considering.

"Our customers love us," Sam had said, optimism (and delusion) as thick in his blood as ever. "We know what books they like. We know what books to recommend. We know them. We care about them. You can't get that at these new box stores, and you never will!"

"That's not what people care about anymore," Will said, feeling more defeated than ever. The recent months had beaten and battered their bank account. "How long are you gonna ignore the numbers?"

"I'm not ignoring the numbers," Sam said, offended. "But I'm not willing to give up on our customers. People like Mrs. Williams, Mr. Jenkins, and Vince Patrella – just some of the people who rely on us, who come in every day, or every week. People we've come to know over the years who have made this place feel like a second home and them like family and friends. There are a few dozen more just like them. These people are loyal."

Will didn't have the heart to tell Sam that two weeks ago he'd seen Mrs. Williams, the same woman who said she'd rather die than step in one of those big soulless stores, walking out of the new bookstore with a bag full of books. Fortunately, she hadn't seen Will. That would have been awkward. But he had seen her, and the writing wasn't just on the wall, it was in every book on every shelf in the bookstore down the street. When someone like Mrs. Williams, a loyal customer for years, was buying books in bulk from the competition, Hidden Wonders would have to fight with both fists for a snowball's chance in hell.

And Will was getting too old to fight losing battles.

Their argument, if it could be called an argument at all, ended as it always did, at a stalemate, neither side willing to surrender or even back down an inch. Sam seemed destined to sink with his ship, making Will more or less stuck, unless he could change the captain's stubborn mind. Sam was fiercely loyal. Though it was one of his best qualities in most areas, it clouded his business thinking and decision making. A little over a year ago, the town's favorite bagel shop next door exploded in popularity. The owner needed to expand, and offered Will and Sam an extremely generous amount to sell their shop so he could knock the walls down, increasing his square footage. Will thought it was a no-brainer. But Sam wanted to stay put. The owner of the bagel shop decided to move when his lease was up, opening shop a half mile away. The opportunity, along with a lot of the bagel shop's customers, would never return.

And now, as closing time – 9 p.m. – inched closer, Will wanted to get to the bar, meet with Sam for some drinks, and hope like hell the conversation wouldn't come up again. Tonight, he just wanted to drink, forget, and have a good time. Tomorrow was his day off, and he intended to sleep in late. Really late. Maybe all day, if he could get away with it.

As Will began cleaning up and getting ready to close, the phone split the silence and sent a shiver down his spine. Before the first ring finished its chime, Will knew something was wrong.

Little did he know he'd wind up spending the entire night in the hospital.

**

Will sat in the hospital waiting room waiting forever for Trudy, Sam's mom, who had to drive from Boca.

Trudy arrived, as she usually did anywhere she went, as a full-on spectacle. She raced over to Will, already half crying, "What happened?"

"A cop friend of mine called and said some men jumped Sam. Beat him up pretty bad. They're not letting me see him though, since I'm not family."

"Oh God," Trudy wailed, "How can this happen?! Where did this happen? *Why* did this happen?"

"According to my friend, the men were calling him 'fag' and 'homo' over and over as they beat him, lots of blows to the face."

Trudy looked around and demanded to see Sam's surgeon. One of the orderlies said she'd get someone. Trudy's eyes bored into Will, "Where were you? Why didn't you stop them?"

"I was at work," Will said. "I was about to close shop and meet up with him. Happened just outside the bar where we meet every weekend. We've never had problems before."

"Is it one of those . . . *gay bars?*" she asked, barely able to push the words from her mouth. Though Trudy had accepted her son's lifestyle when he came out to her two years ago - or at least claimed she did - she could rarely utter any words associated with it. It seemed as if she felt ignoring that part of her son's life would somehow make it go away, returning her life to how it used to be, before she knew.

"Yes, but it's not some seedy joint," Will said, "It's a nice place, with a friendly atmosphere and the drink prices to prove it. We've never had anything like this happen before. There's a few gay-friendly businesses in the area, and this just doesn't happen in these parts."

"So, you go there, all the time?" Trudy asked, her voice thick with accusation.

"Like I said, it's a great place to unwind," Will said, growing impatient and defensive.

"I always knew you were bad news for Sam," she said, wiping tears from her eyes.

"What?"

"It's your fault. He didn't go to places like . . . *that*, before . . . until *you* came along!"

Will wanted to scream.

Do you think I made your son gay? That he wasn't that way before he met me?

But what was the point? That's how Trudy thought, and how she always would. To her, being gay was a choice, and the wrong one. So she needed someone to blame for "making" her son gay. For his entire 40 years prior to meeting Will, Sam had been straight as an arrow. Then BAM!, Will turned his preference like some sort of gay vampire. It was ridiculous, but no easier to change than the weather.

Will bit his tongue, as was custom with Trudy. He'd let her have her drama, then wait for her to calm down, as she always did. Anything else would only make matters worse. Trudy was barely polite to Will on the best of days, even though Sam claimed she really did like him. There was no way he was going to get into an argument or try reasoning with her today. Sam could've been jumped outside of a church, and Trudy would find some way to blame his lifestyle on Will. Besides, some part of Will understood her anger.

She was afraid. Hell, Will was afraid. Civility sometimes went out the window when you were afraid, especially when a loved one's life was in danger.

The sound of the waiting room doors opening heralded the entrance of the surgeon. Trudy went to him so quickly Will didn't have time to follow. By the time he did, he would have felt like he were butting into the conversation. So he stayed put, about 20 feet away, tilting his body toward the conversation while trying not to be too obvious, watching Trudy's reactions for any sign of what might be happening with Sam.

"A coma?!" she cried, "I want to see my son!"

A coma?

Will's heart froze in his chest; the unthinkable suddenly reality – Sam could wind up a paraplegic, regardless of Will's intervention. Had fate found a way around his loophole as it had so many times in the past?

He flashed back to the last words they'd had as Sam was leaving for the day. They were unkind. Will told Sam he was a fool, and they were going to lose everything on what, sentimentality and an unwillingness to let go and lean into the inevitable?

The surgeon led Trudy away from the waiting room.

Will started to follow, but the surgeon, a Greek man with dark eyes and darker hair, turned to him, and said, "Are you family?"

"He's my boyfriend," Will said. "We live together, so practically, yes."

"No," Trudy said, glaring back at Will. "He's not family."

They left Will standing in the hall, devastated, the words robbed from his mouth.

* * * *

CHAPTER 3
WILL BISHOP

Kingsland, Alabama
The Sanctuary
March 25, 2012
Morning

"Jesus, that's a giant cross!" Desmond said, pointing to the massive wooden cross erected overnight, or in the misty morning hours, in front of the church. It dwarfed the original cross, still standing to its left, by almost half, and looked sturdy enough to hang someone from.

"Is there a crucifixion on the schedule today?"

A chill ran down Will's spine. The cross was even more menacing under the light of the sun than it had been in the shroud of his dreams. Given that everyone was already dressed in funeral black, a crucifixion didn't seem entirely impossible, even if Will hadn't seen it in his dreams.

"If you're gonna take the Lord's name in vain, I suppose that's about as close as you can get to an appropriate use of blasphemy." Will laughed, trying to smother his chill.

Desmond said, "This place just keeps getting weirder and weirder."

"You're telling me, 'brother.'" Will said, and they both laughed.

They were on their way to breakfast, about 50 yards from the table, when Desmond pointed to The Sanctuary's front gate. "You know anything about that?"

Will didn't, but it took him approximately one second to not like it a bit. "No idea." The sun was bright above, making the white of the snow scream below. He made a visor with his hand to improve his view, but it didn't help much. "But it looks like we have a visitor."

Brothers John and Rei were standing by the gate, huddled beside a handful of their most intimidating men. The stranger stood in front of the huddle, slightly inside The Sanctuary, too far for details beyond the dark thatch of hair and the familiar darkness Will had seen in his dreams too many times to count.

"Well, what do you think?" Desmond gestured toward the gate. "Does our new friend end up kneeling at the altar of New Unity, or does he get smart in the other direction?"

"Who knows? Has anything turned out as we expected? Maybe that guy out there," Will nodded toward the gates, "ends up on that back there." He threw his thumb behind him, toward the new cross. "All we can do now is watch, and wait."

"Ah," Desmond said, "the end of the world special."

The men fell silent as they approached the breakfast table, which Mary, Paola, and Luca were already sitting at. A few others from the church were also seated at their table, neutering any real conversation.

Desmond pulled out his chair and sat directly across from Will. Both men folded their hands and waited for Morning Prayer. Will smiled at Mary and Paola and Luca, but didn't see Linc at any of the other five tables. There was another few minutes of silence, and when it was clear that neither Brothers Rei or John, or The Prophet, were coming to lead grace, Brother Reginald stood and thanked The Good Lord for all they were about to receive.

Silverware clinked, a few people coughed, and the wood from the bench whispered as members of the congregation shifted in their seats. The silence was so loud it was nearly a scream. Paola couldn't take it. She dropped her fork with a clatter and yelled, "Isn't anyone going to talk about him?"

Will didn't think she and Scott had been all that close, but he kept the thought in the back of his head where it belonged, then reached for Paola across the table. "I'm sorry," he said. "Some people like to grieve in silence. Just because no one's saying anything, doesn't mean they don't care."

"Scott was funny," she said. "He wouldn't have wanted everyone to keep quiet."

"Well then," Will said, "let's remember the good times. How about the time we were stuck in that warehouse for two days and had nothing to eat, and Scott made you the imaginary milkshake?" All eyes were on Will, even the ones that acted like they weren't. "Now what was in that milkshake again?"

"It was a Jolly Rancher flavored milkshake, with rainbow sprinkles, chocolate chips, and magical drops from the sun to keep me warm." Paola laughed, then wiped a tear from her eye. "And it was in a tall glass made from sugar crystals and Saturn rings." Paola started laughing harder through her tears.

That was enough to get others at the table, those who hadn't known him and had no right to really talk of him, to do just that, with more than a fair share of "he's with the Good Lord now," and "the Gates have swung open early for him."

Will saw Desmond trying not to roll his eyes while grabbing Mary's attention. But her mind seemed elsewhere, which would explain the gaze that was nowhere near Desmond. There was a new frosty layer between them that had to be a recent development. He wondered if they'd been in a fight, but the chill was only coming from Mary. He waited for her head to turn in his direction, then swallowed his mouthful of biscuit and said, "You okay?"

Mary nodded. Desmond's eyes moved between her and Will, as though he wanted to know the same thing, and was sure one of them harbored the answer.

Mary and Desmond were always desperate for alone time, but had to wait until after breakfast each morning, when they could sneak away to the garden and steal a few minutes' worth of whispers. But the funeral was scheduled for this morning, so they wouldn't have their usual chance. Any whispers worth stealing would have to be stolen later.

Two of the older women in the congregation, whose names Will didn't know, began clearing the tables as the rest of the congregation drifted like the black cloud it was out of the house, past the church, and beyond the far wall, outside The Sanctuary and to the cemetery in the woods just beyond.

The iron gate whined open to a short, twisting path through the woods, leading to the ancient cemetery. Even if it wasn't ancient by biblical standards, it was ancient for American soil, with a few newer headstones mingled among the mostly Civil War-era graves.

Will's eyes were everywhere, but The Prophet was nowhere in sight. Not knowing where he was made Will feel like a target. The Prophet, Brother Rei, and John had been watching him more intently in recent days. Perhaps The Prophet had seen the same things Will had seen in his dream, and wanted to act before events unfolded as they would. Will's hairs were on end as he searched for The

Prophet. Fortunately, the mystery was cleared before the funeral started.

Brothers Rei and John approached the congregation with The Sanctuary's new visitor one step behind. The visitor and John stayed at the back, as Brother Rei walked to the front and glanced at the hole in the ground, then turned his attention to the congregation. The corners of his mouth were heavy, dipping toward his almost nonexistent chin. He cleared his throat and said, "Before we get started, I must inform you, as deeply saddened as I am to do so, that The Prophet has taken ill, and is on bed rest for the day. He shall be well again soon, but I regret that I must step in and administer today's ceremony."

Brother Rei lowered his head, then clutched the Bible to his chest with one hand while raising the other to the sky. He held his pose for more than a minute, then raised his head and moved his eyes across the congregation. Will wondered if any of the people standing with hands folded and eyes on Brother Rei wanted him to get the hell on with it, or whether they were happy to stand in the stinging cold while he milked the moment of every drop. Brother Rei might be third in charge, but he may as well have been second, the way he enjoyed the spotlight. John was more of a silent partner in the church, while Brother Rei desperately wanted to be as charismatic as The Prophet was.

"We are gathered here together to celebrate a young life ascended to Heaven. Brother Scott was taken from our flock too early, yes, but we have no reason to mourn. For Brother Scott was called Home and ushered through the Gates; Brother Scott now has what we are all waiting here to get. Our Good Brother Scott most certainly received his Heavenly reward for his hard work, ridding this world of Demons, which is what he was in the thick of doing when he was called home by the Good Lord Himself."

That was all Brother Rei managed before Luca fled the funeral, crying.

Will was suddenly grateful that Luca was only a boy inside the shell of a man, giving him the perfect excuse to run off and leave. And since a boy shouldn't be wandering through a Demon-infested forest alone, Will would be happy to do the Good Lord's work and look after him.

Will followed Luca back to his Quiet Spot, where he sat with his head in his chest, buried beneath gangly arms, looking every bit of eight as he did sixteen.

"You okay?"

Luca looked up, nodded at Will, then buried his head back where it belonged.

"What are you thinking in that head of yours? You don't mind telling me, right? You can trust me. Remember, I'm the man with the lobster tacos. I flew you all the way across the country. And plus," Will smiled. "I've known you since you were only eight!"

Will wasn't sure if the joke about his age would upset Luca further, and was relieved when the boy broke into a little laugh. Will took Luca's laughter as permission to sit. "You know," he said, "I'm sad, too."

Luca looked up. "You *are?*"

"Of course. Scott was my friend. And these days, friends are scarce."

"I was mean to him," Luca said. "The last time we talked, I mean. It makes me feel like maybe I had something to do with him not ever coming back."

"You know that's ridiculous, right?"

Luca nodded, but fresh tears fell from his eyes anyway. "I heard Scott call me a freak. But he didn't say it. He thought it. And I heard him. And he knew I heard him, and was even more freaked out. So, I ran away, and when I did, I was kind of wishing I'd never saved him. I know it sounds silly, but I feel like if I hadn't thought that, maybe he wouldn't have died yesterday," Luca cried, loud enough for Will to scoot closer and shush him.

"Not sure it's best to draw attention to ourselves right now with talk of hearing thoughts," Will said in a whisper, even though there was no one around them. He took off his jacket and handed it to Luca. "Cry into this, okay." It was freezing outside, but Will would rather be freezing than heard, and The Sanctuary felt like it was growing ears.

"Don't be silly," Will whispered. "You had nothing to do with Scott dying. Nothing. It happened, and you have to be okay with it. It wasn't like you knew he was gonna die and did nothing to stop it. And even then, fate's gonna do what it's gonna do. It's easier to win an argument with Paola."

Luca smiled, then surprised Will by dropping the subject. He surprised him more by changing it. "Do you think we should be here? I mean, right now, at The Sanctuary. Do you think it's safe?"

Will looked at Luca for a while before he said, "What makes you say that?"

"Because this place feels wrong to me."

"Can you tell me what you mean?"

Luca looked everywhere except at Will, before he finally said, "Just promise not to think I'm weird. I don't want to be weird anymore."

"Sorry, kid," Will shook his head. "No can do. You're definitely weird. We both are. That's what makes us worth talking to in the first place."

Luca laughed, but only for a second, then said, "Is it sometimes okay to do the wrong thing for the right reason?"

"Ah," Will said, finally getting where Luca was going. "You're worried about Rebecca, right?" Luca nodded, eyes still in the snow.

Will wondered which of the hundred things Luca wasn't saying he should ask about first, then went for the shortcut. "What are you worried about? Are you wondering if Rebecca's okay?"

Luca shook his head. "No, I know she's okay. She told me. But I want to help her. I keep thinking maybe I could get her out of there if I tried. I keep thinking I should."

Will raised his eyebrows. "What do you mean she *told you*? Have you been over there talking to her? You have to be careful, Luca. If you're caught, you'll be in trouble, too."

"I can hear her in my head, but she can hear me, too." Luca said. He closed his eyes and swayed back and forth for a second, before opening them again and holding Will's eyes for the first time. "We talk to each other. I know it's really happening, and that it's not just in my head, even if you think I'm crazy."

Will said, "What makes you think I think you're crazy? Didn't we cross the country together on account of a dream?"

Luca nodded. "But this isn't in a dream," he said. "It's in real life. And when it's in real life, with real people, it feels like I'm going crazy. Even though I know I'm not."

"All of it is in real life," Will said. "Even the dreams. And you're closer to sane than almost anyone here, Luca. You're not crazy; you're gifted. And you can't change who you are, so stop trying. You're different than us all. Most likely better, too. Best you can do is not question the gift. Embrace it, and try to do the best you can for as long as you can. Nothing less will do."

Will kept talking, but only in his head. "You've nothing to be worried about. I hear a thought or two myself, here and there."

"You have?" The words were already out of Luca's mouth before he realized what that meant. They'd been speaking without words for a while.

"So, you can hear me, too?" he thought. "Why can't everyone else?"

Will shrugged. "Honestly, kid, I have no idea. My best guess is that they probably could. They just don't know how, or even that they can. Like I said, everyone's weird. Unless they know for a fact that they can do something, most people assume they can't do something that sounds hard or impossible, even if it's as simple as closing their eyes and getting it done. Tell you what," Will put his hand on Luca's shoulder. "Close your eyes and think of something, but don't say a word."

"Okay," Luca said.

Will watched Luca as his muscles relaxed. When his face was placid, Will said, "Now, tell me what you see."

Luca said, "I can see you, and the Man in the Middle. We're all in the courtyard here. And there's fire in the background."

Will felt a cold chill. He could see The Man in the Middle, too. But his view was nowhere near as sharp. Will could see The Man, and Luca, but he could not see where they were, or even himself. "Do you know who he is?" Will thought.

Luca shook his head. In his mind, he said, "I saw him picking petals last night in my dream, or trip, or whatever it was. But I don't know what it means. The dreams are always there, but they never tell me what's going to happen."

"Sounds to me like you have nothing to worry about," Will thought.

"Do you see what's going to happen next?" Luca asked. "I've had bad dreams, really bad. But when I wake up, I can't remember much."

"No," Will thought, realizing it was much easier lying to Luca in his mind. "I've no idea what's going to happen next."

No point in telling Luca what he can't stop from happening, or it will only make the goodbyes that much harder.

* * * *

CHAPTER 4
CHARLIE WILKENS

Dunn, Georgia
March 25
Pre-dawn

Charlie's feet were rooted to the floor, his eyes fixed on the reanimated corpse that used to be Vic, but was now a human-monster hybrid.

Vic's right arm was wet and ebony from the elbow down, just like the monsters' skin. His arm was misshapen into a twisted mockery of a limb, fingers fused together to form an oversized blade-like appendage. His face was corrupted by an army of black veins marching across his skin like spider webs, covering every inch and deepening every crevice. Something pushed at both cheekbones from beneath his skin, forming half circles of withered, darkened pits beneath beady, black reptilian eyes.

Vic opened his mouth and screeched an inhuman cry. The scream sounded as if Vic were trying to dislodge something, or many things, from a prison in his throat. Then

393

he ran toward them, swinging his blade-hand at Charlie. Charlie rolled to the ground, as Adam jumped back, and dashed toward the gate.

Where the fuck are you going, Adam?!

Vic turned around and looked up at Adam, as though he might give chase, then turned back to Charlie, just as he rose to his feet. Something resembling a smile spread over Vic's rotting face, revealing jagged, blackened teeth.

Vic screamed again, that sickly scream that ripped straight through Charlie's brain, and leaned into another attack, this time with his normal hand. His punch landed on Charlie's left ear sending a thunderbolt of pain between his eyes.

"Fuck!" Charlie screamed as he put his hand to his ear. He had no time to consider the pain as Vic charged again, this time landing a strike in Charlie's ribs. Pain splintered through his side while radiating from his left ear.

Charlie doubled over and vomited onto the snow.

Vic stopped, staring at Charlie polluting the virgin white. Charlie wiped vomit from his mouth with the back of his hand, then looked up to consider his next move. Vic stood fixed between Charlie and the car, with its cache of weapons. Charlie chewed on his meager options for bypassing Vic and retrieving the guns, all the while wondering where the fuck Adam had run off to.

Charlie took a step back. Vic remained rooted, staring intently at Charlie with his beady, black reptilian eyes, but did nothing.

What the fuck is he doing?

Charlie backed up again, this time with four long strides, but never breaking eye contact with the freak of nature. Vic still refused to budge.

He's fucking with me; he's waiting to see what I'll do. Maybe he wants me to run so he can chase me down for more of a thrill.

Charlie took two more steps back, placing him steps from the front door. If he could run without slipping in the snow, then maybe . . . Once inside, he could get to the shotgun behind the front door.

Vic continued to stare like a coiled viper. If there were an expression on Vic's face, Charlie couldn't discern it. Vic looked like someone who wasn't home inside his head. If Vic was impaired, even momentarily, Charlie had to seize the chance and run — *now.*

Charlie spun around, planted his left foot, and exploded off of it into a dead sprint, not looking back.

Immediately, he heard Vic's steps falling quickly behind him, fast, and gaining ground.

Fuck!

Charlie reached the front door, turned the knob in his hand, and . . .

Fuck! Adam locked it on the way out!

Footsteps punctuated the promise of death behind him. Charlie spun around just as Vic reached him, blade-hand on the down-swing toward his face.

Charlie inhaled his last breath and prepared to greet death.

A final flinch, then . . .

BANG!

The gunshot cracked like thunder in the pre-dawn darkness, hitting Vic in the back and knocking him forward off balance, causing his blade-hand to miss Charlie's face by inches and decapitate the doorknob instead. Vic fell on top of Charlie, catapulting them both into the door, then onto the ground.

Charlie screamed, pushing and kicking at Vic, who was down but not out, arms reaching wildly to grasp Charlie.

He kicked Vic in the face as more footsteps came toward them. Adam appeared with a rifle, the one they kept near the front gate. He fired again at point-blank range, this time blowing Vic's head open like a grotesque melon, spewing a blackened bloody mess.

"What the fuck was that?!" Charlie asked, getting to his feet and looking at the thing that had been Vic.

"I thought you killed him!" Adam said, staring at the corpse.

"I did!"

"So, not only do we have to worry about these monsters, but the dead rising from their graves as mutants?" Adam said. "Fuck. Me."

Charlie looked up, bug-eyed, and laughed. Adam didn't curse much, so it was funny to hear the words coming from his mouth. "Maybe he wasn't dead? Maybe one of those monsters got to him before he died and turned him into one of them?"

"Like in zombie movies?"

"Yeah," Charlie said. "Unless this is more like that *Invasion of the Body Snatchers* movie, where Vic was some kind of pod person, and had been this way for a long time, just hiding and waiting to come out of his human shell."

"Yeah, but you saw him. He didn't seem right. I think if he were some kinda pod person all along, we woulda picked up on it a long time ago. Besides, I don't think pod people would be such assholes."

Charlie laughed again, "When did you get so funny? Wait. You're not one of them pod people, too, are you?"

"Ha, Ha," Adam said, and then his eyes locked onto Harry, lying on the ground, disemboweled from Vic's blade-hand. Charlie's eyes followed, and instantly, the joy he felt in being alive was severed as they remembered Harry's grisly death.

"I didn't know him that well, but he didn't deserve this," Adam said.

"No, he didn't," Charlie agreed, taking a moment of silence, before turning to Adam. "Come on; we need to get the hell out of here and go find Boricio."

"We're not gonna bury Harry?"

"We don't have time; we need to find Boricio if we're gonna save Callie."

"How are we gonna find him?" Adam said. "He could be anywhere."

"Harry said something about a compound, remember? How many other compounds are around here? That we know of?"

"You think he went back . . . there?" Adam asked, fear cracking the man from his voice.

"We're about to find out," Charlie said, as he grabbed the sack of guns from the car and loaded them into the cabin of the F150. "Let's roll."

* * * *

CHAPTER 5
DESMOND ARMSTRONG

Kingsland, Alabama
The Sanctuary
March 25
Morning

Desmond walked a step behind Mary and Paola on the return march from the funeral, back behind the The Sanctuary walls. He was burning to talk to Mary, but he had no choice but to wait. They were flanked by the congregation on all sides; Desmond couldn't help but feel that he was a dissenting buoy in a sea of similar thought. And in a world where The Prophet, Rei, and John all had the power, the wrong word at the wrong time, overheard and reported, could get them all in trouble, or maybe a box.

The congregation scattered at the gate, everyone going to get out of their black clothes and into the day's chores. Desmond felt a swell of hope, now seconds from finally being able to talk to Mary. He turned to Paola, so he could ask her if she'd mind if he and Mary had a few minutes alone, when Will was suddenly beside them.

"So, how did that go?" he asked.

Desmond felt a flash of irritation, but it wasn't Will's fault. Desmond said, "Oh, you know Brother Rei, such an elegant speaker. I haven't been so moved since I evacuated my bowels this morning. Scott deserved better than that. How is Luca? Everything okay? The kid seems to be taking this especially hard."

Mary pulled Paola closer to her and shot Desmond a look.

Will leaned down toward Paola and said, "Hey, would you mind going and checking on Luca for me? I'm sure he'd love that. He's okay, mostly just nerves. It can't be easy to be small inside, walking around in that big body. But I'm sure he'll open up to you. Always has. Besides, he's worried about you. Even mentioned it to me earlier at breakfast."

Paola looked down, then quickly back at Will. "I feel bad about this morning," she said. "I wasn't trying to make anyone upset, especially Luca."

"Sometimes it's best to simply say what's on your mind. You *did* get the table talking about Scott, after all, right?" Will winked at Paola and she smiled. "And I don't think Luca's upset, but I know he'd love to talk to you. He's over at his Quiet Spot right now."

Paola nodded, then hugged her mom and headed toward the Quiet Spot.

Desmond was grateful to Will for taking care of Paola, even if that wasn't what he was trying to do. With Will, you never really knew. Now if only Will would disappear, too, he and Mary could finally start talking.

"Everything okay?" Will addressed them both, but he was looking directly at Mary.

She nodded, then said. "I think I'm like Luca – a heavy case of nerves."

Will told Mary everything would be okay, that it was always hardest in the valley of a dip, and a few more random things that made little sense to Desmond. He had no idea how much they meant to Mary, and until they were alone he'd have little space to find out. Will seemed even weirder than normal. Though, if he thought about it, Desmond thought everyone seemed a little weirder today. That meant it was probably him. No one was weird in a way he could put his finger on, except Mary.

Mary was weird because she'd never seemed so far away.

Will said his goodbyes.

To Desmond's relief, Mary said, "I really need to talk to you, Des," a second later.

Desmond smiled. "Thank Christ, I'm not crazy. I could tell something big was on your mind. What's up?"

"Not here," she shook her head. "It's big and I want to know we're alone. Let's find somewhere less crowded."

"Fine by me," Desmond said, taking her hand.

They made it two steps before they were stopped by John, with the new stranger standing beside him.

"Desmond, Mary," John bowed his head after each name, "there's someone I'd like you to meet." The stranger stepped forward and John said, "This is Boricio. The Good Lord has led him to us. He feels he is home now, here at New Unity, and would like to contribute to the congregation and The Sanctuary as much as possible. You two remember what it was like to be new; I was hoping you might oblige to make Boricio feel as much at home as you were made to feel upon arrival."

Perfect.

Desmond stepped forward and shook Boricio's hand, then introduced him to Mary. Something about the stranger made him bristle, but Desmond had no idea what, and couldn't exactly trust his instincts since he was smart enough to realize he was acting paranoid. He should at least wait for the guy to give him a reason before hating him automatically. Of course, Desmond would have disliked pretty much *anyone* that John introduced him to at the exact moment he was about to finally get some alone time with Mary to find out what's had her acting distant all morning.

"So, what brought you here?" Desmond asked.

Boricio looked around the compound as though he owed his breath to the safety of its walls, even though he'd only been behind them for a few hours. "I have to confess that I believe Brother John here hit a home-run at the batting cages. The Good Lord must have led me to you just this morning. There's no other explanation. I was lost, and figured I'd probably never be found again, wandering through the woods with no idea where I was or where I could go."

Boricio shook his head and rubbed the crease in his forehead. "Had a bad run-in with a group of wild folks not too far from here just a while back. It was a guy and two girls, took me in like we was family. Lived there a while, until they got all sorts of sinful ideas and tried to lure me into the rat's nest of their evil ways. I left as soon as I could, straight out the back, but they gave chase. Tried to kill me. I managed to escape, but just barely. And only because The Good Lord saw fit to deliver me here."

Boricio looked around The Sanctuary in silent gratitude again.

John said, "Boricio has fought off many of the Demons, too."

Boricio nodded like his neck had fresh batteries. "Sure did, been fighting them since the late of last October. Should've known there was evil in the house of sinners since there were so many Demons around their part of the woods." Boricio waved his arms around the courtyard. "Aren't none of them here, though. In fact, I was getting chased by two of them Demons just this morning while I was following

The Good Lord's path to your blessed doorstep. But soon as I was spitting distance from the gate, both them Demons turned back around, screaming that horrible scream, like a banshee ripping off a Band-Aid. They went running off in the opposite direction like they found a shortcut back to hell on the far side of the forest." Boricio looked solemn as he finished his story. "I've made war on maybe a hundred of them Demons since October, but I ain't never seen 'em run scared like that before. That's how I knew I'd found my home. I'd be safe in the bosom of The Good Lord. I'm lucky to be here."

Mary squeezed Desmond's hand. "It's just so dangerous out there," she said.

Huh?

Desmond was confused, and trying not to get agitated. Mary had been in a hurry to leave The Sanctuary. And now she was hinting that she wanted to stay?

Why?

Boricio was full of shit. Desmond figured the stranger was simply using his smarts. The guy knew how to survive. From the outside, The Sanctuary looked plenty safe. If Boricio was smart enough to survive on the outside for half a year, he was smart enough to survive in here, too. Even if that meant acting like a religious nut.

Desmond tuned out as John started telling Boricio that there was no luck. The Good Lord had led the way, and they were all better off for it. One new mouth to feed, but two hands to help build the church, *blah blah blah.* Desmond was crafting an exit to the conversation so he could get Mary alone, at least long enough to empty her mind of whatever was giving it weight, and pulling him down with it.

Boricio told Desmond and Mary how nice it was to meet them again, then turned his attention to John, asking him about work schedules, and seeing if maybe there was something he could do to help everyone out. He claimed he was a whiz in the kitchen, but Desmond was happy to hear John say that the kitchen staff was well taken care of. Desmond didn't want the stranger touching his food.

Desmond and Mary clearly weren't needed, so they excused themselves from the conversation, then made it to the area behind the barn without further interruption. Luca and Paola were now walking around the hangar, Paola talking animatedly, though Luca still looked sad.

Mary was softly crying before they got to the benches, though Desmond could tell she was trying her hardest not to. "What's wrong, Sweetie?" he said.

Mary didn't make him wait. Through a controlled sob, she said, "I'm pregnant."

Desmond couldn't find his tongue through the thick tangle of sudden shock. At first, all he could do was stare, then he pulled Mary close and started petting the back of her hair. Finally, he said, "Are you sure? How can you be certain? You haven't actually taken a test have you? Maybe whatever happened in October has affected everyone's cycles?"

Mary cried harder, and Desmond regretted all four of his questions, especially the last one.

He repeated the first question anyway. "Are you sure?"

Mary nodded. "I know my body, and trust my instincts. There's a baby inside me, Desmond. *Our baby.* I'm sure of it."

Desmond laughed, so he could feel alive instead of numb. "You're *sure* of it? Now you're starting to sound like Will!" He laughed.

Desmond had no idea if Mary found it funny. He thought he could feel her smile, but her face was buried in his chest as she surrendered to a shuddering sob. He let her catch her breath as he continued to stroke her hair. "We have to stay," she finally said. "It's too dangerous out there, at least on our own. We don't know what sort of dangers are waiting and I'm only going to get bigger and bigger. From what we've seen, there are no doctors or hospitals anymore, Desmond. This is it."

"There aren't any doctors here," he said.

"But there *are* two midwives, at least. Plus heat and food and guns and a lot of other stuff a baby needs to stay safe. My big baby might be old enough to handle it out there," Mary glanced toward the gates. "But my new baby doesn't stand a chance." She looked at Desmond and held his eyes. "*Our* new baby doesn't stand a chance out there."

Desmond said, "I'll do whatever you want, go wherever you want, do whatever you think is best. But this place creeps me out. The sooner we leave, the sooner we can find somewhere to settle down."

"Where Desmond?" Mary had stopped crying, but she was skating along the razor's edge. "Where else can we find someone to help us have our baby? We thought we found safety at the farm, and you saw what happened there. If John and the people here hadn't come, we'd all be dead. All of us."

She was right. John and the nutjobs *had* saved them.

"We'll find someplace safer, with normal people that we don't need to worry about. Wherever we go," Desmond said, "*I'll* be there. *I'll* help you. We'll find someplace safe. We'll be safe. We did it before; we can do it again. People were having babies for thousands of years before the first hospital was ever imagined."

"Yeah," Mary agreed, "and they had the infant mortality rate to prove it."

Desmond nodded toward the box with the young girl being punished inside. "How about that, Mary? You want our child to grow up in a place where he or she might get tossed in the box when it cries too loud?"

He would have loved to hear Mary's comeback, but they were suddenly interrupted by Rei, looking even more smug than normal.

"Yeah?" Desmond said, not even trying to hide his irritation.

"I was wondering if either of you two have seen Brother Will. I would very much like to have a word with him."

"I saw him a bit ago, but I'm not sure where he went." Desmond said. "What's up?"

"I had something I wanted to share with him. Pay no mind; go on with your talk. I'm sure I'll find him shortly." Rei made it three steps before he turned back and said, "Oh, I almost forgot. Brothers John and Boricio would like your help over at the church, Desmond. They're waiting for you now."

Then he turned and looked at Mary, with a wolfish smile that made Desmond want to rip every tooth from the fucker's mouth.

"Sarah was wondering if you could help her prepare for our new Brother's stay. She's waiting for you now." He turned and walked away, not waiting for an answer.

Desmond and Mary knew they were being watched, so they wiped their eyes and each walked toward their assignment. He hoped she would listen to reason, and that they'd be gone from The Sanctuary before much longer.

The end of the world had jumbled man's laws, and Desmond wasn't sure how much longer he could stay before he made sure Rei quit breathing for good.

* * * *

CHAPTER 6
WILL BISHOP

Will waited until lunchtime, when the guards thinned to nearly nothing, just one man on the main house roof and one at the front gate, then made his way to the rear gate leading to the cemetery.

The rear gate was left unguarded, secured with only a padlock – easy enough to pick open with a paperclip and a tension wrench.

He'd have to be quick. If he wasn't back before lunch was over, he'd have a tough time getting in undetected, and would probably wind up sharing a cell with Carl, wherever the hell they were holding the kid. Or worse, inside a box beside the girl, Rebecca.

Will picked the lock, slipped through the gate, stepped from the path and raced into the woods three inches deep with snow, still frozen from the night before. His eyes scanned the forest, hoping like hell he wouldn't find any monsters. He didn't think he would, but to hear people talk, you'd think the woods were infested. Maybe they were, but everything looked eerily quiet at the moment. No birds chirping and no animals foraging, nothing but a light, cool breeze and creaking of trees.

Where is it?

He'd seen it so clearly in his dreams; it hadn't been far. Will was fairly certain it was just south of The Sanctuary, circled by forest on all sides except the west, which faced the front entrance.

He glanced at his watch. 12:35.

Lunch would be over at 1 p.m., and then the back of The Sanctuary would be filled with workers, laboring on the church.

Will walked deeper into the woods until the stone wall of The Sanctuary was only a suggestion. He wondered if he should have gone north of The Sanctuary. If so, he was screwed. He'd been walking a while and wouldn't have time to make an about face that mattered.

His heart raced as he glanced at his watch again.

12:45.

It was as if time were speeding up to conspire against him.

Where is it?!

He was turning back in defeat when he saw what he'd left The Sanctuary to find.

The white tarp covering the car, exactly as he had seen it in his dreams.

He raced over, whipped the tarp off, then drew in his breath with a whistle.

There it was, just as he'd seen in his dream. Some sort of modified BMW Z8. If the dream was correct, which of course it would be, the guns were in the trunk. Will searched for the tree he'd seen in the dream. The tree with the hole in the trunk.

It took him a moment to find. Once he did, Will reached into the dark, damp hole, and found the keys The Sanctuary's new visitor had hidden. He carefully pushed the trunk button, hoping like hell he wouldn't accidentally set off the alarm. The trunk popped open, putting the large, black bag of weapons on full display.

Will grabbed the bag, which felt like it weighed 50 pounds, then shut the trunk, put the bag on the ground, and pulled the tarp back over the car. He slid the car keys into his pants pocket, and glanced at his watch.

12:54

He raced back to The Sanctuary, heart pounding in his chest as he sucked in deep mouthfuls of freezing air.

At the wall, he squatted down and opened the bag, careful not to get snow on his pants. He withdrew a Glock and a box of bullets. He slipped the shells into his pocket, and the gun behind his waistband in the small of his back, hidden by his jacket, then hid the bag against the outer wall, behind a small cluster of trees, where it wouldn't be seen unless someone was looking directly at it.

With the bag concealed, Will raced to the gate, scanning the yard beyond. He could hear others, not too far off, but had yet to see them. The gate was fairly well hidden at the rear of the property, behind the barn and maintenance shack. Unless someone was in the rear of the garden, behind the barn, or walking along the rear wall, he was reasonably covered. Will stepped inside the gate, closed it, then retrieved the padlock he'd taken when he left and clicked it shut.

He turned around, and saw Brother Rei standing there.

"Hello," Will said, acting perfectly normal, no idea what he'd seen.

"What were you doing?"

"I thought I heard someone out there," Will said.

Brother Rei eyed him suspiciously, then walked toward Will and looked outside the gate. "Did it sound like a person?"

"I'm not sure," Will said. "I thought so. But it could have been a demon, maybe?"

"I'll have some men search outside," Brother Rei took Will by the elbow, leading him away from the gate. Will hoped they didn't search so well that they found either the weapons or the car.

"Come with me," he said. "I've been looking for you. We need to talk."

Will swallowed the lump in his throat, and followed Brother Rei back to the main house, the gun in his back a 12-ton stone that might fall out and crush his cover at any moment.

**

Brother Rei led Will to a room on the bottom floor of the main house. Will didn't know if the office was Brother Rei's, The Prophet's, or someone else's, but it was sparsely furnished. Just a desk, with two wood and leather chairs on either side, and a large metal filing cabinet against the rear wall. On the desk was a manila folder with a stack of papers inside.

"Have a seat, Brother Will."

Will sat in the seat in front of the desk, as if he were about to interview for a job, rather than sit through the interrogation he expected. Will had seen the way Brother Rei was watching him lately, like a dog trying to divine the meaning of life. Brother Rei knew something was off about Will, and was trying to figure out exactly what it was. Or maybe he thought something was off about the whole lot of them, and Will was the easiest to go after. Mary and Desmond would defend one another, as they would Luca or Paola. Linc was roughly the size of a shit brick house, and men like Brother Rei never went after men like Linc unless the odds were heavily stacked in their favor.

Will was the weakest link, the one most likely to break their group's chain.

"I'll be right back; I just want to tell the others not to disturb us," Brother Rei said, excusing himself from the room and closing the door behind him.

Will looked around, plotting the sudden escape he might have to make. The office window was barred, as were most of the windows on all three of the houses, so jumping out the window was out of the question. The room was small with no other doors, so if things went south, he'd have to go out the way he came in, then contend with whoever was standing guard.

"I'm sorry," Brother Rei said, re-entering the room and taking a seat in the leather chair behind the desk. "Now, let's get to know Brother Will a little better."

"Okay," Will said, shifting uncomfortably in his chair, gun pressing hard against the small of his back.

"A little birdie told me that The Prophet isn't the only one who dreamed of October 15 before it happened. That you, too, had visions."

"Well, I'm not sure I'd call them visions," Will said, not sure where Brother Rei was headed with his line of questioning. "They were more like dreams that happened to come true. And it's been months since I've had any."

"You and I both know that nothing just *happens*, right?"

"I suppose," Will said.

"And what did these vis . . . *dreams* tell you?"

"Not a whole lot," Will lied. "Just bits and pieces, really. The one thing I remembered most was the date, of course. And that a lot of people would disappear all at once."

"Rapture, you mean?"

"Well, I'm not sure what to call it," Will said. "Nor did my dreams explain it, really."

"And how long have you been having these *dreams?*"

"Decades, on and off."

"And you never thought to warn anyone?"

"Well, I warned people I worked with at the Air Force. They thought I was crazy."

"People can be doubting of The Truth. So, what did you do in the Air Force? Did you fly?"

"A bit, at first, but then I was a researcher, of sorts."

"Of sorts?" Brother Rei said, eyebrows raised. "What does *that* mean?"

"It's too complicated to explain," Will said, wishing he'd said something with a thinner skin of truth. The truth was something he couldn't explain to most people, let alone a fundamentalist who saw things in two ways, either of God or the Devil.

"Why, because I'm just a dumb rube who doesn't understand technical jargon?" Brother Rei said sharply, his eyes no longer disguising his disdain for Will.

"Did I do something to offend you?" Will asked, surprised at how quickly Brother Rei had dropped the courteous act. Will wanted to calm the man, and get the hell out of the room before things got out of hand. *This* was not part of the dream, and Brother Rei's interference was a danger to *everything*.

Brother Rei smiled, though his smile had the warmth of an igloo. "How did you come to meet the boy? This *child* with such powers?"

"Luca? I dreamed of him," Will said. "Something told me I'd meet him, and I did."

"*Something.* Not God, though, right? Because God doesn't speak to you?"

Will wasn't sure what to say. There wasn't much room for navigation. He could tell the little weasel wanted to pick a fight; it was all Brother Rei could do to keep his fist from suddenly swinging at Will. This man was a bully, a power-hungry one at that. Will had seen his kind, dealt with his kind, plenty of times before. He was a petty, little man with inadequacy issues, looking to make a name for himself, however he could.

Brother Rei might have been looking for a reason to spar with Will, but Will was smarter than the weasel by a wide berth. Will wouldn't give in to the attempts. He would remain calm in the face of Brother Rei's fury, no matter how quickly it rolled to a boil, or how high the bubbles rose.

"So, tell me, Brother Will. How *close* are you to Luca?"

Will didn't like the innuendo in Brother Rei's voice or the arch in his left eyebrow when he said 'close.' Had Brother Rei discovered his secret, or was he simply guessing? In any event, homosexuality didn't equate to pedophilia, and Will would have to hide his outrage if that's where Brother Rei was going with this.

"What are you asking?" Will met Brother Rei's dark eyes, almost daring him to voice his ugly suspicions.

"Just trying to figure things out, is all," Brother Rei said with a devious smile. "Do you think Luca is possessed?"

"What?! That's crazy."

"Do you not believe in demonic possession? Have you not seen enough of what's happened outside, or been paying attention enough to know what it means?"

"Don't you have better things to do with your day than spend it asking me questions about my faith? What is the point of all this?"

"The point, Brother Will, is to determine which side of eternity you and your little group are standing on. Brother John may have been fooled by your act, but I'm not so naive and trusting as he."

"If you don't trust us, then why have us here?"

Brother Rei smiled at this as if it were some kind of joke, and that it was all he could do to keep his laughter contained. He leaned across the desk, lowered his voice, and said, "You're right; you shouldn't be here. Please, let yourself out."

Will was confused, "Out of this room, or leave The Sanctuary?"

"Both. Go tell your friends their time is up. The Sanctuary offers no solace to sinners."

Will felt the acid churn in his gut.

What have I done? I can't get the rest of them kicked out.

"Listen," Will said, trying to smother the flames of his reckless behavior. "I don't know what I've done to cause offense, but it wasn't intentional. I've abided by your rules. All of them. And I've not spoken a word against your customs. I've helped in every way I've been asked. So, if there's something I've personally done to you, please forgive me. But don't take it out on my friends. If you want me to leave, I'll leave right now."

Brother Rei stared at him, then sat back and folded his fingers on his desk.

Whatever the weasel had expected to happen, Will had thrown him with his offer. Brother Rei's eyes, and the uncertainty lurking like fear within them, said he was contemplating his next step with caution.

"You will leave? Just like that? Right now?" Brother Rei asked, surprised.

"I'd like to take a few of my things, and tell the others I'm going. But yes, I'll leave."

"And what will you tell the others? That I pushed you out, made you go away, gave you an ultimatum?"

"No, because then they'd leave here with me, and I don't want that. I don't have to believe what you believe to think they are still safest here. I even told them so when The Prophet asked Mary to choose here or outside. I've never been one to stay too long in one place. They know that, and aren't likely to think much of it."

Brother Rei leaned forward a second time. "The Prophet and Brother John are kind men. The Prophet has already once allowed the wrong people into our Sanctuary.

I, however, was not a kind man before coming here. And I have no problem tapping into that darkness to preserve the light of this holy place. I will allow you to leave, but you must do so today. And you must convince the rest of your friends that this was your idea. Because even though The Prophet gave them a choice, I will never allow them to leave, at least not with the child."

"Luca?" Will asked.

"Yes. He is a gift from God, and it would be an affront to allow him to be corrupted by your world. If they attempt to leave with him, they will die. Each and every one of them, including the girl."

"I can't believe The Prophet or John would allow that," Will said.

"The Prophet isn't doing especially well. He's come down with something vile. To be blunt, I'm not sure he'll live to see the completion of his church." The corner of Brother Rei's mouth crinkled, just enough to make Will certain he had something to do with The Prophet's sudden illness.

"And John? Certainly you don't think John will stand by and let you take control of this place, let alone murder his friends?"

"John is not a concern," Brother Rei said. "I have won the loyalty of my brothers. If there's a war for the heart and soul of The Sanctuary, have no doubt, I will be the victor. I have God, and the men, on my side."

Will stared at him, then smiled.

"Why are you telling me all this?"

"You're leaving," Brother Rei said. "And I have two guards outside this room right now to ensure my absolute safety. These men will be your shadow until you leave. And you will leave promptly after dinner. I'll make a big announcement, let everyone know how truly sorry I am to see you go. You will be given a car and some supplies. Then we're done here, do I make myself clear?"

"Yes," Will said, anxious to get the hell out of the tiny room.

Will stood and headed for the door, tempted to turn back, and put a bullet in Brother Rei. Maybe three. But that would be changing things, and Will knew that was forbidden. Brother Rei was in the dreams of what was to come, so that meant he was still alive. Even if Will were to get a shot off, fate would intervene long enough to keep the weasel breathing.

Will was strapped in, committed to the roller coaster ride, all the way to the end. He knew all too well the dangers of attempting to change fate.

* * * *

CHAPTER 7
LUCA HARDING

Luca wasn't feeling well before lunch, but he didn't say anything to anyone until he had a mouth filled with meat he couldn't chew, let alone swallow. Everyone gave him looks that said they were sorry he was sick, except for Brother Rei, who gave him a look Luca didn't understand, even though it made him feel a little bit black inside.

Luca excused himself from the table, then crossed the courtyard and went into his room. He slipped into bed and turned toward the wall with his hands cradling his stomach. Since Scott was gone, Luca had the room all to himself. The woman who cleaned the house, Sister Louise, was scrubbing the hallway on the other side of his door. Luca could hear her thoughts and they were making him sad. Louise was nice on the outside, and always smiled whenever she said hello, but today Luca could hear her thoughts, wondering if Luca were indeed possessed.

He turned toward the window, wanting to find Rebecca, since he lost her in his dream last night. He'd been worried about her all day, and was glad that the funeral took place outside The Sanctuary so she didn't have to hear Brother Rei talking about Scott's "Heavenly reward," which he got when he was fighting the bleakers, or the Demons, as everyone at The Sanctuary always called them.

Luca kept listening for the sound of Rebecca's thoughts, but her thinking was nowhere to be found.

Listening for people's thoughts, he'd discovered the prior day, was like TV channel surfing, like his dad used to do. Sometimes his dad would know what he was looking for and go straight to that channel. But most times he didn't. When his dad didn't know what he wanted to watch, he would point the remote at the screen, press the arrow, and flick from show to show until he found a station that looked promising. Often, his dad would watch the channel for a few seconds, lose interest, then move onto something else. When he finally found something entertaining, he'd drop the remote in the "Remote Boat," then sip his glass of water, smiling. Picking up on people was the same way, but less entertaining.

If Luca knew whom he wanted to hear, or when he was looking at the person directly, getting in their thoughts was easy. But when he didn't know, he had to do a lot of *dipping*. *Dipping* was what Luca called it when he had to go into someone's thoughts just long enough to figure out whose mind he was inside.

He kept trying to find Rebecca's thinking, but he couldn't go dipping since the only person he could hear thinking was Louise.

"He picks his nose . . . and all that urine around the toilet! That's all bad enough, but it's his eyes that are the worst. That boy's been branded by the Devil as sure as he misses the bowl."

Luca didn't want to be inside Louise's head anymore, but he still couldn't find Rebecca. He was almost ready to turn back to face the wall, since his tummy hurt less in that direction, when he heard her.

"Are you trying to find me?"

"Rebecca!"

Luca heard her think in a giggle. "Yay! I found you," she thought.

"How long have you been looking?"

There was a moment of silence, then Luca heard, "All morning." There was another moment of silence then she added, "How was the funeral?"

"Terrible. I left at the beginning. I was crying like a big baby. Everyone probably thought I was stupid."

"That's not true," Rebecca thought. "No one thought you were stupid. They understand that you're just a kid."

Luca thought. "They didn't understand that you are just a kid."

Rebecca went quiet.

He said, "I'm sorry" in his head.

"It's okay."

"Where did you go last night?" Luca wondered.

"I'm not sure. I think I went into a different part of the dream. I looked for you but I didn't see you anywhere. I kept looking, but I couldn't find you. I was lost for a while. And I couldn't escape from the man who was watching me. He was watching both of us, actually. At the same time, too. Like he had eyes all around him. I wanted to follow him because I thought he might show me where you were. But I was too scared. I ran away when he saw me behind him."

"That's The Man in the Middle," Luca thought. "Did he say anything to you?"

"He said, 'You can't watch the watcher, unless your eyes are made of sky.' He disappeared into the snow after that. Is The Man in the Middle bad?"

Luca had to think before he thought his answer. "Yes, I think he is. But since I'm not scared of him, I don't think he can hurt me."

"Why?"

"Because the voices didn't say anything bad was going to happen. I think The Man in the Middle has to stay inside the Terrible Scary." Luca didn't want to think about The Man in the Middle or the Terrible Scary anymore, so he wondered if Rebecca wanted to go on another trip. She said yes, and the next thing they knew, Luca was back in Las Orillas, in the middle of a freshly mowed lawn, looking at his old house with Rebecca beside him.

"Is that where you used to live?"

Luca nodded.

"It's really nice," she said. "We didn't have anything like that. What did your parents do?"

Luca thought about it, but then felt bad that he couldn't remember. Then he wondered if he'd ever known. Was 8 old enough to know what your parents did for work? Yes, of course it was. It had to be. Did he not know, or could he not remember? Luca finally said, "I'm not sure," though saying it out loud made him feel like he lost something important.

He said, "Come on!" then took Rebecca by the hand and ran inside the house. No one was home, but that was fine. Luca wanted to show Rebecca his toys, not his family. He showed her his Lego collection, including his TIE-Fighter and his newest prize, the Ninjago Fire Temple.

"Isn't it awe-awe-awe-awesome?" Luca sang, just like he did all through late September and early October of the previous fall, back when the Lego Ninjago Fire Temple was the pride of his bedroom.

Luca caught his reflection in his closet mirror, then dropped his Lego dragon on the floor where it shattered to pieces.

He had expected to see his 8-year-old self. They were in his house and his dream, after all. But the young man looking back at him hadn't been a boy for some time.

"It's okay," Rebecca said. "You can still like Legos."

Luca smiled, then showed Rebecca his favorite books, his light saber collection, and his three favorite Nerf guns. She even watched him play the Zelda video game and sat beside him while he beat his favorite boss. When the boss was dead, Rebecca told Luca he was cute. He turned from the screen, dropped his controller, and told her she looked pretty, even without her hair.

Rebecca touched the top of her head, as though she had forgotten, then lost her happy face to a sad one. "I'm so ugly now!" she said.

"You're not ugly at all." Luca shook his head. "You're awe-awe-awe-awesome."

Rebecca laughed and told Luca he was nice. She said she hadn't really known too many boys, especially nice ones. And though she had *thought* Carl was nice, she was wrong. "Have you seen Carl?" she asked.

Luca shook his head. "I haven't seen him since the day they took him away. I know they're keeping him somewhere else. Linc told me it's a place called The Hole. Do you know where that is?"

Rebecca nodded. "I've never seen it, but it's in the basement of the women's house. That's where they put people when they're *really* bad."

"Oh."

Luca was silent for a while, and didn't really know what else to show his friend since she was way too old for any of his sister Anna's toys, and too young for anything in his mom's room.

"Do you miss your house?" Rebecca asked.

Luca scrunched his nose. "I'm not sure. I guess I do. I miss my mom and dad and Anna. And I miss my toys. But I'm forgetting what I really miss, instead of what I'm supposed to miss."

"What do you mean?"

Luca shook his head. "I don't know how to tell it." He sighed, "I don't know where I put the memories. It's crowded in here." Luca pointed to his head. "And I think I might be running out of space because there's new stuff I don't understand, and the old stuff that I do understand is getting harder to find."

Before Rebecca could ask Luca to explain, there was a knock at the door.

"Who is that?" Rebecca said, startled.

"I don't know," Luca was already on his feet and on his way to the front door. He opened the door and was instantly shocked to see Will, though it was barely Will at all.

Almost Will stepped inside the house, not formed like Luca or Rebecca.

"Hi Will," Luca said.

"Who are you talking to?" Rebecca asked.

Luca turned to Rebecca. "My friend, Will. You can't see him?"

Rebecca shook her head.

Luca turned to Will. "Are you really here?"

He had to ask since he could barely see Will, a semi-invisible shadow with Will's wild hair and beard and general shape, but none of his skin and little of his coloring.

"Good, you can see me," Will said, "I needed to tell you something, but I haven't got long. Brother Rei is asking me to leave the compound tonight, after dinner."

"What?" Luca said, upset, "Why?"

"Because he knows I'm on to him for being a bad guy," Will said. "I don't have time to get into it now. I'm not sleeping like you are, and this isn't exactly easy for me, but I needed to reach you privately since they've got people watching me. Please, Luca, I need you to be brave; for me and you, and everyone else, including Rebecca." The ghost Will nodded toward Rebecca, even though she couldn't see him. He turned back to Luca. "I need you to lie low, and convince the others to lie low with you. Be discreet, and trust no one but Desmond, Mary, and Paola. I'll be back as soon as I can. I promise."

"But, but . . . Where are you going?" Luca was trying hard not to cry, but wasn't doing very well.

"Not far," Will said. "And I'll stay safe; I promise. I need you to do me a favor. Are you up for it?" He put his hand beneath Luca's chin and raised his face to meet his eyes.

Luca nodded.

"I need you to let Desmond know there's a gun in the tank in the bathroom at the end of his hall, along with a set of keys to a BWM parked in the woods on the south side of The Sanctuary, beneath a white tarp. Got that so far?"

Luca nodded.

"Great job." Will smiled and Luca smiled back. "There's also a bag of guns behind a cluster of trees on the outside of the south wall, at the back of the compound."

"What's happening?" Luca said, afraid, but still trying not to cry. "Are you gonna be okay? Will I see you again?"

"Yes, you'll see me tonight at dinner. After that, I have to leave. But I promise I'll be back soon. Just swear you'll do what I said; tell Desmond and Mary everything the next time you're all alone, okay?"

Luca agreed. Will told him not to be afraid, but he had already faded away before he finished his sentence.

Luca blinked his eyes open, somehow knowing what he'd find.

Even though he was in the real world and away from the dream, the Terrible Scary was everywhere around him, covering him like a blanket.

Luca had never felt so close to the middle of it all.

* * * *

CHAPTER 8
CHARLIE WILKENS

Somewhere in Alabama
March 25
Mid-morning

"You sure you're gonna be able to find this place?" Adam asked as the morning sun beat a glare into the windshield.

"I'll find it," Charlie said, for the hundredth time in the past hour.

"I sure hope so," Adam said, "Because I think we're lost."

"Do you have anything productive to say?" Charlie snapped, no longer able to bury his irritation. Adam said nothing.

Sometimes, Adam seemed like two different people. At times, he was the nice, overly friendly dude who knew exactly what to do in a moment, like when he saved Charlie from freezing to death from the killer storm or shot the monster Vic seconds before Charlie would've been a dead man. But other times, like now, he behaved like a semi-retarded man-child who didn't know anything about anything, and was full of doubt and annoying questions. It was a wonder to Charlie how this Adam managed to even dress himself in the morning. If Charlie could find a way to split Annoying Adam from Cool Adam, he'd do it in a heartbeat and drop that other fucker off at a rest stop somewhere on the highway, tie a big, red bow around him, leave him for the monsters and never look back.

Of course, Charlie couldn't do that. He was stuck with both Adams, like it or not. He watched as Adam shoved an entire pack of gum in his mouth, a stick at a time, while laughing like an idiot. Charlie rolled his eyes, turned his attention back to the road, and tried to figure out where in the fuck he was.

"Check the glove compartment; see if Harry left any maps in there."

Adam leaned forward, then said, in a voice muddled by a mouth full of gum, "Mo-thwing in here."

"Of course," Charlie said, slapping the steering wheel with his palm. Pain shot through his arm. He remembered doing the same thing in the car after the storm, and how badly it hurt.

I have to stop doing that!

"So?" Adam asked, mouth full of marbles.

Charlie turned slowly, "What?"

"Wha we gon . . . do?" he said, barely able to talk around the gum.

Fucking idiot.

"I don't fucking know! Don't ask me again, or I'm gonna shove one of these shotguns up your ass!"

"Je-bus," Adam said.

"And spit out that fucking gum; you sound like a retard!" Charlie said.

"Sowwy," Adam said, then pulled the gum from his mouth, in a big sticky, saliva-coated wad, rolled down the window, and threw it outside. "Sorry," he said, mouth now free of gum.

Charlie didn't say anything. He knew he should apologize to Adam, that he was only snapping at him because he was stressed, but he was far too annoyed to fake an apology. So he kept driving, eyes peeled for anything familiar, anything that might lead him to the compound where they'd been held captive five months earlier.

"What if Boricio's not there? And what if those people remember us?" Adam asked.

"I dunno," Charlie said, not snapping, and actually considering the question. He reached into his jacket pocket, then ran his fingers over the cross that Callie had made for him.

"It's for good luck," she'd said. "I figured we could use that more than anything right now, right?"

"Yeah," he had said, and hugged her.

Now, as he thought back on Callie's gift, Charlie wished he'd hugged her harder, showed more appreciation than he had. He wasn't used to getting gifts, particularly from girls, so he thanked her, said it was awesome, but felt maybe he should've said more, talked about how well it was carved, or something! He loved the cross enough to hide it so Vic, or anyone else, wouldn't steal it. But he hadn't explained that to Callie, nor did he even tell her he was hiding it. One day, for some reason, he simply thought to do so. Callie never mentioned the fact that Charlie had hidden the cross. He wondered if she had wondered where he'd put it. Maybe she thought he didn't like it and threw it away. He hoped that wasn't the case. He considered her now, prisoner of whoever took her, alone and thinking that Charlie didn't like her gift. That image made his eyes water.

He blinked, refocusing on the task at hand — figuring out where the hell they were.

"She's gonna be okay," Adam said. Dumb as he sometimes was, he was intuitive enough to know what was plaguing Charlie's mind.

"What is that?" Adam asked, pointing to a black van about a quarter mile ahead, pulled to the side of the road.

"Is that like the one that took Callie?" Charlie asked, heart racing.

"Hard to tell from here, but could be."

"Get the guns ready," Charlie ordered.

Adam grabbed a shotgun from the bag behind their seats. He made sure it was loaded, even though he'd done so at the beginning of the ride, then grabbed a rifle for Charlie.

As they drew closer, they noticed the back doors of the van were wide open. Snow piled and flowed into thick forest on either side of the road. Charlie wasn't sure if the van on the side of the road with open doors was a good sign or not. He wasn't sure if Callie would have fled into the snow-dense woods. Hell, he wasn't even sure if this was the van used to abduct Callie. But it was a black van and there was no snow piled on it, so it was likely recently used.

Charlie eased off the gas as they pulled up behind the van, coming to a full stop about five car lengths back. Charlie analyzed the scene — the van, the road, the woods, everything. The back of the van was empty. A black wall with a sliding window separated the back of the van from the front. Charlie figured it made the perfect prisoner transport vehicle.

The distance made it impossible to tell if anyone was in the front of the van. He considered driving around to the front, but decided he'd rather be on foot so he could get a better shot off, if needed.

"See anything?" Charlie asked Adam.

"No, nothing. What should we do?"

"Let's investigate," Charlie said. He stepped from the van and onto the road. "I'll take the driver's side; you take the passenger's. And check the snow over there for footprints."

Adam stepped out and walked along the side of the highway, eyes alternating between the passenger door and the snow, approaching the truck directly opposite Charlie.

They walked together in tandem, guns raised. "Don't shoot unless you're sure it's not Callie," Charlie warned, voice low. "You understand me?"

"Yes, sir," Adam said, eyes bolted on the van ahead.

Say what you want about Adam; in times like this, he was pretty fucking intense, and kept his eyes on the task at hand.

They were maybe 10 feet away. Charlie strained to see the mirrors on the side of the truck, to get a look at the driver's side. The windows were tinted, almost black, making it impossible to see inside.

"See anything?" Charlie asked Adam.

"Nothing," Adam said.

"OK, let's go for the front. Remember, do not shoot until you're sure."

"Got it," Adam said.

They reached the back of the van, then fell from one another's sight, each on one side of the van. Charlie kept his eye on the door as he closed in, gun aimed straight at the window. He hoped *he* wouldn't accidentally shoot if Callie was in the front seat.

He was about five steps from the front passenger door when Adam screamed from the other side, and then fell quiet, his scream muffled.

"Adam?!" Charlie called out.

No answer.

Fuck, fuck, fuck.

Charlie backed away from the van, rifle raised squarely at it, hands shaking, waiting for someone to run from Adam's side and hoping like hell he didn't accidentally shoot Adam or Callie.

He never saw the shooter that hit him from behind.

* * * *

CHAPTER 9
DESMOND ARMSTRONG

The Sanctuary
March 25
5:47 p.m.

Desmond stared in the mirror. It was hard to believe it had been just months since he left his home in Warson Woods forever. He looked like he'd aged a half decade, if not the full 10 times around the sun.

Desmond was fine living life without luxury. He'd lived plenty of his early years going without. But he'd be a liar if he didn't admit to missing some of the finer things from the yesterday now gone forever. From the scalding shower in his finely tiled bath, to the L'Occitaine shaving bar and brush, to the ridiculously thick towels.

Hell, he'd gladly settle for the wine cellar and nothing else. Looking like shit was fine; feeling like shit, not so much. And he'd love nothing more than a bottle of Pinot.

Desmond combed his hair back, which was longer than it had been in forever, put on some fresh clothes for dinner, then, like clockwork, raced downstairs and joined up with Mary, Paola, and Luca, as they walked toward the main house for dinner. Linc was a few paces ahead, walking beside two brothers from the congregation.

Before Desmond had a chance to wish the group a good evening, Linc broke rank with the brothers, then fell back and into step with the Drury Crew. "Did you hear?" he said, addressing them all at once.

"Hear what?" Mary asked.

"Will is leaving tonight. Not sure what's going down, but apparently he talked with Brother Rei, and words were said, I dunno."

Desmond said, "Who told you that?"

"Brother Reginald. But Brother Mark told him." Linc's voice dropped to a whisper. "If Will leaves, does that mean we're leaving, too?"

Desmond wasn't sure if Linc was asking for himself, or if someone had sent him to find out. And really, Desmond didn't trust him either way. Linc had gotten too friendly with the others during their short time there. He'd steadily drifted to his own side of The Sanctuary from Day One forward, and wasn't really talking with the Drury Crew as much. Desmond felt bad for not trusting him since Linc had always been so nice to them, and had saved their asses more than a few times in the prior months. But survival meant staying alive, and that meant keeping watch over both sides of your shoulder. Linc was so spooked by what happened at the farmhouse, he was more than willing to trade freedom for safety. If Linc was comfortable living with a cult, he had to be willing to pay the rent, even if that meant turning on his old friends.

"I don't know," Desmond said. "Mary thinks we're safer staying here. Why is Will leaving? Are they forcing him out? Isn't there anything you can do to get Brother Rei to change his mind?"

Desmond didn't think Linc had a shred of influence over Brother Rei, or any of the brothers for that matter. But this could provide a good indication of Linc's loyalties.

"Would if I could, believe me," Linc said as they entered the house and walked to the dining room. "I like the crazy old coot as much as you, but from the way I hear it, Will wants to leave. Was *his* idea to go. Said he had itchy feet and wanted to get to someplace where the spring would come up pretty."

"I haven't seen Will since this morning, and he didn't say anything about leaving, so I'm pretty sure that Brother Rei must have something to do with this," Desmond said.

Luca said, "That will be great when Will's gone."

Linc raised his eyebrows. "You know something I don't?"

"I'm using sarcasm!" Luca said.

Everyone laughed, and Luca blushed. He'd been trying to use sarcasm for the last few days, but had yet to properly use it a single time. Desmond put his arm around Luca and pulled him close. He wanted to ask the boy if he was okay, dig deeper to see if he knew anything, since he didn't seem particularly surprised. But he didn't want to do it in front of Linc.

"Well, see ya," Linc said, then took his seat at another table beside Brothers Reginald and Mark.

As soon as Linc was out of earshot, Luca whispered. "Will told me to tell you all to let him go. He has a plan and he said you have to trust him."

Desmond had to swallow every one of his 17 questions as John approached the table, pulled out a chair, then sat directly across from them. John never sat at their table. "Good evening, Brother Desmond," he said.

Desmond nodded, and even managed to speak without gritting his teeth. "Good evening, Brother John."

"I'm sure you've heard the news," John said. "Brother Will will no longer be with us here at New Unity after dinner. He has decided to leave the safety of The Sanctuary to embrace the unknown beyond our walls."

Desmond didn't have time to respond. John had barely shut his mouth when Rei commanded the head of the main table, hands folded and head bowed, patiently waiting to make his announcement.

With every set of eyes upon him, Rei parted his arms and raised his chin to the sky. Desmond made it through the prayer with gritted teeth, then chewed his bottom lip as Rei went through his song and dance of an announcement, spilling nothing but the scum on the surface of empty lies.

"I regret to inform you that tonight is our final evening with Brother Will," he started. Will entered the dining room with two brothers a little too close behind him. *Escorts for the prisoner.* Will smiled, then took the seat closest to the door. Rei smiled at Will, then continued. "I have begged and pleaded with Brother Will. I've practically fallen to my knees to keep him here with us. But he must heed the call of his heart, even if it sends him into the foaming mouth of Satan himself."

Rei stared at the floor, as though Will's decision was breaking his heart. "But we will wish him well on his way, and pray for him daily. Perhaps our collective spirit here can help to quell whatever unfortunate calamity awaits our Brother on the other side of The Sanctuary walls."

Rei shook his head and hovered in silence, like a televangelist's pregnant moments, just before he asks for the sale. If Rei was auditioning to take over The Prophet's role, he'd nailed the performance. When he raised his face to the crowd, Rei said, "There is no solace beyond our walls. But the Good Lord does, and always will, see fit to protect the soil of our Holy Land. We pray he sees fit to protect one of our Brothers, too."

Rei raised his glass in the air. "We wish you well in the world outside!"

"We wish you well in the world outside," the room repeated, glasses in the air.

* * * *

CHAPTER 10
BORICIO WOLFE

The Sanctuary
March 25
6:40 p.m.

Dinner tasted about one short and curly better than a sack of fresh mildew and old pussy, but what the fuck did you expect from a bunch of cornbread eating Bible fuckers? Boricio had offered to go into their kitchen and turn their slop all sweet and spicy, but the Bible fuckers had declined. They liked their food like they liked their lives, boring.

Just one of the billion and one dumbfuck decisions they seemed to specialize in, here in Bibleburg. The place had approximately dick in common with what Boricio had expected to see. It was nothing like it had been the previous fall, enough to make Boricio figure Bibleburg was under new management. The motherfuckers in Round One had meant business. And while there was business going on up in here - that you could guaran-fucking-tee- but what it was, Boricio didn't have a goddamned clue.

He'd figure it out, though. And he wouldn't waste his fucking time looking for a needle in a haystack. Best way to find a needle was to torch the entire fucking haystack, then come back with a magnet. So as soon as Boricio figured out what sort of needle he was looking for, he'd come back with the flamethrower.

Of all the dumbfuck decisions Boricio had seen so far in Bibleburg, the inconsistent guard shifts and unlocked houses were by far the dumbest. He would have little problem ruling this roost. But for now, he'd examine the situation.

Patience wasn't exactly the sharpest tool in Boricio's box. And while he liked playing character, and watching gullible fucks suck on his lies like they were the throb of a cock, he'd waltzed through the front gates looking for answers. But he had yet to find a single fucking one. No Charlie, no Adam, no Vic. And the bitch he killed back in New Orleans on Oct. 14, the one he'd seen two times since, both up in that window in the house across the way, and on the side of the road – both places fucking with his ability to see shit clearly – well, she was nowhere to be found either.

Boricio also wanted to know how many of the motherfuckers behind the walls were sipping the Kool-Aid because they liked the sweet taste of the sugar, and how many of them were pretending to like it since they weren't serving it outside The Sanctuary, where the "demons crawled through the forest." Boricio smiled. To hear the folks in charge tell it, the world was crawling with monsters like crabs in the cunt hair of a French Quarter whore. But that was bullshit. They were out there, sure, but any cocksucker with a few full clips had little more than dick to worry about. Boricio could smell bullshit, whether it got flushed or not. And it was ripe as a maggot-covered body behind the gates of ye ole Sanctuary.

Of course, the place did have a few amenities.

Even though he'd been close enough to smell the slick of a slit, he'd not tasted the dew. And there wasn't much worse than getting clearance from Mission Control and losing the blastoff. Fortunately, The Sanctuary had a few women Boricio could split right open. Even better, they were the sort of bitches Boricio liked. Churchgoing chicks were always the biggest sluts in the bedroom, down and dirty, and ready to do the kinkiest shit. Took them a while to start, but once you got them going, well ye-fucking-haw!

Boricio figured he had everyone's number, except the fucker with the quiet eyes full of ideas, the one who knew Boricio was beer battering a pan full of bullshit. Boricio had played the *I should've known there was evil in the house, what with all those Demons circling their part of the woods banshee ripping off a Band-Aid* bullshit with just about every fucker in the place. Quiet Eyes was the only one who'd stared right through it.

The one fucker, John, he knew Boricio was full of shit, too. His eyes said so. But whatever his game, Boricio's seemed to fit in with his plans, whatever they were. That wouldn't keep John alive forever, but it would sure as hell keep him alive for now.

The Sanctuary seemed to be split into three camps. Those with The Prophet, which Boricio hadn't seen hide nor hair of yet, and those with Brother Rei. There was a revolution coming, Boricio could smell it like a rotting corpse. Then there was the third group, led by Quiet Eyes. The fucker with the quiet eyes had a few other fuckers in his group, though Boricio couldn't tell exactly who all quite yet. The Godfather had taught Boricio a helluva lot of shit worth learning, but none more important than *keep your enemies closer.* He had a lot of shit to figure out before he burned the haystack to ash. Who better to ask than the one fucker in the place who probably wouldn't want him to know shit?

Boricio slid between Quiet Eyes and the stuck-up looking bitch, who were knee deep in private conversation. The two of them had been trying to grab some minutes together all day, and you'd have to be retarded, blind, or all of the above not to notice. Boricio wedged himself between them, then pointed out the window toward the large wooden box it seemed like everyone inside Sanctuary was trying too hard to ignore. Boricio knew what it was, figured it was the same box Dead Guard Walking had been talking about when he had ole Boricio on his knees, just before Boricio made him eat the fat side of his baseball bat.

"What's in the box?" he said.

"What do you think it is?" Quiet Eyes didn't turn from Stuck-Up Bitch.

"I think it's a punishment box," Boricio said.

Quiet Eyes moved from Stuck-Up Bitch to Boricio. "A punishment box? You say that with familiarity."

"Oh, yeah," Boricio nodded. "I went to school up in Arkansas. Was a small school that my daddy said would give me a good education, of the sort that came with The Good Lord's blessing. I never had to do no time in the box, but my friend Jimmy Appel had to do a full day on account of him taking the Lord's name. And my other friend Robby did two days for taking Sleazy Suzy off-campus without a chaperone."

Boricio wanted to laugh out loud at how Quiet Eyes wasn't buying a syllable of his bullshit. Boricio almost took it for granted, how easy it was to fool the foolish, since 49 out of 50 fuckers would believe whatever shit you told them, so long as you stared 'em in the eyes when you said it, and made sure to throw in an '*aw shucks*' every once in a while.

"Where in Arkansas?" Quiet Eyes asked.

"Up around Subiaco," Boricio said, not missing a beat.

Quiet Eyes didn't push the point. He said, "Yeah, it's a punishment box. Right now it's holding a little girl named Rebecca."

Boricio whistled. "What'd she do?"

"She snuck out of here with an older boy. The two of them went on a picnic." He turned to Boricio. "What do you think? Does the punishment fit the crime?"

"Well," Boricio said. "That does seem mighty harsh to me, but if we ever needed to refine the old rules, it's now. Wouldn't you say?"

Quiet Eyes didn't answer. Neither did Stuck-Up Bitch. A young guy who must've been part of his crew answered instead. "That's my friend, Rebecca, in there. And she doesn't deserve to be in there at all."

Boricio got a sudden flash of something he didn't like, and he got it from the kid, who had his hand out before Boricio even knew what he was doing. The kid's hand was halfway to his when Boricio realized where he'd seen him before.

It's the kid from my fucking dreams.

The one who goes from young fucker to old.

The one who can see right through to Boricio's middle.

On the outside, the kid looked like he could've been anywhere from 17 to 20. But Boricio could see right through to his middle, too, and could hear the chanting of *awe-awe-awe-awesome* looping in his mind.

Boricio shook the kid's hand, holding it as long as he could, absorbing the boy's memories, watching him play in the bedroom of an empty house with a young bald girl, Legos assembled in half-finished wedges scattered across the floor. Boricio pulled back with a horrible feeling that he'd lost some of his life as time turned soupy inside him.

What the fuck?

The man-boy stared at Boricio, and the mind fuck he was feeling was like nothing else he'd ever felt before, at least not on this side of being awake.

Boricio went on autopilot, answering questions and doing his best to make sure everyone felt comfortable and relaxed around him, except for Man Boy and Quiet Eyes and Stuck-Up Bitch, and teenage Stuck-Up Bitch who had come up beside her. People thickened around them as more members of the congregation crowed about to hear Boricio's tales of survival and hunting Demons on the way to his new life at The Sanctuary.

The more the congregation laughed, the more Boricio could feel Quiet Eyes and his Three Fuckerteers pulling farther away.

Boricio wanted to break from conversation and follow the Fuckerteers so he could see where they were going, but John was suddenly beside Boricio with his hand on his shoulder. Boricio pretended that the hand on his shoulder didn't make him want to break it off at the wrist and find some wolves to feed it to. He said, "Yes, Brother John, how can I be of service?" instead.

John said, "I'd like for you to come with me, if you can spare a minute. I think you'd enjoy talking to Brother Rei. He's dying to learn more about you. Not just your past, but what you're good at now. He wants to make sure you're as happy here at The Sanctuary as you can be. He'd like to talk to you about how you see yourself fitting in."

John walked off toward the main house, and Boricio followed.

He had to get his shit together. He was losing himself to the mess in his mind. He didn't know what to do, where to go, whom to kill, or how to do it. As is, shit was bad. Boricio always had the edge because he was always in control. If Boricio lost control, he'd lose the edge, and anything could happen then.

Boricio was also pissed as fuck that his crew had decided to bail. Maybe he'd made a mistake coming back out here to find them. *Sure would be fucking nice to have some back-up right about now. Maybe Chuckie Fuckstick would have an idea or two.*

What the fuck, Boricio? Get your fuckin' act together. Who the fuck cares if those twats go their own merry fuckin' way. Team Boricio only needs its star playa to be a winner, and that's its hung-like-a-lion, blood of a pirate, captain.

That pep talk and his holier-than-thou surroundings had never made Boricio want to kill more.

No one was safe.

He wanted to kill all the Bible fuckers for fucking the Bible, the Stuck-Up Bitch for looking like a stuck-up bitch, and her daughter for sharing the bitchy DNA.

Boricio figured he'd have no choice but to kill the kid who could see to his middle.

But Boricio would have to start with Quiet Eyes, especially since he finally figured out what it was that pissed him off so much about the motherfucker.

Quiet Eyes thought he was better than Boricio.

Boricio could practically smell it, like a stench on his body.

And no one was better than Boricio.

* * * *

CHAPTER 11
WILL BISHOP

Fort Lauderdale, Florida
Nov. 11, 1995
Morning

It was one of those dreams. The kind he hadn't had since a year earlier, when he'd first been warned that Sam would be injured by the drunk driver.

In this dream, warning, or blackened promise, Sam died lying in his hospital bed. Never opened his eyes, never said a word, never saw that Will was beside him. He just faded into the long kiss goodnight. In the dream, Will cried out to whatever *thing* pulled the strings above the prophetic dreams that plagued him, "Why?! Why couldn't you warn me?"

"*We did, last year, and you found a loophole,*" an unknown voice whispered from the warm womb in the middle of his dream. "*We found a loophole to your loophole. You can't change fate. And now it's time to correct the error. Loopholes go round, Will. Everything in a circle. No escape.*"

"But he wasn't supposed to die in the original plan! He'd only been paralyzed," Will shouted to the unseen voice.

"And he was . . . until you interfered."

Will woke to the ache of the uncomfortable waiting room chair, the sound of Trudy's voice pulling him from the mire. "Do you want to see him?"

"I thought I wasn't allowed," Will said, surprised.

"Yeah, well, you know how I can be," she said, attempting a smile. Her eyes and nose were red from a long night of crying.

"How is he?"

"Not good," she said. "There is a lot of swelling in his brain, and right now, anything could happen. He could wake up and be fine, or wake up with brain damage, or . . . He could stay in a coma and be a vegetable, or . . . die."

Trudy's mouth opened into a painful grimace, a long string of saliva hanging until it popped, as she let out a long wail.

Will hugged her, and held her tight as she cried on his shoulder.

"I'm so sorry," Will said, now crying himself.

"He really loves you," Trudy said. "I'm so sorry that I gave you such a hard time. He must hate me so much."

"Don't worry about it," Will said, hugging her harder. "He loves you, too. He thinks the world of you, Trudy. He could never hate you. Not ever."

They hugged a while longer, until the nurse appeared, a broomstick-thin black woman who looked like she just started her shift. The same nurse from his dream.

"Are you ready?"

"Yes," Will said as she led him to Sam's room. Trudy said she'd wait for him in the waiting room.

**

Will nearly fainted when he saw Sam getting eaten alive by an army of wires, all being fed by the bank of machines behind him.

There was a tube in his mouth, electrodes crawling all over his body, IVs, and a catheter tube, which emptied Sam's piss and stored it in a bag. His face was swollen and violet, a severe gash marked his left cheek, where surgeons had stitched his skin back together. His head was shaved and bandaged.

Will's knees buckled as he drew closer, and he swallowed his grief.

The nurse hovered in the background, "I'll be back in a few minutes. If you need anything, just call down the hall."

Will thought about the dream he had before Trudy woke him. He shrugged the déjà vu from his shoulders, recognizing the nurse from the dream. She had left him alone in the room in the dream, too. Minutes later, Sam was dead.

No, no, no.

Tears painted his face.

Please, God, whoever, don't do this to him. He is such a good, kind, sweet man. I've never known anyone so selfless and caring as Sam. Someone who would give you the shirt off his back even if it were snowing.

Will thought back on how they'd met, five years earlier at one of those gaudy chain stores, no less. They met in the poetry section. Will noticed Sam staring blankly at the neat rows of books for more than five minutes, and wondered if he were checking him out. It wasn't often Will saw anyone in the poetry section, let alone another guy, except the occasional college student trudging through a paper or looking to impress a girl.

"Are you familiar with this stuff?" Sam asked.

"A little," Will said. "Looking for a gift, or something for yourself?"

"Neither," Sam said sheepishly, "I'm trying to impress someone."

"Ah," Will said, "And is this someone a classical romantic, modern, maybe a fan of beat poetry?"

"I have no clue," Sam said, "He's this cute guy I saw, and I . . . Ah, I'm just gonna come out with it. I just wanted to strike up a conversation with you."

Will smiled, surprised that the guy was gay, since Will had a pretty damned good gaydar, but also surprised that he was approaching Will. He seemed a bit too pretty to be attracted to a guy like Will, who was a bit too casual about his appearance.

"I'm sorry," Sam said, "This is so awkward. I never do stuff like this. But I saw you here last week, and I wanted an excuse to talk to you, but I've gotta be honest, I don't like poetry. I'm a Lawrence Block guy. My name is Sam."

"Will," Will said, shaking the man's hand, firm but soft.

"You into poetry?" Sam asked.

"A bit," Will said, "I used to have a big collection, but I moved around a lot, and don't really feel like building the bookshelves again. So, I come here on the weekends and thumb through some classics, and check out what's new."

"That's cool," Sam said, shuffling his feet on the carpet, obviously trying to think of something to say.

"You're new at picking up guys?" Will said so matter-of-factly that Sam burst into laughter.

"Is it that obvious?"

"Well, most guys don't dress up so nicely on a Saturday morning to hit the bookstores, unless they're leaving their John Hancock on the first page."

"Was that a compliment?" Sam asked, flirting fairly well for a rookie.

"Maybe," Will said, smiling back. "Tell you what. How about I recommend a good poetry book, and you tell me which Block book I should buy."

"OK," Sam said, as Will took his time perusing the shelf for a great first read.

Will could feel Sam trying not to look at him. Will would have blushed if he were a few years younger. He wasn't a committed relationship guy, and hated to let himself get carried away with the idea of new relationships. He preferred them short and sweet. Sam seemed, even in their first exchange, serious and long-term. Will would entertain the notion, though, and see where it led. He moved closer to Sam, caught his scent — a light cologne he didn't recognize, a bit of lavender, but not overpowering like many men wore. This scent accented Sam, not defined him. Will loved the confidence.

"Okay," Will said, walking toward Sam with two books in his left and one in his right. "Good things come in three," he handed the first book to Sam, "and I figured these were good to start."

Sam looked at the collection of Poe. "Really?"

Will shook his head. "No, not really. He's just someone you're supposed to like. Start here instead." He handed Sam a copy of *Tarantula* by Bob Dylan. "You'll love that," he said. "Dylan at his best. Twisting words like they were tiny tornadoes, better here than on a lot of the records. Like Guthrie and Whitman got stoned together. It's great, I promise."

Sam was wearing the widest smile Will had ever seen in a bookstore. Will held up a copy of e. e. cummings.

"Isn't this another one I'm supposed to like?" Sam asked.

"Well, yes. But because he's great, not because your teacher told you to. Cummings is a master of metaphor and blather. He'll have stupid, random words and phrases thrown in a poem, then suddenly make you laugh out loud with the beauty of a perfect phrase, right there in the middle of his mess. Like a rose in a war zone. Hidden meter, gorgeous imagery, comfort, and inspiration. Plus, it's sexy."

Sam's smile finally stretched itself all the way into a laugh.

Will continued.

"Cummings said one of my favorite things ever: 'To be nobody but yourself in a world which is doing its best, night and day, to make you everybody else means to fight the hardest battle which any human being can fight; and never stop fighting.' Buy this book. You will read it often."

Will handed the book to Sam. Their fingers touched, and Will felt a chill. The good kind, not the creepy kind he got from so many men.

Sam led him to the fiction section and picked out a book, *The Sins of the Fathers.* "You'll love it," Sam said. "Maybe?"

Will smiled, "Maybe."

They met for coffee a week later so Sam could rave about cummings. Will read his book cover to cover, then picked up the next in the series. "Pretty damned good," he said. "I've never been much of a fiction guy, save for some old science fiction stuff back when I was young. But I liked it; thank you."

Will hadn't thought he'd like crime fiction. And he hadn't thought he'd like a long-term relationship. He was happily wrong on both accounts.

The coffee turned to dinner, turned to six years later, turned to now — Will standing in the ICU, watching his love leave the world of the living.

He touched Sam's arm, hesitantly, afraid he might set off alarms, or cause Sam to die on the spot.

Sam's eyes opened.

Will's heart swelled.

The dream was wrong! Which means that . . .

No, don't jinx this.

Sam's eyes tried to surface through confusion, just like his tongue tried to get itself to talk. Maybe he finally realized that he was hooked to a ventilator; his eyes and tongue stopped trying at the same time.

"You're in the hospital," Will said softly, "But I'm here now. So is Trudy."

Sam's eyes filled with water. Will hoped he wasn't feeling much pain.

"Don't try to talk; you're hooked up to a ventilator. I should probably get the doctor."

Sam shook his head no, his eyes now tearing, and he spoke.

"Don't, Will. I'm dying."

Except he hadn't spoken.

He was thinking. And Will was hearing it.

Will was certain he was imagining it, wanting to hear Sam speak to him, but no, Sam's voice spoke again.

"I'm scared."

Will turned to him, crying, "I'm scared, too."

Will turned, and called out, "Nurse! Doctor!" Then Will hit the alarm beside the bed.

The monitor began to beep faster as alarms rang on the machines.

"What's happening?" Will asked the staff rushing into the room.

"Sir, I'm gonna need you to wait outside," a surgeon said. One of the nurses stepped in front of Will to push him away.

"Will? What's happening?" Sam called out in his mind.

And then Will was outside the room, looking in through the window.

That was the last thing Sam would say, if Will had even really heard his thoughts.

"Will? What's happening?"

447

He died afraid, as his lover was wrestled from him. Inside, Will died that night, too.

He thought he'd found a loophole.

He'd saved Sam from one fate only to deliver him to a worse one.

Will walked down the hall and found Trudy, but could not bear to tell her she missed Sam opening his eyes. Fate might be cruel, but Will was not.

* * * *

CHAPTER 12
WILL BISHOP

The Sanctuary
March 25, 2012
7:11 p.m.

The cold night air was as cruel as the goodbyes, freezing Will's joints even beneath the thick pants and jacket he wore. Will walked to the car, a black Honda, which John said was his to keep, along with a bag of supplies.

Will wished they hadn't been waiting outside by the gate to see him off. Yet, there they were — Mary, Desmond, Paola, Luca, Linc, and even John. Brother Rei kept a respectable distance, surprisingly, back at the porch in front of the main house. He couldn't tell for certain, but he thought the weasel was smiling.

Desmond was first to say goodbye, reaching out to shake Will's hand.

"I'm sorry to see you go," Desmond said, pulling Will into an embrace.

"Luca told me. Don't worry," Desmond whispered.

Will pulled away, and Mary came to him, tears in her eyes, "Thank you so much for saving Paola. I will never forget your selflessness and kindness. Or our many weird conversations where I always felt like a kid in grammar school pretending to keep up."

She laughed through the tears, as did Will.

Paola hugged him, "Goodbye, Mr. Will. Thank you for everything."

"Anytime, sweetheart. You stay good for your mom, okay?"

She smiled, wiping tears from her eyes.

Luca was next, the closest thing to a son he'd ever have — this child turned teen in the span of months. Tears streamed down Luca's face, real tears, even though Will told him he'd be back. Maybe Luca knew more than he'd let on. Maybe he'd had the same dreams Will had. Or maybe the boy had read his mind, even though Will thought he'd been able to guard those thoughts.

Will hugged him, hard, both of them crying.

"Thank you," Luca said, collapsing completely to tears.

"Please, come back," Luca thought. *"Please don't forget us."*

"I will. I will find a way," Will thought back, unsure whether Luca could hear him.

"OK," Luca thought, like a blanket on Will's uncertainty.

Will left Luca a final thought: *"I'll meet you in your dreams. Call on me if you need me. You'll know when the time comes."*

Luca nodded, and Will winked.

Linc was next. He pulled Will into a big bear hug. Surprisingly, his eyes were wet, too. Guy was a big old teddy bear inside, after all. "You take care of yourself, alright?"

"You, too," Will said, eyes meeting Linc's. "And take care of them like they're family."

"Sure thing," Linc said, a bit shaken as if Will had called him out on his betrayal. "I will protect them like they're my own. And if you change your mind and come back, our doors are open," Linc said with a smile so sincere he must've believed the words, and not been part of the plot to have Will exiled.

John was last in the line. He had a smile on his face that seemed odd, even odder than he normally was.

"We're going to miss you," he said. "Please, feel free to come back, anytime."

"OK," Will said, reaching out to shake the man's hand.

Will felt his body go dead cold, as if he'd shaken hands with Death himself. He met John's eyes and the two exchanged a lingering gaze with equal unease. Will was sure John felt something, same as he did.

Will could see the pieces in his head, mostly in place. *John* was not John after all. This was a big development and something the dreams had overlooked.

Will bid the group a final farewell, eager to put The Sanctuary behind him before John realized he knew what he really was and stopped him. He had to get away and plan. He started the car, heard Luca and Paola call, "Goodbye, Will!"

He waved as he drove out the gates.

As Will drove and The Sanctuary grew smaller in his rearview, he knew it wasn't the last time he'd see the place. It was, after all, where the battle would soon occur. The battle that would result in Luca's death.

And try as Will might to find one, there were no loopholes.

* * * *

::EPISODE 12::
(SIXTH EPISODE OF SEASON TWO)
"REVOLUTION CALLING"

CHAPTER 1
BORICIO WOLFE

1987
Lauderdale Greens, Florida

Boricio had been playing Pik-Up Stiks with Ricky for about 15 minutes, and had been bored for 14 of them, when he decided he would hurt the kid.

He wished there were other kids on the street he could play with. It would have been nice if they had cool toys, or more interesting personalities, but he would've settled for a pulse. Ricky wasn't just the most boring boy Boricio had ever met; he was the only other white boy on the block.

There weren't many white kids in Boricio's neighborhood. Weren't many white adults, either, and Joe didn't let him play with "the darkies." The white people had left seemingly overnight, and the property values plunged, effectively turning the neighborhood into a ghetto of peeling paint, broken windows, and endless yards of chain link fencing off lawns of concrete and rust.

Boricio had seen pictures of the neighborhood from back in the old days. They had a fire safety assembly at school one time, and the fireman showed them slides of life in the city, before the neighborhood went to hell and the smelly rock was sold in the streets. It seemed like everyone on his street was a buyer, even his own mom. Maybe not Ricky's mom. Boricio had never smelled the smelly rock at Ricky's. He wrinkled his nose imaging the smell of the smelly rock's smoke, like cat pee and burning plastic.

The neighborhood was pretty in the slides from *back then*. There had been so many trees and green lawns. Most of the trees had been replaced by patches of hard dirt with a few spindly branches sticking out like fingers.

Boricio's street had no trash cans. There used to be a few when he was younger, but that was before the Fourth of July that some kids filled a bunch with firecrackers. The bottoms of the plastic bins were blown out and garbage exploded everywhere. The city came out and cleaned up, but hadn't replaced the cans. So, now people just threw their bags out on the curb, which invariably were torn into by stray animals, and nobody cared enough to clean up the resulting messes.

Boricio never really liked Ricky, though he used to like Ricky's older brother, Julian. Julian was 13, five years older than Boricio. He was nice to Boricio, showed him dirty magazines and let him use his slingshot to shoot at the cans on the lawn and the cats in the alley. He let Boricio hang out with him, whenever he had to watch Ricky anyway. Julian didn't really like Ricky all that much either, called him a fag all the time.

He would often disappear, taking different girls into the back of the house and leaving Boricio and Ricky alone, and bored. Granted, it was better than being home and listening to Joe scream at his mom, or worse.

Boricio couldn't play with Julian anymore since Julian was sent away a few months ago. Ricky didn't know where he'd been sent to, only that it was for his own good on account of their mom saying Julian was gonna grow up bad if she didn't do something quick. Julian once told Boricio that his dad left about an hour after Ricky was born. Boricio figured that made the two of them lucky. Boricio's real dad had left an hour after he'd been born, too. At least their mom never ended up with a Joe.

Boricio didn't want to play with Ricky anymore, but he didn't want to go home. So, Boricio balled up his fist, just like Joe, and clocked Ricky in the left ear as hard as he could. It was mostly out of curiosity, wanting to see what would happen, though a little was from the stuff that comes when your inner hate starts to simmer, but instead of taking his turn.

Boricio had taken plenty of hits, but had never thrown one, not like Joe gave him, anyway. He wasn't exactly sure what to do, but figured it couldn't be too hard since Joe did it all the time. Ricky had the sticks in his hand and his eyes on the pile, so he never saw Boricio's fist.

Ricky's face filled with surprise, the emotion quickly followed by pain, then fear – in an order that fascinated Boricio, even though all three flashed by in less than a second. He used a punch to Ricky's gut to knock the wind from him, then erupted in laughter as Ricky exploded in tears.

Ricky doubled over the scattered pile of sticks, clutching his stomach, which made Boricio picture Joe, and the way he smiled down on Boricio when he was doubled over just the same.

Ricky cried "NO!" as Boricio's foot landed hard on his face. It was the last intelligible sound he made, everything after that was just screams and cries and sobs and whimpers as Boricio started on Ricky with his fists, then finished with a pile of sticks, grabbing them in handfuls and stabbing them all over Ricky's twitching body.

Suddenly, a scream.

Ricky's mom, who rushed over to the boy to make sure he was okay. The boy was bloody, but he'd live.

Then she grabbed Boricio by the back of the neck, dragging him away, as Boricio kicked, swung, and cursed at her, trying to break free.

But she was holding on to the back of Boricio like he was the buckle of a belt.

"Let me go, you dumb bitch!" Boricio cried.

Ricky's mom didn't say a word. She dragged him across the yard, and then the street, until he was standing on his bottle-littered porch while Ricky's mom pounded her tired knuckles on the broken screen.

Boricio's mom was at the door a moment later, eyes bloodshot, hair hanging in damp and clumpy ribbons. The smell of cat piss and burning plastic poured from the house.

Ricky's mom was screaming so loud, Boricio could barely make out a word she was saying, and wasn't sure how much his mom would be able to gather. She sure looked like she had a problem standing there listening, though she knew she couldn't leave.

"You're raising a monster!"

"He almost killed my son!"

"How can he do that? They're friends!"

"I'm calling CPS immediately!"

"You all deserve to get locked up!"

The last thing Ricky's mom said before throwing Boricio through the doorway and marching back to her house was, "Your boy is broken."

Broken? That would explain a lot.

Boricio's mom slammed the door and slapped him across the face. "You think I need this shit now?" she yelled, her face as red as her eyes.

Boricio didn't cry, but he did fall to the floor and crawl backward toward the kitchen. She was wearing the look that meant his body was gonna hurt real bad, real soon. At least it wasn't Joe. Joe was worse. Much worse. Most of the time his mom protected Boricio from Joe, kept him safe from the worst of his temper. Kept him out of the dark room, away from the hotplate, safe from the baseball bat. But tonight, Boricio might not be so lucky.

"Just wait until your father gets home!" his mother screamed, her foot landing smack in the middle of Boricio's crumpled body. He cried. She said, "You don't have anything to cry about you crazy, cocksucking parasite!" She finished her sentence with a hard kick to her son's side. Boricio felt like he was bleeding inside instead of out. The doctor had said that was the most dangerous kind.

His mother kept kicking him and screaming: "You dumb shit, diarrhea for brains, more trouble than you're worth, stupid sonofabitch! I will NOT be yelled at, and I will NOT be humiliated, and I will NOT be threatened. That dumb bitch outside did all three. Because of you!"

She stopped kicking and Boricio stayed in a pile crying. She said, "That's nothing, Bo. You wait until Joe gets home. He's gonna make sure you're sorrier than a skinned cat." Then she left the room, slamming the door so hard that a picture frame hanging in the living room fell and broke. The picture was the last school picture taken of Boricio, way back in kindergarten.

"Fuuuuck!" his mother screamed.

The smell of cat piss and burning plastic bled through the crack beneath her door and spread like a fog through the house.

Boricio thought about leaving since home was the last place in the world he'd want to be when Joe got home. But Boricio had no idea where he could go. He didn't have any food or money, and the farthest he'd ever been out of the neighborhood was to school a couple of miles away. Leaving the house would be scary, but less scary than whatever his mom would do once she opened the door, and a world better than Joe.

Boricio cried harder, thinking about what would happen when Joe walked in the door.

Once he could breathe again, he went to the kitchen and took the four packs of Ramen from the cupboard and put them in his backpack, along with two cans of Shasta, a box of powdered potatoes, and some mustard. He added a change of clothes, then turned on the TV to think. His mom would be in her room for another couple of hours, at least. He had at least six before Joe came home. That gave him at least an hour to think.

Boricio watched a rerun of *Family Ties* and wondered how much of it was bullshit. Sure wasn't like any family he had ever seen. That, and *The Cosby Show. French fried fucking lies*, as his mom would say.

Boricio figured that *maybe* life could be all happy, funny, and loving like it was on TV, if he could get to a place where it still looked like it did in the old days. Maybe if he was lucky, he'd find a family like that one day. Boricio had a few teachers who told him he was smart. The same teachers who stared at him with big, sad eyes when they asked him what was wrong at home. It was the only question he never answered. The teachers were right, Boricio *was* smart. He wasn't about to fink on Joe and wind up six feet under.

Family Ties ended, and Boricio stood from the couch, turned off the TV, slung his backpack over his shoulder, and headed toward the door. Halfway there, he turned back and grabbed the White Pages from beneath the phone that had been disconnected three months earlier. Enough people had used the words *child*, *protective*, and *services* together for Boricio to know that maybe someone there could help him.

He thumbed through the C pages, found what he was looking for, and then tore the page from the book and shoved it in his pack.

The other side of his mom's door was still silent. Boricio figured it was now or never, then crept toward the front door. Joe opened it before he could.

Boricio's heart nearly exploded in his chest, and the look on his face must've been all guilt, because Joe stared at him hard.

Joe wanted to know where Boricio was headed off to with the backpack, and when he opened it up to a change of clothes and Ramen, plus the paper with hotline numbers for CPS, his eyes went blacker than black, which meant he was about to get meaner than mean.

Boricio cried, "NO!" then turned and ran as fast as he could. Joe was faster, grabbing Boricio by the neck and throwing him to the floor.

Boricio's mom opened her bedroom door and even though she threatened punishment, she begged for Joe to stop.

But it was too late.

It was always too late once you let the monster out.

* * * *

CHAPTER 2
LUCA HARDING

Kingsland, Alabama
The Sanctuary
March 27
Morning
Two days after Will left

Luca looked across to Paola, sitting in the back of the room at the desk beside him, obviously uncomfortable in the long, dark-blue dress she'd been forced to wear after Mary decided they would stay at The Sanctuary.

Luca didn't mind his change in clothes, wearing dark slacks and a long-sleeve, light-blue shirt with suspenders; it made him feel more like he matched the body life made him wear.

"This looks like a children's classroom," Paola whispered. "I'd rather be washing dishes and cleaning."

"It's all ages," Luca said.

"Shh," 11-year-old Tammy Watson whispered from up front, casting a nasty look back to Paola and Luca, even though the teacher had yet to arrive.

Paola stuck her tongue out. Tammy's eyes widened as if Paola had said the F-word.

Though the classroom was on the bottom floor of the children's house, the room's interior looked just like a schoolroom, complete with a chalkboard, chairs with desks attached, and colorful pictures on the wall. There were six kids in the classroom other than Luca and Paola, ranging from ages 6 to 15. There were 20 chair/desk combos in the room, and though Luca usually sat up front, he followed Paola to the back of the class. It was her first day, and he didn't want her to feel alone.

"So, what do you do all day? Learn Bible stuff?" Paola whispered.

"Yeah, and regular math, and English stuff," Luca said. "It's not bad."

"Ugh, you're one of those kids who *liked* school, aren't you?"

"Yeah, didn't you?"

Paola rolled her eyes, "Um, *nooo.*"

The teacher, Ms. Autumn, a young brunette with a pretty smile and beautiful blue eyes, arrived just after 8, apologizing for being late.

"I'm sorry," she said, "I was helping Sister Theresa with something. Good morning, class."

"Good morning, Ms. Autumn," the children said in chorus.

Paola looked at Luca with narrowed eyes, "*Oooooh,* I see why you like school so much; you have a crush on the teach."

Luca went red-faced at the accusation, and was about to deny it when Ms. Autumn said, "Ah, we have a new student, Miss Paola Olson. Say hello to Paola, class."

"Hello, Paola," they all said, including Luca, who giggled while doing so. Tammy Watson shot Paola a dirty look as she said her hello.

"Why don't you tell us a bit about yourself, Paola?" Ms. Autumn said.

Paola went from jaded to shy in seconds, "I dunno, I'm 12. I'm from Warson Woods Missouri. And I like hanging out with friends, going to the mall, and playing video games. Well, I did, anyway."

"Welcome to our class, Paola, we're glad to have you," Ms. Autumn said as she sat. "Now, let's begin with our morning prayer, shall we?"

Paola gave Luca a weird look as he folded his hands and closed his eyes. He didn't remember the prayer, but he kept his mouth moving as though he knew every word. He peeked over at Paola, grimacing through the prayer, and smiled. She opened her eyes and caught him, then furrowed her eyebrows in playful anger, which made him almost giggle out loud.

He closed his eyes, since he didn't want to erupt in a laughing fit and get in trouble.

As Ms. Autumn began talking about the day's lessons, Luca found his mind drifting to Will, and wondering if he was okay. Luca hadn't seen Will since he left two days earlier, in real life or in his dreams. He hoped he was okay.

Though Luca was sad Will had left, things had been running smoothly at The Sanctuary ever since.

Desmond and Mary told John and Brother Rei that they would stay at The Sanctuary, a decision Luca knew they'd been fighting about, from the snippets of conversations, and thoughts, he'd overheard, though he never intended to eavesdrop. Once they made their decision, they were all given new clothes like the rest of the people wore.

Now that they were officially part of The Sanctuary, Luca noticed that people were thinking less bad things about him and the others. They were starting to accept them, though some people, like Tammy, didn't care for them at all. Tammy, Luca had discovered while accidentally tuning into her thoughts, was jealous of Paola's beauty. Luca thought it was odd, considering that Tammy was pretty. But she was blonde and pale, and secretly craved to have Paola's olive skin and dark hair. Tammy's nastiness was almost an obsessive string of thoughts. Thankfully, Luca was now learning to tune out people's thoughts.

When Luca first began hearing other people's thoughts, the voices poured through like a whole bunch of radio stations all tuned in at once, and it was too much. Now, when he wanted to, he was able to tune out everyone completely and stay in his mind with his own thoughts. He didn't like the constant chatter and negative thoughts of others. Now, however, Luca was tempted as he watched Paola doodling on a piece of paper and ignoring Ms. Autumn, to get in her head and hear what she was thinking.

Things had been weird between them since he started talking to Rebecca, even though Paola had no idea that Luca was hanging out with her every night in the little trips he took outside his body. Nobody but Will, and Rebecca, knew he could do that.

Things had already been weird between them since he saved Scott. Once he grew physically so much older than Paola, she started acting different. Maybe she sensed he had a crush on her, and wasn't sure how to respond. He was, after all, really 8, and not the 16 years his body now appeared. The whole thing was weird, and Luca noticed how even Mary and Desmond looked at him different, like they didn't want him being friends with her anymore. They were afraid he'd have sex with her. While Luca's knowledge of sex was extremely limited, he couldn't deny that the body change caused him to think about girls a lot more. Not to mention, he was always "popping boners," as Jimmy had called it.

Last night, when Luca and Paola were joking after dinner, Luca heard Mary's thoughts, even though he wasn't trying to eavesdrop.

Don't you dare make a move on my daughter.

Luca heard the thought, clear as if it had been his own. He turned to Mary, and caught her staring at him. A moment passed between them, and she quickly turned, as if she knew he'd heard her thought.

He left her head, but not before he felt something. It wasn't in words, but rather an emotion — fear . . . of him.

Luca liked Mary; he thought of her like a mom, almost. So, her fear of him made him sad. He didn't want to be the target for her Mama Bear rage, and was offended that she felt that way about him, like you might an outsider. They'd known each other for months, and Luca thought he'd earned more trust from Mary.

Besides, Luca didn't even feel the same about Paola anymore. Not since Rebecca, anyway.

Even though Rebecca was locked in the box outside, he felt as if she'd been by his side nearly every night.

Over the course of the past few nights, they'd journeyed to the mountain, his home, a lake she used to swim in, and even Disney World, or at least the version informed by TV and painted by Luca's imagination. They even went on rides, and though it couldn't possibly have been real, it felt real to them. Though Rebecca was locked in a cold box with barely any food or water all day, she was having the time of her life when she closed her eyes at night.

Luca felt like they'd known each other for years, not days. In many ways, Rebecca, at 13, was closer to Luca's age, than Paola, who seemed way older than her 12 years, and was growing more jaded by the day.

Rebecca would be freed from the box after her week was up, and Luca couldn't wait to finally see her in person. But he was also afraid. Once she got out of the box, her mother, and the others, would surely be keeping a close eye on her. If she even talked to a boy, let alone Luca — the outsider — they might both wind up in boxes.

Luca tried not to think about the stuff that would stop him from enjoying his time with Rebecca. Even if they had to spend the next year together only in their connected dreams that weren't really dreams, it was a lot better than nothing. Luca wasn't sure what romantic love was like, or if it was possible to feel it so quickly for someone — someone you technically didn't even know in person — but he felt *something* for Rebecca. If it wasn't love, it had sure fooled his heart.

So, why am I still wondering what Paola is thinking?

I have to listen in. Just one more time.

He closed his eyes, and tuned into the voices. But he didn't hear Paola's.

Instead, he heard Black Pieces, the voices he hadn't heard since they came to The Sanctuary.

"Hello, Luca. I missed you."

"Black Pieces?" Luca thought, excited and a bit nervous that his old chess-mate had resurfaced.

"Yes, I've been looking for you." Black Pieces said, his voice today like Cheshire Cat's from *Alice in Wonderland*, but with a bit of a hiss at the end of his words.

Luca felt a chill. *"What do you want?"*

"He's here, isn't he? The Man in The Center, Man in the Middle, whatever you're changing voice is calling him today. I feel him with you."

"Yes," Luca thought, *"But he's not like he was in the dreams. He's not killing people."*

"Not yet, but you know the dreams can't be changed, right? Because they're not dreams."

"Yes, they can. I can change them."

"Do you even remember what happened in the 'dreams,' Luca?"

"No, not everything. I haven't been having them lately. I thought maybe they wouldn't come true. Maybe things would be okay."

"Yes, I see what you've been doing, but I wouldn't get too attached."

A vision flashed before Luca: Rebecca's dead eyes staring up at him. She was skinny, and her skin blue, as if starving and cold.

"No," Luca thought. "*She's not going to die!*"

Dark Pieces laughed.

"*She's already dead, silly. Heh-heh. She died two nights ago. You've only been imagining that she's still alive. Tsk, tsk, you're even more messed up than they said you were. Poor Luca's first love is a dead girl.*"

"No!" Luca thought. Or *thought* he thought, but then realized, by the stares from his classmates, that he'd shouted it out loud.

"Are you okay?" Ms. Autumn asked as the kids up front giggled. Paola stared at Luca, concerned.

Luca's heart pounded, and he felt short of air, sucking in deep breaths, his thoughts a jumbled mess.

No, she can't be dead!

Luca got up from his desk, heart pounding in his throat, and said, "I don't feel so good," and raced from the classroom, into the hall, and out of the house, headed for the Box of Shame.

* * * *

CHAPTER 3
LUCA HARDING

Luca raced from the women's house, toward the courtyard where the Box of Shame stood in the morning sun and last night's four inches of snow.

He could feel eyes on him: workers at the church, a couple of men in front of the barn, Brother Rei and John, who were standing in front of the hangar, and surely the men in the guard towers over each of the houses. He heard snippets of thoughts, people wondering what he was doing. One man wondered if he should shoot Luca.

Luca didn't stop running until he reached the box. He pounded on the box, his hands hurting in the cold air as his fists met the wood. He cried out, "Rebecca!"

Nothing but silence.

His heart froze.

No, she can't be.

All those journeys taken together, all their conversations, stories, secrets, and laughs shared in the past two nights, were they all in his head?

He continued to bang on the box. "Rebecca!!"

Behind him, one of the men shouted, "Hey, get away from there!"

Luca could hear footsteps approaching, though he could see nothing but the wooden box in front of him with its heavy wooden bar locking the poor girl inside. He put his hands beneath the bar, and pushed up. It was lodged tight, so he pushed harder, putting his feet into it, but his feet were slipping in the snow.

Please, please, please be alive!

"Hey!" the same man shouted.

"Get away from there!" another shout. It was Brother Rei, racing toward him, John close behind.

Luca looked at them, then back at the bar, giving it another desperate push. He had to get the box open before they got to him. He pushed with everything he had. The bar lifted and swung aside.

Footsteps closed in, and he could hear breathing, and their thoughts:

I'm gonna kick his ass.

You little fucker.

The boy is possessed!

He's dead!

Luca pulled the door open and his heart stopped. He saw Rebecca inside, eyes closed, skin blue, unconscious, maybe dead. He reached in pulled her out of the box — she was so cold — and gently laid her on the ground so he could try to heal her. A hand caught his hair and pulled tight, yanking him back. Brother Rei.

"Let go!" Luca screeched, trying to break free, and get to Rebecca. "I have to save her!"

"You're coming with me!" Brother Rei said, ignoring Rebecca who had yet to move and was dead or dying. There were more than 50 adults at The Sanctuary, at least 10 in the courtyard, not including guards, and yet nobody was helping Rebecca.

"Someone, please help her!" Luca cried out, still trying to pull free from Brother Rei's tight grip on him.

A couple of the men looked down at Rebecca, but remained passive.

"She's dying!" Luca screamed as Brother Rei's hands went around Luca's waist, and pulled him farther away.

"Let go of him!" a voice shouted.

It was Desmond, who'd come running from the barn.

Brother Rei held his grip tight, "He's going in the hole!"

Desmond dropped to his knees beside Rebecca, then felt for a pulse. A moment later, he began to perform CPR on Rebecca. The crowd of people around them had grown to nearly 20, but only Desmond was helping Rebecca.

"Get him off of her!" Brother Rei commanded to one of the men.

Brother Andre, a big, red-bearded man, almost as large as Linc, grabbed Desmond by the right arm.

Desmond spun around, gripped the man's hand, and twisted it behind him hard, then thrust Andre to the ground. Two more men ran toward Desmond.

"She's dying!" Luca screamed.

"Let God decide her fate!" Brother Rei shouted, holding his hand out to command the others to stay put.

Luca used the slippery snow to his advantage; he spun, dipped down and slipped out of Brother Rei's grip, then came up and elbowed him beneath the left eye.

Freed, Luca dropped to the ground and scrambled to Rebecca's side. One of the guards, Brother Terry, thrust a rifle at Luca, "Get away from her, or I will shoot."

A loud shot rang out, and Brother Terry dropped the gun, clutching his bloody, mangled right hand, crying in disbelief, "You shot my hand!"

Luca looked up to see Desmond holding a pistol, and waving away the others. "Back the FUCK off!" he shouted.

471

"Everyone just hold on," Linc said, stepping forward with his hands up. "Let the kid help her. I've seen him do it before."

Luca put his hands on Rebecca's face — so cold — then closed his eyes in search for her soul.

He found her on the mountain, in their spot where the swing and rose bush had been during their first trip. Only now, there was no swing, rose bush, or lightning bugs to light the darkness swirling in the clouds overhead. Rebecca was in a heavy black coat, on her knees in the snow, back turned to him and looking down at something he couldn't see, her long, red hair flowing in the wind.

Her hair is back!

Luca stepped toward her, and heard her murmuring. As he drew closer, he saw her pulling petals from one of the roses with a million petals, saying, "He loves me; he loves me not," over and over.

"I'm here," Luca said, but she either didn't hear him, or was ignoring him, as she kept counting the petals, tossing them to the ground. As he circled around her, he saw there must've been 500 petals on the ground in front of her splayed blue dress, which flowed over the snow like a blanket.

"He loves me, he loves me not," she said, oblivious to his presence, her eyes closed.

"Rebecca," he said, kneeling down in front of her, "I'm here."

"He loves me, he loves me not ... "

He reached toward her hand as her fingers plucked a petal free, and touched her.

Her eyes opened wide, but they were all black.

Luca jumped back, startled.

She kept counting, "He loves me, he loves me not ... " only now her eyes — her alien, black eyes — followed him as he backed away.

"*Rebecca?*"

"He loves me, he loves me not ... " she said, ripping petals from the flower, faster now, though her dark eyes never left him.

"She can't hear you," a girl's voice said behind Luca. He turned and recognized the older teen from the pictures Rebecca had shown him at her house — her sister. She wore a long, black dress, which blew around her like a tapestry in the wind.

"Alexis?" Luca said.

"She's gone," Alexis said, no emotion on her face.

"No," Luca said, "She *can't* be gone. I can save her."

"Just let her go. She's better off here, where Mother can't hurt her."

"No!" Luca said, "I can protect her!"

"No," Alexis said, "no one can. It's too late. Too late for all of you. He's bringing them all."

"What?" Luca said, "Who?"

"The Man in the Middle; he's not who you think he is. And he's preparing to eat you all."

Rebecca gasped, sucking for air, then caught her breath as her eyes went from black to blue. They were both back at The Sanctuary, with Desmond holding off an angry mob.

"You're alive!" Luca said, eyes tearing up as he hugged her.

"Luca?" she asked, her voice thin and shaky, "What happened to you? You look older."

Luca looked around and saw that everyone was looking at him with wide eyes, shocked into silence.

Desmond looked down at Luca and nodded his head, "You look about 25 now, buddy."

Rebecca's mother, who must've seen what happened, came over, practically pushing Luca out of the way, and fell to her daughter's side, crying, and holding Rebecca, "I'm so sorry, baby."

She looked at Luca, eyes red, "Thank you."

Luca said, "You're welcome," then noticed something.

Luca saw the movement too late to warn Desmond, as a man slipped behind him, and punched him in the back of the head, knocking him to the ground, out cold. It was only after the man picked up the gun that Luca recognized who it was — Boricio.

Boricio looked at Desmond's gun oddly for a second, as if he'd recognized it or something, then turned it over in his hand and handed it butt end to Brother Rei.

Two pairs of hands grabbed Luca tight around his arms and yanked him away as Rebecca screamed, "No!"

* * * *

CHAPTER 4
RYAN OLSON

Elmore, Georgia
Feb. 26
8:17 p.m.

Ryan had hoped to reach Alabama by nightfall, but they'd had to flee the highway five times thanks to the seemingly endless piles of vehicles littering the road. The world around them was pitch-black, slowing Ryan's driving to a crawl.

If the moon was out, it had been choked by the low-hanging churning dark clouds.

Driving on the highway in complete darkness was an accident waiting to happen, as they'd discovered two nights earlier when they plowed into a stalled VW at full speed. If Ryan believed in miracles anymore, he'd consider it one that they all escaped without a scratch. Their Honda Odyssey however, wasn't so lucky.

Ryan, Carmine, and Gramps found themselves stranded and having to walk two miles, inching Gramps along in a wheelchair, and praying to find shelter before the monsters found them.

Their luck had lasted a little longer, leading them to a hotel just off the highway where they found another van, an older Econoline with a full tank of gas, which is what they were driving now.

"We gonna find a spot soon?" Carmine asked from the back of the van as they hit a logjam of dead metal, making them backtrack in a snaking line away from the highway.

"Yeah," Ryan said, "You all want to find a house, or a hotel?"

"Whatever's first," Gramps said from the back, "I need to use the facilities something fierce."

"OK," Ryan said, getting off the highway and driving into a small nothing town.

Ryan killed the headlights, and drifted through darkness, not wanting to attract any attention. The main street stretched for a bit before they found anything worth finding — a strip mall. They passed the strip mall, then turned down the first connecting street, searching the neighborhood for homes that looked secure and vacant, finally killing the engine at a cul de sac with 13 houses. They picked the two-story house at the end since it offered the best view of the entire street.

Ryan pulled into the driveway, turned off the engine, and rolled down his window, listening to the night for sounds of creatures.

"I remember when the sound of night was like music," Gramps said, "Back when I was a kid, we used to go to my Grandpa's house out in the country, and I remember opening the window so I could listen to the crickets sing. To a city kid used to hearing traffic as music, it was almost magical."

"Sounds like the magic is gone," Ryan said, "I haven't heard crickets, or seen much insect or animal activity, since

October. It's like whatever took the people got greedy and took everything else, too."

Gramps started to say something about the rapture and animals, but stopped when something grabbed his attention outside the van.

"Do you hear that?"

"What?" Ryan asked, reaching for his pistol, before he heard the sound a second later.

"A helicopter?" Ryan said, confused. "I haven't seen one of those since October!"

"Let's flag them down!" Gramps said, "It's the government, and they're looking for survivors."

Gramps started to open the passenger door, even though he'd have to wait for them to get his wheelchair from the back.

"Wait, Joe!" Ryan said, "We don't know for sure who or what they are, or even if they're looking to *help* anyone."

"Have some faith, boy!" Joe said, "That sounds like a Black Hawk, and that means armed services, or maybe FEMA or something, someone able to help."

"Let's just wait to see if they come closer before we get out of the van. We don't need to be outside screaming our heads off and attracting the creatures. If they come, I'll hit the lights and honk the horn to get their attention, if they're even looking."

"OK," Gramps said, wrinkles crinkling with agitation.

Though they'd gotten along well the past three days since Ryan was attacked, Gramps could be on the cranky old man side at times, especially when his blood sugar dropped. It wasn't like Ryan was feeling himself since the attack, either. Though his body had mended remarkably well from the gunshots and bite wound, and despite feeling stronger than he had in years, he was also feeling irritable with excruciating migraines, which hurt bad enough to make him vomit. Worst was the pain-inducing sounds it seemed that only he could hear. Initially, it sounded like a light ringing in his ears, but then the ringing grew more distinct, like the buzzing of an insect. Dozens, maybe hundreds.

The buzzing came and went at random intervals, a few minutes here and there. Usually, it was a minor annoyance. Sometimes the pain was so loud, not in his ears but rather his head, that it was as crippling as the migraines.

Add to that a lack of a full night's sleep since they began keeping watch, and it was easy to see why his, and everyone's, nerves were rawer than usual.

There was also the little issue of their journey.

Ryan had to convince Gramps and Carmine that they couldn't stay in their apartment any longer, that it was no longer safe now that the monsters had locked onto their location. And while Gramps was a helluva shot, he was disabled and unable to run if necessary, a fatal liability. Gramps resisted at first, headstrong and full of pride. In the end, he relented, admitting that yes, there was definitely strength in numbers.

But the issue of *where* they would go was a simmering debate. Gramps wanted to head to Virginia where he had an old friend, Harry, he wanted to check on. Ryan insisted that they first go to Alabama, where he believed his ex-wife and daughter were, thanks to the dreams he'd been having since the attack.

"Yeah, but you're going off a dream. We don't even know if that's where they are, assuming they didn't vanish," Gramps said. "At least with Harry, I know where Harry is, if he's still here."

"Yeah, well I knew where Mary and Paola were, too," Ryan argued. "They were at their house, but had to leave, remember? What are the odds that your friend Harry stayed in one spot? And if he's still there now, then there's a good chance he'll still be there after we find Mary. Besides, I'm looking for two and you're looking for one. And my two are family."

"Come on, Gramps," Carmine had said, "He's right. It's his *family*. They're more important than a friend, aren't they?"

Gramps apologized and agreed, and they began their trip. However, Ryan felt like the old man was rushing him at times, in a hurry to get to Alabama to either find Mary and Paola or not, so they could get on to Virginia. If it came to that, and Ryan's family wasn't in Alabama, Ryan was going to have to *really* upset Gramps. Because when it came right down to it, Ryan had no intention of going to Virginia, *unless* he found his family. If he didn't find Mary and Paola, he would circle the state until he did. He hoped it wouldn't come to that, as he didn't want to pull rank, and didn't want Gramps and Carmine going off on their own, since Carmine was just a kid, and still unable to take care of them both. They needed Ryan.

Besides, he'd come to like them.

They listened for the sound of the chopper to come closer, but instead, it faded away.

"Aw, hell," Gramps said, "OK, let's go inside. I need to whiz."

**

Ryan took the first watch, at the upstairs bedroom window, watching the street for any sign of a threat. It was nearly 2 a.m. and Carmine, who had the next shift, lay sleeping in a bed just feet away from the chair Ryan was sitting in. Gramps slept in the room next door.

From past experience, Ryan figured they were safe as the monsters generally only seemed to go into homes when they saw or heard something inside. As long as the three of them kept quiet, it wasn't likely anything would come bursting through this house, of all houses on the street, hunting for people. At about 2:14 a.m., Ryan was finding it hard to keep his eyes open. He fought the urge to nod off by drinking warm cans of energy drinks. Unfortunately, that also made him have to pee — a lot.

He went to the bathroom, then back to his spot in front of the window. The shades were drawn almost all the way, save for a sliver through which he spied the street below. Five minutes after he pissed, Ryan saw a pair of monsters at the other end of the block, where his street met the main connector road.

Ryan hoped like hell they'd keep right on going. Instead, they stopped, staring down the cul de sac. Ryan's heart began to accelerate as his breath froze. He reached down blindly behind himself, his fingers fumbling for the gun.

The creatures turned their gaze in his direction, though he doubted they could see him a full block away. They must've heard, seen, or smelled something of interest, since they started to lope down his street, headed toward his house.

Fuck!

Ryan looked down at Carmine, wondering if he should wake the boy, or wait until the monsters drew closer. If he woke the boy, he risked startling him and shattering the silence of the house, which would put them in graver danger. So he waited, watching the street below.

The pair of creatures was halfway down the block, eyes on one of the other houses on the left. They lifted their heads high, as if sniffing something through their slits for noses, then turned their attention back to the end of the street and seemingly on Ryan's house.

Fuck, they can sense me.

Go away, go away, FUCKING GO!

The creatures stopped dead in their tracks, as if they'd heard his last command, turned around, and began to bound away, on all fours, like wild gazelle running from a lion.

What the hell?

Ryan's head started to throb, and the buzzing sound hummed in his ears again. It grew louder, as if someone were cranking up the volume in his brain. His stomach churned as he grew dizzy and nauseous. He hurried out of the room and into the bathroom, found the flashlight on the sink, clicked it on, shut the door behind him, then fell to the floor over the toilet. Before he even had a chance to determine if the bowl had a floater, he vomited forth a bag of Chili Fritos and three energy drinks.

Oh God!

His stomach was churning, painful cramps pinching his gut from all sides, as he continued to splatter the toilet with puke. His head continued to buzz like hornets were swarming through his ear canals.

His hands gripped the cold bowl tight as his arms shuddered, continuously spitting until he was all finished retching, and the sound faded from his head.

He swallowed, turned, and grabbed a towel off the towel rack. He wiped his mouth, collapsing against the bathroom wall, exhausted. As he sat on the floor, his eyes grew heavy, and he thought about going to sleep right there. *Just a few minutes.* The monsters had run away, after all.

But what were they running from?

What scared them so bad?

Ryan didn't want to consider that something *worse* than the monsters might be lurking nearby. Perhaps they'd seen or heard the helicopters, even though Ryan hadn't. Maybe the monsters could hear at longer distances.

No, that's not it.

You know what happened.

His inner voice had obviously figured out something his conscious mind hadn't yet assembled. He felt like he should know why they ran, but was coming up empty. He tried to think back on the moment, and then he heard the sound of something wet.

He rose to his feet, carefully, his head still throbbing, and still feeling waves of vertigo.

Where is that sound coming from? The toilet?

He grabbed the flashlight and cast its beam into the bowl, where he saw his vomit, black and thick, alive with inch-long writhing things, like worms or maggots. There had to be hundreds, if not a thousand, in the bowl.

Jesus, what are those?!

Were those in me?

Then the light caught movement, something racing across his left arm.

No, not on it, but *in it*, just beneath the skin.

What the hell was that?

He thought he was seeing things, floaters in his eyes, shadows, *something!* But when he cast the light fully on his forearm, he saw the shapes writhing beneath his flesh. Worms, just like in the toilet.

He stared in disbelief, revulsion growing, and threatening to make him return to the toilet to vomit up whatever else was in him.

What is happening to me?

His mind began to pull at the thread of his question: the weird dreams he'd been having where he was running with the creatures, like a pack of animals; the weird buzzing sounds; how he'd healed so quickly from wounds that should have laid him up for weeks if not killed him; how the creatures turned tail when he thought at them to go.

The answer unspooled before his mind's eye, leading him back to a sickening conclusion.

He was infected.

* * * *

CHAPTER 5
MARY OLSON

Kingsland, Alabama
The Sanctuary
March 27
4:01 p.m.

Paola was nestled deep into her mother's chest, sobbing, but Mary petted her head and pushed her deeper. "It's okay," she soothed, "We'll figure this out."

Paola tried to make words, but couldn't. Through fresh tears, she finally confessed. "I'm scared, Mom."

"I know, honey, I know."

"Do you think Desmond's okay? What do you think they'll do to him? Will they throw him in the box, like they did to Rebecca?"

Mary held her tighter. "Everything is gonna be okay. I'm sure Desmond is fine. The situation was getting out of hand, and they had to disarm him. Things were confusing. People didn't know what Luca could do, because they hadn't seen it. Desmond had a gun, so he looked like the

483

aggressor. That Boricio guy was only trying to help. And no, I don't think they'll throw him in the box, not at all. I think they'll ask him a few questions. Then he'll be back with us, telling us his stories."

Of course, Mary didn't believe a word that left her mouth. While she hated lying to Paola, it was better than the alternative. She had no clue whom to trust, which was partly why she shuddered when Paola said, "Do you think there's anything John can do to help?"

"I'm not sure," Mary said, "but I'll find out right now."

She hated the question, but hated her answer even more. Mary told Paola she'd be right back, then left to go find John. She found him talking to a pair of Brothers. She called his name, and he turned to face her. "I'm so sorry about what's happened, Mary."

"Does that mean you know what happened?"

John said, "You mean what's happening now, or what happened a few minutes back when our buddy Desmond was waving a gun in the air, a gun he shouldn't have had? Brother Rei will want to know where it came from. Safety is the most important consideration for everyone at The Sanctuary, after all."

"Yes," Mary agreed, "especially for Desmond right now. I'm sure that after what happened to Rebecca, turning up ice-blue in a box, and Carl, who no one has seen for days, you can appreciate my concern."

John's face softened, though it was closer to the jelly of missing emotion she'd seen since arriving at The Sanctuary, rather than the simmering sorrow she'd known during their time at the Drury Inn.

"I need to know what you know, John. Please, I deserve it. You know that's true."

"I'm really sorry, Mary, but I really, truly don't know anything. Desmond is with Brother Rei right now, probably getting questioned. I promise I'll do everything in my power to make sure Desmond's punishment isn't harsh. He was only acting to save the child, after all. Everyone could see that."

Mary said thank you, then turned her back to John. She wanted to ask if she could see Rebecca, but didn't want to push it. She hadn't seen her, or her mother, Sarah, since the incident. Mary wanted to go check on them, make sure the girl was okay, but wasn't sure where they were. They may have been in the women's house being tended to by Angela, a former nursing student who lived at The Sanctuary. Wherever they were, it was surely under guard.

Mary was on her way back to Paola, but decided to find Linc instead. He may have grown distant, but Mary understood why. He'd grown quickly accustomed to life at The Sanctuary; that didn't mean he would turn his back on any of them, especially since Desmond and Luca were being held, both because they were trying to save a little girl. Linc had tried to intervene in his own way, after all.

She found Linc standing guard at the front gate, alone.

Linc almost seemed like he'd been expecting her.

Mary spilled her guts, but kept her tears inside.

Linc listened to everything, then said, "I don't know much right now, other than Desmond and Luca are with Carl in the hole."

"The hole? When will they get out? Are they okay?"

"Sorry," he shook his head. "I don't know. And I can't really ask. None of the Brothers I talk to knows a thing, and it's not like I can ask Rei. He definitely doesn't trust me. He sees me as one of you. No offense." He met Mary's eyes.

"None taken," she said.

Linc smiled, then continued. "At best, he thinks of me as no better than John, and I don't think that's any help to you at all."

"No better than John?" Mary said, "I thought John was up there with The Prophet at the top of the chain of command."

"Exactly," Linc said. "John has the ear of The Prophet, and his trust. Rei doesn't like it." Linc lowered his voice to a whisper and stepped closer to Mary. "That's just one of the things that makes the guy so dangerous. Rei's totally out of control, Mary. If he's not put under control, and soon, we're all gonna pay. The Prophet is strict, sure, but at least he kept everyone safe. Strict as he was, he'd never allow a little kid to die. Rei said it was God's Will, but if you ask me, we sure as hell didn't leave God with much of a choice."

Linc looked around to check for any extra sets of ears before he continued. "Something's happening, Mary. And it's happening quick. I think Rei is planning something, maybe has been for a while. And I'm not sure whom I can trust, other than you all."

"What are you saying?" Mary asked, a new thundercloud of dread rolling into her mind.

"I'm saying I don't think it's a coincidence that The Prophet has gone sick just after our arrival. I think we upset the apple cart and pushed Rei to speed up some plans he's got brewing."

"What's wrong with The Prophet?" Mary asked. "Do you know?"

Linc shook his head. "No idea, but Brother Stephan said he was making some awful terrible sounds while he was on watch."

"What sort of sounds?"

"Loud, like he was choking on something. But they stopped right before Brother Stephan was about to head in. Brother Stephan knocked on the door and asked if The Prophet was okay, and he said yes, so he didn't think much of it until the next day. Brother Rei has been the only person in or out of the room, lately. Not even Brother John has been in."

"I thought John was The Prophet's right hand," Mary said.

"Yeah, but he's been weird, lately. Like he's not even paying attention anymore. Rei's planning a revolution right under his nose, and he's not batting an eyelash."

"You think he's in on it? John and Rei are tight, right?"

"I don't know what to think," Linc said.

"So, they're plotting a revolution?"

Linc nodded. "Yeah, from what I gather, they had it planned before we arrived. Us coming here derailed them a bit, forced them to regroup, maybe. But I also think it helped speed the plan up. It's happening, sure as shit. I'm worried we're in the middle. Been worried since the whole thing with Will went down. Nothing's felt right since."

"How many do you think Rei has on his side?"

"Not too sure," Linc shook his head. "Let me think." He closed his eyes a moment, then opened them back, along with his mouth. "There are about 50 adults at the compound total, I'd guess. I'd say at least a dozen are with Rei lock-step, maybe more. I can't say for sure. But something is gonna go down. It's gonna be big, and it feels like hours more than days. I'm surprised that nobody's come to relieve me of my post yet, which makes me think that at least some of the guards are still loyal to The Prophet."

"You realize how much danger we're in, right? I mean us, specifically." She grabbed Linc by the arm and whispered through gritted teeth. "If there's a power struggle and Rei wins, we're goners, I know it. He's crazy, and he hates us."

Every cell inside Mary was terrified that Linc would betray the Drury Group, and that she'd already said too much. Had he said as much as he did to see where her loyalties stood? Or was he being honest? Her gut and the look in his eyes said she should trust him. Besides, it wasn't as if she had anyone else left to trust.

She held Linc's hands and pleaded. "You have to help us, however you can."

"I'm on the front gate until Brother Barry returns from his break. I'm on prison guard duty after that, so long as Rei doesn't change his mind before then. I'll see how they're doing and let you know."

"What are we going to do about Rei?" She asked.

"I dunno, Mary. I'm thinking on it. I'll let you know if I come up with something before shit hits the fan."

Mary thanked Linc, then left, running back to Paola and trying to ignore the waves of acid sloshing along the shores of her stomach. The *knowing* she'd always felt was whispering a certainty she couldn't accept.

She and Paola were going to die. Along with the child growing inside her.

* * * *

CHAPTER 6
DESMOND ARMSTRONG

Desmond woke in the darkness, bound to the wall in a T shape, his head throbbing and arms burning. His feet were bound to the floor. He was able to move them, just slightly, and heard the sound of chains rattling when he did.

The smell of piss and shit was rancid in his nose.

Where am I?

The room was pitch-black and cold.

"Hello?" he said, hesitantly.

"You're awake," a familiar voice said, though it sounded different, a bit deeper than he remembered.

"Luca?"

"Yes, are you okay?"

"Yeah," Desmond said, trying to pull free from the arm restraints, with no relief.

"Carl is in here, too," Luca said, "I think he's sleeping. Carl?"

No response.

"How long have we been in here?" Desmond asked, "And where are we? Do you know?"

"Since this morning. I think it's nighttime now; I'm not sure," Luca said. "We're in the basement of the women's house. It's like a dungeon."

Probably the room where Brother Rei interrogated Carl.

"Did they take anyone else?"

"Anyone else?" Luca asked.

"Did they go after Mary, Paola, or Linc?"

"No, I don't think so."

"Good," Desmond said. "Is Rebecca okay?"

"Yes, but Brother Rei put her back in the box not too long after one of the women examined her and made sure she was okay."

"How do you know?" Desmond asked.

"Because I can talk to her in my head," Luca said.

Desmond laughed. "Of course you can."

"You don't believe me?" Luca asked, hurt.

"No, it's not that. I was just laughing because you're like some sorta magical wonder. You heal people; you can hear people's thoughts; you turn into a 25-year-old man. What else can you do? Can you leap tall buildings in a single bound, or at least get us out of here?"

Luca was quiet for a second, "No, but I know someone who can."

"Who?" Desmond asked.

"I'm trying to reach Will. If I can get to him, he knows where there's some guns and might be able to come back and save us."

Desmond liked the idea, but wasn't sure if Will could pull it off on his own, even if he were 20 years younger and a bit less weird. "You can talk to Will?"

"Yes, before he left he told me to call him when we need him. He seemed to know we would need him soon. I think he dreamed all this. I've been trying to reach him for a little while. I'm not sure if he's too far or maybe he needs to be asleep, but I'll keep trying."

"Good," Desmond said. "Thank you."

Then after a moment, Desmond asked, "Can you reach out to Mary and Paola?"

"I can hear their thoughts, sometimes, so I know they're okay right now, but they can't hear me if I try to talk to them."

Desmond sighed with relief that they were okay, though he wished Luca could converse with them. Then he felt a twinge of doubt, and thought maybe Luca was only imagining that he could hear people's thoughts. Desmond didn't really doubt, so much as he wanted to know for certain.

He thought in Luca's general direction, "*Say Amen if you can hear me.*"

Nothing.

He repeated the thought, this time louder.

Nothing.

One more time, and this time Desmond screamed it in his thoughts.

A moment later, Luca said, "Amen."

"*You heard me?*" Desmond thought, "*What took you so long to answer?*"

"What do you mean?" Luca said.

"*I said it three times,*" Desmond thought.

"I wasn't tuned into you," Luca explained. "I can only hear if I'm tuned in, and I don't like to tune in on people if they don't know it. But I heard you the one time, when you screamed."

Oh shit, I wonder if he heard all the things I've been thinking. I wonder if he knows the things Mary and I have been thinking about him and Paola. Shit, Desmond, stop thinking, he's gonna hear you.

Desmond tried to change his thoughts, almost certain Luca had heard the last few, if he'd not heard them before. He decided to hedge his bets, and try to think good things.

"I like you, Luca. We all love you. You're family to us. Yeah, you've spooked us a few times, but we still love you. Mary was just worried. You know how mothers can be, right? Paola's her baby girl. Even though you're 8 in real life, you're a teenager, well, hell, now you're 25. You can understand how protective she feels, right?"

"It's okay, Mr. Desmond," Luca said after a minute of silence. "I understand. I'm getting out of your head now, so don't worry."

Desmond wondered if Luca really left, and felt a flush of shame and guilt, but also a bit violated. How long has Luca been able to listen to their thoughts? How often had he spied on them?

Everyone thought things they'd be ashamed for others to pick up on, from petty to perverse. Any number of times Desmond might have mentally told someone in their group to fuck off, or wished them dead, even if he didn't really mean it. He was certain he'd thought of Luca as creepy any number of times, and even wondered if the boy was a threat, a time or two.

Desmond's unguarded thoughts probably made him seem like a monster to an eight-year-old, especially one so sheltered and innocent as Luca had been. Hell, Luca could've picked up on Desmond thinking Paola looked pretty, and misinterpreted it as him being a pervert, even though he didn't think of Paola in *that way*. Perhaps worse, Luca had picked up on the dirty thoughts Desmond had about Mary, who he *did* think of in *that way*, thoughts that had grown dirtier the longer they were separated at The Sanctuary. The things he thought about doing to her.

Oh God, he must think I'm the biggest pervert ever.

He hoped Luca saw through the stray thoughts to the real Desmond, the guy who was loyal and kind; the guy who loved them all like family, and would die to protect them. He hoped Luca would judge him on his actions, instead.

Desmond felt invaded and ashamed, but at the same time, he had to take Luca at his word. The boy was a kind, gentle soul, and if he said he wasn't peeping into their thoughts, Desmond had to believe him. Luca had been privy to Desmond's every thought, so if he had been tuning in, surely he'd have seen the good and bad, and judged Desmond fairly. Desmond was sure that compared to the others at The Sanctuary, his thoughts were downright decent. He could only imagine the depravity running through someone like Rei, who probably got off on torturing small animals, or people, while making others watch. And who knew what weirdness ran through John, who seemed so straight laced, but whose weird smile hinted at something weird or wicked underneath.

Desmond tried to think of himself before he broadcast THAT image, and polluted whatever innocence Luca still held onto. He imagined a field of flowers, cleansing his mind's canvas.

The sound of locks on the outside of the door severed Desmond's thoughts and tensed his body. Light spilled into the room from outside as shadows fell on the stairs and footsteps echoed into the chamber.

Desmond took advantage of the light and scanned the dungeon to get an idea of what was what. The room was ten by ten, with concrete floors. He was strapped to the wall facing the steps, while Carl and Luca were strapped to opposite walls to his left and right, respectively. Carl looked up, groggy and emaciated. Desmond wondered if they'd even fed the kid since locking him down here days ago. His pants were stained with shit and piss. His shirt, like Luca's, had been removed and his chest was covered in purple and black bruises. Luca, thankfully, showed no signs of abuse — yet.

Jesus. Is locking someone up not enough of a punishment? They have to torture him? If they tortured Carl, one of their own who happened to disobey "the law," what the hell will they do to us?

Desmond swallowed, waiting for Rei.

Rei stood at the top of the stairs for a moment, out of sight, probably trying to make them anxious. He then descended the steps slowly, seeming to savor each step as if it were delivering a wound that he would be echoing soon enough.

"Tisk, tisk, tisk," the weasel-faced fucker clucked as he stepped into view and walked up to Desmond, stopping just inches from his face.

"What *have* you done? Breaking our Laws? Shooting one of our Brothers? God don't take kindly to acts of violence against your Brothers, Desmond."

"I was trying to save Rebecca," Desmond said, "Since nobody else seemed willing to step up. Or aren't the lives of children as important here?"

"She was in God's hands, and from the looks of it, she wasn't dead, was she? Who do you think you are to step in and try to intervene in God's plans? Do you think you're above Him?"

Rei removed the belt from his pants and took his time winding it around his fist, as he spoke, "Answer me, Desmond, are you ABOVE the Lord Almighty?"

"It wasn't God who put her in a box," Desmond said.

Rei smiled, pulled the belt tight, then swung, hitting Desmond hard beneath his right ribcage.

"Fuck!" Desmond screamed as pain ripped through him.

"Ah, there it is, the Devil's filth coming from your mouth," Rei said, his eyes flashing a glimmer of hate as he swung again, this time hitting Desmond in his gut.

Desmond took the punch in silence this time, though the pain was no less acute. He would not give Rei the satisfaction of hearing his cries.

"No more filthy Devil words?" Rei asked, hitting him again in the gut.

Desmond winced as Rei stepped closer. "You're a manly man, aren't you Brother Desmond? You're strong. You know everything, and all the ladies love you, eh?"

Rei punched him again, this time in the center of Desmond's chest, emptying his wind.

"Stop it!" Luca shouted as Desmond gasped for breath.

Rei spun on the ball of his right foot, and raised a fist at Luca, "You want some, too, boy?"

Desmond didn't want Luca taking his punishment. He called out to Rei, "Hey, pussy, you gonna hit a boy? Why don't you take my chains off and we'll settle this, just you and me, since you think you're so tough?"

Rei turned back to Desmond, eyes on fire, just inches away from Desmond's face. He reached down, grabbed Desmond by the balls, and squeezed tight.

Desmond cried out, unable to hold the pain inside, as Rei squeezed tighter and pulled. Rei's little weasel mouth pinched in a tight, angry smile.

"All balls, eh, big boy?" Rei said.

Desmond spit in his face.

Rei's face went bright-red as he wiped the spit away with his sleeve, and allowed the buckle to fall as the belt uncoiled from his hand like a whip.

Desmond braced for the whipping, but Rei turned instead to Luca, and swung, hard, hitting Luca in the head.

Luca screamed, blood seeping from a wound in his temple.

Rei turned to Carl, and whipped him, the buckle slashing Carl across the left cheek.

Rei took another swing, this time hitting Carl in the chest, then turned back on Luca and began lashing at him, leaving bright-red marks and dark trails of blood criss-crossing Luca's chest.

Luca writhed in pain, crying out.

"Stop it!" Desmond screamed, as Rei kept whipping the boy, now on his sixth lashing.

Luca was in tears, begging Rei to stop.

"Please!" Desmond cried out, defeated, tears running down his face. "Please!"

Rei turned slowly to Desmond as he began to slide the belt back through the loops in his pants, "Don't you ever disrespect me, or The Sanctuary, again, or I will bring your bitch in here next, and her child. And I'll teach you to fear the Good Lord's wrath."

Rei punched Desmond a final time, under the left ribs, and Desmond wailed.

Rei spun around, pulled the chain dangling from the light fixture, and cast the room into darkness. He marched up the stairs, opened the door, then slammed it shut and locked it, leaving Desmond alone with his pain and the sobbing from Luca and Carl.

I will fucking kill you.

* * * *

CHAPTER 7
BRENT FOSTER

Milner, Georgia
March 24, 2012
Morning

Brent and Ed raced up the hotel stairwell as aliens exploded through the doors downstairs.

"You got a plan?" Brent panted, out of breath and trailing Ed, despite being almost a decade younger.

"Nope," Ed said cooly, continuing until the stairs ended at the top floor, well lit by the skylight in the center of the hotel's roof.

Before Brent could ask what they were doing next, Ed handed him his shotgun and was halfway up the ladder leading to the rooftop.

He waited below as Ed pushed the hatch open.

The echoes of aliens screeching, clicking, and clambering up the stairway made the stairwell sound like a living, breathing death trap of madness. Brent's heart raced as he handed Ed's gun back and started climbing the ladder.

Go, go, go, go!

He hoped to God he'd reach the top and close the hatch before the aliens caught up to him.

Brent hauled himself onto the roof and rolled out of the way as Ed glanced down with his shotgun, then softly closed the hatch.

Ed stayed down, surveying the shopping center parking lot. The hotel was the tallest building in the plaza at 12 stories high, and they were smack dab in the middle of the roof. If they stayed low enough, they wouldn't be seen by the aliens that might still be in the parking lot.

"What now?" Brent asked, "Can they climb ladders?"

"Probably not, nor do I think they'll realize we're up here, unless they hear us."

"And if they do?" Brent asked, "What then?"

"Then we hope we don't run out of ammo before we kill them all."

Brent pulled his pistol from his waistband and looked at it, wishing he'd thought to bring a rifle or shotgun before the kid stole their bag of weapons. There were five bullets left.

Fuck.

"Come here," Ed said, "let's get away from the door, so they don't smell us. Step softly."

Brent followed Ed toward a large room on top of the roof, which Brent figured was probably the utility room for the hotel. They leaned against the wall and waited for the roof hatch to pop open.

After an uneventful half hour or so, Brent broke the silence that had stretched between them, "So, how long until we can go back down there?"

"I dunno," Ed said, "I'd wait until morning."

"You want us to stay up here all day and night?"

"You got somewhere else to be?"

Brent sighed, and shook his head, now wishing he'd thought to bring some pillows and blankets with him, too.

"I'm sorry about the kid stealing our shit," Brent said, even though he wasn't sure why Ed was pissed at him. It wasn't *his fault* that they were robbed.

Ed didn't say anything, simply stared at the sky, deep in thought, or something.

"Where do you think the kid went? Think he's still somewhere in the hotel?" Brent asked.

"If he is, he's gonna need those weapons."

"Maybe he came up to the roof," Brent suggested, thinking that maybe he was in the utility room behind them.

"No, the hatch was locked from the inside. Nobody's up here but us."

"So, where the hell did he go? We would've seen him slip out downstairs, right?"

"Maybe he got past you and slipped out one of the other exits," Ed said. "Why are you so worried about whether the kid got away? He stole from us. If the aliens don't get him, I might go looking for him."

"He's just a kid," Brent said.

"Yeah? And what if he decides to shoot us? Will you sit back and let him because he's *a kid*, or will you fire back?"

"Fire back, of course."

"Well, he may as well have shot at us by taking our weapons. If we stayed downstairs, we might have wound up dead. Or at least you would've been killed."

"What do you mean *I* would have been?"

"You've got a shit gun, you're slow, and you're remarkably out of shape for a thin, young man. They would've gotten to you before me."

"And you'd let them?"

"I'm not your babysitter. We're working together, but if you can't keep up, you can't expect me to always bail you out. I'm looking out for me first. That's the only way I can ensure my daughter's safety."

Brent said nothing. After all, what could he say? That Ed was being a big jerk? This was life now, and Ed was a no-nonsense, kick-ass soldier, spy, or whatever the hell he was prior to October 15. Brent would have to hold his own and hope to hell he could keep pace. That was his only chance of seeing his family again, assuming he and Ed could even get back to their planet.

Brent had assumed they could, that Ed had some idea how to get back that he wasn't sharing. But now, on top of a hotel out in the middle of nowhere, he wondered why he'd allowed himself to believe that. It wasn't as if Ed had said they could get back. It wasn't as if Ed was a scientist or someone who even understood how they'd managed to get sucked over to a parallel world. Ed was a soldier simply following orders in hopes of keeping his daughter alive, and maybe, if the other girl was still alive, finding her.

What if the powers-that-be at Black Island were simply using Ed as a pawn? What if they had no idea how, or no desire, to deliver them back to their world? Besides, why would they? If their goal was to repopulate the planet and start over, that probably meant they needed everyone on the island. Why would they allow anyone to return home? Unless . . . they planned to come over, too.

Brent wanted to ask Ed all these questions, and a hundred more, but was afraid of the answers. Ed was a practical guy. He wouldn't tell Brent something just to make him feel good or to give him hope. If anything, Ed might shade things negative, so he could manage Brent's expectations. Brent opened his mouth to ask Ed what the odds were that they'd ever get back home.

But then his mouth closed.

Because truth was, Brent needed to preserve the illusion that he may someday see Gina and Ben again.

* * * *

CHAPTER 8
BORICIO WOLFE

Soon as Boricio took the gun from Quiet Eyes, it seemed like every sanctu-fairy in the fucking place was willing to bow down and swallow his load, starting with the head sanctu-fairy himself, Brother Rei, or Brother Rainbow Brite, as Boricio had taken to thinking of him.

Rainbow Brite looked at Boricio, eyes full of surprise, while Boricio did his best to look like he couldn't believe it himself. He sure as hell didn't see any reason to let the fairy fuckers know he could do that shit any time he wanted during any one of the 60 minutes the Good Lord had given an hour.

"Brother Boricio," Brother Rainbow said. "That was excellent work. New Unity needs more good men like you." He looked around at the cluster of onlookers, then turned his eyes back to Boricio, though Boricio knew every word was meant for them.

"There's a place here for you," he said. "An important one. The world has changed, and we've had to change with it. The Good Lord has blanketed our lives with more mystery than ever, first striking The Prophet ill, then bringing sinners to the surface. Yet it is all for the best," he scanned the crowd, then turned his eyes back to Boricio. "For now we can deal with the sinners, cast them where they belong, and establish a more effective leadership to keep us safe in the most uncertain days the world has known since the flood."

Brother Rainbow turned his face grave and stroked his chin. "We need men, real men like you, Brother Boricio, men whose true allegiance is to Heaven and all its Glories; men who won't cower in the face of the enemies of the righteous."

Boricio smiled wide, then said, "I wouldn't know how to shrink from the enemies of the righteous if I tried. I've been all across this lonely land, Brother Rei. And I'm here to stay as long as you'll have me. I'll do whatever must be done. Until the Gates of Heaven swing open, Brother Rei, you can count on me."

Brother Rainbow smiled, then put his hand on Boricio's shoulder and led him from the onlookers, and John, who seemed to be off in his own little mental Wonderland. Once they were a few dozen yards away, Rainbow took his hand from Boricio and lowered his voice.

Boricio was monkey fucker-curious to see what the head monk from the Holy Order of Beer-Battered Bullshit had to say.

"The Prophet is a good man," Brother Rainbow said. "Great, even. A true visionary. But he has fallen gravely ill, and I cannot believe the Good Lord doesn't know exactly what He is doing. The Prophet is ill because his time has passed. We can never forsake him for all he has given us, for building The Sanctuary, and keeping us safe. Without him, we'd be at the mercy of the Demons."

"There is no doubt he's made some mistakes." Brother Rainbow shook his head, as though the realization made it too heavy to hold straight. "The Prophet wanted to bring people into New Unity to reform them. He believed everyone deserved a chance, and that it would only take a person so long before they recognized the obvious choice."

Brother Rainbow shook his head. "But that's not right. Only the Lord's children, those who have truly accepted Him and His ways, should be allowed to wait for the Gates to open. There is, after all, only so much Sanctuary to go around. A small congregation limits much of the danger."

Brother Rainbow pointed to an empty bench. "Would you sit with me, Brother Boricio?"

Boricio nodded, then quietly followed, wondering if it would be easier to cover the rainbow in red and fuck his shit up now. Boricio resisted the urge. It would be best to wait things out. Let the brother shepherd his sheep, right over the rainbow, where it would be easier for Boricio to gather the flock.

Boricio listened as Brother Rainbow poured more bullshit into the pan, frying it nice and hot. Boricio kept nodding along; his nods punctuating the Brother's obvious insanity and delusions of grandeur.

Once Boricio figured Brother Rainbow was finished making his points, he looked down as though embarrassed, and asked, "What's happened to The Prophet? I mean, what's wrong with him?"

"He's been struck ill, and it looks like he won't be coming back. And though I hate to say it, I feel a bit envious that he is going to meet his Maker, while we must stay here and fight the Good Fight. The Prophet will finally be reunited with his family. But it does leave us at a loss for leadership. A congregation must have someone at the front. And that front must have someone by his side. Do you follow me, Brother Boricio?"

"Through a Demon's nest and back," Boricio said. "But what about Brother John? I thought you two were leading this congregation together?"

Brother Rei smiled like a vulture, "I've not yet determined where John's loyalties lie. If he is with us, then he will have a place at our side. But if not, he may need to be dealt with. Do you understand what I'm saying, Boricio?"

Boricio returned the smile, "Consider me the top soldier in God's Army. I will do whatever you need me to do to restore unity to this church."

Brother Rainbow's eyes glimmered like a pimp who just found his prize bitch. However, it wouldn't be long before Boricio would show that his pimp hand was strong, and Brother Rainbow would see who the real bitch was.

"God has truly blessed us with your arrival," Brother Rainbow said, hardly able to keep the boner hidden in his robe. "Now, if you'll excuse me, I have some business to tend to. Peace be with you, Brother."

"And with you, Brother," Boricio said.

Boricio looked around his new home, widening his smile along with the glance. *Yup, this will definitely fucking do.* He had everything he needed: high walls, ample weapons, and plenty of sheep he could march off the ends of the Earth, or keep in front of him to defend from a "demon" attack.

There was a war on its way, that was sure as a long sit in the shitter after a longer night pounding shots. Boricio had to figure out which side of The Sanctuary he wanted to be on. War was good when it delivered you up top.

Boricio's choices came in a pair: he could either help Brother Rainbow Brite pull off his little coup, or he could set him up and side with John and The Prophet, looking like Pope Boricio to every Sanctu-Fairy in the place.

John, along with Quiet Eyes, was one of the only people here who wasn't buying Boricio's bullshit, though. Did that make them threats to remove or potential allies? Boricio didn't want dumbasses running his empire, but at the same time, he didn't want anyone smart enough to come after him. He needed someone with just enough ambition to be a great Number Two, but no desire for all the glory. Someone like ole Charlie boy.

He wondered again where his crew had gone off to.

Had they been fucking dumb enough to abandon him? Or had the "demons" gotten them? Once he got control of this place, maybe he'd expend some people to go looking for the balance of Team Boricio. He'd either make them pay for their betrayal or welcome them into the new Kingdom of Boricio.

Boricio considered his options and allegiances a bit more, wondering whom to side with. Either way, he was pretty sure he could make things work and rise to the top of the fucking food chain faster than you could fuck a desperate housewife.

* * * *

CHAPTER 9
DESMOND ARMSTRONG

The Hole
Early evening

Linc came in to check on them after dinner.

Desmond was surprised that Rei trusted Linc enough to let him down in the hole. Perhaps Linc was in league with Rei, after all. Linc's eyes widened at their injuries, but he didn't say anything. Given that the door at the top of the landing was still open, Desmond suspected that another guard was standing by, so he couldn't take Linc's lack of reaction to mean too much.

Linc whispered to Desmond, "It'll be okay," and then left. Mercifully, he'd left the light on, either an act of grace or forgetfulness. Either way, it was nice to be out of the darkness.

After Linc left, Desmond noticed that Luca was squeezing his eyes shut. At first he thought Luca was crying, perhaps in pain from the belt, even though he'd said he'd be okay earlier. But after a few minutes, Desmond realized that Luca was trying to connect with someone, perhaps Will.

Desmond said nothing as Luca's face vacillated between serenity and horror. He still couldn't get over the boy's most recent change. Just when Desmond had finally grown used to his instant evolution from small boy to teenager, he was now trying to get his head around what should've been a smaller jump that, shockingly, was not.

Desmond would have considered Luca's first couple of leaps in growth a scientific impossibility if he hadn't witnessed them with his own two skeptical eyes. Despite having seen Luca's healing of others three times, the change in Luca physically was so drastic that Desmond could barely believe he was the same person. The starkest change was in Luca's eyes, though there was a hint in his posture and a clench in his jaw. Other than the slight pause before he answered a question, when the new Luca seemed to search for the perfect way to say something, just like the old one, all traces of the boy had disappeared. The change was so unsettling, Desmond had a difficult time looking at him, which was why he was trying to get more comfortable while Luca was using his mind to find Will.

Luca finally opened his eyes to find Desmond staring at him. Desmond looked away, embarrassed. "Hey," he said. "Any luck?"

Luca nodded. "I found Will. He's going to help us tonight, as soon as he can get here."

"And you're sure you're not imagining any of this?" Desmond felt bad asking.

"Yes. I'm going to try to reach Linc, now."

"Bad idea," Desmond said. "We don't know whose side Linc's on. A lot's changed since the farmhouse, you know."

"He's still Linc," Luca said. "He's still our friend. He left the light on for us, didn't he?"

"I'm not saying he's *not* our friend, or that Linc would ever want to harm us," Desmond struggled for the right words, unsure of how much of Luca was still eight.

"Things are different now," Desmond said. "The human mind will do anything to protect the body. Right now, I'm guessing Linc's in survival mode. If he thinks Brother Rei will help keep him alive, well, that means Linc's likely to find his words more magnetic than ours."

Luca was quiet a while, then finally said, "I already looked in his mind when he was in here. He's okay. He's trying to think of a way to help us. He and Mary, both."

"Mary is going to do something? You talked to him? He heard you?" Desmond said.

"He didn't hear me, I don't think. I was tuning in to him, though. And Mary asked for his help. He told her yes."

"How's he gonna help us?" Desmond asked.

"Not sure. Anyway, it might be best if we told him what to do, right? I'm gonna try to find out from Will what he wants Linc to do. I'm going to try and push a thought into Linc's head. Not sure if it will work, but I'll show him where the bag of guns is outside."

Desmond cringed. It was one thing trusting Linc to go along with his plan, but another altogether to tell him where the guns were. That was their last line of defense. But then again, that defense was nothing if they were chained up in the hole. Desmond was about to ask how far away Will was when the door up top opened again. Rei stepped into the chamber and began to slowly pace the room.

"How are you boys getting along down here?" Rei looked up at the light, "Ah, I see that someone left a light on for you. How thoughtful. Who was it?"

Desmond didn't want to get Linc in trouble, so he kept his mouth shut.

Rei approached Desmond, "I asked a question. I expect an answer. Have you so quickly forgotten what happens when you don't obey me?"

Desmond met Rei's eyes. He would sell his soul to the Devil right now to break free the chains and put an end to the weasel's smile.

"I think it was Linc," Desmond said.

"Ah, Linc. Your friend, Linc, right?"

Uh-oh.

"How cozy are you and Linc?" Rei asked. "What sorts of things does he tell you?"

"Nothing," Desmond said. "He's pretty much ignored us ever since we got here. He's a traitor as far as I'm concerned, to let you hold us down here like this."

Rei stared at Desmond as if trying to decipher what was true and what was lie.

Rei began to pace again. "You see, Brother Desmond, I hate to think that my fellow brothers are sneaking around like rats behind my back. I don't like rats very much."

Desmond nearly laughed at the irony: a weasel that didn't like a rat, but the pain in his body told him to resist the urge. They only had to last a little while longer until Will, and maybe Linc, would help them break free.

Keep your mouth shut, and try not to piss Rei off. Just wait him out.

Rei kept pacing, saying over and over, "I really, really don't like rats."

What's he getting at? What does he know?

Suddenly Luca was in Desmond's head, "*Oh no.*"

"*What?*" Desmond thought.

And then it happened.

Carl opened his mouth.

"They're planning an attack," he sputtered. "The old man is coming back!"

Rei's eyebrows rose as he looked from Carl to Desmond, to Carl again, and then back to Desmond. "Is this true?" he said.

Desmond was stunned silent. He and Luca had been talking about everything out loud, without any thought that Carl might betray them.

"*I didn't even think to look in Carl's mind to see if he was on their side,*" Luca thought to Desmond. "*I'm so sorry.*"

Rei's eyes went back to Carl. "Go ahead, Brother Carl, I'm listening."

"The creepy kid can do stuff with his mind. Said he was talking to the old man a while back, and to Linc just now."

Rei smiled, chewing the delicious news. "Well, how about that? So, Linc *is* working with you?" He stood just inches from Luca. "So, you have a window to the whispers in our minds? Pray tell, boy, what am I thinking?"

Luca closed his eyes tight and said nothing.

After a minute of mutual silence, Rei turned to Carl. "What else did they say?"

"Luca said that Will is gonna help them break out of here. And Linc is gonna help them. And something about a bag of guns or something."

Brother Rei kept smiling, telling Carl he'd done excellent work, and that it was always a glorious day at The Sanctuary when the Good Lord's work was done. The flock was never prouder than when one of its own learned a valuable lesson and chose virtue over sin.

Rei unfastened Carl from his restraints, then handed him a pistol from beneath the folds of his robe. "Welcome back, Brother Carl. Please, go to Brothers Gerald and Evan. Tell them the time has come. Then get Brothers Peter and Boricio and round up Linc and bring him here to me. If anyone tries to stop you or stand in your way, shoot them where they stand. The Good Lord will decide what happens to them after that."

"Thank you, Brother Rei," Carl said, bowing. He left the torture room without looking behind.

"So, what is this about weapons?" Rei asked, smiling.

"He's lying," Desmond said, "He just wants out of here. And you just let him go. He's playing you for a fool."

Rei stepped closer to Desmond, "You think you're so damned smart, don't you?"

Desmond said nothing.

Rei began to pace again, and then disappeared up the steps for a few minutes.

Luca looked at Desmond, afraid.

"Don't say anything," Desmond thought. *"He might be listening at the top of the stairs."*

Rei returned with a pitchfork, holding it up for Desmond to see. "What do you think would happen if I plunged this into your boy's stomach?"

Rei turned to Luca and aimed the pitchfork at his stomach. As the sharp prongs grew closer, Luca closed his eyes, either out of fear, or desperation to reach Will before he died.

Desmond was about to say something to bring Rei's attention back to him, when footsteps fell into the chamber.

Carl returned, shoving Linc inside the torture room with two guards walking behind him, Peter and the full-of-shit sycophant, Boricio. Linc looked at Desmond with defeated eyes.

"Brother Boricio, would you please help Brother Carl tie our new guest to the wall so we can get to the truth and finally leave all of this ugliness behind us?"

Once Linc was secure, Rei smiled a sickening smile, then thrust the handle of the pitchfork hard into Linc's chest, knocking the breath from his body.

"While the Good Lord decides if you're worthy of breath, I want you to consider the meaning of the word 'Truth.' If you do manage to retrieve your breath, well, I'm guessing that means the Good Lord would like you to share what he's left on your tongue."

When it sounded like Linc was finally done choking, Rei said, "Now, I hear you all are planning 'an attack.' Tell me how many traitors there are among us? I want a name for everyone, and then I'll release you immediately. I hold no grudges. Just ask Carl." Rei gestured toward Carl who still had his gun trained on the prisoners, as if they posed a threat, fastened to the wall.

Linc gathered his breath as though he were about to spill every secret inside him, then did the unthinkable by hawking a giant wad of mucus into Rei's face. Desmond smiled, hating himself for ever doubting Linc.

"Fuck you," Linc said to punctuate his action, clearly not giving a fuck what Rei might do.

Rei looked ready to boil. Desmond winced imagining what was about to happen to Linc. Suddenly, footsteps echoed down the steps as another of his men, Brother Chris, raced down the steps and shouted, "Brother Rei!"

Rei wiped the spit from his face, dabbed at his chin with his robe, then turned toward Chris. "Yes," he said, voice calm but laced with an insanity that sent a chill down Desmond's spine.

"What is it?" Rei said. "And I dare say, this had *better* be worth the interruption."

"I'm sorry," Chris said. "You wanted to know if there was anything happening with Mary or John. Something's happening with them both right now. Mary just ran into the men's house. She was frantic, demanding to see John."

"Very well," Rei stepped toward Linc until he was just inches from his face, almost daring him to spit again. "We are far, far from finished here. When I return, you will tell me everything, or you will die."

Rei turned to the room. "Brothers Carl and Chris, follow me." He nodded toward Boricio and Peter. "You two stay here and guard the traitors. Empty your guns into anyone who looks at you funny."

Rei smiled, turned, and led the way up the stairs.

Brother Peter held his gun nervously in front of him, aimed at the prisoners. Boricio smiled at Desmond, a smile too wide to worship a loving God.

Luca closed his eyes tight, and Desmond wondered where he was going.

* * * *

CHAPTER 10
MARY OLSON

Mary and Paola were alone in the reading room of the women's house when she heard the commotion in the courtyard, looked out the window, and she saw Linc being led to the basement under the women's house.

Mary couldn't swallow her anxiety any longer. The part of her that *knew* they were in imminent danger was screaming. And doing nothing was the same as doing something to make everything worse, for all of them.

Mary turned to Paola, who was sitting on one of the two sofas reading a book. "I want you to stay here and stay safe," she said. "Hide if you need to. Only come out for me, no matter what. I don't know what's going on, but it isn't good." She stared in Paola's eyes. "Do you promise me you'll stay safe?"

Paola nodded and let her face say, "I love you, Mom," since her words wouldn't.

Mary gave her a tight hug, then ran to the men's quarters, and burst through the door, yelling for John. He was downstairs in seconds. She grabbed him by the shoulders, in hysterics before the first words left her mouth. "I need your help, John. I'm begging you."

"What's going on?"

"It's Brother Rei; he's making a move to topple The Prophet. We're in the way; you're in the way; we're all in the way. This ends badly John. I *know* it. You have to believe me; you have to help me. I'll stay. We'll all help The Prophet rebuild the church. But we have to stop Brother Rei tonight." Mary's voice cracked, her sanity bleeding from the seams.

"Really?" John said, his voice full of surprise, but his eyes not at all.

"Come upstairs," John said to Mary, as he glanced at two of the men milling about in the living room, "and tell me everything."

John led her upstairs and outside to the balcony, where they could have some privacy.

The courtyard was buzzing with activity; men and women were watching them from below but were unable to hear them.

"Tell me everything," John repeated, his eyes meeting Mary's.

"Brother Rei, he is planning something big. And I think now that he's got Desmond, Luca, and Linc all locked up, he's gonna make his move. I can feel it. Linc said he'd heard whisperings among others, too."

"So, they're coming after me?" John said, as if amused by the prospect. If he were scared or nervous, he hid it well. This was not the same John who was freaking out at the Drury and wanted to get the hell out of Dodge before shit hit the fan. This John was almost cavalier about the threat. Maybe even welcomed it.

"Aren't you worried?"

Brother Rei stepped through the doors and onto the balcony before John could answer, and was standing before them in two strides.

Rei had a gun in his hand and pressed it into the flesh of John's temple before anyone had time to register the action, much less stop it. John's eyes widened, and Rei pulled the trigger, filling the night with thunder and permanent memory. A sloppy glop of dark crimson showered Mary's face. John's body, miraculously standing for several seconds after half his head went sloshy, collapsed to the floor.

The courtyard erupted in screams, echoed by Mary, who stared in shock.

If he killed John in cold blood, no doubt we're next.

Rei turned to the huddle of Brothers who'd followed him. "Grab her," he said, pointing to Mary. "Then bring me the girl. She'll be hiding, but easy to find. Tear the houses apart if you must. This ends tonight. Let's see how much Brother Desmond is willing to lose."

Mary stared down at John's corpse, and her entire body flooded with adrenaline as her inner *knowing* deepened, the cancerous thought trying to convince her of what she refused to believe — that these were the final few moments of her life.

If the knowing was right, so be it. But she had to save Paola.

The Brothers shoved her forward at gunpoint, forcing her downstairs and out the front door.

The feeling of impending doom was punctuated by the sight in front of her. Two Brothers dragging Paola toward them.

"Mom," Paola screamed.

Brother Rei let them embrace only so he could rip them apart before leading them to their deaths.

* * * *

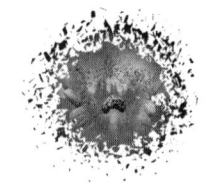

CHAPTER 11
LUCA HARDING

"Please, let us go," Desmond pleaded with their captors, Brothers Peter and Boricio.

"Shut up," Boricio snapped.

"So, you're gonna turn on The Prophet, too?" Linc asked Brother Peter, his voice dripping with accusation. "This is how you repay the man who took you in and saved your life?"

Brother Peter looked down at Linc, not in anger, but with pity. "I'm not turning on anyone. The Prophet isn't coming back. And Brother Rei is the only one brave enough to keep leading us from the darkness."

"What about John?" Linc said, "You think he's gonna stand by and let you all take over? There's more people loyal to The Prophet and John, than Rei. You ought to get on the right side while you still can, *brother*."

"I *am* on the right side," Brother Peter said, through gritted teeth. "I stood by and watched while The Prophet opened his doors to one and all, without a care in the world of what kind of danger that exposed us to. Letting in sinners, polluting the well, and drawing the Demons closer! It is our faith that keeps this place pure and safe from the Demons. Letting in sinners allows cracks in the fortress that the Demons will use to gain access and destroy The Sanctuary!"

"Please, Brother Peter, I know you're a good man," Desmond pleaded. "You know Brother Rei will kill us. Are you going to let him kill Mary and her daughter, too?"

"If they're righteous, God will spare them," Brother Peter said.

"Yeah, right," Linc said sarcastically.

"Enough chit-chat," Boricio snapped, shoving his pistol in Linc's face. "I am sick and fucking tired of hearing all you motherfuckers goin' on and on about stupid shit. Forgive my French, Brother Peter, but facts is facts — this is a New World Motherfuckin' Order where only the strong survive. Just so happens, The Prophet is fat, old, and weak. And Brother Rei and his men here are ready to do what needs to be done. Can I get a witness?"

"Amen!" answered Brother Peter.

"So, I don't wanna hear none of your gums flapping, unless you're ready for Boricio to punch your ticket to knock, knock, knock on Heaven's Door tonight."

As Desmond and Linc shut their mouths, defeated, Luca closed his eyes, and reached out into the world, searching again for Will. Each time he'd gone out, he came up empty. Will was nowhere to be found, and Luca started to wonder if the monsters had gotten him.

"Please, Will, you have to get here now! Something really bad is about to happen."

Luca waited in the darkness for a response, but heard nothing.

Then he heard the sound of gulls.

Luca opened his eyes and found himself on the warm sands of Las Orillas beach, standing on the boardwalk, the hot sun on his skin, the smell of salt in the air, and the sound of gulls squawking over the crashing surf. He was 8 years old again, and wearing his red Spiderman swimming shorts, which made him smile. He'd forgotten he even owned them.

"Luca?" a voice called.

Will?

Luca looked up to see the lobster taco stand, with Will in his bright-green T-shirt, smiling and handing a taco to a teenage girl in a red bikini. She took it and joined her friends, a group of surfers carrying their boards toward the showers. Luca ran toward Will, smiling, and calling out, "You're here!"

"Hey, Luca, how can I help you?" Will asked, oblivious to what was going on in the real world.

"It's happening! Brother Rei has locked us in a dungeon beneath the women's house. He's gonna kill us all, I know it."

"I know," Will said, the smile vanishing from his face. "I saw it in the dream."

Luca stared at him, confused.

"What do you mean you knew? Why didn't you warn anyone?"

"It wouldn't have mattered. We can't change what's meant to be, no matter how much we might want to. Even when it's what you want more than anything else in the world. There are no loopholes to get around fate."

"Am I going to die?" Luca asked, tears in his eyes. "Who else? Is Rebecca going to die? Paola? Mary or Desmond?"

Will shook his head, "Don't ask, Luca. Just do what you feel is right when the time comes. You'll do the right thing. I know it. I'm coming back now, and I'll do what I can. But

I've seen what's next, and I can't say it's going to end well. But you have to trust yourself."

"Are you going to die?" Luca asked.

"Don't worry about me," Will said, reaching out and tussling Luca's hair. "I'm coming as soon as I get past these monsters."

"Where are you?"

"I'm holed up in a shop about a mile away. I ran into some monsters, but I'll be there as soon as I can. I promise," Will said, then vanished like a broken transmission, as did the world around Luca.

He was again in darkness, death looming on the horizon.

He heard a sound ahead in the darkness, and realized he wasn't back in the dungeon, but in a hallway. Light bled through cracks around a door at the end of the hall. Luca approached the bleed and found himself in a bedroom he'd never seen before, a room with gray walls and a tattered New York Jets poster on the wall. A boy, about his age, 8, was curled up in his bed, crying.

"What's wrong?" Luca asked.

The boy yanked his covers aside, surprised to find someone in his room, "Who the hell are you?"

The boy had dark hair and intense eyes. It took Luca a moment to recognize where he'd seen them before, but there was no mistaking the child.

"Is your name Boricio?"

"Who the hell's asking? How did you get in here?" the kid asked, getting out of his bed and stepping toward Luca, fists balled and ready to strike.

"Get out of my room, kid, or I'll slit your fucking throat!" Boricio said, grabbing a box cutter from his nightstand and waving it at Luca.

"You won't do that," Luca said.

"Oh really, why not?"

"Because now I see the real you. You're not the Man in the Middle. You're the Man with Broken Pieces."

Boricio turned his head sideways, recognition spreading across his face. "You're that kid," Boricio said, but in his adult voice, "You're Luca."

Luca nodded.

"Get outta my head!" Boricio screamed, throwing his fists back and leaning toward Luca, as if his scream alone would send Luca flying back into the door.

"We need you to help us," Luca said. "Please. You have to kill Brother Rei before he hurts anyone."

"Why the hell would I do that?" Boricio spoke, still an adult voice coming from the child's body.

"Because I know you're good," Luca said. "I can see it."

Boricio looked down, his hair falling in his face, and his head and shoulders convulsed as if he were crying.

"You couldn't be more wrong, kid," Boricio said, laughing as he looked up. He was now adult Boricio, eyes bright with rage.

"GET OUT OF MY HEAD!!"

Fear flooded Luca's body as Boricio took a swing with the box-cutter, and came inches from Luca's face. Luca wasn't sure how he knew, but some part of him did — if he were hurt in this place, he might never wake up.

Luca turned, opened the door, and fled into the darkness of another, longer, nightmarish hallway.

Luca heard footsteps behind him as Boricio chased him fast into the blackness.

Ahead, Luca saw a door slightly ajar, light coming from just beyond. He didn't even stop, instead, threw his body into the door, then crashed through and found himself in his own bedroom. Footsteps grew faster and louder. Luca slammed the door and locked it, just as Boricio's footsteps stopped sharply outside.

"You think it's funny to invade people's heads? Do you, you little fuck?!" Boricio screamed from the other side of the door.

"No, I was just trying to ask you to help us," Luca whined.

"Boricio don't help anybody but Boricio. Ah, this is a nice house you've got here, kid." Luca could feel the hallway outside his doorway changing into his house, even if he couldn't see the change taking place.

Boricio was now in his head. Luca could feel him like an itch in the back of his brain. Now it was *he* who wanted Boricio out of *his head*.

"Let's see what you've got lurking in here, eh? Ah, is this your sister's room? Ooh, lookee, lookee a picture. She is a sweet little thing, ain't she? How do you think she'd like it if old Uncle Boricio paid her a visit?"

"Get out!" Luca screamed, trying to wake up and return to the dungeon. But the world he'd so easily crafted with Rebecca was now refusing to cooperate.

"What's that Nietzsche quote? 'Be careful when you look into Boricio, because Boricio also looks into you.'" Boricio laughed.

Luca heard Boricio stomping around the house, slamming doors, seemingly searching for something which Luca couldn't even guess at. Luca became certain that if Boricio wanted, he could use one of the doors to ravel back to Luca's real house and even back through time, to kill Luca and his family.

He had to get Boricio out of his house, and his head.

"What secrets does little Luca hide in here?" Boricio asked. The sound of glass crashed in the living room.

The walls of Luca's room began to shake violently, like they might fall in on him, or fly away at any moment.

"Show me your memories!!" Boricio screamed, his voice echoing in Luca's head like some sick funhouse trick.

"No!" Luca screamed opening and closing his eyes fast, as if it that might bring him back to the real world.

"Show me!" Boricio screamed, and ran, slamming into the door hard.

Luca was shaking, unable to move, cold sweat and warm piss running from his body. He was certain that if he let Boricio see his memories, the Man with the Broken Pieces would somehow take over.

"Ah, I see, you don't want to show me. That's not very hospitable of you, Luca."

Luca heard Boricio's footsteps, then the sound of a door slamming. The garage door.

What's he doing in the garage?

Moments later, footsteps again, and Boricio clearing his throat.

"One more chance, Luca. Open the door. Let me in."

Luca couldn't move.

"Little pig, little pig, let me in," Boricio sang as he began shaking a container. Luca listened, trying to figure out what the splashing sound in the hallway was. Then he smelled it — gasoline.

He's gonna start a fire!

"I'm gonna huff, and I'm gonna puff, and I'm gonna burn your fucking house down!"

Flames erupted in the hallway along with the sound of Boricio's laughter. "Roast, little piggy! Roast!"

Luca screamed. He was trapped.

Suddenly, he heard a sound outside the window. Scratching.

He turned and saw Dog Vader outside clawing at his window.

"Dog Vader!" Luca exclaimed, rushing to the window. He unlocked it and began to pull the window open, when the door behind him burst open and Boricio walked through, entirely engulfed in flames, but unharmed.

"Come here, lil' pig."

Luca lifted the window and shoved the screen forward, crumpling it as he dove through the window, and landed not outside, but in another hallway.

Dog Vader was gone, much to Luca's sadness.

And another door appeared at the end of the hall.

Luca walked to the door, praying this would be the one leading back to reality. The door creaked open before his hand even touched the knob.

He was in a church, light pouring through stained glass windows, casting the church in a rich sea of colors. The pews were empty, and a boy stood at the front before an open coffin. The boy was Boricio, but a bit younger than the last version Luca had seen.

Luca walked to the front of the room, and stared inside the casket. A skeleton of a woman was tucked within the velvet. She looked like she might have been pretty once, but the years had not been kind to her.

"Is that your mother?" Luca asked.

Boricio turned, this time not hostile, but staring, emotionless. "Yes, I should have stopped Joe. She might still be alive."

"I'm sorry," Luca said. "Are you sad?"

"I don't feel anything. I know I'm supposed to. It's not like I want her to be dead, but I just don't care. Not anymore."

"Why not?" Luca asked.

"Because I'm a monster. The shrinks all say I should be locked away."

Boricio turned to Luca, eyes wide and vulnerable. "Do *you* think I'm a monster? Are you scared?"

Luca stared at him, "You're not a monster. You're just . . . broken."

"Broken?" Boricio asked, confused.

"Yes, something is not quite right in your head. Something that should have been different, but it's not. I can feel it."

"So, I can't help it?"

"Help what?" Luca asked.

"Being a monster."

"Maybe I can," Luca said, and reached out.

"What are you doin', ya queer?" Boricio said, pushing Luca away, but too late.

Luca grabbed his hand, and their fingers locked as bright-blue light flashed between their palms, warm at first, then burning hot, growing so bright it quickly eclipsed the room.

"What did you do?!" Boricio cried out as the blue light engulfed them completely.

"I have to show you something," Luca said, even though he wasn't sure where they were going.

**

They were suddenly in the living room of a large, spacious house overlooking the sea.

"Where are we?" Boricio asked, still a child, eyes wide in amazement. "This is some house! This yours?"

Luca shook his head, "No. But I feel like I should know where we are."

Boricio's brow furrowed, "Me, too. I feel like I've been here before."

The sound of keys came from the other side of the front door.

"Uh-oh," Boricio said, "Someone's home. They're gonna bust us."

The door opened and a young dark-haired boy, around 12 or so, came in holding four plastic shopping bags stuffed with groceries. He walked right through Boricio as if he weren't even there.

"He can't see us," Luca said.

Boricio looked at the kid as they followed him into the kitchen, watching him set the sacks down on the black granite counters. The kid looked up and called out to someone who was still outside, "You got it all?"

"Yeah," a man's voice said from outside, "Just getting the mail."

"OK," the boy said as he began to unpack the groceries.

"He looks so familiar," Boricio said, stepping just inches away from the kid. "Holy shit! Is this me?"

Luca's eyes widened. It *was* Boricio, a 12-year-old version.

"It *is* me! He's got the same scars on his arm," Boricio said, pointing to two circle scars on his left forearm, identical to those on his own arm.

"Joe gave me these when I was six," Boricio said. "So, is this the future me? I'm a happy kid in this nice house?"

"I dunno," Luca said, confused. Something was different about this dream, and this Boricio, than the others, but Luca wasn't sure what.

Suddenly, the 12-year-old Boricio was joined by a second Boricio, an adult version.

"No, this shit never happened," the adult Boricio said, staring at the house. "This isn't my past or my future."

The 12-year-old Boricio finished unpacking and looked toward the living room. "Any mail for me, Dad?"

"Dad?" adult Boricio said, his brow knotted in confusion. "I got a Dad who owns a rich bitch pad like this?"

"No, it's just junk mail," a man said, still out of sight.

His voice is so familiar.

Something weird was happening. Weirder than any of the dreams or mind trips Luca had been on. Luca racked his brain trying to figure out what his brain was only sensing.

Boricio's dad emerged from outside and closed the front door, "Just junk mail," he said, throwing the junk mail on the counter. "Thanks for putting the groceries away."

Luca stared in disbelief at Boricio's dad. *It can't be!*

But it was — Will.

Adult Boricio's eyes stared in disbelief, "What the beer-battered bullshit?"

Twelve-year-old Boricio looked at both versions of himself, now seeing them.

"What the ... ?" they all said in unison.

The blue light that had engulfed Luca and Boricio erupted like lightning, buzzing and crackling, then struck all of them at once, including Luca.

And in a flash, they were back in the dungeon.

**

Luca opened his eyes, his body alive with electricity flowing like fire. He looked down. The wounds on his chest were gone.

"What the . . . ?" Desmond said.

Everyone was staring at Luca and Boricio in a daze of confusion, or awe, or both.

Boricio stared back, eyes wide and frightened. "What did you do?" he said to Luca.

"What happened?" Brother Peter asked.

Boricio turned to Brother Peter, and shook his head, then looked back at Luca, staring as though his gaze could solve the puzzle.

Suddenly the door swung open, footsteps clopped down the steps, and Mary and Paola appeared, with Brother Rei behind them, holding them at gunpoint. "This shit ends now," he said. "You are all going to tell me who is planning what, or I start shooting, starting with the children."

* * * *

CHAPTER 12
RYAN OLSON

Ryan stared at his arm, watching the worm-like shapes swimming beneath his flesh.

He pressed hard, trying to squish one of the fuckers, but it was too quick, or his skin too fleshy, to do anything but force the worm to redirect its path. There were maybe 15 or more shapes writhing beneath his skin, on his left arm alone.

God knows how many are inside the rest of my body.

Panicked, Ryan moved closer to the mirror, flashing a light across his face, searching for movement. Nothing there.

Yet.

He pulled his shirt up to check his chest, and nearly vomited when he saw hundreds of tiny shapes moving beneath his chest, stomach, and sides.

"Fuck!" he screamed, feeling invaded and disgusted.

He felt a burning need to find something sharp to tear them from his body. *Now!*

Seconds after Ryan screamed, Carmine knocked on the door, "You okay?"

"Yeah. Just go!" Ryan said, unable to keep the escalating panic, revulsion, and rage from his voice.

He had to do something to get these things out of his body.

Ryan's disgust of insects, and anything else that slithered through dirt, was borderline phobic. The thought that these things, now splashing in the toilet, were also inside him, was too much to bear. If they were beneath his skin, and in his stomach, where else had they migrated to? His brain, his heart?

How long until they inflicted permanent damage?

His body shook, and cold sweat coated his hair and flesh as Ryan racked his brain in search of a plan. He could make himself puke, but that wouldn't get rid of the ones under his skin. These parasites, whatever they were, wouldn't surface on their own. They would either multiply and turn his body into a festering host, or they'd die out, in time.

But he couldn't wait that long. He had to get them out *now!*

Another knock on the door, Ryan turned to the door, angry, "What?!"

"You okay?" Gramps said from the other side. "Carmine said he thought something was wrong."

"Go away!" Ryan screamed, staring in the mirror at his sickening reflection.

Ryan bent over and retched into the toilet again, more black bile and worms spilling into the bowl, and all over the floor.

"Fuuuuuck!" he screamed while puking more of the living bile from his body.

He wiped his mouth with the towel, then looked in the mirror again and saw a slight flash of movement beneath the flesh of his right cheek.

Oh God, no.

He moved in closer to the mirror to inspect.

More movement.

He yanked the mirrored medicine cabinet door open so fast, the mirror shattered against the wall and glass shards fell into the sink below. He searched inside the cabinet for something sharp enough to tear his flesh, while whatever was beneath his cheek began to bulge, as if it were trying to come out on its own.

At first, nothing. Then his eyes found a suitably sharp object — the shards of mirror in the sink. He grabbed a jagged triangle piece and brought it to his face, its point centimeters from his bulging flesh.

Stab it. Stab it now!

Another knock on the door. "Ryan?" Gramps said.

"Go away!" Ryan said, his voice hoarse, dry, and barely his own.

He watched as his cheek bulged like a hand pushing through a plastic bag until his flesh opened in a bloody hole and something black, with pinchers, oozed from the hole. This worm, or whatever, was bigger than the things in the toilet. As thick as a caterpillar, at least.

Ryan was paralyzed with fear and disgust as the black caterpillar-like thing pushed itself from the wound and scurried onto his cheek, with hundreds of tiny wet, black legs.

Ryan screamed, dropped the piece of mirror into the sink, and grabbed the caterpillar, then pulled on it, tearing the rest of its length from his cheek, like black rope, as the hole in his face ripped wider. Oddly, he felt no pain, only disgust as the insect continued to stretch to nearly a foot and half in length as he pulled it out, then threw it into the sink along with chunks of bloody fat tissue.

He reached up to his open wound, blood dripping down his face and neck, trying to push the tear closed. It was too large; there wasn't enough skin in place to cover the gaping hole.

On the other side of his face, more movement.

More insects.

Ryan screamed a long, animal cry and grabbed the doorknob, which was slippery in his bloodied hands, and whipped the door open. Gramps and Carmine stared at him in horror. If they'd had guns, he was sure they would have shot him on sight.

"What the ... ?" was all Gramps could get out, his eyes large and worried.

Carmine was speechless.

Kill them!

The voice spoke in the back of his head, not foreign, but his own, a craving to hurt them both. To rip into their flesh. To end their lives, and chew on their guts.

He reached out, toward Gramps, his fingers splaying impossibly wide, and shaking. Bones shifted beneath his hands and fingers, causing them to crack and bend at unusual angles, as if his fingers were somehow growing new joints. The agony was too much. He screamed and, at the last second, swung himself into the wall, avoiding Gramps.

His hand punched through the plaster of the wall, and Ryan looked back at Gramps and Carmine, and wanted to say sorry, or something, but all he could do was scream, as Gramps put his hands in front of Carmine to protect the boy.

As if he could.

The buzzing began again in Ryan's head.

Ryan had to get out of the house before he killed them both.

He pushed himself off the wall and launched down the stairs, then out the front door, trying to contain the growing scream within, until he was far enough away not to attract the monsters to the house where Gramps and Carmine were hiding.

Have to get away, far away.

Ryan ran faster than he'd ever run in his life, not caring who or what he ran into. If he ran into the creatures, let them kill him now. That would be better than ending up as a host for their worm-like offspring, or whatever was inside him.

As he ran, he felt movement in his body — his guts, his arms, and his face — as if the things inside him sensed his panic and fear, and were growing more active in response. He reached up to the hole in his face and probed, his wet fingers searching the bloody fat for more insects. He tore something away, but wasn't sure if it was part of him or the insects.

He kept running, adrenaline and fear bleeding through him, alongside the panic and disgust. He was maybe five streets away when he finally screamed, continuing to run as he wailed, until his body was exhausted and his voice was all gone.

He passed two of the monsters, maybe the ones he'd seen before, and glared at them, daring them to come at him. They stared at him with knowing, as if he were no different from them.

The buzzing returned in his head, louder than ever. He slapped his hands over his ears to silence the sound and shook himself violently for extra measure, but there was no silencing the misery burrowed into his mind.

The buzzing had patterns, like language, almost. If it was language, was he hearing the monsters around them in the world, somehow communicating telepathically. Or was he hearing the voices of the untold number of insects swimming within him, communicating with one another on how to best fester inside their new host?

He screamed again, his voice cracked and throat raw, until the buzzing started to die.

He kept running, thinking now of Mary and Paola, and how he'd never see them again. He was infected. He was going to die like this; he was certain. Die without ever seeing his daughter again.

He collapsed to the ground, in the middle of the street, and wept. Not for himself now, or at least not for his physical self and the things that ravaged his insides.

Ryan cried only for his family.

Memories swirled through him: everything he'd done, all the guilt, how he'd abandoned his family for what, a stupid, superficial girl with nice tits who wasn't a tenth as smart, caring, or loving as Mary? If he hadn't cheated, he would be with them right now. Whether that meant with them in the post-apocalypse, or with them in the graveyard, it didn't matter – he'd be *with them*.

Instead of alone.

He wished like hell he could go back in time, to before it all went wrong, and make things right. There was no way he could go to Mary and Paola like this, and let them see what he'd become, or worse, pass the infection to them.

He sobbed into the cradle of his bloodied palms, rooted to the ground, and decided he would die right there. He would wait until death claimed him, one way or another.

The buzzing grew so loud it drowned out everything else. He sat in the street, kneeled, head in his hands, rocking and crying, begging God for a merciful death. He wished he'd thought to bring the gun with him. He would end it all right now.

Then a light came from above.

God?

He looked up, finally hearing the sound of the chopper's rotor blades, which had been drowned out in his cranial buzzing.

"Stay put," an electronically amplified voice said as the chopper descended upon the middle of the street.

Ryan did as the voice instructed. Was this the help Gramps had promised would come? Or was this death?

Either way, Ryan was ready.

The chopper landed and two armed men, in black paramilitary outfits and sealed helmets attached to air tanks on their backs, rushed toward him.

One of the men flashed a weird blue light on Ryan, then turned to the other, and through a speaker said, "He's infected."

The other man raised his gun and fired a shot into Ryan's neck.

Ryan smiled at the thought that death had come so quickly.

But he wasn't dying.

Instead, Ryan fell to the ground, immobilized, his world a blur. The men lifted his limp body and carried him to the chopper.

If they're not killing me, what are they doing?

Is this help?

Ryan tried to speak, to tell them about Gramps and Carmine, to go help them too, but he blacked out before he could utter a word.

* * * *

CHAPTER 13
"JOHN"

As *John's* body hit the ground of the balcony, the thing that wore *John's* body like a stiff suit the past few months, and was nameless before that, was freed from its mammalian shell.

When the humans left the room, *It* left *John's* husk through his mouth, then floated in the air, in its true form, like liquid smoke, lighter than air, flowing back into the house, in search of a fresh host.

It had forgotten how good it felt to be in its natural state.

But it needed a human body in order to fight. And *It* was itching to fight. *It* was surprised to have become so embroiled in such petty human matters as vengeance. Perhaps *It* had spent too long in its human wrapper, and had taken on a few of the species' lesser qualities. Nonetheless, *It* wanted revenge. Now.

Brother Rei would pay for his betrayal. The humans were a wretched species, and *It* was tired of waiting to extinguish them. *It* would kill them all, except the child, Luca, and perhaps the new visitor, Boricio. There was something about them *It* needed to understand.

Whatever *It* was waiting for, whatever the voices promised, would have to wait. *It* needed to feed – NOW. *It* flowed past Brother Eric, who stared, eyes wide in horror, at *Its* true form.

Brother Eric reached for his rifle and fired a shot, but guns had no effect on *It* in this form.

It flowed faster, snaking through the hall and drifting up the stairs, sensing the perfect new host, lying crippled in bed, practically dead – The Prophet.

Brother Saul, one of The Prophet's right-hand men, stood guard in front of the door. When Saul saw *It* coming, he screamed.

It entered Saul's mouth, finding his core in seconds, taking over the shell and using it to open the door to The Prophet's room.

The Sanctuary's self-righteous leader lay in bed, nearly dead thanks to whatever Brother Rei had done. *It* knew Rei was plotting something. *It* had allowed it, even, not really caring much for the games of mortals, as *It* had more important things to plan.

It didn't realize that Brother Rei would betray *John*, though.

It left Saul's body, floating out and over The Prophet's bed, gathering strength before bursting in through the man's mouth. Then in *It* went.

The Prophet put up a decent fight, but was no match for *It*, who seized control within a minute.

The Prophet stood from his bed and stretched out its new husk, feeling exhausted and frail. *It* didn't like this husk; it was obese and felt tired. But this was the husk that was most useful at the moment, the one that would make people obey.

It looked down at Saul, who was gasping for air, looking up at The Prophet with a confused, scared expression.

The Prophet stepped past Saul, then went forth into the world to wreak havoc.

It walked down the stairs, still in his pajamas, past several of The Prophet's followers, staring with wide-eyed disbelief. They were surprised, and mortified, "Sir, your mask," one of the men said.

The Prophet felt no need to hide *his* burned face any longer.

"You're okay, Prophet! Praise the Lord, it's a miracle!" another said.

The Prophet ignored everyone, leaving through the front door and approaching the main gate.

Brother Roderick stood guard, the only one on gate duty. He held a rifle at his side, and a vest with ammo, ready for war at a moment's notice. He was The Sanctuary's best shooter by a mile. When Roderick saw The Prophet coming, he straightened his back and stood taller, "How can I help you, Prophet?"

The Prophet locked onto the man's gaze until he was subservient to any command.

"Give me the keys to the gate," *The Prophet* said.

"Yes, sir," Roderick said, handing him the keys, unable to resist *The Prophet's* instructions.

"Now, go forth and kill them all, except Boricio and Luca." *The Prophet* flashed images of the child and Boricio into the man's mind, in case he didn't know who was who. "Kill the other guards first."

"Yes, sir," the man said, then marched toward the main house and opened fire on the guard perched on top. Then he turned and took out the next guard. The third guard managed to get a shot off, but it missed. The puppet's shot didn't.

A woman in front of the women's house screamed, followed by another. Roderick opened fire, cracking the woman's skull open in one shot. He then marched toward the main house, firing upon men as they emerged.

The Prophet turned his back on the violence and went to the front gate, slipped the key into the lock, sprung it, then pulled open the gate.

More gunfire erupted in the distance behind him as guards returned fire on Roderick. *The Prophet* didn't flinch, but walked out of The Sanctuary and into the woods. He looked up to the sky as it started to snow. He opened his mouth, and let out a shrill scream — his call to the things that were an extension of himself.

Come feast. The time is now.

* * * *

CHAPTER 14
DESMOND ARMSTRONG

Rei shoved Mary and Paola down to the ground at gunpoint, forcing them to kneel in the center of the room, next to Linc, as they cried. Peter, Carl, and Boricio stood behind Rei, guns ready.

Rei pushed the pistol into Linc's temple. Mary winced, then shuddered. "Tell me who the others are," he said. "All of them. Now."

"I don't know anything," Linc cried. "I swear."

Rei clicked his tongue. "Tisk, tisk. That's the wrong answer, Brother Linc."

"You're not gonna get anything from him, because he doesn't know anything to tell you!" Desmond screamed. "No one here trusts us enough to tell us anything!"

"Tell me now, or I kill the girl first," Rei said, without a whisper of apology.

"I don't fucking know!" Linc's voice cracked, tears running down his cheeks.

"Too bad," Rei said. He aimed his pistol at the back of Paola's head, held it steady for a pregnant second, then pulled the trigger, sending a bullet sailing through the back of her head, then exploding out the front of her head.

Desmond and Luca both screamed "No!" as if they could somehow turn back time and stop the moment from happening.

"YOU FUCKER!" Desmond screamed, struggling to break free his shackles.

Paola's eyes widened at the sight of infinity as her body fell forward, face first into the ground. Mary screamed in anguish, as she crawled toward her daughter and cradled Paola in her arms.

Mary looked up from Paola, eyes on fire, then leapt to her feet and charged toward Rei. But he was expecting her. His fist landed in her stomach and his foot on her knee.

Mary dropped to the floor, wailing and crying, her pain so animalistic and raw that it tore like a knife through Desmond's heart.

Rei took a step toward her, lowering his gun on the way.

"No!" Desmond screamed. "She's pregnant!"

Rei looked up at Desmond, "Tell me what I want to know. Names. Plans. Now."

"I swear," Desmond said, breaking down, "I don't know."

Rei shook his head, then pulled the trigger, shooting Mary in her stomach. Mary looked up at him and screamed. He put a bullet through her head, ending her anguish and her life. And the life of her unborn child.

Their unborn child.

No!

Desmond, Luca, and Linc cried in a symphony of shared torment. Linc started to get up, but Peter put his gun in the back of Linc's skull.

Outside, a Fourth of July's worth of gunfire erupted behind a Halloween's worth of screaming. And then they all heard the unmistakable sound of monsters outside, shrieking, clicking.

"It's started," Rei said. "Well, I guess I don't need the names any longer." He turned and headed for the stairs. "Kill them all," he said to his men. "Including the kid."

"This isn't over," Desmond screamed. "I'll tear the life from you, you motherfucker!"

Rei was already halfway up the stairs when Desmond swore he heard the sonofabitch laugh.

Peter and Carl took aim at Linc and Luca. Boricio aimed at Desmond.

Desmond winced, waiting for the blast and the arrival of death.

Death didn't show.

Desmond opened his eyes a half second later to the sight of Boricio's hands suddenly divided between two guns. In a ballet that Desmond could barely fathom, Boricio pulled Carl into his hands and knocked Peter to the floor, then kicked Carl in the back of his calf, sending him down in a painful kneel, while he took aim at Peter.

Peter shielded his face and body with his hands, inching backward toward the stairs. Boricio emptied his clip without flinching. Bullets ripped through his flimsy shield of flesh and tore his body to pieces. Boricio dropped the empty gun on the floor, then slammed his fist into Carl's face, before delivering another blow to his liver.

Carl fell, doubled over and screaming. Boricio casually walked to the far side of the torture room, retrieved Carl's dropped gun, aimed it at its former owner, then pulled the trigger twice. Blood pooled through the room, soaking the floor and everything on it, including Desmond's love and her beautiful daughter.

Boricio said, "Brothers love; Boricio 30," then started freeing the prisoners, one by one. Desmond wasn't sure what Luca had done to switch Boricio to their sides, nor did he have time to ask or figure it out.

He raced to Mary and Paola.

There's a chance!

Desmond dropped to the ground, feeling for a pulse in Mary and Paola and finding nothing. Both were dead. He looked up at Luca, heart brimming with hope.

"Luca, can you save them?" Desmond pleaded.

Luca kneeled down in the pool of blood, eyes tearing, as he closed them and placed his hands on Mary and Paola's hands.

The room grew silent and heavy with expectation as they watched Luca attempt to work his miracles again.

Outside, the world continued to erupt in chaos.

Boricio stood at the top of the stairs, "Don't worry; I got the door."

Desmond turned back to Luca, whose eyes were squinting tight, as he appeared to be trying hard to focus.

Please, God, if you're up there, please, please, save them. They don't deserve this.

Luca's eyes squeezed tighter, his hands now shaking on the women.

Desmond's breath was caught in his throat, along with his heart, watching anxiously, waiting for the moment the boy would do what he'd done three times before.

But nothing was happening.

Linc glanced at Desmond, fear in his eyes, then back down to Luca.

While Luca had brought three people back from the brink, never had he brought someone back from death.

Perhaps some miracles were too great for whatever was working through him.

Desmond's heart turned to lead and he swallowed. The minutes were stretching, and Luca collapsed in tears.

"They're not answering," he cried out, and looked up, grief-stricken, "I'm so sorry, Desmond. I can't."

Desmond fell to the ground, his world shattered.

Chaos continued to reign outside. Screaming, gunfire, and the sound of monsters. All hell was breaking loose.

But nothing would compare to the hell Desmond would rain upon Brother Rei.

Desmond stood up, and ascended the stairs, taking a gun from Boricio, and walking out into the night of death.

* * * *

CHAPTER 15
BRENT FOSTER

After nightfall, Ed spotted the aliens, seven of them, leaving the hotel in a pack. They mulled about, looking around the cars, then headed toward the underpass running beneath the highway.

"That all of them?" Brent whispered.

"I think so," Ed said, fishing a pair of mini binoculars from his tactical jacket, then training them on the group.

"Whatcha lookin' at?" Brent asked.

"I thought I saw something different about one of them ... oh Jesus."

"What is it?"

Ed handed him the binoculars. Brent focused on the pack of aliens. One was indeed different, and by different, Ed had meant nearly human in form. Its skin wasn't like the infected but rather exactly like the aliens' – dark, wet, and lit from within.

"Is it human? You ever seen anything like that?" Brent asked, handing the binoculars back to Ed.

"I dunno if it's human. And no, that's a first, that I've seen anyway. It's like some sort of alien-human hybrid, but it's a more severe transformation . . . an almost total transformation."

"Could it be what happens if the infected progress all the way?"

"I don't think so. The scientists have had infected for long periods of time, studying them, and I've not heard of anything like this. Of course, they don't tell me everything, so who knows?"

"An evolutionary step," Brent pondered. "How?"

"I don't even want to say what I'm thinking," Ed said, slipping his binoculars away as the aliens vanished beneath the highway, and hopefully kept going right on down the road and far from the hotel.

"You're thinking Black Mountain, aren't you? Experiments?"

Ed looked at Brent. His grim expression was all the confirmation Brent needed.

"Do you think they're experimenting on people?" Brent asked.

"If they are still operational, then I have no doubt they would experiment on people, infected and uninfected alike. After all, our own scientists are looking to cure whatever this is, and kill an unknown enemy."

Brent thought back on all the stories he'd read as a teenager: "scientific" experiments by Nazis, vivisections on humans by Japan's Unit 731, and even his own government's radiation, toxins, and disease "research" on unwitting victims. As long as there was an enemy, or underclass to exploit, there would be scientists willing to treat humans as lab rats. A chill ran down Brent's spine as he thought of the Gina and Ben of this world now being probed by Black Island's scientists, assuming they were still alive.

He thought of Ben's parallel, still more human than not, clinging to his infected mother, while she, who was more progressed in her transformation, shunned him. The pain the child must've felt soured Brent's heart as if it were his son.

But it's not. Stop thinking like that, or you'll never get back to them.

"Think it's safe to leave now, or you still want to wait until morning?" Brent asked.

"I think we should get some rest," Ed said. "I don't wanna go down there while it's dark. The good thing is, we can both sleep. Not much chance of them sneaking up on us up here."

"First, I have to piss," Brent said, and walked over to the other side of the utility room to take a piss he'd been holding in for far too long.

He was thirsty, and his stomach was growling. The shopping center in the plaza was so close, yet at 12 stories below, so far. He couldn't wait to hit it in the morning. Assuming they made it through the night.

**

Brent woke to the sound of distant laughter.

He jolted awake to the blinding morning sun and reached for his pistol. He found it, and turned to see Ed already on his feet, shotgun in hand, inching toward the edge of the roof in an impossibly low crouch to find the source of the sound.

"What is it?" Brent asked.

"Well, lookee here. Seems our little thief came back to the scene of the crime."

Brent looked down and saw the dirty-looking child walking with a woman with long brown hair, wearing jeans, black boots, and a black leather jacket. She was holding a shotgun slung over her shoulder, no doubt one of theirs. They were checking car handles, and were five cars away from Ed's van.

"No, no, no," Ed said, racing to the hatch. "I'll be damned if they take our ride, too."

Brent followed, woefully behind, as Ed raced down the stairs like a man possessed.

Ed reached the shattered front doors just as Brent was stepping into the lobby. Ed raced out, gun aimed, "Get the hell away from there!"

Shit, Brent thought, pushing himself to catch up. When he did, he was caught in a standoff with everyone, except himself, aiming guns at one another. Brent raised his pistol and aimed at the kid since Ed had his shotgun aimed at the woman. He hoped he wouldn't have to shoot a child, even if he was a rotten thief.

"We want our weapons back," Ed demanded.

"What weapons?" the woman said.

"To start with, the one you're holding, and then the rest of the bag the brat stole from us."

"I'm not a brat!" squealed the kid in a bratty voice.

"They're not yours," the woman said, her eyes hidden behind shades, which made Brent think of Sarah Connor, hunting terminators. "You looted 'em, same as anyone. Everything is fair game, now. Go find another gun shop."

"They're ours," Ed said sharply. "We're with the government. Those are government-issued weapons and ammunition, and your taking them is a federal crime. Believe me when I say you don't want to cross the government now, unless you want to wind up dead or in a cell. And the courts are a bit backed up, what with the lack of judges and juries these days."

The woman stared, "Who are you with?"

"Homeland Security, and I'm going to give you five seconds to put down your weapons, or we'll shoot you both."

"How do I know . . ." the woman began to ask, but her voice was severed by Ed.

"Five."

"Wait; how do I know you're who you say you are? You got a badge or something?"

"Four."

The child looked nervous and blinked, looking at the woman, "What do we do?"

"Three."

"Wait," the woman said again, "I want . . . "

"Two," Ed said, "Put the fucking guns down now!"

The woman lowered her gun and placed it on the ground, and the kid followed.

"Get the guns," Ed instructed Brent. "Now tell us where the rest are."

"They're in the grocery store over there, where we've been hiding out," the woman said. "I'm sorry; we didn't mean to take your stuff."

As Brent grabbed the weapons, Ed squeezed off a shot at the kid.

The bullet sailed just past him, but caused him to scream.

"Next time you steal from me, I won't miss." Ed said.

"Hey!" the woman yelled, "I said we're sorry! You don't have to be such a dick!"

Ed ignored her, and said, "Lead us to our weapons, or you'll see just how big a dick I can be."

The woman took off her glasses, and glared at Ed with her fierce, blue eyes. He pointed with his gun, gesturing for her to start walking in front of them. She looked young, maybe in her mid-20s. The kid, who looked around 12, was probably a brother or someone she teamed up with on the road.

As they walked to the store, the woman asked, "So, what's your name, Mr. Homeland Security?"

"Doesn't matter," Ed said. "Keep walking."

"Is he always this grumpy?" the woman asked, turning and grinning at Brent.

Brent wanted to say nothing, to stay as serious as Ed was, but the mischievous part of him hadn't been let out in a while. Plus, Ed *did* gross him out with all that talk of eating a pregnant spider.

"Yeah, he used to work at the DMV before becoming an agent. He's a teddy bear when you get to know him, though."

"No, I'm not," Ed said, not even looking at Brent, keeping his eyes, and gun, trained on the woman and child in front of them.

"Aw, did someone not get enough love as a child?" the woman asked. "My name is Lisa, and this is Billy. It's a pleasure meeting you both."

She stopped and offered her hand to shake.

Ed pointed with the gun, "Keep walking."

Ed turned to Brent, "She a relative of yours? She sure is chatty."

Brent laughed, hoping Ed would return the laugh, but he stayed corporate.

"So, you're with the government. Can you tell us what the hell happened? Where everyone went? What the fuck these monsters are?"

Brent wanted to say they're not monsters, but aliens, but kept his mouth shut. He wasn't sure what information was still classified. There was no disguising the fact that these things were running rampant, but *what* they were, that was still top secret shit, perhaps.

"That's classified information," Ed said in his gruffest voice.

"Ah, so it was you all that made the world go poof? I figured as much."

Ed didn't respond.

When they neared the grocery store, the woman pointed inside and said, "Your stuff is in there, inside the manager's office. You think you can leave us something?"

"Like your boy left us? No. Besides, as you said, there's plenty of stores you can find what you need."

"You're the government; you're supposed to help us!" Lisa said, turning back and casting an exaggerated angry look at Ed. Though she was likely serious, Brent couldn't help but notice how good she was at banter. She was probably a rather successful person before Oct. 15, like one of the power networkers he used to run into on the job — someone who could get anything, meet anyone, or find out anything through the power of their words alone. The opposite of Ed, who couldn't persuade without a weapon or the threat of violence.

"Where are you two going?" Lisa asked. "Are there others out there? Other than the people who killed our friend the other night, and chased us here?"

"Yes, there's others," Ed said, surprising Brent with his candor. "At a place called Black Island, up by New York City."

"Never heard of it," Lisa said.

"Most haven't," Ed said.

"So, can you take us back there? Is it safe?"

"Yeah, it's safe, but we're not headed back for some time."

"Why not?"

"Because we're looking for someone," Ed said.

"Who? Wait, lemme guess . . . Classified?" Lisa said as she pulled the double mechanical doors of the grocery store open, and slid inside. The kid was right behind her.

"That depends, do you know anyone named Boricio?" Ed said, as they followed the duo into the grocery store.

The minute they breached the doorway, rifles were pressed into their heads, held by men in black gear similar to their own.

Lisa turned and smiled.

"Wow, Black Island has approximately shit on Black Mountain Guardsmen."

* * * *

CHAPTER 16
LUCA HARDING

At the top of the stairs, Luca looked at Boricio. "Thank you," he said.

"You can give Boricio the Blue Ribbon later, and maybe teach me the magic mind bayou voodoo you do so well. Right now, it's time to keep the balls swinging in their sacks and kill us some fuckers."

Luca didn't know what happened, what he'd done to Boricio, or if he'd done anything at all. Nor did he know what to make of the scene he saw or the lightning that struck him and the three versions of Boricio. He wondered if that jolt had something to do with his inability to bring Mary or Paola back. Maybe his healing powers were gone.

Or maybe he just couldn't bring people back once they were dead.

His heart was broken, even more so for Desmond, but they had no time to nurse their wounds now. The Sanctuary had become a battleground, as the men, women, and children fought the demons with guns, shovels, and anything they could find.

The courtyard was bathed in the orange glow of the children's house, which had caught fire. Corpses, at least a dozen humans and maybe nine of the demons, lay on the ground. Luca saw the mean girl from his class, Tammy, lying on the ground in front of the barn, choking up blood. One of the monsters came out of the darkness, and landed on her, it was on all fours like a beast. It grabbed both her arms and ripped them from their sockets, then ran off with the souvenirs. Tammy's dead eyes stared at the churning clouds in the night sky above as blood spurted out of where her arms had been, adding more red to the snow.

Despite all she had done, Luca wanted to run to her, and try to save her.

Then he remembered Rebecca, and couldn't believe that he'd forgotten about her in all that had happened. His eyes found the box Rebecca had been in, turned over on its side in the middle of the courtyard, open and empty.

Oh God, she's dead, too.

He scanned the chaos, searching for her. Maybe she'd made it into one of the houses, where he could hear gunshots as the people tried to fight off the monsters.

Luca searched the corpses, praying not to find hers.

Boricio raced off, firing shots at one of the creatures and then another.

Luca turned, confused, overwhelmed by the cacophony of noises both external and the flood of frightened thoughts all around him. These thoughts were even louder and more powerful than the others, though, as he could also *feel* the fear, and pain of the people of The Sanctuary as they fought for their lives.

Luca dropped to his knees and closed his eyes, oblivious to the danger of doing so, as he reached out into the madness to search for Rebecca's thoughts. People and monsters both raced past and bumped against him. He tried to ignore them until he heard her.

"Luca are you out there? I'm so scared. Please . . . "

Then something slammed into Luca, knocking him back. He opened his eyes to see one of the demons on top of him.

It looked down, eyes gleaming, mouth open, rows of jagged teeth ready to bite.

An explosion of thunder, and the monster's head erupted in black goo.

Boricio appeared, firing a second shot, which thrust the rest of the monster to the ground.

Boricio yanked Luca off the ground. "Not a good time to be napping, kid!"

Luca was stunned and disoriented. The world was speeding by in a blur, and he just wanted to retreat. Close his eyes and go back home.

But he had to find Rebecca. Though he couldn't close his eyes and concentrate, he still tried to listen for Rebecca's voice again.

Boricio fired at another monster, dropping it in two shots, then turned to Luca.

"Looking for Strawberry Shortcake, kid? Follow me and we'll find her together." Boricio handed Luca a pistol, then said, "I imagine you've got dick of an idea how to use that, right?"

"I've never used a gun."

"Ever play with toy guns in the backyard?"

Luca nodded.

Boricio held his gun in the air and aimed. "It's exactly the same as toy guns. Point at what you wanna kill, then pull the trigger till it's dead. If you don't think, it goes faster. Now come on."

Boricio raced through the courtyard, gun in the lead. Luca followed.

It was easy to feel safe and strong behind Boricio. He seemed fearless, even when there were monsters running toward him. He never flinched, just raised his gun, aimed, if he had time, then pulled the trigger until the monsters stopped moving. Once, when one of the monsters was faster than Boricio and he couldn't get his gun raised in time, he used his fists instead.

Luca cringed at the sounds of Boricio's flesh sloshing into the monster's slippery black skin. The creature cried like a swung cat, probably shocked by Boricio's lethal attack. Boricio spun himself behind the monster, then kicked it from the back. When the creature landed on the ground, Boricio aimed just above its slit for a nose, pulled the trigger, then laughed. "Will you look at that gallon of demon goo! You could tar the fucking highway with that shit!"

Boricio led them through the courtyard, through the madness, in search of Rebecca.

The roar of gunfire started to dim, as the crowd began to dissipate from between the houses. The hangar was now the busiest part of The Sanctuary, as members of the congregation abandoned their faith, piled into cars, and floored pedals toward escape. A hundred feet or so from the hangar, Luca saw one of the brothers dragging Rebecca behind him, as she kicked and screamed and thrashed in the dirt. She saw Luca and cried for help.

Luca broke into a run.

The Brother, whom Luca didn't recognize, saw Luca and turned and fired a shot, but it whizzed right by. Luca didn't dare fire his gun for fear of hitting Rebecca. Instead, he raced at the man, who let go of Rebecca and steadied his aim at Luca, holding his pistol with both hands.

Luca raced ahead, staring right down the chamber of the man's loaded gun.

Is this how I'll die? Is this what Will wouldn't tell me?

He had to get to Rebecca. He didn't care about the threat. Nor did he need to.

Boricio's bullets found the man true and killed him before he could squeeze off another round.

Luca reached Rebecca, frightened out of her mind, and crying. He collapsed to the ground beside her and pulled her close.

"Are you okay?" he asked.

Rebecca wept into Luca's chest. "They killed my mom," Rebecca cried.

"I'm sorry," Luca said, then turned to Boricio, who was right behind him, eyes on the lookout.

"Get us a car," Luca said, "And keep Rebecca safe. I need to find Desmond."

Boricio made a face that was sort of like a smile, though Luca couldn't really tell.

Linc appeared, blood all over his clothes, and holding a pitchfork covered in black demon blood. "Where's Desmond?"

"I dunno," Luca said. "Let's find him while Boricio gets us a car."

Linc nodded his head as Boricio took Rebecca's hand from Luca, and led her toward the hangar, saying "Whatever you say, G.I. Junior" as he walked off, laughing as he fired at monsters and anything else that stood in his way.

The chaos around them was dying, but the nightmare was just getting started. There was a black inside Luca's mind he couldn't see through. The only thing that made things okay was the glimmer of Will in the distance, roaring toward them as fast as he could.

* * * *

CHAPTER 17
DESMOND ARMSTRONG

Desmond found Rei behind the barn, just as Rei finished off one of the monsters.

Desmond had a shot from about 40 yards away, but Desmond didn't want to dull the vengeance with a ranged shot in the back. No, that wouldn't do. He wanted to experience Rei's death up close.

He wanted to see the lights leave his eyes.

Desmond should have taken vengeance when he had the chance.

Rei heard him coming, spun around, and fired. He missed, but the sudden shock of Rei's shot caused Desmond to duck and weave. Rei bobbed from view before Desmond could recover his aim. Desmond was on Rei seconds later.

Desmond kicked the gun from Rei's hand. Rei managed to grab Desmond's right wrist and squeezed hard, wrenching Desmond's gun away. The pistol fell to the snow, and Rei jumped toward it.

Desmond fell atop him, got him in a headlock, and pulled back just as Rei's fingers grasped at the gun handle.

Desmond rolled back, pulling Rei with him, and away from the gun.

Desmond squeezed Rei's neck with all his might, choking the life out of the weasel.

"Die, fucker, die!" Desmond said through gritted teeth, squeezing even tighter.

Rei struggled, his legs and arms flailing wildly, attempting to break free.

Desmond squeezed tighter, then reached up with his free arm and gouged Rei's eyes out, thrusting his fingers deep into Rei's warm eye sockets, puncturing balloons of blood that seeped forth.

Rei screamed, shaking even more violently.

Die, you fucker. Die, die, die!

A moment later, Rei obliged, his limbs falling limp to the crimson snow.

Desmond collapsed into tears of grief for Paola, Mary, and their unborn baby.

Just when Desmond was about to renew his vengeance upon Rei's lifeless corpse, Linc and Luca appeared. "Desmond!" Luca called out.

Desmond stood up, gave a final scowl at the deceased harbinger of death, then began to walk toward his friends when his back, then stomach, erupted in explosions of pain. He looked down just in time to see a monster's hand sticking through his guts.

* * * *

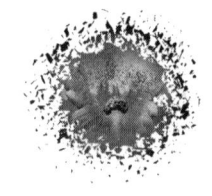

CHAPTER 18
LUCA HARDING

Luca screamed to warn Desmond, but he was too late.

The creature dropped Desmond's dead body in the snow, then opened its mouth wide, screeching at Luca and Linc.

Linc, with only the pitchfork, could not attack the demon. It ran toward them, at full speed.

Luca raised his pistol and fired at the rapidly approaching doom. Linc held his pitchfork out, ready to strike.

One of Luca's bullets connected, and the creature rolled to the ground in a shriek just short of them. But it was not dead.

Linc stabbed the beast through the head. Now it was.

The rear gate burst off its hinges as a fresh wave of the creatures raced into the grounds of The Sanctuary.

"Fuck!" Linc screamed, "Let's go!"

Linc and Luca raced toward the hangar and the hope of escape with Rebecca and Boricio. The creatures, at least eight of them, were hot on their heels.

Two cars screamed from the hangar, plowing right into one of the several creatures scattered outside the hangar, waiting for them. Both cars made it to the front gate.

Luca hoped to God Boricio was still in the hangar, waiting for them, and that they could get to his car in time.

Luca wasn't sure how many bullets his gun had left, but he doubted many. And while there were plenty of scattered weapons lying next to corpses in the snow, he didn't think he'd be able to get to any before the monsters made a meal of him.

He swallowed, preparing for death, when Boricio and Rebecca raced from the hangar entrance in a black Escalade. Boricio whooping and hollering so loud, Luca could hear him outside the car's cabin, even above the roar of the engine and screeching from the monsters.

Boricio tore through a cluster of creatures, then swerved toward Luca and Linc.

The monsters were just steps behind, and gaining ground.

Luca raced toward Boricio, pinched his brain, and thought, "*Run them over.*"

"*Gotcha,*" Boricio thought.

Boricio was angling the Escalade directly at them. At the last possible moment, Luca shoved Linc to the side and onto the ground just as Boricio sped past them, striking a mob of creatures, sending some flying backward and crunching others beneath the Escalade's oversized tires.

Three creatures raced past Linc and Luca, eyes now on Boricio's truck.

Luca sat up and took aim, hitting two of the creatures as the third veered off toward a new target, one of the Brothers who was fleeing from the main house.

The courtyard was momentarily cleared. Boricio drove up next to them, rolled down the driver's side window and said, "What the French fried fuck are you waiting for? Git your asses inside!"

Rebecca opened the back and they climbed inside. Linc slammed the door shut just as another monster landed on the Escalade's roof, quickly followed by another.

Another two sprung onto the hood, their claws ripping through the Escalade's metal and digging deep into the engine.

A shrill and sudden ringing filled the night, followed by an explosion. The main house erupted in flames. Then the second house echoed, with a second detonation sending it to splinters.

The third house was already on fire.

Boricio gunned the engine, but nothing happened.

"Fuck my asshole with asphalt!" Boricio's face was beading with sweat. He gunned the engine again. The silence seemed louder the second time.

"Alright, folks," he said, turning to the backseat. "Looks like we're gonna have to run from here to there," He nodded toward the barn. "There's at least three of them greasy motherfuckers outside, maybe five. Anyone got bullets left?"

Luca handed Boricio his gun so he could check.

"Okay, we've got one bullet left. Awesome."

The car started to shake violently. The clicking and screeching outside the cabin was deafening, as though the monsters were determined to be heard.

"We've got slightly less than no time. You trip, stumble, think, or breathe, you'll end up a couple hundred pounds of demon chew. You run, and don't stop. First one to look behind them is a rotten egg forever. I'm gonna bust this door open and run as fast as I can in the other direction." Boricio pointed to the church that would never be finished, then pointed at Rebecca. "You wait five seconds, then open the door and run as fast as you can. Miracle Boy will follow. Linc, you go last, or with Luca. Don't look behind you, no matter what. I guarantee every one of them fuckers'll be following me. I'll lead 'em in the other direction, then circle back round to the barn."

"What if you don't make it?" Luca said.

"I will."

"But you only have one bullet."

"Boricio don't need guns," he said, handing the gun to Linc. He opened the door and roared, then charged from the truck like a raging bull. The monsters followed. Rebecca counted to five, then opened the door and raced for the barn. Like Boricio said, they were clear. Every one of the fuckers was following him.

Luca watched Boricio a moment longer. Boricio was still in full sprint when he suddenly dove to the dirt, landing between a pair of fallen brothers. He picked up one weapon and carefully aimed, then emptied it of its few remaining bullets, dropping two of the demons. Boricio grabbed another gun, then rolled away just as a demon landed beside him. Boricio stood and blew off its head, then pivoted his body and pulled the trigger twice, sending a pair of charging monsters into the snow.

Luca had seen enough and looked at Linc, "OK, I'm going."

Monsters were crawling over The Sanctuary's stone walls from all sides, black shadows over white snow, like a sun setting on forever.

Luca got out of the truck and ran for his life.

He reached the barn, Linc just behind him.

Someone screamed, but Luca didn't dare look behind him.

He darted through the smaller of the barn doors, where Rebecca waited.

Her eyes were wide in horror.

Luca turned to see a creature about to pounce on Linc. Somehow, Linc managed to roll and avoid its swipe, but slipped and was unable to get up before the monster descended on him.

Luca grabbed a pitchfork leaning against the inside of the barn, and raced out toward the demon before it could kill Linc.

Just as Luca was about to plunge the pitchfork into the demon, a second one came out of nowhere, and slammed into him, sending him to the ground, and knocking the weapon from his hands.

Luca screamed as the creature rolled on top of him, mouth gnashing and shrieking.

Four shots rang out, and the monsters fell to the snow, their hot, black blood steaming the cold ice. Boricio appeared, gun in hand, and scooped Luca up and shoved him inside the barn. Linc followed them inside, just as more of the things appeared behind him.

Linc slammed the door shut just in time, and pressed his weight against it, trying to keep them from breaking through. The door rattled and shook, as the creatures pounded.

Little pig, little pig, let me in.

Only now it wasn't Boricio trying to break down the door, but the demons outside.

Luca looked around. The barn appeared to be sealed off on the ground level, but there was an open door up top, in the hayloft. If the demons were able to get up there from the outside, there would be no way to keep them from getting inside.

Boricio looked at the hayloft, then at Luca.

"You got any miracles in that noggin, you better crack 'em open and get to scrambling."

Luca said nothing.

And just then, two creatures appeared in the hayloft's opening.

They'd gotten in, and more would follow.

* * * *

CHAPTER 19
WILL BISHOP

Will put a bullet in the last of the monsters, then wiped his mouth on his sleeve. He took a final look around the store, then ran to the car outside and climbed in.

He pressed the pedal as far as it would go, as though pushing the car harder would change the future's history.

Will had seen a lot of yesterdays go by. Even if the dreams didn't decide the future, they never lied. When you tried turning the dreams into liars, they snitched to Fate and *that fucker, Fate,* made everything worse.

Will didn't know how it could be worse than what he'd seen, but he also knew it could be. He couldn't argue with the dreams, couldn't try to turn them into liars. He could only hope there was something else on the other side of the vision, another angle to the prism he couldn't quite see. Not a loophole, but an opportunity to do something.

Will kept on driving because the alternative was letting that fucker, fate, make everything worse. The dreams showed that Will had to be at The Sanctuary. He should have been there already, in fact.

He was late.

What would that mean?

After 10 minutes, Will saw orange on the night's horizon where The Sanctuary should have been.

It's burning.

Will drove faster, until he arrived at the gates that were no longer there, and drove into where The Sanctuary used to be. There was nothing standing or breathing. Every building was cinder or ash, trails of smoke snaking into the darkness above. Charred remains of structures and corpses littered the snow in black and red.

It was worse than he'd seen in the dreams. Much worse.

Will got out of the car and stepped onto the death grounds, searching for any signs of life.

His heart ached as he looked around. A little girl, maybe 6, lay in a pool of blood just outside where the main house had been. Her stomach had been gouged open, and blood still poured from her mouth. She was clutching a burnt doll, and her eyes were open in a permanent death stare. She was but one of the corpses, and but one of at least three children he could see in the immediate area.

Oh God.

The only building still standing somewhat was the barn, but flames were quickly lapping at what was left of it.

Snow continued to fall, faster now, as if it could cover the dirt, grime, and blood.

Will moved toward the burning barn as two figures appeared, silhouetted in fire.

Boricio and Luca, blackened from smoke, and bloody.

Will approached them.

Luca's eyes were wet, his mouth struggling to make a sentence.

Finally, he stared at Will, then swallowed and said, "They're dead . . . They're all dead."

Will looked away, hedging for a second.

There are no loopholes.

"Not everyone," Will said, reaching into his jacket. A tear rolled down his cheek as he pulled out the pistol, aimed at Luca, and pulled the trigger.

TO BE CONTINUED ...
IN
YESTERDAY'S GONE: SEASON THREE

WANT TO KNOW WHAT HAPPENS NEXT?

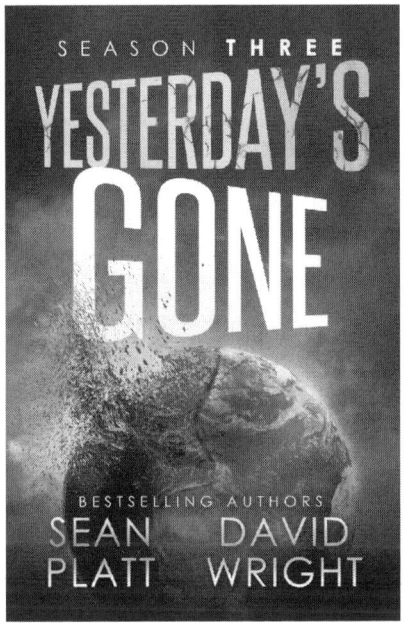

The story continues in *Yesterday's Gone: Season Three*
SterlingandStone.net/book/yesterdays-gone-season-three

CONVERSATION WITH AUTHORS SEAN PLATT AND DAVID WRIGHT

(NOTE: Oct. 2013 This conversation originally appeared at the end of Episode 7. We've moved it to the end of the season compilation so it doesn't interfere with the narrative.)

We've gotten some great feedback from readers since Season One of *Yesterday's Gone*. We've also gotten a lot of questions from both readers and fellow writers. In January, we put out a call for questions and sat down (virtually, since Sean and I live in different states) to discuss the questions.

Here's the conversation:

January 2012

WHAT INSPIRED *YESTERDAY'S GONE?*

DAVID: As Sean and I watched the digital publishing revolution unfolding, we saw an opportunity to do something we've long wanted to do but would never have gotten a chance to do under traditional publishing — serialized fiction. As fans of Stephen King's *The Green Mile*, and serialized TV like *The Wire*, *LOST*, *Carnivale*, *Deadwood*, *The Sopranos*, *The Walking Dead*, *Mad Men*, *Breaking Bad*, and a bunch of other shows, we LOVE the whole concept of "To be continued . . . "

Given that traditional publishers don't even embrace the format with *proven authors*, there was no way in hell they'd touch the format from a couple of unknown writers. But that's the thing about this revolution, the power has shifted, and now writers like us can write the things we want to write.

Conventional wisdom says there's not a huge audience for serialized fiction. But we feel that's about to change with e-books. We've gotten great response from readers for *Season One*, and have since heard from many writers who are planning to pursue serialization.

SEAN: Serialized fiction isn't really new, it's actually a really old way of doing things. It's how Dickens released the majority of his work. Readers love open loops and cliffhanger endings because it gives them more to think about, pulls them deeper into the narrative, and gives them a deeper connection with the characters, as well as investment in their story. And that's what an author wants most, for their reader to care about their story.

I love TV. But the TV I think about when I'm not watching, are the shows that leave me asking questions and wanting answers. It's a ridiculously fun way to watch a story, so surely it would be a ridiculously fun way to write one, too.

And it was. Just as television shows are shot with scenes out of order, that's how we wrote *Yesterday's Gone*. Dave wrote his scenes, and I wrote mine, then we went into post production together, edited into a unified story with the best possible flow.

We're thrilled that it worked, both for us as writers and you as a reader, because our inspiration flies far beyond this title. Writing *Yesterday's Gone* has been so much fun, and so creatively rewarding, we can't wait to follow it up.

WHAT HAPPENED TO THE WORLD? WHAT KEPT THESE PARTICULAR PEOPLE ALIVE?

David: You're going learn what happened to the world real early in the season. That's one of the answers we knew we HAD to answer early on. One of the criticisms I heard for *Season One* is we (the writers) didn't answer that many questions. One person even suggested the theories that we posited were ridiculous and showed no understanding of quantum theory. The thing to remember is that the speculations about what happened in *Season One* were from the mouths and minds of the people trying to figure out what the hell happened. The explanations weren't informed in any way by knowledge, but rather people with limited knowledge, trying to figure shit out.

Imagine if you and your friends woke up and most of the world was gone. Unless you're a scientist, or well-versed in scientific theories, you're probably gonna say more stuff that sounds crazy and far-fetched than things which make sense. As a reader, you are limited to what the character whose point of view the chapter is told from, knows.

That being said, you'll get a peek at someone a bit closer to the original event early in *Season Two*.

As for what kept these particular people alive, that would be spoiling one of the bigger secrets. Sorry.

SEAN: I'll add that this was one of the most rewarding parts of writing the second season for us, was really putting all of this together. When we started writing, we didn't necessarily know what happened to everyone, though we'd certainly batted around a few ideas. But by *Season Two*, we needed to know a lot more about our world, even if the characters didn't.

Dave did a lot of the heavy lifting for this part of the story, and did an amazing job threading everything together. I couldn't be happier with the story's direction, or more proud of the world building that's been done since the first season concluded.

WHO WAS YOUR FAVORITE CHARACTER TO WRITE? WHO WAS THE HARDEST?

DAVID: I know Sean's answer to this before he gives it! My favorite was probably Brent Foster, only because he's similar to me. Brent is an overworked journalist with a young son, trying to do the best he can to keep his family together and doing what he feels to be the right thing even as he distances himself from his family.

I approached his story thinking, *how would I respond?* Some of his scenes in *Season One*, particularly the one where he lay in bed with his son and came to the realization that he was an absent father, were difficult to write because it was an admittance of my own feelings to that effect. I actually cried when I finished that scene.

The hardest to write for me was probably Boricio, because that is all Sean's creation, and his dialogue is way over the top. It's hard for me to get the voice just right, and we don't want Boricio to become a caricature of himself. It's a fine line. I think Boricio's dialogue might be the closest we've come to disagreeing with each other. Arguments over Boricio could be an entertaining inclusion for a book! Sean: "Why can't we call him a cum-colored cracker?" Me: "That doesn't even make sense!"

SEAN: Ha, that's too funny. Dave's not exaggerating. We actually have that e-mail. There's no doubt, I love writing Boricio and even have fun rewriting Dave's interpretation. He's a ridiculously over-the-top character, sure, but I do think we fill him with enough fun to make him a blast to read. I thought he would be more polarizing than he was. I figured some people would love and some would hate, and it would be around half and half. But it seems like most people enjoy reading him. My wife's the best litmus test. When I read Boricio's parts out loud and she's smiling, I know I've done a good job. I would even give Boricio his standalone series, but Dave won't let me. So you need to speak up, send him an e-mail, and let him know how wrong he is. GO, TEAM BORICIO!!!

As far as the most difficult to write, that's Luca for me, by far. Part of him is easy because I have a son his age, but my son isn't fighting voices in his head, or aging years in seconds. Getting his voice just right is difficult. It's also funny that some of the criticism for the unrealistic dialogue of Luca are things I've taken directly from my own son. BONUS FUN FACT: My son is named Boricio and knows about the character, though he only knows he is a "bad guy" and doesn't know any specifics.

WHAT WAS THE BIGGEST CHALLENGE IN WRITING *YESTERDAY'S GONE?*

SEAN: Knowing the story we wanted to tell. We never wanted to build out so much of the story out that we left nothing to discover along the way, but we also didn't want to leave so much to chance that we wrote ourselves into a corner, or made the story a molecule less than what the reader deserved.

Finding the *just right* between the magic of surprise and the intelligence of plotting was instrumental to delivering the best stories possible. But it's hard to know where that *just right* is. Because the first season started from nothing, we were able to make up more of it as we went along in the first couple of episodes. By the end of the first three episodes, we were much more focused on specific spots the story needed to hit so we could deliver a more rewarding payoff at the end.

Season Two has had a different sort of process. We've had to script our story out with more precision this time, from the start. But we are extremely pleased with the results.

DAVID: Timing. The biggest challenge was making it all come together in a way that keeps a lot of the mystery, yet reveals enough in character development and storyline to keep readers hooked. A lot of times, especially in the horror genre, the story falls apart after the mystery is gone. We'd love to leave readers in the dark as long as possible, but at some point, they need to have an idea what's happening or they lose faith that YOU know what's going on.

I think the writers of *LOST* faced a lot of unwarranted (in my opinion) criticism because many viewers thought they had no clue what was happening late in the game. We NEEDED to understand and refine the back-story before starting *Season Two*. Because if WE don't know what's happening, then we're gonna make mistakes. We have a fairly big reveal coming in *Episode 8*, one I *wanted* to hold off on delivering until the end of the season, but if we did that, the story would have suffered. So, we're answering questions, yet raising new ones, as all the best serials do.

I think we were learning as we went along in *Season One*. This is certainly the most ambitious thing I've worked on, and I think we're hitting our stride now.

HOW MUCH OF THE STORYLINE WAS MAPPED OUT AHEAD OF TIME? DO YOU KNOW HOW IT WILL END?

DAVID: In the very early stages, we wrote the first episode without ANY idea of what was going on aside from a very basic premise — On Oct. 15, most of the world's population vanished. Write what happened next. We were each assigned to write our own characters with minimal direction, and then we traded our pages, and began to piece the puzzle together. I was shocked by how little we changed and how well our ideas meshed. We then brainstormed the rest of *Season One*, and a bit beyond, and got busy writing.

Very early on, I knew a few things, such as some of the key cliffhanger sequences well into *Season Three*, and how the whole thing might end. I plotted a good chunk of *Season One* out, but kept things fluid, open to change as the characters and situations presented new ideas. Some of the best changes were ones we'd never planned and which came up in our brainstorming sessions.

In short, we planned out a lot of the first season <u>before we finished the final draft of *Episode One*</u>, and then into *Season Three* as we worked through the first season.

SEAN: *Yesterday's Gone* started with only a premise, and quickly grew cooler with every conversation and fresh pile of pages. We realized early on that we had to know where we were going, not just immediately, but long-term. We wanted our story to have the same sort of vibe as cool, serialized TV, but we didn't want it to meander to nothing, shedding its audience like dead skin along the way, as many great shows have done.

This usually happens because there isn't an endgame in mind. So, it was important for us to keep things as open as possible so that the creative possibilities never dulled, while building the mile markers required to make sure we were going the right way.

We have an idea of how our story will end, but not necessarily how every *character's* story will end. We need more time to live with our characters before we can conclude their stories. We love them, and if we did our jobs, you love them, too. So we want to make sure we end things in a way that respects the story as well as the characters themselves. Dave has pushed this from the beginning, character arc over everything else.

HOW DO YOU BOTH HANDLE WRITING CHORES?

SEAN: David and I have different ways of putting our stories together, depending on the project. One of the ways we work best is when Dave builds the house, and I come in to landscape the grounds and decorate the interior. That's largely how *Yesterday's Gone* has been put together, especially in the second season. But the best parts of the project for me have been during those brainstorming sessions when the pieces of our story click together between laughs and gasps and *ohmygod's*.

We each write our pages, pass them between us, then usually get on the phone to discuss what worked, what didn't, and how to blend things better the next time. Though we've been writing together for over three years, we live hundreds of miles apart, and have only met one another in person twice. So, I pace my basement in circles, or turn the treadmill on low, while we shoot the shit and hash it out. I think much of *Yesterday's Gone's* magic is dusted in those moments when we're building our story out loud. And I think part of that is because we often speak in terms of how our story would play out if it was shot for television.

DAVID: I think we bring out the best in each other's writing, each with our own strengths. We both write and edit an equal amount of each other's stuff, though we vary on stories, or even within chapters, who will be taking lead. It comes down to whoever has the best idea for that particular story. Sometimes, we'll handle our own first drafts of the segments, and other times, we'll write story beats or prompts for the other to flesh out. It's a very fluid and fast process that has an energy I'd never have working solo. If left to my own devices, I'd still be perfecting my first unpublished novel.

IS IT EASIER OR HARDER TO WRITE WITH ANOTHER WRITER? DO YOU EVER GET INTO ARGUMENTS OVER WHAT GOES ON THE PAGE?

DAVID: Sean and I work remarkably ego-free. We listen to one another's ideas and never worry about who gets credit for the stories. When we first started publishing, we had to consider whose name would be first on the book covers. The first idea we had was to go with whoever was lead on that story. However, we decided to just stick with one constant branding: *Sean Platt & David W. Wright*.

It doesn't matter if people think Sean wrote something I did, or vice versa. *Though, I did write all the really cool shit! And Sean wrote the parts you didn't like as much :)*

The thing you need with a co-writer is trust. Trust to carry out a vision, trust to respect what you're doing, and trust that they'll tell you when something isn't working on the page. It's kind of like marriage, except without all the sex (though Sean keeps propositioning me!) and arguing, two people working for a common goal and more concerned with the final product than individual accolades.

SEAN: I'm a collaborative writer, so I probably prefer to write with someone else. I'll probably always have at least one project going on that is just mine, but I write fast and love working with others. When you have a great writing partner, ideas are easy, and verbal riffing is ridiculous fun.

In three and a half years, I can't remember a single argument over whether or not something went on the page. Dave will make suggestions, and I take them on first call. The opposite is true, too. Dave and I have wonderful, creative harmony. I'm sure there will be something one of us has to fight for at some point in the future, but we haven't seen it yet.

Our creative differences are more like creative preferences, and while there is a wider gap in business philosophy, creatively it's as easy as walking.

HOW MANY "SEASONS" WILL YESTERDAY'S GONE RUN?

DAVID: We're writing it as three seasons. I don't want to spend too long on it. There's too many different stories we want to write this year! I have this cool, year-long story I'm itching to write, unlike anything I've ever seen. We're also working on two more serialized projects, and a host of other books.

We won't rule out a fourth season if demand is there AND it makes sense for the story. But right now, we're planning for three, and I'm not padding to make room for a fourth season just because the books are selling well. Of course, if someone wants to pay us a few million, we'll pump these things out for the next 10 years, and even help design the action figures.

Just kidding.

Maybe.

(**UPDATE: November 2012.** As we worked through the second and third seasons, we realized there was no way to tell the entire story we have planned in three seasons. We've since decided on six seasons, though most of the answers we set forth in the first season *are* answered by the end of the third season. *Season Four* also marks a decidedly significant break from what happened in the first seasons. I can't explain more without giving a lot away, but we've organized *Seasons Four* through *Six* to be much easier to follow and far more streamlined than the first three seasons.)

SEAN: I love the idea of three seasons, but I'd be happy to write another three after that if the demand was there. Any time we have an audience eager for something, and we can deliver a satisfying story with both character and quality, in a world that we love, I'm 100 percent on board. However, as Dave said, there are SO MANY stories in our story garden and we just can't get to them all, so it might make more sense just to start with something from scratch.

HOW IS SERIALIZATION WORKING FOR YOU?

SEAN: I'm thrilled so far, and readers seem to really love the format. I've yet to see anyone not enjoy the option to buy the titles either one at a time, or all at once in the full season. And most of our *Season One* buys (of the full compilation), it seems, have come from people who downloaded the first episode for free and were hooked. Which is awesome. I see this as a huge opportunity for storytelling, and there is nothing in my writing or publishing life that I'm more excited about than seeing where it takes us.

DAVID: Great! Before we launched *Yesterday's Gone*, I heard and read a lot of naysayers dissing the format. Some people didn't think serialization could work and doubted that readers would WANT to be kept waiting. I disagree. I love books and shows that leave me hanging until the next dose, so I'm guessing I'm not alone. There's an audience there, you just have to find it. And self-publishing presents us just the opportunity to find the readers who get what we're doing.

WILL YOU BE DOING OTHER SERIALIZED BOOKS?

DAVID: We're working on a paranormal romance for the young adult market. We're also working on a spin-off to our short story, *The Watcher*, from the *Dark Crossings* book. Sean's also working on a few things in different genres. I wish I didn't need sleep so we could write all the things we'd like to write this year!

SEAN: Oh, yeah! I would tell you how many things were on the drawing board between us, but then you'd call us crazy, or liars, or maybe something worse, so I'll just say yes with an extra exclamation point!! (or two)

AS A READER, DO YOU WISH THERE WERE MORE SERIALIZED TITLES?

SEAN: Absolutely. I would love to read high-quality serials, as it's always interesting to see what other writers are doing. And as a fan, I just love the open loops. I'm thrilled that there are as many superbly scripted television shows as there are. I think it's a golden age of TV. I'm really looking forward to the new season of *Mad Men*, which is an achingly long two months away!

DAVID: As I've mentioned many times in the past, I LOVED Stephen King's *The Green Mile*. And I loved comic books when I was younger (and before they cost more than most kids can afford to keep up with). I've heard from writers who are now doing serials, or planning to. I've been too busy writing to check out any of the titles, but I can't wait to find one that hooks me in like King did.

WHAT HAS YOUR BIGGEST SELF-PUBLISHING OBSTACLE BEEN?

SEAN: Asking our readers to do things they may not be used to doing, such as leaving a review. Because we're self-published, it is much harder for our work to get discovered. Every review helps. As does every Facebook like, Twitter tweet, or e-mail to a friend. The reviews we do get have been excellent, so that's really rewarding for us and lets us know we're on the right track, but as a percentage it's slightly small, so it would be nice to have more reviews on the original season, as well as the season we're launching right now. If you're reading this and want to help get the word out about *Yesterday's Gone*, or anything else Dave and I are writing right now, it really will make a difference. Leave a review. Short of buying books, it's the most helpful thing anyone can do to ensure we're able to keep bringing stories to you. We read and appreciate every review.

DAVID: I think getting word out was the toughest thing, along with reviews. It's hard to get noticed. You're competing with bestselling authors and indie authors alike. There's no shortage of quality books to read. We just have to reach out to those who most enjoy the kinds of stories we're writing. And judging from the reviews and e-mails, we've found our people! Or they've found us. Either way, I'm thrilled to have them along for the ride!

HOW DO YOU DEAL WITH NEGATIVE REVIEWS?

SEAN: Fortunately, we've only had one outright bad review. We had a couple of three star reviews that were totally fair. I appreciated what the reviewers had to say immensely. And that sort of feedback helps us grow as writers and entertainers. The review sections provide an invaluable opportunity to learn from our readers so we can develop the stories they most want to read.

We recently got a one-star review from a reviewer who hated the book from top to bottom. That's fine, I don't expect to please everyone. It wasn't constructive criticism so much as bitter ranting, but that was fine. I had no problem with the review itself. But the reviewer also attacked some of the five star reviewers, saying that we must have planted them, even calling one of our most loyal readers and reviewers a troll. That is poor behavior, and I just had to say something. It's okay to badmouth our book, but you can't badmouth our readers.

DAVID: Oddly, one of my favorite reviews was from someone who gave one of the episodes (or maybe it was the season) three stars. They had some issues with some elements of the story, which I completely respected. The cool thing about the review, though, was that they didn't outright trash the book. I DON'T LIKE THIS BOOK, THEREFORE, NOBODY SHOULD OR WILL. Instead, the reviewer wrote how fans of specific titles would likely enjoy the book. I loved that they were objective enough to say that.

As a writer, I don't think you ever stop learning, and sometimes that means learning from your critics.

Thank you to everyone who sent in questions! We appreciate you taking the time to be part of the conversation!

* * * *

POST-SEASON INTERVIEW
WITH THE AUTHORS

(**Note: Oct. 2013**) *This is an interview with our original editor, Matt Gartland, (we've since had the season re-edited) who interviewed us as a bonus for the season compilation. If you haven't yet read Season Two, and you're one of those weird people who reads the back of the book first, you might want to wait and come back to read this AFTER you finish the season.*

In other words, spoilers below!

Interview conducted February 2012

MATT: So, after that ending, what's next?

DAVID: I can't say anything other than find out on June 19.

SEAN: Ditto.

MATT: Season 1 was a tremendous success. How did that challenge you in Season 2 to at least meet, if not exceed, your high standard of creativity?

SEAN: Season 1 was an amazing creative experience, and really drove us to do something different than a lot of what was happening with self-published fiction. Season 1 was about establishing the world and proving it would work.

Proving that readers would return week after week, then come back after hiatus hungrier than ever.

Season 2 was about building on that world, and rewarding returning readers with a narrative that was tighter and better, and grew along with them. We wanted to do more and say more, and do everything better. We wanted to start strong, and finish with an ending that made readers say, "WOW! What happens next?!?"

DAVID: The big fear lurking in my mind was the whole "sophomore effect" you read about where musicians, novelists, and TV and movie producers attempt to duplicate what worked so well the first time only to come up short, or worse, fail miserably. But when it comes down to it, I saw areas for improvement over season 1, things we'd learned during the first season, that we could apply to the second. So, in my mind, Season Two would be better. And looking back now, I believe it was.

Now the trick will be topping an insane season finale! I'm glad we have a month or two to think about it!

MATT: How did your process change from Season 1 to Season 2? And more generally, how do you both continually look to tweak and improve your process Season to Season and episode to episode?

SEAN: The exchange between Dave and I gets better by the day. A weekly series is a demanding task, so communication must be fluid, honesty must be everywhere and professional shorthand must be tight. Season 1 started out making it up as we went along. Dave would write his characters, I would write mine, then I'd polish them all and he'd blend them together. This worked beautifully.

Season 2 was more plotted, and has gone even better. Dave is pencils and I'm ink. Some stuff he writes note for note, and some stuff is just a sketch. I fill in the blanks and color the pages. We'll be carrying this flow with us to our next serial, *ForNevermore*.

Also with Season 2, we've had the awesome work of our editor, Matt Gartland, who has helped us have great copy produced at a tremendous clip.

DAVID: The overall process was relatively the same, but we had to work much faster with a goal of releasing a new book each week. As for tweaking, I believe the more you write, the better you get. So we keep writing and aiming for that perfect blend of story and character that defines serialized fiction for us.

MATT: What new inspirations did you weave into the fold of the storytelling in Season 2 that weren't there in Season 1?

DAVID: Our opening sequences in Season One weren't exactly gripping. Between seasons, we were watching back-to-back episodes of *Breaking Bad* and LOVED how that show often opened up with something compelling and then circled back to deliver WHY it was compelling. *LOST* did that with its flashback openings from time to time, also.

So we opened up Season Two with the attack on the farm where the Drury group was staying. That was the biggest shift in writing this season, the opening sequences. Start strong or start compelling, or start weird, even, and then come back and tie that into the current timeline. We didn't follow that formula in every episode, but overall, I think the openings were much better this season.

SEAN: I think our inspirations were mostly carried over from one season to the next. The biggest change was that we were writing for an active audience the second time around, and that changed the mood. It was wonderful to have readers waiting each Tuesday. One of the best parts of my year so far for sure.

MATT: What "magic" can you share about how well you produce such captivating stories at such a high velocity?

SEAN: I think speed is our key. Dave and I have written together for three and a half years, and I've had to write thousands of words a day professionally for all of that time. The velocity has always been there, as has the quality. That's how I made my living. But now I'm getting to point that velocity toward something I love, while doing it with a creative partner who makes the writing fun, and deep, velocity isn't the problem so much as deciding which stories we want to tell next!

DAVID: Trying to keep up with Sean! And prodigious amounts of diet soda.

MATT: What was the hardest scene or episode for each of you to write, respectively, and why?

DAVID: The hardest episode was Episode 11, "The Loophole." I wanted to write a romantic storyline with elements of fate, destiny, and choice which would set the stage for the season finale in a big way.

The big challenge was that we were asking readers to care a lot about Will, who had to that point been only a background character. So we had to slow down the plot to introduce Will's back story. Initially, the Big Reveal at the end of Episode 11 was that Will had foretold his own death. But there was no parallel in that and what happened with his boyfriend, or in Episode 12.

Sean and I brainstormed and then it hit us ... Will didn't see his own death. He saw Luca's! Will wasn't trying to protect *himself*, he was trying to protect someone he loved. That revelation changed everything, bringing not only Episode 11 full circle, but it set up the season finale perfectly.

Episode 11 was the hardest, but it was also the most rewarding. I'm not sure how many readers consider it a favorite, but it might be one of my favorite things I've been a part of.

SEAN: Boricio's origin. I really wanted to get that right. It's important to get Boricio just right, and he's definitely the most specific character I've ever written. That scene needed to say everything, and it had a lot of heavy lifting. Boricio is obviously central to the story, and it's important that readers care about him, even if they hate him. That scene had a helluva job to do, and when I read it out loud to my wife, I knew it did it. It may not be the best scene in the series, but it's my favorite. So far. Probably.

MATT: Did you ever feel, individually or collectively, that you were writing yourselves into a corner? If so, how did you work out of that?

SEAN: Ha, a bunch of times. Not really, but we would have if we weren't careful. We have our straight lines because of Dave. I'm more haphazard than he is, and would miss the details that help keep *Yesterday's Gone* in key. Whenever we had something that looked like it would lead down a dead-end, we untangled it together. That made the final section of Season 2 take a little longer than we'd planned, but the payoff was explosive and totally worth it.

DAVE: I worry about that stuff a lot. There's a lot of tiny details to keep track of, and it's easy to overlook something as you're writing. Before the season began, I started a chart and even a secret website to keep track of all the data so I'd better remember it. But with the speed we're writing, I don't have time to keep track of every little thing. So far, I think we've done a pretty good job, save for a few minor continuity errors which I'm fixing as I find them.

There's also a concern when killing characters off, where I need to make sure I'm not killing an idea I had for later in the series which required that character. So far, we've avoided writing ourselves into anything too bad. Knock on wood.

Not an easy thing to say given how the season ended.

MATT: What do you hope your readers interpret from the messages interwoven into your characters and the story arcs overall?

SEAN: I think everyone sees life through their own prism, and I'm happy as long as people are reading and enjoying what we create. I never sit down with an agenda. I write the characters as people, and have them react how I think they would react in that situation. I think the same is true for Dave. If someone wants to read something into what I've written, for good or bad, that's there side of the prism and nothing more. I'm happy if a reader sees our work as an honest interpretation of life, even if the circumstances in the story are extraordinary.

DAVID: My primary goal is to entertain, to create a world that you will want to spend time in. We've got a broad base of characters and ideas within the story, so there's no overarching political, religious, or philosophical worldview we're driving at.

I love that people have connected with the characters, though, and have found something deeper within the story to enjoy.

I'm attracted to writing about dark subject matters, and part of that is to better understand why people do what they do or how people respond to horrible situations. I'm fascinated by stories of redemption and corruption for much the same reason. Why do people go bad? Can bad people become good? Those are themes I tend to drift toward.

And though it's not intentional, I try to show a sense of hope in the world. However, I'm pretty sure that people who read our books will think I have a pretty twisted idea of hope.

MATT: Do you feel the reader base is accurately understanding your narrative, characters and all? Or do you feel that there's something that they just aren't "getting?"

SEAN: I've not seen any evidence that the readers aren't getting it. The reviews have been wildly encouraging. I've only seen one where I'd say the reader didn't get it. If there was confusion, I imagine we'd see that reflected in reviews or in our Goner's newsletter, but we've not seen it in either place.

DAVID: Yeah, they get it. At first, I was worried that people might not care for serialized fiction, but that hasn't been the case at all.

I get email every day from readers who get it and are enjoying the ride. I'm surprised how many readers have reached out to us. It's easily the best part of our job, connecting with people. There's still some people who prefer to read the full book all at once, but they still enjoy the roller-coaster type ups and downs in our story.

MATT: So much has already been written in this saga. How do you keep it fresh at this stage?

SEAN: We're not modeling *Yesterday's Gone* after written work so much as televised work. The TV serial is an art form and vibe we're trying to capture with *Yesterday's Gone*, and the upcoming *ForNevermore*, and all our titles.

Treating it like a TV series allowed us to do some new things creatively, and I think that's paid off in the reader experience.

DAVID: We keep it fresh by following the road we started down and telling the story of these people. We respect the story and the characters. We started out wanting to do three seasons. Sean and I talked it over, though, and realized that we'd need at least four seasons to tell the story properly. I don't see it going much longer than that, though. There's too many other stories to write.

That being said, if we had a great idea to return to this series in the future, or any series, we'd never close the door completely.

MATT: Do you have a finale already conceived for the series? Or is the serialized storytelling truly serial in that there is an indefinite end point?

SEAN: We know *when* it will end and approximately *how* it will end. It's serialized in spirit, not necessarily in fact.

We don't want to tire our readers or bore ourselves. There are too many stories to write. Our road is clear, but we're not sure exactly how we'll cover the distance in between.

DAVID: I know what will happen to a few key characters. I'm waiting for the others to show me their endings. There IS an end-point to this series, though. But there's also a lot more to happen between now and then!

MATT: Is serialized fiction turning out the way you had hoped and dreamed it would? How about for your readers; is the reader response what you were hoping it would be?

SEAN: It's been exactly as I hoped, and I CANNOT wait to get started on Season Three. June 19 seems so close, yet so far away! Reader response blows me away, and I can't wait to kick the story harder in the balls for the third season. The reader response makes me want to impress them more. Least we can do to say thank you for all the support.

DAVID: Sean was always more optimistic than I was. I was afraid people might not want to wait for the story to be continued. I knew *I* loved the format, and *hoped* that others would, but I couldn't be certain until we put the story out there and found out.

And response is turning out even better than I'd hoped! Even more impressive, is the number of people who are rooting for us to succeed! These are people who are connecting with us through this story. They're buying our books, telling their friends, writing to us, and leaving reviews. In doing so, our readers have made our writing dreams a reality. We're humbled and thankful for how readers have responded.

Thank you!

MATT: If you could start over from the very beginning of *Yesterday's Gone*, including the *pilot*, what would you do differently?

SEAN: I would remove some of Luca's infantile language. That's one of the only things some readers have questioned, and understandably so. I've seen a few comments about how the author must not know any 8 year olds and that Luca must be slow. My son is Luca's age, and my daughter is two years older. My son, Ethan, is extremely bright. But he turns small when he's sad or scared. And if his world went away, he would be terrified enough to see the world in terms of "terrible scary." Knowing what I know now, I would spend more time developing the thought that he was feeling infantile, not slow.

DAVID: Like I said earlier, we didn't really give much thought to opening sequences before this season. This is even more evident in Episode One, which quite frankly, opens up pretty damned slow for a post-apocalyptic book.

While we've drawn a large audience, I can't help but think that the slow open is not representative of the overall series, and we likely lost some readers in the opening pages. I'd love to go back and just change the beginning of Episode One a bit, just to bring the action in earlier, set up the stakes right away.

In fact, I might just do it in the next few weeks. I won't change anything which affects the timeline or history, just the opening sequence. If I do it, I'll leave a note in the Author's Notes to indicate what I did, in case anyone is re-reading it and thinking they lost their mind, "This isn't how it originally opened!"

Other than that, I love how the series is playing out. I can't wait to take what we've learned with *Yesterday's Gone* and bring it to Young Adult paranormal genre with *ForNevermore* next week!

* * * *

FIND OUT WHY READERS CAN'T GET ENOUGH
COLLECTIVE INKWELL

To see all our of our books, visit:
www.SterlingandStone.net/
collective-inkwell

ABOUT THE AUTHORS

Sean Platt is the bestselling co-author of over 60 books, including breakout post-apocalyptic horror serial *Yesterday's Gone*, literary mind-bender *Axis of Aaron*, and the blockbuster sci-fi series, *Invasion*. Never one for staying inside a single box for long, he also writes smart stories for children under the pen name Guy Incognito, and laugh out loud comedies which are absolutely *not* for children.

He is also the founder of the Sterling & Stone Story Studio and along with partners Johnny B. Truant and David W. Wright hosts the weekly Self-Publishing Podcast, openly sharing his journey as an author-entrepreneur and publisher.

Sean is often spotted taking long walks, eating brisket with his fingers, or watching movies with his family in Austin, Texas. You can find him at sean@sterlingandstone. net.

David W Wright is the co-author of several horror series, including the bestselling *Yesterday's Gone* and *WhiteSpace*, as well as the disturbing standalone books, *12* and *Crash*.

Dave is also the curmudgeon co-host of the weekly Self-Publishing Podcast, he invites listeners along on his journey toward better health on the strikingly personal The Walking Dave podcast, and regularly rants about his many pet-peeves on the ridiculous podcast Worst. Show. Ever. (which should never be listened to by anyone, ever).

Dave is an accomplished and intermittent cartoonist who lives in [LOCATION REDACTED] with his wife and son [NAMES REDACTED]. Dave cultivates the perfect level of paranoia and always carries a decoy wallet in case he gets mugged. You can stalk him at dave@sterlingandstone.net or visit his personal blog at www.davidwwright.com.

For any questions about Sterling & Stone books or products, or help with anything at all, please send an email to help@sterlingandstone.net, or contact us at sterlingandstone.net/contact. Thank you for reading.

Printed in Great Britain
by Amazon